I0606661

Everything was going so well, and her life would have been perfect—if someone wasn't trying to kill her…

Reverting to her home screen, Kingsley noticed someone had left her a message. With no caller ID, her curiosity piqued—who had this number? She opened the message.

The voice was female and husky—that of an unrepentant life-long smoker. "Youse in danger. Some bad ass in County Prison after you. Brags he's gots help on the outside. Watch ya ass."

Click.

Kingsley stared at the phone then hit redial.

"The number you are trying to reach is no longer in service…"

Had to be a wrong number but, still, her hands trembled.

Kingsley Ward survived two vicious attacks, only to be targeted by the perpetrator's partner. She should be safe—with the psychopath in prison, awaiting trial for her young husband's murder—and by publicly swearing that she cannot identify the killer's partner. She'd just caught a glimpse—but that's enough. And the partner knows it!

Kingsley has worked hard, reinventing herself, away from her prestigious Philadelphia family, as head of commercial lending at a small, rural bank. Buoyed by new friends, meaningful work, and an amazing new man, she fails to grasp that *honor among thieves* is a real concept and that she is in eminent danger. As the star prosecution witness, her failure to testify could free two felons in unrelated cases. Or are they connected? As the plot to silence her gains momentum, Kingsley struggles toward redemption and a new life, finding allies in unexpected places. Haunted by nightmares and guilt, she vows to see justice done—that is, if she lives long enough to testify.

book two opens, Kingsley is recovering from her attack and getting ready for the trials, both on her attack and on the loan scam. With Miller in jail, Kingsley should be safe, except that Miller has a partner who calls himself Steven Turner. Turner is determined to get Miller out of prison help him silence Kingsley. Thinking she is safe because she lied and told the police, and the media, that she never saw Miller's partner, Kingsley goes on with her life, even falling in love. But dark clouds are gathering on the horizon, and she needs to pay attention before she's caught in a deadly storm. With enchanting characters that you can really identify with, an intriguing mystery, and a number of plot surprises, *Redeeming Trust* is one you won't want to put down. ~ *Regan Murphy, The Review Team of Taylor Jones & Regan Murphy*

ACKNOWLEDGEMENTS

Many people deserve my humble thanks and appreciation for sharing technical knowledge, sage advice, inspiration, proof reading, and for saying, "Keep going! It's good." While some thanks are specific to this novel, others are being thanked-forward for work in progress, lest I lose the opportunity.

Writing is solitary work, yet a host of helpers seem to crowd by eight-my-ten-foot office. Some are no longer living, like my parents Jose M. and Elizabeth Shannon Arburu, and my Grandmama, Lucy Ward Shannon. Their wisdom and expressions sneak into my work. Others—especially my gifted teachers—whisper encouragement when needed.

Friends who share their special gifts are my angels. Thank you, Polly Brockway, Barbara Ann Hughes, Linda Meyer, Mary Ann Hayes, Mary Ellen Richards, Margaret Funk, Kristen Bergman, Forensic Pathologist Neil A. Hoffman MD, The Rev. Cannon Karl L. Kern. And my readers, especially the book clubs who have invited me into their circles.

Where would we be without public libraries that perpetuate our literate society—free—and their librarians, patrons, and volunteers? Bless you for enabling readers of all ages and situations to feed their passion. My particular thanks to the Berks County Public Library System and the Reading Public Library for promoting local authors and providing children's programs.

I am indebted to the MWA's New York Chapter for their friendship, direction, programs, and stimulating events. Independent booksellers, especially The Mysterious Bookshop in Manhattan, deserve our gratitude and patronage.

To my publisher, Black Opal Books—my enduring gratitude for nurturing my novels into print and for tolerating my idiosyncrasies. I am indebted to my editor, Lauri Wellington, to Faith for her patience and devotion to detail, and Jack for his beautiful artwork. Black Opal's dedicated staff handles myriad details and challenges with professionalism and grace. You are the best.

Redeeming Trust

Nancy A. Hughes

A Black Opal Books Publication

GENRE: MYSTERY-DETECTIVE/THRILLER

This is a work of fiction. Names, places, characters and incidents are either the product of the author's imagination or are used fictitiously, and any resemblance to any actual persons, living or dead, businesses, organizations, events or locales is entirely coincidental. All trademarks, service marks, registered trademarks, and registered service marks are the property of their respective owners and are used herein for identification purposes only. The publisher does not have any control over or assume any responsibility for author or third-party websites or their contents.

For Bill
Thank you for making dreams come true.

Prologue

Unseasonable heat and humidity smothered County Prison's exercise yard. The inmate who called himself Miller, always prefaced by Mister, jabbed a blunt finger into his palm to punctuate another escapade of underworld intrigue that revealed no names or traceable details.

A motley crew hung on his every word, some out of fear, some admiration, and some from the same morbid fascination that rivets gapers to wrecks.

One gangly kid remained after the others had drifted away. Abruptly Miller turned on the new kid who had asked entirely too many questions. "Whatcha in for?" Miller demanded.

"Some kid stashed drugs in my crib. It's all a mistake."

"Yeah, right."

"What about you?"

Miller spat on the ground. "Mur—der." He tasted the word like a delicacy. "Other shit they won't prove." He bared his teeth in the kid's acne-riddled face, pleased when the kid flinched. "Gettin' sprung from this hell hole."

"'Cause you didn't do it?"

Miller stepped into the kid's personal space, and the youngster backed up. "Because the witness won't live to testify. No witness? No case."

The kid drew several slow breaths and faked a nonchalant look while mauling an ant with his toe. "That's cool." He was trying to hide shaking hands behind his orange jumpsuit. "So, Mr. Miller, sir, sounds like you're smarter than any of them. How are you going to get out? Got help outside?"

With cougar-like speed, the big man lunged at the hapless kid's throat, half lifting, half hurtling him against the brick wall. "They're still looking for the last piece of shit who tried to deal information." Blocking everyone's view with his massive body, he ground the kid's head into the wall. "Nobody rats me out, ya got that?"

Miller loosened his grip, and the kid bobbed his head, leaving a bloody streak where his flesh grated against the wall.

"I'd find you, just like the asshole banker who threatened to expose me. He had an *unfortunate* accident." Grinning about his sordid solution, Miller lowered the kid, half patting, half smacking his face. "Listen, kid. I'll make you a deal. See my buddies over there?" He made a small jerk toward two huge, pumped, and tattooed prisoners. "Little guy like you gonna need some protection, if you get my drift. No one hurts my friends. You'd like my protection?"

"Yes, sir! Of course!"

"It's gonna cost you."

"What do you want? I don't got no money. No way to get drugs."

Miller grasped the boy's shoulder, giving it a shake with his oversized paw. "When your mom visits on Sunday—"

"How'd you know she was—"

"I know everything 'round here. You're gonna start giving Mommy messages for her to send to an email address that I give ya."

"She doesn't have email."

Miller rolled his eyes. "The library does! You tell Mommy that you've made a powerful friend who will not let any of these psychopaths hurt you. That is, if she sends messages for me."

"What if she won't? What if she's scared? What if—"

"Oh, she will. Trust me. She will." *Perfect! That was too easy to even be fun.* Miller strode off to gather his minions.

☙❧

In the dense forest beyond his cabin, Miller's partner tackled the first order of business that came to his email in code: obliterate all trace of John Miller's identity. Destroy all forged documents—driver's licenses, auto registration and proof of insurance, PI licenses, military discharge papers, et cetera—anything that could link either of them to their *business*. He blended the shreds with wild animal scat in a galvanized bucket. That he buried in the woods.

What should Miller's partner call himself for his next incarnation? He scanned a commencement program from a large Philadelphia public school. First name: he liked Stephen. No, better with a *V*. What goes with Steven? He loved Piscatelli, Shesniak, and Winchester, but joking aside, he needed *ordinary*. A last name so innocuous that nobody would question its spelling or if he was related to so-and-so in Scranton. Snyder, Ott, Turner. Turner? Steven Turner.

His eye fell on White. Steven White, a.k.a. Steve. No, Turner was better. Done. Mentally, he started a fresh page in his life. With forged documents in order, he could pursue new business ventures. And springing John Miller from County Prison topped the list. He felt itchy to get back to the hunt and execute his brilliant plan for his partner.

Several prospects had contacted him via one of the phones he dedicated to his new business, which he'd advertised on an obscure soldier-of-fortune Internet site. Discreet inquiries, his specialty, usually led to big prizes and a shit-load of money. He would not take any shortcuts, however, like Miller had done. That had led to his downfall.

Miller's client had wanted certain competition eliminated. Completely. Emphatic that there be no connection between the client, his associates, and the victim. Miller had charged extra to background those connections. The client was just another idiot who couldn't succeed without someone tipping the scale. No problem. Weeks of surveillance had revealed that the young doctor's habitual behavior made staging an accident easy. Checkmark.

The new Steven Turner internalized the lesson that Miller had failed—to always cross-reference similar names. A human resources banker-client had merely wanted sensitive documents recovered from an employee's apartment. The employee would not be home. Her apartment offered easy access via a fire escape obscured by mature trees. The woman who stole said documents couldn't possibly complain without incriminating herself. Piece of cake for big bucks, which led to a much bigger prize.

Except—the two targets being related never occurred to Miller. Ward was too common a name. The bank-target woman—Kingsley Ward—had surprised him, catching Miller in the act, forcing him to neutralize her. She never should have survived, but she had. Miller subsequently suffered the consequences of targeting high-profile people. That had disastrous consequences.

Worse—he'd taken for granted that the victim would grieve her dead husband, then bury herself in good causes. Instead, she was bent on revenge. Miller said he would never fail backgrounder 101 again. Or so Miller had communicated through a reliable insider in prison where he awaited his trial.

The newly christened Steve Turner ticked through his agenda. The banker who hired Miller in the first place was a dead issue—literally. *Check.* But that woman, intent on testifying against Miller, was not. *That score must be settled.* It was payback time for his friend for saving his ass in the war. *Semper fi, good buddy. Her days are numbered. This job is pro bono.*

Chapter 1

Kingsley Ward's days, no matter how pleasant, morphed into abysmal nights, where restorative sleep was a stranger. Her mind simply would not shut up. Part of her brain felt it must keep alert, lest the killer sneak up on her. A *ping* on the metal fire escape might be an acorn, a squirrel—or a footstep. A barely perceptible movement of air could be the killer or her beloved Pandora, chasing a mouse in her dreams. Even the wind seemed to mutter death threats. The killer's howl, vowing to kill her, screamed so loudly that she'd startle awake. Disoriented. Unsure if she were still locked in her kidnapper's trunk.

Sometimes in her nightmares, she thought she could smell him before she could make out his features. His cloying anger took on shape in the darkness. His pervasive stench that she couldn't place—sweat, booze, garbage, putrification, and sulfur—was she smelling death? She opened her mouth to scream, but nothing came out as she scrunched, exposed, into a void, shrinking from eyes that pierced the darkness, stabbing her with their venom.

His wrath bellowed curses. "You! You will pay!" The scream that awakened her must have been hers.

She slid from her bed, steadying herself by the rice-carved poster, her bare feet grateful for the recognizable touch of her late Grammy's Persian rug. Her eyes swept the room for orientation, locking on the glowing coach lamp outside her second-floor apartment in the small city's historic district.

I'm safe, she tried to convince herself after getting her bearings.

Kingsley replaced her sheets with dry bedding. Pandora crept from under the bed, weaving her fluffy body through Kingsley's legs while casting questioning eyes at Kingsley's.

"It's all right, baby. Just a dream," she said, soothing herself as much as the cat.

She flipped on lamps throughout her apartment to dispel every trace of the darkness. Her computer awakened, she opened the document she'd saved as *my testimony* to review the crimes as they had unfolded. She rehearsed the details for two different trials, terrified that she would get rattled and enable her husband's killer, John Miller, to walk.

Of lesser importance was the trial of the loan scam's mastermind, a plot she had exposed at her bank. He, too, might walk without her testimony, but a white-collar criminal held no terror for her. That the two cases could possibly be linked, however, haunted her. Could she prove it? But at what expense? Peaceful dreams would continue to be interrupted, like a switch that triggered sheer panic, until the whole matter was settled.

Kingsley yearned for peace and prayed for a normal existence now that the *alleged* perpetrators of the two crimes had been identified. She should be enjoying her growing relationship with an extraordinary man as well as the job she had managed to snag.

But panic crept from its hiding places, thwarting her efforts when least expected, knowing the killer's accomplice was still out there. She kept telling everyone that she could not identify him, but convincing herself of that lie wasn't working.

However absorbed in her new life, terrifying memories stabbed like exploding light bulbs. The horrifying murder of Andrew, her twenty-four-year-old husband. Her own escape from the killer's clutches. Reinventing herself in rural obscurity, separate from Philadelphia and her influential family, only to uncover criminals in her new bank. Too much. Way too fast.

Of course, she had seen a therapist. Just thinking about those two appointments made her smile. Perhaps it was his solemn demeanor that caused her extroverted personality to turn the hour into a social encounter. In no time, *she* was interviewing *him* as she tried unsuccessfully to lure him out of his shell with upbeat conversation.

During the second session, she had lost it, dissolving into laughter when he said, "If you contemplate hurting yourself, call me first." What flashed through her mind was herself, poised like an Olympic diver on the roof of a ten-story building. But no! Wait! I can't jump without calling Dr. What's-His-Name first. When she finally could speak, she had mopped her eyes and thanked the therapist for his cure. Remembering the look on his face made her chuckle. No doubt he was sure she was certifiable.

As a pale November dawn backlit the park across the street from her window, she commanded herself, *get a grip!* From her favorite window-seat perch and wrapped in her favorite shabby robe, she sipped strong black coffee as she watched the daylight normalize her world. Andy had been gone fourteen months. No, not gone. Dead. Murdered. But the world had revolved a full circle plus two additional months.

For one full year, she had struggled alone to adjust to a world without Andy. Before depression swallowed her whole, she had impulsively made a clean break and fled Philadelphia to accept a new job in rural Pennsylvania. Now, blessed with new friends and the wonderful man who had entered her life, she acknowledged that once again *Grammy had been right—in life's darkest moments, you've got to have faith that things will get better.* If only the nightmares would cease.

ↄ∽ↄ

A fresh day, with its semblance of normalcy, started typically in Kingsley's commercial lending department. From the pile of message slips left by her administrative assistant, she studied the one with Marle's terrified smiley embellished with horns. The assistant district attorney would appreciate a call at Kingsley's earliest convenience. She glanced at her calendar. November. Could the bank's former EVP Frank Ziegler's trial for the loan scam be scheduled anytime soon? She'd been led to believe that it wouldn't take place until spring or maybe next summer. Hopefully, never, should he take a plea.

With Ziegler free on bail, his attorney wasn't pushing for *speedy*. And the prosecution might need time to develop stronger evidence. No doubt the ADA wanted to review, in excruciating detail, how Kingsley had unraveled the twelve-million-dollar loan scam that began with a solitary misapplied commercial loan posting. Obviously, Ms. ADA wanted to keep the details fresh in Kingsley's mind.

Again she would ask if Kingsley had identified the voice of the mastermind she had overheard arguing with the deceased loan officer, the latter having been murdered in a cover-up attempt. With nothing new to report, and unwilling to fabricate a plausible lie to advance the case against Ziegler, Kingsley dropped the pink slip into the trash.

The vacillation between danger's stimulation versus the enormous relief that the mundane provided left her with pent-up energy, poised to explode, followed by periods of exhaustion. She loved her job in rural obscurity, a complete change from the big city. Here, she'd accepted a prodigious opportunity for someone so young with a fresh MBA.

Her dedicated colleagues, amazing customers, and loyal new friends inspired her. But no matter how blessed, lucky, or productive she felt, Andy's death was fraught with unanswered questions that niggled beyond conscious thought.

❦❧

Kingsley bolted from Keynote National Bank's elevator and dashed into the second-floor back-office restroom. Concealed in the farthest stall, she willed herself not to throw up as a fresh spasm of cramps gripped her belly. If only she could keep that dreadful pill down for another thirty minutes.

As another white-hot slash nearly eviscerated her, she knew that if anyone offered to shoot her, she'd beg them to do it. Maybe she should end this nightmare surgically. What good was her plumbing if her dreadful miscarriage had rendered it useless? But just twenty-seven? Wait. The doctor had urged her to wait. To do nothing drastic, because research was full of surprises.

As the nausea lessened, she sat on the seat, wriggling until she found a position that gave her a modicum of relief. She wasn't expected back in Lending until the department head meeting, and nobody would miss her until then. Feeling a teensy bit better, she couldn't help smiling. Talk about blowing her image. How would it have looked if the head of Commercial Lending had thrown up all over executive staffers and visiting dignitaries from the fed?

She should return to her office but resisted the urge to give up her comfortable position, in case the nausea and pain shot through her again.

The heavy exterior door crashed open, startling her as two women erupted into the restroom in mid-conversation. "Anyone here?"

Knowing she might have to linger and not wishing to explain her dilemma, Kingsley kept quiet. Obscuring herself wasn't difficult because the stall doors came to the floor and stayed closed unless someone tested their availability with a finger's touch.

"Sorry you didn't get the promotion in June. I thought you were a shoo-in."

"I was, until that outsider whore Marle stole it from me."

Kingsley startled. Marle? They were talking about her administrative assistant. Bright, professional, enormously qualified—*yeah*, Kingsley thought. *I wouldn't have wanted to compete against her*. Kingsley had no doubt that the speaker, who sounded so unprofessional, was not corporate office material anyway.

"And then that Ward witch dropped in from nowhere and seduced that gorgeous Todd Henning. I hope something terrible happens to her. A friend, who vacationed in Haiti, brought me an authentic voodoo doll. Got it in the back of a desk drawer, along with a hatpin."

"Surely you don't really believe in that shit."

"Makes me feel a hell of a lot better."

"You are e—vil!"

Kingsley was stunned. Tempted as she was to erupt from her stall and demand to know what could be more terrible than having her young husband murdered and herself nearly killed, she remained frozen and silent. *Doesn't that woman read newspapers?*

Besides, Kingsley was intrigued about what they'd say next.

"Then why so happy?"

"Something far better's come along. My ticket to real money. A secretarial position opened in Trust. I nailed my interview."

"You got it? But isn't that a lateral move? How do you figure it's worth big bucks?"

"The real prize is the senior VP. The word is that he came on to a widowed client—gorgeous, rich, educated, politically connected. She saw right through him and distanced herself. But not without confiding to friends."

"Because…"

"He's married. Not separated, much less having a divorce in progress. With a little digging, I learned that he's had several affairs over the years. He has a weakness for younger women. He's ripe for the plucking."

"And just how do you do that?"

"By following the formula. Sexy but corporately acceptable clothing, a tiny whiff of intoxicating scent, detectable only at close range. The best make-up. Becoming indispensable. And research—his likes and dislikes. For instance, if he likes jazz, ask his opinion about an upcoming concert for which I was unable to get a ticket. Or which sushi bar he recommends for my visiting girlfriend. Learn everything about him and use it to my advantage. Let him conclude that I'm soulmate material."

"But kiddo—he's old."

"Fifty-seven and eight months."

"That's crazy. At twenty-eight, you could do a lot better."

"Depends upon your definition of better. His salary is huge, he drives a Mercedes, belongs to the best country club. I could get used to that life."

"But the wife—"

A soft laugh. "Remember that socialite widow? His come-on line was 'there hadn't been much of a marriage for some time.' Translation, he's looking for sex. And to upgrade. How hard can it be to make him feel like he's an extraordinary stud?"

"He could use you then dump you."

"Girlfriend, I cannot lose! Best-case scenario I get a rich boyfriend—maybe a rich husband. Worst case, I sue the bank for sexual harassment. They'll settle quickly and quietly for big bucks to avoid bad publicity and looking stupid because there's no policy against employee dating. And there should be. Most corporations have them. I'd just claim he forced me to keep my job. Now, you must come shopping with me. I need the right bait."

Kingsley searched her brain for the new term. *A hustle*. That's what she was. And if she'd wanted Marle's job, did she have a target in Lending? Toilet one flushed and then two, followed by the sound of running water. Kingsley tried to glimpse the women through the tiny crack where the door met the frame.

"This one works," the hustle said to her friend after she'd worked her way down the washbowls in Kingsley's direction. Through the sliver, Kingsley made out a short, skinny figure with a cap of dark hair that reminded her of a chickadee. A bit of her profile revealed a slice of plain face, but not enough to identify her. The door swooshed open and air-braked shut.

Huh! In spite of Kingsley's education and experience, this level of immorality still shocked her. Couldn't get a man her own age, much less a single one, so she targets an older guy, his marriage be damned, who would be flattered into divorce court by this greedy little bitch.

Kingsley realized she'd forgotten her problems. She

willed her body and her resolve to just get through the rest of the day. As she rubbed her hand down her distended belly, she imagined the hustle sticking her hatpin into the voodoo doll's stomach.

Gathering her briefcase that she'd leaned against the stall's tile wall, she washed her hands, grimacing at the tired face she saw in the mirror. She needed a little blush, a dab of fresh lipstick, and a pleasant expression to face the rest of her day.

Compulsively, she bent to examine the healing suture-line on her crown, which had been shaved in the ER. Little by little, the puffy line was receding, and a half-inch regrowth was obscuring the psychopath's bludgeoning. If only emotional damage healed that quickly.

Still, had Grammy's pottery vase not splintered, lessening the effect of her attacker's blow, she would be dead or brain damaged. She fluffed her auburn curls that her brilliant stylist had created to camouflage the damage.

Grammy—the sainted lady who had died when Kingsley was ten. A widow who had taken over her late husband's CPA business and infused Kingsley with her determination, work ethic, and love of gardening. On summer mornings when Kingsley was little, Grammy would gather the flower vases, spread newspapers on the kitchen counter, and ask Kingsley's opinion about which stems were *done for*.

After setting the survivors in fresh water, they'd go to the garden where Grammy gave Kingsley real grown-up scissors and let her cut whatever she liked.

Grammy's favorite china vase with its raised iris motif waited with the others on the counter. One awful morning, Kingsley's elbow bumped the vase, sending it crashing to the hardwood floor. Horrified, she cried inconsolably. Grammy had hugged her, insisting that the vase was *just a thing*, and together they'd fix it. With special epoxy, they'd patiently reassembled the chunks like a jigsaw puzzle until Grammy proclaimed it *good as new*.

Kingsley's mother had produced the vase from Grammy's attic treasures for Kingsley's first apartment. Knowing it would never hold water, Kingsley arranged silk snapdragons that reminded her of those long-ago summers. Had the killer grabbed a sturdier weapon instead of that vase, which had given way along its fault lines, she would be dead.

Exiting the express elevator on Four, Kingsley spotted Marle at her desk in the Lending Department cubicle nearest Kingsley's private office. She couldn't help grinning at Marle's beautiful face, its lovely features framed by perfect cornrows, her lithe body dressed as professionally as any senior officer. Kingsley motioned her into her office.

"Do you have everything you need for Department Head?" Marle asked.

Kingsley swiveled her chair toward the small pile on her credenza beneath her window-wall and nodded. "Marle, I'll never be able to thank you enough for everything you've done for me since I joined in September. I could never have managed without you. Not just your exceptional skill, but all the personal interference you ran for me. I promise, life going forward won't be such a circus."

Marle grinned. "Crime fighting could be addictive.

I'm just glad you weren't killed. Not everyone could have uncovered a huge loan scam, much less gone after a murderer." She shuddered.

Kingsley reflected on the strangest year of her life. Andy, her wonderful husband, murdered. Fleeing Philadelphia and the media circus to begin life anew, only to come face to face with his killer. And now there was Todd, the EVP newcomer and president-elect with whom she was falling in love. Her life was spinning, hopefully, to settle quietly in a world of family, friends, and the work that she loved. Could anyone guess she felt terrified?

"Marle, when I arrived, we immediately plunged into big problems in our lending portfolio. I've been terribly remiss in not asking about your career plans and what I can do to advance them. Did you have competition for your job?"

"I heard it was advertised in-house first. Dissatisfied, they opened it up to outsiders. That included me. I interviewed with Jeffrey Johnston in HR, then with Shirley Granger, who heads the HR and the Branch Administration Division, and finally with Nathaniel Frasier here in Lending. I suspect I nailed the job when Mr. Johnston asked me to get back to him if I had other offers. I didn't take that seriously, though, because HR types like applicants to think the job is theirs for the asking. String candidates along so the employer can pick and choose. I did tell Mr. Johnston that I wasn't interested in Ms. Granger's area, branch administration. That my goal was corporate banking in general and lending in particular. That could have killed my chances."

"You liked what you saw?"

"Who wouldn't? I had my associate degree in business—all transfer classes—and Keynote will reimburse me one-hundred percent for every additional business course I take if I get an A, eighty percent for a B, and so on. I volunteered that in five years I envisioned myself with my bachelor's degree, working in lending, and starting MBA courses. Business law, perhaps. I guess they liked that."

"You might make assistant officer before you finish your bachelor's degree. If I can help you in any way, please let me know."

"Speaking of Jeffrey Johnston, may I ask if anyone has news about what's happened to him? It's no secret that he's suspected of being involved in the loan scam and that he vanished the same day two of the embezzlers were murdered. Gossip has him enjoying the islands or at the bottom of the Schuylkill River. I feel so sorry for his wife. I'm relieved she didn't have to resign from RE/MAX."

"She's an excellent realtor. Everyone from her office circled the wagons. They take teamwork literally."

Marle flipped a look at her watch. "Got your mail, if you want to go through it before Department Head." She made a quick U-turn to her desk, returning with a bundle of business mail and inter-office envelopes. "Looks like you have an admirer," she said, proffering a pink envelope that was sealed with a heart-shaped sticker.

"Where did that come from?" Kingsley asked, noticing its lack of postage, return address, and only her name typed in large caps.

"The branch. It was among items sent in their inter-office envelope. Aren't you going to open it?"

Kingsley bet that Todd Henning had slipped it into the mail, yet that didn't feel right. The conservative man oozed corporate correctness and safeguarded their budding relationship by keeping all personal matters off campus. With no policy in place to prohibit such dating, he was particularly sensitive to setting high standards that others could follow. "No, I'll open it later. Thanks."

The upbeat department-head meeting progressed smoothly as each Lending head reported on numbers that should nail an exceptional fourth quarter and support the year's increased profits and earnings. Outsiders would smile if they could see how excited numbers people could get about the minutiae assembled on spreadsheets. Kingsley felt a flush of appreciation for these experts, especially Margaret Stiles, the head of Residential Real Estate Lending, who had shepherded her from day one.

She and Assistant Controller, Barrie Brown, helped thwart the multi-million-dollar loan scam, the fallout from which was ongoing. In the process, they had become fast friends.

Back in her office, Kingsley closed her door, plopped into her soft leather task chair, and indulged in opening the pink envelope. She extracted a Hallmark notecard that she anticipated had been blank inside and scribed with his personal note.

She'd need a special memento box to contain such treasures—perhaps something Victorian, unlike her somber banking accessories. She had kept every last card and note from her late husband, Andy, the box now relegated to a top closet shelf. That, she might never be able to toss. Relishing the present, she looked at the back, which was blank. Grinning uncontrollably, she opened the card. And shrieked so loud that Marle came running without pausing to knock.

"What is it? What's wrong?"

Kingsley grabbed her mouth with her hand, the note card having fallen to her desk. She couldn't speak. Marle snatched it, the horror quickly registering in her eyes. A simple line drawing of a woman, dangled from a noose, beside which was typed, *die bitch!*

Marle darted back to her desk and rummaged until she found the inter-office envelope from the branch. Grabbing her phone, she speed-dialed security and demanded their immediate assistance.

Chapter 2

Keynote's head of Security, Charles "Chas" Wasleski; Shirley Granger, the senior VP under whom Human Resources and Marketing reported; branch manager Connie Davis; and Marle met with Kingsley in the Human Resources conference room to discuss Kingsley's anonymous threat.

Connie spoke first. "Our tellers take turns opening and sorting the mail that comes into the branch. Most is branch business, but we also forward pieces that pertain to other areas. You'd be surprised how many outsiders think that the branch *is* the bank. My teller remembered this particular piece, which arrived in a larger white envelope, addressed to the marketing department, requesting it to be forwarded to the branch's attention. Marketing sent it to us, unopened, in an interoffice envelope. Like Russian dolls. Seeing Kingsley's name, and assuming it was personal, the teller added it, still unopened, to Lending's batch."

"Did anyone keep the original envelope?" Chas asked.

"Afraid not," Connie said. "I checked as soon as you called, but the trash was already gone."

"Kingsley, do you have any idea who might do this? Might it have been a sick prank?" Shirley asked.

Kingsley sighed. "I overheard an exchange between two women in the second-floor restroom. They didn't know I was there." Succinctly she reiterated their conversation. "She referred to me as 'that Ward bitch.' Oh! And she hoped something awful would happen to me. I think she was just blowing off steam—maybe having a bad day. Venting disappointment for not getting a plum position, which might have meant a promotion to a higher pay grade."

"Did you recognize her?"

"Not really. A slice of a petite white woman's profile, having short, straight, dark hair, a narrow face and pointed nose. Probably worked on the second floor. Why else would she be there? But she could be anybody, and I just caught a glimpse through the crack where the stall door meets the frame."

"Could you see what she was wearing?"

"Fuchsia on top with a black pencil skirt." To puzzled male expressions, she translated, "Hot pink."

"Anyone else?"

Kingsley debated, questioning the wisdom of discussing her assailant, John Miller's accomplice, but chose to brush it off. "The police and the district attorney know there's another guy out there who was involved with Andrew's killer. But he'd have no reason to come after me. The newspapers made it quite clear, in several articles, that I did not see his face, nor could I identify even the gender of a 'mysterious second person.' I wanted them to quote me on that—thought it would buy me a degree of protection." She paused, summoning calm before adding, "Besides, it's the truth."

"What happens now?" Shirley asked Chas.

"Given that Kingsley is a key witness in Frank Ziegler's loan scam trial, and also has identified John Miller as her attacker, I'm turning this threat over to the police. I'll check first with Mr. Kramer. As CEO, he'll probably want to keep the bank's attorneys in the loop." Clear zipper bags enclosed the death threat, its pink envelope, and the inter-office envelope that originated at the branch.

Back in her office, Kingsley toiled through loan applications, but her attention was shot. Her ever-perceptive AA collected the Department Head meeting's supporting documentation from a pile on Kingsley's credenza that she could process. "Leave that for tomorrow," Kingsley said. "And thanks for your moral support today."

The alarm on Kingsley's watch gave her permission to take another painkiller. She dug the vile little thing out of her purse and downed it with an inch of that morning's cold coffee. She would go home, knock down a shot, and curl up on the sofa with her beloved Pandora.

Not wanting to jar her ravaged body unnecessarily, she opted for the elevator rather than her customary jog down four flights of stairs. Seeing the express to Four and Five stalled in the lobby, she opted instead for the *everybody* lift, the light indicating it was en route from Five. She wasn't surprised to find it empty—nobody left the executive's bastion and the Controller's Department anywhere near five o'clock. She stepped in.

The elevator whizzed past Three but braked hard on Two. Even the tiniest stutter made her belly twinge. For all its over-the-top elegance, the elevator was technologically challenged. She grabbed the brass rail and braced for the jolt. The door slid open. Shirley Granger entered first, straight-faced, without acknowledging her. Always a friendly, supportive colleague who had just dealt with Kingsley's threat, Shirley made no attempt to greet her. *Odd*, Kingsley thought.

Security chief Charles Wasleski filed in after a short woman whose face was obscured by the much-larger passengers. As they rearranged themselves for the ride, the slim woman stepped sideways. She appeared dazed until her red-rimmed eyes locked on Kingsley. The woman's face transformed into a mask of pure hatred.

A shoulder bag dangled from her right arm. An open cardboard box, anchored by her left hip, held personal items—framed pictures, an empty pen holder, a coffee mug, a partial box of granola bars, a curious doll from which protruded several hat pins, and an open box of pink notepaper. If looks could kill, Kingsley would be on a slab in the morgue.

The hustle! She must have been identified and pounced upon with immediate consequences. She wouldn't have a legal leg to stand on. Pennsylvania was an *at-will* commonwealth, meaning an employer could fire someone without reason and without notice. Unless the employer discriminated by age, gender, race, disability, et cetera, they could fire employees if they didn't like how they wore their hair, or for no reason whatsoever.

A competing bank had drawn the community's ire

when a junior officer was fired because the president wanted her job for his best friend's daughter. In spite of her flawless five-year record, their excuse was that "they weren't comfortable with her." She hired an attorney and sued, the case being settled quickly and quietly, but not before the shenanigans were publically aired. Accounts were closed. Editorials written. Lesson learned.

Great, Kingsley thought. Just what I need. Another enemy. An eternity later the elevator bumped down. Kingsley hung back until the others exited, then headed toward Lending's side parking lot. She observed the trio, lock-stepping a different direction toward the second floor's designated lot. Should she inform George Whoever, the hustle's intended target, that he'd dodged a bullet? Absolutely not.

෨෨෨

The newly baptized Steven Turner exited the highway and climbed the long driveway of the industrial complex that faced Keynote National Bank. From his vantage point high on a hill, he could monitor the bank's front, right, and rear parking lots. Armed with high-power binoculars, he settled to watch and to wait. He couldn't help admiring the opulent building with its horizontal bands of rose granite and natural stone that alternated with copper-pink windows.

Lights on tall standards winked on, dispelling early November's dusk. Gardeners were packing up their trucks, having yanked frostbitten annuals to substitute potted evergreens and hollies around which they had been tucking spring bulbs. The towering fountain's waterfall slept for the season. Chimes bonged five o'clock, quitting time for most employees. They gushed from the exits, like fans leaving a victorious Penn State football game, hoping to beat rush-hour traffic. Everyone looked eager to reclaim their private lives.

To kill time, Turner reviewed the floor-by-floor plans that identified the bank's corporate headquarters, main branch, and back-office operations. The executive suite and controllers department consumed all of Five, lending on Four, HR on Three, and so on. Commercial Lending's reserved parking spaces were one hundred yards below him.

Glancing left and right for unwelcome attention, he focused his binoculars for a better view. There—the Ward woman's old Lexus. Why the trust-fund bitch didn't trade up stupefied him. While he was contemplating his best plan of action, something far better caught his attention.

He felt his eyes widen as a fortuitous opportunity unfolded in the rear parking lot. Two big men—one in a navy suit, the other in gray dress slacks and a black leather jacket—were escorting a tiny woman toward the back row. The woman was carrying a small open carton, a purse slung over her shoulder. When leather jacket attempted to grasp her forearm, she jerked it away, giving the man a look that could kill. Perfect! She had been fired.

With only one exit onto the highway, Turner knew exactly what route she would take and where he could wait unobserved. From the armrest he extracted an envelope addressed to a county jail employee that contained a message and a self-addressed stamped envelope that would come back to his new post office box. If this young woman proved herself, he'd continue to use her. Then he'd mail envelope number two to John Miller in the county jail.

He followed the ex-banker's Ford Focus for two miles into her well-maintained suburban condo complex. He grinned. That gal's got to be over-extended. He braked at a curve before her group of twelve parking places, giving her time to exit her car and rescue her box from the trunk. He then parked near the Focus. At the most advantageous moment, he called after her exiting back.

"Miss! Oh, miss! You dropped something!"

He knew she couldn't resist taking a quick glance at her box, then turning her attention toward the voice. At the precise moment she looked toward him, he waved crumpled bills over his head. "Bet you'd have no idea where these fell out of your pocket." Seeing her suspicious face, he added, "I'm sorry. I didn't mean to startle you. Here—I'll just set them on the back of your car." He started to turn with a little wave of his hand.

"Wait," she called, readjusting the carton on her hip and edging a little closer. She set the box on the trunk and dug into both pockets, shaking her head. "It's not mine. Thanks anyway." As a breeze caught the crumpled bills like tumbling oak leaves, she leaped to stop their escape. Her eyes widened, as anticipated, at their denomination.

"See? It must be yours. Look, miss, I was supposed to meet someone here an hour ago, but she's a no-show, and nobody else has come through here. Maybe it's too early for working folks. If we just leave the bills, here on the ground where I found them, someone else will be celebrating her good fortune."

He inched closer to the trunk, picked up the money, and pretended to examine it. "Kind of dirty—probably been on the pavement for days. Whoever lost it won't know where." He straightened the crumpled bills. "A fifty, two tens, a few ones. Here! You take it. It's your lucky day."

He watched the turmoil and the *tell* it produced on her face. He extracted a paper from his pocket. "The young lady I was supposed to meet here gave me the wrong address. I've circled the complex repeatedly, but the numbers don't go this high. I could have checked with the office but thought better of it. She probably changed her mind or just didn't know how to say no to my offer. A pity—it's such easy work."

His target picked up the box and started to leave, but then reversed direction. She set her box back on the lid of her trunk. "What kind of job is it?"

"I have wealthy clients who wish to give anonymous gifts to deserving people. Having made their fortunes, they want to pay back. An individual can accept a gift under $25,000 without paying the gift tax."

"How does that work? I mean, if it's anonymous?'"

"I'm given the name of the beneficiary. I copy the letter my employer has drafted to the person in my own handwriting. I cannot deliver the letter myself because, after the first communication, I could be followed. So I hire someone to drop off the initial letter when we know that person will not be at home. It does not go through the mail. It's kind of like playing secret Santa."

"How do they get their gift?"

"The letter includes a reply card and stamped envelope, like a wedding RSVP, which another of my employees can identify as coming from the beneficiary. That person will then put it, unopened, in a larger envelope and mail it to a post office box. I have a key to retrieve the correspondence. If the beneficiary accepts the gift, they will be notified to retrieve an envelope at a particular bank branch. That envelope will contain the gift."

"What's the catch?"

"There is none. Think of it this way. Suppose you're extremely wealthy. Or a middle-class person who's able to pay your bills and make charitable contributions. And you choose a worthy charity, such as the American Red Cross or the Goodwill. You wouldn't see who ultimately benefits, right? Now suppose you've already donated to lots of charities, underwritten a hospital or library wing or emergency shelter, and you want to do more. Another scenario is broken families, grandparents irrevocably separated from children, parents, grandparents, or siblings who would not knowingly accept 'charity' from a relative who prospered, perhaps at their expense. You get the idea?"

"I think so. It sounds very noble."

"I'm sorry. I'm babbling." He motioned to the money he'd found on the ground. "Enjoy your good fortune."

She appeared to stifle tears. "I'm not feeling lucky. I got fired today. My big mouth got me into real trouble. I'm half expecting a visit from the cops."

He motioned to her attire, as if painting a picture. "I'm sure a professional person like you will have no trouble finding employment. In the meantime, don't employers give people they've downsized a severance package? Unemployment compensation? That should give you time to find something better. Even go back to school."

As he was speaking, he was delighted to see her sadly shake her head *no* to each scenario he had proposed. He reached into his pocket for a business card case and extracted one. "Here. Maybe you'd like to be a messenger for me." She studied the business card, turning it over to inspect the Christian scripture—about being more blessed to give than to receive.

"What would I have to do?"

"Well—what my no-show had agreed to do. Hang on a minute." *Bingo! She's perfect.* He handed her an envelope that was addressed to a woman. "Ground rules. Do not, under any circumstances, open this letter or keep a record of the recipient. For my employers' safety, from time to time, we slip in a little test."

"How would I get paid?"

He tugged his wallet from his hip pocket and extracted a one-hundred dollar bill, which he folded into her shaking hand.

"Are you sure this is legal?"

"Absolutely."

"What about taxes?"

"If I were you, I'd declare it as miscellaneous income. As if you were babysitting, shoveling snow, cleaning houses, or doing IT work from home. You never want to screw with the IRS!"

"Well, I guess—"

"If this works out, there will be other deliveries to make."

"How can I get in touch with you?"

"If you give me a number where you can be reached, I'll leave a message. You can use the cell phone number on my card. However, I cannot impress upon you strongly enough that our work is extremely sensitive and confidential. You cannot tell anybody about it. Not your husband, your boyfriend, your parents, your girlfriends—you get it?"

"I don't have anyone." Barely a whisper.

"And you are…"

"Nicole Smith," she said, initiating the handshake.

"Steven Turner. Nice to meet you." He handed her envelope number one and the hundred-dollar bill. "One last thing. Some merchants don't take hundreds. Ask a bank teller to break it for you. Or deposit it into your account. Bankers know a forgery from the real thing."

She was smiling as she climbed the steps to her condo, its number being committed to his memory.

As Steven Turner prepared to return to the highway, he couldn't help grinning, knowing how foolish he would look to the casual observer. If this young woman did exactly what she was told, he'd have an avenue to extract John Miller from prison. As soon as the return envelope finished its circuitous route to his post office box, he'd send John Miller a birthday card from his Aunt Mary. John would know that the game was afoot.

Nicole Smith unlocked the entry door to her four-condo cluster and peeked out the vestibule's side window. As surreptitiously as possible, she scanned the parking lot and driveway that looped throughout her development. The man who approached her was taking his good old time to get into his car. He seemed to be writing something in a tiny notebook while glancing her way. Keeping back from the glass while maintaining a clear view, she noted the man's car—an older BMW. If only she had binoculars she could read the plate.

That man's showing up as he did couldn't be a coincidence. Paranoid and suspicious by nature, she had noticed the car's distinctive front grill when it had followed her convoluted shortcuts home. After her unceremonious ejection from Keynote's corporate headquarters, she'd half expected someone would make damned sure she didn't re-enter the bank. As if she'd go postal, for god's sake.

Slowly the man got into his car, backed from the space, and continued in her direction on the one-way loop. When he slowed momentarily by her mailbox and the short flight to her door, she flattened herself against the interior wall. She listened and only peeked when she heard the motor retreating. Frozen, she glanced at the envelope, still in her hand.

With shaky fingers, she unlocked her second-floor condo, entered the security code, and shut, bolted, and chained the steel door. She dropped her carton and purse on her dinette table. Without shedding her coat, she examined the mysterious envelope she'd agreed to deliver. The seal, she realized, was minimally glued, and with very little coaxing with a Ginsu knife, it yielded without blemishing the flap or the envelope.

She tugged latex gloves from a dispenser under her kitchen sink and pulled them on, taking care not to leave fingerprints on the envelope. She sat at the table and extracted a tri-folded sheet of expensive stationery and a return envelope like she had sent to RSVP wedding invitations. The return envelope was empty.

With surprising excitement, she read a sweet letter, which enclosed a small gift and a request to return the envelope with a note. Nicole wasted no time booting up her computer and printer, scanning and saving the note and the envelope's address to her hard drive. Then she made a paper backup of both as well. The copies she stowed in a flat canvas bag that she concealed at the bottom of her laundry hamper. She really should get a safe deposit box—if she ever worked at a bank again. Fat chance of that.

Late that night, at the designated time, she discarded her paranoid thoughts. Grabbing her car keys and purse, she imagined the lucky recipient as she set off to play secret Santa.

Chapter 3

After tossing her briefcase into her Grammy's old Lexus, Kingsley headed toward her new home. As she passed under the canopy of ancient oaks and maples into the city's historic district, she felt renewed by its elegant charm. Graceful Victorian street lamps dispelled November's gloom. The 1800s industrialists, who built their fortunes and these mansions, embraced Queen Anne, German Gothic, Georgian Revival, and Victorian Romanesque architecture. They valued craftsmanship and spared no expense, even bringing craftsmen from Germany. Three-story brick and stone homes sported bay windows, turrets, dormers, and mansard roofs, some with arched windows, ornate porches, and lavish landscaping. Gingerbread in traditional colors trimmed gabled eaves.

Parking around back in her personal spot, Kingsley circled the slate sidewalk to the wrought-iron gate that led to the porch and her upstairs apartment. The stained and beveled glass windows and exquisitely carved walnut door excited her appreciation for living history in a country obsessed with tearing down to build tacky.

As she mounted the Victorian mansion's porch steps and opened the exterior door, her landlady met her in the vestibule. Kingsley had loved the landlady immediately when she had rented the entire second-floor apartment in August. A devout Christian who had no use for degenerate culture, Thalia Weber had repeatedly turned down producers who wanted exterior shots for their movies. No inducement could budge her as she adamantly insisted on maintaining the spirituality of her special home. Her spunk and vitality reminded Kingsley a bit of her Grammy.

"Dear, I didn't want to blindside you with strangers. The fellow upstairs, working on your locks, is Lew. He's from Adam's Locksmiths. Maybe you've seen their trucks? 'Adam's Your Key?' Sound familiar? They're good, trustworthy people. I know Lew from my church. Even though that very bad man who attacked you is locked up in jail, I want you to feel as secure as possible." She handed Kingsley two sets of three keys. "In place of the doorknob and lock combination, there's a brass thumb latch that looks authentic. Lew is installing two deadbolts above it. I'm also entrusting you with a front-door key." She indicated the largest key, without insulting her with *don't lose, share, or copy it.*

"I need a remedial course in motion detectors."

"Yes, I remembered to tell Lew all about it. We don't want a repeat of September, now do we?"

Kingsley felt her face flush. Had she not been running late and failed to reset the security alarm to prevent Pandora from setting off the motion detectors—again—

perhaps John Miller wouldn't have gained easy access to her apartment, even though the police insisted that no lock could stop an expert, determined psychopath like him. And he'd entered via the fire escape outside her living room window that faced the rear parking lot.

Lew met her as he exited her apartment onto the upstairs landing. He patiently took her step by step through the ultra-high-tech security system, finally proffering a little cheat sheet that translated the manufacturer's complicated verbiage. He waited while she unlocked both deadbolts, approached the keypad, and let it know she was home.

"Now lock up and re-enter again, just to make sure that you've got it." She did, and she had. Lew raised his fist to knuckle-bump hers, and she happily returned the gesture. He clattered down the steps, which reminded Kingsley how glad she was that they were not carpeted, making it even harder for someone to sneak up on her.

With emphatic meows, Pandora emerged from beneath the couch. Kingsley scooped up her gorgeous feline and ran a fingertip from her snowy white face to the longhaired tuxedo cat's fluffy black tail. Startling, Pandora's ears perked, body arching, wriggling from her mistress's hold, and streaking down the hall to Kingsley's bedroom in the farthest reaches of the apartment. Silly cat, she thought, turning left from the entry into her study. She set her briefcase beside her desk and glanced through the tall windows toward the softly lit park across the street.

As Lew's van pulled away, a familiar black SUV took its place. Todd! She darted into the bathroom for a badly needed pit stop, lathered her hands with lavender soap, and grimaced at the weary face that was beyond quick repair. By the time she opened the door to Todd's smiling face, Pandora had crept down the hall, peeked around the corner, and then on her belly, slinked back toward the bedroom. Todd shrugged. "That's one female I'll never charm."

Kingsley hung his wool dress coat on her antique stand in her office and welcomed him into her sanctuary with a hug and quick kiss. "Like a drink? If so, you can fix me one too. It's been a scotch kind of day."

Inside the narrow, U-shaped kitchen, he fetched rock glasses and poured two fingers of their favorite antidote while she hunted salted cashews and napkins.

"Thought you should know, first off, that I saw a copy of your death threat."

"How? I don't even have one. Security scarfed it up, bagged it, and handed it off to the police, just like that."

"Warren shares practically everything with me. He's distancing himself from the day-to-day, letting me run with anything *bank* as opposed to the holding corporation. His focus, he maintains, is the board, the fed, the analysts, the shareholders, and the big picture, but I suspect he's had about enough. That he's positioning me to take over so he can retire. And our president, Doug Neiman, is a lame duck. Just anchoring that position until the end of the year."

"That's great! Congratulations, President Henning."

He held up his hand. "Not so fast. Next year holds make-or-break challenges for our little bank if we don't want to be sold, due to—"

"It's not that little. Our footprint is in seven counties and growing."

"—obsolete technology, crushing turnover, checks and balances to institute, products we should have launched years ago, security problems. And we need an in-house daycare to retain single parents. That I will champion. Kingsley, we've got to launch forward! And then there's Frank. He's up to his neck in the loan scam, but he could still beat the charges, especially with an excellent attorney like R. Samuel Roth. Big Sam is famous for pulling off miracles, and, accordingly, earns big bucks."

Kingsley did not mention, nor did she remind him, that she had overheard the perpetrator-mastermind speaking to an unidentified co-conspirator—someone she believed was connected to the Executive area of the bank. Someone she could not place, nor had she heard him speak again, in spite of eavesdropping whenever possible. Could he have been an outsider?

"So what do you think? About the death threat?" she asked.

"That you ticked someone off." He appeared unconcerned. "Any ideas?"

"Loan applications we turned down were just business. I made sure those applicants understood our rationale. One couple had the down payment to purchase a farm. But they had no capital to purchase equipment, animals and feed, or money to live on until they turned a profit. We talked about their business plan, long-term goals, how to position themselves for their future. In the end, they decided to buy the land, rent it for crop farming, keep their day jobs, and stay in their doublewide while their savings grow. And so on."

She decided not to tell him about her altercation with the *hustle*. Not only had she not wanted anyone to be fired, but the scenario smacked of chick problems. A man wouldn't even have noticed, much less brought it up. She'd discuss the incident with her buddies, Barrie Brown and Margaret Stiles.

"Could you possibly—"

"Of course," Todd said, reaching for her empty glass.

"Wait. This is more than refilling my drink. I've decided to set up a trust in Andy's name with the insurance settlement. I received the draft of the documents. Could you take a peek? I'd appreciate your input."

"Do you have them handy?"

She padded sock-footed into her office and snagged two envelopes she had received from her godfather and family attorney, David Wentworth. She extracted the contents from one, which he scanned.

"Mind if I take these with me?"

She smiled and handed him the envelope. "That's not the big favor." She paused until he looked up from the page he was reading. "Would you feel comfortable coming with me to meet Andy's parents and helping me explain the trust? That is, if you have time and wouldn't find it awkward or—"

"Of course. It would be my pleasure. Whenever you're ready. I've got to tell you—it was generous of you to accept the heating oil company's settlement offer. The driver sped across the overpass and was overdue for a break. You could have held out for much bigger bucks."

"I don't need the money. I have a good job, no debts, and Grammy's trust. And I have zero interest in bankrupting that family's business. Grammy would say, 'More money does not make more happy.' In all fairness, Andy wouldn't have died if his car hadn't been pushed into that truck's path."

"Guess it's best not to remind anyone of that."

She sighed, lost in thought for a minute, visualizing the fireball captured by the media. Four thousand gallons of blazing fuel, its heat so intense that it melted the overpass, torching nearby vegetation and buckling the highway's pavement below.

"The Saturday after Thanksgiving works for the Wards. I'm afraid that I've neglected them shamelessly. And they'd like to meet you. By the way, my parents are delighted that you accepted their invitation for Thanksgiving."

"Your mom sent the sweetest note, underscoring that it was *their* invitation and thanking me again for 'all that I did' after you were attacked and hospitalized."

"They can't give up hope that a strong man will save me from self-destruction."

Todd laughed. "Personally? I feel sorry for any bastard who messes with you with nefarious intent."

ი‌ᲔᲔᲔ

Charlotte Unger could not procrastinate one minute longer. The kettle had whistled but had cooled entirely too long to steep tea. The heat that she'd wasted! She couldn't concentrate on anything other than that ugly stack of bills. She peeked at the teetering pile, wishing she had the nerve to just trash it, insisting that they must have been lost in the mail. She sighed, gathering her resolve to tackle the pile as soon as the water reheated. Setting her grandmother's vintage Revere Ware kettle back on the burner, she turned the knob, willing it to hurry. Within sixty seconds, it whistled.

She draped the teabag's soggy string over her mug that read *STRESS!* and calculated the time it would take the used bag to approach a decent beverage. She stole a peek at the pile, its top envelope bearing the power company's signature robin-egg-blue color. She'd turned her little row home into a laundry, stringing clotheslines in the basement near the old furnace to avoid using the dryer. She'd placed buckets in her shower to capture the water she'd use to wash dishes. She'd even worn her underwear while bathing to postpone using the washer.

Every plug on every appliance that ate watts with its greedy little lights had been pulled. She didn't need stupid reminders, like her rinse agent needed refilling. Every bulb in her tiny row home had been reduced to forty watts. This was no way to live. This was *his* fault, and she saw no way out. If she lost the house, she'd end up in a homeless shelter. Where would she keep her clothes? Would she be fired from her IT job at County Prison for looking unprofessional?

She sat at the scarred kitchen table, tea at her elbow, to sort the pile. A final notice here, a final-notice there, several second notices to her left. Subscription reminders, junk mail, and political ads she tossed on the floor.

What little wages she had that had not been garnished

kept a roof over her head. Charity programs reduced her oil bills to a minimum, and her church paid the water bill. How embarrassing.

By now, she understood why she hadn't seen it coming. Her husband had paid the bills. He'd kept the checkbook. He would scarf up the statements before she could see them. Having come from a desperately poor family, and having parents who had been children of the Great Depression, she had absorbed their obsessive worry about money. When they died and left her fifty thousand dollars, her panic over money was too ingrained to uproot. How grateful she was when her loving husband offered to manage their household accounts.

And then came the brutal shock that rattled her world. He had sobbed, tears and snot wetting his face and his shirt, about the sharks he could no longer pay. That they'd kill him to set an example, not *if*, but *when*, because of his gambling debts. Their dear little row house with its front porch, rockers, and potted geraniums for which they'd paid cash from her inheritance had been remortgaged multiple times, and now was in default. And she'd signed the papers without reading them. The accounts—empty. Savings—gone. Insurance—canceled. And he had insisted that he could do better by investing what she could spare from her paycheck rather than letting her participate in the prison's retirement program.

All that was left of her loving husband was a letter she'd found on the kitchen table, explaining why he must flee. It pleaded for her forgiveness. That he'd make it up to her, find a way to repay their debts and make everything right again. In the following five years, she'd heard nothing from him. A pro bono attorney had managed to separate her from their joint accounts and handled the divorce. Her husband hadn't shown up to contest it, enabling her to keep the house. Luckily, her car had been in her name, on which she carried the minimum insurance required by law.

She riffled through the envelopes again. What was this? An ad? Someone wanting her to buy a timeshare? A cemetery plot?

Her name was typed with no return address, and the stamp had not been canceled. She grabbed the paring knife with the skinniest blade and carefully removed the minimally attached stamp to reuse it. Curious, she slit open the mysterious envelope. A letter, written on heavy stock, got right to the point.

> *Dear Charlotte,*
>
> *First, let me introduce myself. Your maternal grandmother and I were first cousins. As a wild young man, I got into all kinds of trouble, eventually landing in prison. The family disowned me, which is probably why you don't know I exist. Now, in my eighties, and with no family of my own, I'm anxious to make restitution for the sins of my youth. Enclosed is a little gift. I've taken the liberty of enclosing a self-addressed stamped envelope. If you'd jot a note that I found you at the correct address, I'll send you what I can spare. Thank you for letting an old man do something decent.*
>
> *With love,*
> *Your Great Uncle Wallace*

Fingering the one hundred dollar bill lovingly, Charlotte leaped to her feet, happy-dancing to the kitchen drawer where she kept odd pieces of decent notepaper. She thought hard about what to say, not comfortable wailing about her dire circumstances. Instead, she told him she'd apply his gift to the most urgent bill, thanked him with genuine gratitude, and hurried to her mailbox to post her response and put up the flag.

What would she pay first? The mortgage she'd managed to cover from her paycheck from County Prison, thanks to her friend, Margaret Stiles, who was Keynote National Bank's compassionate VP of Residential Real Estate Lending. Charlotte didn't know what she appreciated more—Margaret's clever financial insight or her compassion. She not only dissuaded Charlotte from filing for bankruptcy but also devised a plan to lower her debts and preserve her credit rating.

Charlotte extracted the Chase credit card bill and did the math on the back of the envelope. Struck by an idea, she decided to call their customer service number and beg their understanding for additional time. Might their angel reconfigure their compounded interest? Ultimately, she'd make the minimum payment for whatever debts were most urgent. She would have logged onto ancestory.com and investigated her grandmother's tree, but she'd long since canceled her Internet service and sold her computer to buy food.

Chapter 4

Kingsley speed-dialed Todd's cell phone the minute he double-parked below her bedroom window. "Go around the block, make three turns, and then take the alley into our lot. It's okay to ignore the tow-away sign. I have a pass for your dashboard."

Ten minutes later, she heard his familiar tread as he scraped the balls of his feet on each step. She grinned, guessing he wore holes in the leather prematurely.

Throwing open the door before he could knock, she took in his six-foot-two frame, elegant yet casually dressed in a purple pin-striped shirt, navy blazer, sage slacks, and camp moccasins. She bet that his briefs matched the shirt. Far from telling a man how to dress, she had casually mentioned that her family did not play touch football. The adults were more the walk-in-the-woods types.

Eying the Coleman cooler and a Styrofoam container in her foyer, he sniffed the enticing aroma. "Just what time did you get up?"

She didn't confess that a nightmare and panic attack

had jolted her from sleep before four. "I baked yesterday, and put the meat in the slow cooker last night at six." He peeked into the Coleman.

"Pulled pork—my Aunt Beth requested it—heavenly pumpkin pie, and frozen chocolate pie are on ice. Some of the family stays over, and hence it's a two-day event."

"Are we? Staying over? I didn't bring—"

"No. I told my family that we had to get back. They didn't press or insist that we stay. If you'll grab the Coleman, I can manage the desserts."

"Heavenly pumpkin pie…"

"A secret family recipe, chiffon-like, that everyone loves. Years ago, I asked Aunt Beth for her recipe. Big mistake! Huge! I inherited the job, which takes forever. But—the good news—it makes too much for one ten-inch crust. I saved the excess in custard cups—a little treat for when we get back."

As they circled to the lot, Kingsley stopped, resting the cooler on the flagstone walkway. "Hold up a minute." He paused, following her gaze. "Just look at these trees."

Overhead, the last vibrant reds, yellows, and oranges clung to the canopy in spite of November's progression. Invigorated, she hoisted her cooler and approached the Lexus.

"Mind if I drive?" he asked. "I'm still having fun with my new ride."

She redirected her path toward Todd, who was flicking imaginary dirt from the Explorer's pristine black paint. She looked around appreciatively. Could this area have been where the original carriage house stood? Had the much smaller houses on the parallel street once been part of this property? If only she could go back in time—see history before sprawl happened. Maybe the Historical Society had pictures.

Todd ambled to the Lexis, scrutinizing the ten-year-old vehicle. "Hey, Kingsley? Did you know your tires won't pass inspection?" He inserted a penny into the tread, which exposed President Lincoln's entire forehead. "And the car has a September inspection sticker."

"Which gives me nine or ten months to replace the tires. They're fine for now."

"No, the date says you're two months overdue. I'm surprised the cops haven't spotted it by now. You must be one conservative driver."

Frowning, she read the stickers on the windshield. "Damn. One more thing to do. You better drive. The cops have promised sobriety checkpoints over this holiday weekend. It would be just my luck to be stopped for the wrong reason."

Todd aimed the SUV east on the turnpike, then exited onto the Schuylkill Expressway toward Philadelphia. Following Kingsley's directions, he headed south on the Blue Route. "How did it get its name?" the New England transplant asked.

"Decades ago, this badly needed highway was a line on a map. Some say there were three proposed routes in different colors, the chosen one being blue. It remained a blue line for so long that one young couple bought a house in its path, raised and launched their children, divorced, and sold it before the house was condemned."

"It's not called the Main Line?"

"That's a reference to the train that enabled wealthy

businessmen to build large homes in the new suburbs and commute to downtown Philadelphia. I'm guessing that's the same time-frame as the construction of the historic district where I rent. St. Davids, where my parents live, is one of the towns along the Main Line."

"So you're from the right side of the tracks…"

"No tracks. In fact, when you see the property, you'll feel like you're out in the country. It's one of the newer 'old houses.' Why do you keep looking in the mirrors? We practically have the road to ourselves." She craned her neck to sweep the left lanes and those to their rear, recognizing the same truck that had kept pace for miles.

Damned imagination. She could deal with nasty people in face-to-face confrontations, but the great unknown terrified her. She shook it off and focused on observing Todd as they approached her home turf. She remembered how she used to evaluate potential boyfriends by getting their feet under her parents' dining room table. And nobody had been a better fit than Andy and his family. *Stop it! Do not go there.*

"What are you thinking?"

She snapped to the present. "I should warn you— there's at least sixty adults, and they're going to be very curious about you. And my cousins' teasing will be downright obnoxious." He glanced at her as she studied papers, raising an eyebrow in an unspoken inquiry. "It's my cheat sheet. Dad is one of six siblings, and my first cousins range in age from ten to forty. I've scanned their most recent photos and need to check names. "The youngsters are tricky—take Suzy and Sally—one is my youngest first cousin, and the other is the daughter of my oldest cousin. So she's a cousin once removed, or something like that. They're as alike as two peas in a pod, and I don't want them to think I don't care enough to remember who's who. And every year, given their age, they change so much."

Just as she returned to the sheets, Todd yelped a string of expletives, yanking the wheel to the right, overcompensating, and plunging the Explorer into the swale. Their seatbelts locked, pinning them, finally relenting. The vehicle tipped precariously for a few seconds, teetering on the grassy swale. The SUV hung, suspended on its two right tires. Instinctively, they leaned hard to the left, taking care not to rock their fragile position.

An eternity later, it righted itself with a *thunk*. "You okay?" he asked, as she peered fearfully out her window at the precipitous incline. "We'll need a tow—just sit very still." He reached for his phone.

Above on the highway, a red sports car screeched to a stop on the berm. Two girls in Temple University sweatshirts ran to the top of the embankment and peered down. "You okay? That guy could have killed you!" one yelled. "I thought he blew you clean off the highway."

Fingers to her mouth, she pierced a whistle while the other girl waved frantically to oncoming traffic. A pickup and a BMW pulled in behind them, disgorging a half dozen jocks in similar gear, like clowns who had been crammed into a VW bug. They lined up in a row, stunned.

"Stay put," the linebacker-sized driver of the pickup called. "We'll pull you out. Don't move." He executed a precise three-point turn on the wide shoulder, angling the rear of his pickup toward Todd's trailer hitch, leaving a gap.

Kingsley watched in her side view mirror as the jock pulled on welder's gloves and connected a chain to his hitch. He slid down the bank to Todd's open window. "Will it run?" he asked.

"I didn't hit anything. Just lucky, I guess. A rock could have wrecked the transmission."

"You game to give it a try? If not, you could call for a tow."

"And miss her family's reunion? Where I'm Exhibit A? I'm game if you're willing."

He grinned at Todd's attire. "Excuse me for insulting your intelligence, but you don't look like a mechanic. Put it in four-wheel reverse. I'll give my truck some gas to pull the chain taut. Then give it a little gas until you feel your tires bite into the grass. Don't floor it if they only spin. Easy does it. When they bite, steer backward. Steady." He laughed. "And for God's sake, don't hit my truck!"

With a clank, Kingsley heard metal on metal as the guy attached the chain's hook.

"Can't thank you enough. Just for stopping and helping."

Her heart thudded so hard that she could feel her pulse pound in her neck. Her instincts screamed that she should bolt from the car and run uphill to the road. But given the pitch, opening the door could upset their precarious balance. Instead, she held fast to the dashboard and gripped the roof handle.

The truck's engine sounded incredibly loud, but maintained an even throttle as she felt the small stutter of the chain tightening.

In moments that ticked glacially, Todd eased into gear, gingerly touching the accelerator, left foot suspended over the brake to toggle the pedals if necessary. The wheels spun in the long, matted grass as he adjusted the gas with rapt concentration.

When the tires grabbed, he maneuvered the Explorer out of the swale and safely onto the berm. The audience cheered as he beamed, pumping the guys' hands. Kingsley hopped out, showering the girls with her thanks. "You could have kept going. Not gotten involved. God bless you!"

"Wish I'd paid more attention to that jackass's pickup and license. Called nine-one-one and reported him," her passenger said.

"Wouldn't have done any good," the other girl said. "It was splattered with mud."

Once underway, Kingsley loosened her grip on her phone. She had nine-one at the ready, prepared to add one more one if they'd started to roll. Reverting to her home screen, she noticed someone had left her a message. With no caller ID, her curiosity piqued—who had this number? She opened the message.

The voice was female and husky—that of an unrepentant life-long smoker. "Youse in danger. Some bad ass in County Prison after you. Brags he's gots help on the outside. Watch ya ass." Click.

Kingsley stared at the phone then hit redial. "The number you are trying to reach is no longer in service…" Had to be a wrong number, but still, her hands trembled.

She tried to continue her family's saga. "I don't want to give you the wrong impression—alone, they're conservative, traditional people. But together, they know how to have fun. One warning—under no circumstances take even one taste of Uncle Bart's homemade wine. It isn't. Wine, I mean. He trades with some good old boys in Appalachia when he goes hunting. That stuff burns with a blue flame."

Exiting at St. Davids, Todd slowed through quiet back roads to the Alderson's' secluded property, its access road bordered by limestone walls discarded by the settlers who once cleared the land. Those farms were long gone, replaced by ten-acre estates. Yesteryear squirrels had planted the oaks that interlocked in a 100-foot canopy.

Kingsley scanned late fall's progression, remembering the aroma of burnt leaves, once a common practice, but now prohibited by environmental law. Her brain conjured the distinctive scent, but mostly the time she had spent with her father who doted on his only child. Continuing the short distance, they approached the mowed weeds that bordered the Alderson's front lawn. A youngster waved bright orange sticks as if directing a 747.

Sarah Alderson flung open the door as they climbed the front steps to enter the grand foyer. Kingsley bet her mother had been pacing from the kitchen to the dining room windows for the better part of an hour. They set their load on the round Persian rug to be swept into hugs.

Henry Alderson crossed the upper gallery and took the curved stairway two at a time. "Princess!" She hugged him. "Todd, welcome!" Henry pumped Todd's hand. "We're delighted that Kingsley could pry you away from that bank, if just for the day. Thanks for driving. We worry about holiday traffic."

"Henry. Enough!" Sarah focused on them. "They've got to be starving." Henry picked up the Coleman and Sarah snagged the Styrofoam cooler, and together they headed through the large dining room that fronted the right quadrant of the Georgian mansion. "Todd, how shall I fix your eggs?" Sarah asked.

Kingsley rejoiced that traditions persisted. A quick glance into the living room, to the left of the foyer, revealed card tables set up for the children. Each was set with sterling flatware and a bud vase of fresh flowers on a white linen cloth. While the youngsters complained about their relegation to the kids' tables, they secretly enjoyed just being children whose manners would not meet adult expectations. After pictures and feasting, they could swap party clothes for jeans and bolt outside to escape supervision.

Henry clapped Todd on the shoulder and steered him through each knot of family, his approval apparent. Kingsley suspected her parents had dribbled an ongoing report about Todd, especially his arranging her bodyguard at the hospital after she had been attacked, embellishing the narrative with Todd's promotion at the bank.

Would they make it impossible for him to ease from her life if their relationship tanked? What if it didn't progress as her family seemed to promote it? What if he chose to distance himself from her family's smothering? That could be awkward, especially at work. What if…

Her mind drifted to Andy. She'd only known Todd, whom her parents now viewed as the heir apparent, for a few months. The human version of replacing a battery. Her dad was entirely too excited, overdoing the hero's welcome. *Oh, Dad.*

She slipped into the powder room to regain her composure, wishing…what?…that she could magically divide her life and live a duel existence? In the past with Andy and in the present with this new life? Had she gone with Andy that dreadful night, her entire trajectory would be different. *Shake it off.*

She took deep breaths, eyes closed, willing her mind to a calm, quiet place, to pinpoint that elusive thing that left her wrenched and bereft. She'd made a clean break, leaving Philadelphia. Made a new life that had forced her to grow. She could not go back and forth. Andy was too much a part of Thanksgiving. That was it.

Emerging, she spotted her dad with Todd by the elbow, embellishing another family story. Their brass dinner bell sounded, saving Kingsley from her convoluted emotions. A hush fell over the family. Kids froze, midcavort, and adults gravitated to seats, identified with place cards made by the youngsters. Henry Alderson's voice echoed from the foyer, where the entire family could hear him. The children hungrily eyed the platters piled with Thanksgiving specialties while their parents gave them an eyeball warning.

"Welcome!" he intoned. "It is my pleasure to introduce the newest members of our family."

A ten-day-old baby girl, who looked unconcerned, was presented to oohs and clapping. He continued through the newlyweds and guests, finally introducing Todd. Great Uncle Martin received recognition as the family's patriarch, but the deaths of his sister and a distant in-law were noted.

On cue, Henry beckoned Suzy and Sally center stage. Together they said, "Please fold your hands and close your eyes for our prayer." Their voices reverberated throughout the house.

> "For these and all thy many blessings,
> Lord make us truly thankful. Amen."

From the living room corner, Aunt Beth struck the first note on the baby grand that announced another tradition. Everyone burst into "God Bless America." Kingsley stole a peek at Todd, who was standing by the kitchen door, wearing a carver's apron. *Of course! He's been given the honor.* Hand over his heart, he was belting out the anthem, his baritone floating her way. Her eyes welled as the emotion of family swept her with love and appreciation. She swallowed hard. What if Todd slipped away? She had absolutely no faith in *forever*. Not anymore. Not after seeing poor Andy's burnt body in the morgue.

∞∞∞

Charlotte Unger searched the pantry, hoping she'd find something tasty that she'd overlooked behind the oatmeal, the rice, and the canned vegetables that remained of her monthly rations. When the calendar caught her eye, she dissolved into tears. It was Thanksgiving Day. Her joy over having a day off with pay dissipated as the lonely hours dragged by.

She remembered celebrations with her late family, the mountains of food and happy people. Now she had declined several invitations because she had no money to contribute a special dish and a hostess gift. Several charities hosted wonderful meals for the needy, but she had a job and felt she'd be stealing from families with hungry children to feed.

In happier days, she'd been a volunteer and remembered the newspaper photographers who could not resist a photo op at the expense of desperate families. What if she'd been caught in a picture? And people at work saw her taking advantage? She shunned the idea of volunteering to serve, hoping to snag a meal for herself.

Even though there shouldn't be mail today, she secretly hoped she'd get another envelope from Great Uncle Wallace. With the weather unseasonably warm, she approached the curbside mailbox coatless. She paused, hoping, pulled down the door—and could not believe her eyes. There, in the farthest recess, was another envelope just like the one she had previously received. Typewritten with no postage. Her angel had been there when she wasn't looking. With trembling hands, she tore open the envelope, not waiting to slit it neatly.

Three one-hundred-dollar bills! She could not believe it. Three! And, as before, there was a note and a return envelope addressed to a post office box in another county.

My Dear Charlotte,

Happy Thanksgiving! I have so much to be thankful for this year, especially the lovely letter you enclosed in my envelope. You are very welcome. I wish I could take you out for Thanksgiving dinner, but I no longer drive, and the kind staff where I live has been cooking for days. I am fortunate, indeed, to be able to afford a nice place to live.

Instead, please accept the enclosed gift to buy special treats. Lest you feel guilty about self-indulgence, I've made an anonymous donation to your local food bank. Thank you, again, for letting an old man have some vicarious enjoyment this festive season.

Affectionately,
Great Uncle Wallace

Charlotte's mind went blank for a minute until she remembered the not-so-employee-friendly grocery store that had the audacity to be open on a holiday. Grabbing her purse, she counted what remained of her cash and decided to spend it on gasoline first. How many times had she coasted into work, fearful that she would run out! She might use a bit of this gift to buy a monthly bus pass.

In the grocery store, she went straight to the manager's office and knocked on the door. Nobody answered. A checker, whose badge identified him as an assistant manager, approached her to help.

"I received a gift from my great uncle, but I can't tell if it's real," she said. "Can you?"

The checker examined the bills, running his finger over their surface and holding them up to the light. He grinned.

"Happy shopping," he chirped, handing back the bills and returning to his duties.

Picking up the latest sales flyer, Charlotte urged herself to stay calm. Meat that she could freeze might be problematic, as her ancient fridge was making strange noises.

Upbeat music that oozed through hidden speakers added an air of festivity as she pushed a large cart throughout the store.

Canned yams and green beans, she decided, were cheaper than fresh, but she'd treat herself to a John F. Martin's ham shank, its bone perfect for making bean soup. An hour later, she approached the same checker and was surprised that her purchases totaled less than sixty dollars. "I hate to ask you, but could you possibly break my other two hundreds? I'm afraid other merchants might think they're counterfeit."

"Sure, hon." He counted out twenties, tens, and some ones. "Y'all have a happy Thanksgiving."

"I think I just did." She hurried home with enough food to last several weeks.

She left the non-perishable items in a bag on the floor, opting instead to thank Great Uncle Wallace. Being careful again, not to sound needy, she devoted two out of three pages to upbeat thoughts, little snippets about her job, and wishes for his well-being. At least he'd know that she had a good job and appeared to be doing all right on her own.

Chapter 5

Following dessert and coffee, Henry clapped Todd on the shoulder, motioning him toward C. David Wentworth, Henry's college roommate and Kingsley's godfather. "David and I have something about which we'd like your opinion."

"He's all yours," Kingsley said, noting her dad's formal manner of speech, which experience identified as *rehearsed*. "I promised I'd help in the kitchen."

"Shall we?" Henry steered them into the library and closed the glass doors that separated his office from the foyer.

Kingsley, her mother, and aunts finished organizing the leftovers and drying the sterling, which they grouped on the dining room table. Kingsley elbowed her mother, drawing her toward the library's glass doors. They peeked. Todd and her father, hands in pockets, were looking up at the eaves through the open casement windows. Her dad was pointing to various features.

"I bet they're discussing house restoration," she said. "Todd dreams of restoring an historic farmhouse with ten or more acres—that is, if he finds one that meets his expectations. Last month he invited me to help him check out a few that were on the market, but something was dreadfully wrong with each one."

"He's not going to do that just for himself," Aunt Beth stated flatly.

Kingsley's mother and aunt smirked at each other and then at her.

Kingsley sighed. Exasperated. "He was looking long before I met him—he really hates condos and has loved Colonial history since he was a boy." The women, however, were rolling their eyes, clearly not buying her explanation.

Kingsley ambled toward the kitchen windows that overlooked the flagstone patio below. Enjoying the unseasonably warm weather, families were gathered in groups around tables, circulating pictures. One of Henry's sisters was taking notes on the tablet that held their sign-in sheets. Kingsley wondered if Todd's name was being recorded for posterity.

୧୭୧୭

In Henry's study, Todd noted that the desk chair did not face the splendid view of the gardens, but rather the foyer. Not fond of distractions? Keeping an eye on the comings and goings? A glass top protected the desk's finely-tooled leather surface, which held one small stack of file folders. Interesting. On the side walls, cherry bookshelves rose to the ceiling, holding all manner of books—history, biography, best-selling novels, and most interesting to him, old leather-bound volumes and a shelf that might contain first editions. A ladder was slid to a far corner. Todd smiled. A family who appreciate books.

Henry rolled his leather task chair from behind his desk and positioned it to form a triangle with his guest chairs. As if cued, the three sat. Todd instinctively knew where this *meeting* was going. Were they going to ask his intentions, subtly or directly? He smiled at the archaic thought. Nope. Considering what he knew of this protective family, however, he guessed they had formulated an assignment for him.

"Todd, David and I would like your opinion on something that's bothering us. Kingsley sounds positive that her attacker's accomplice isn't a threat. We don't believe that for a second. Except for her testimony, the preponderance of evidence against Miller is circumstantial. If the accomplice is bent on revenge, she is not safe. We'd like to hire a bodyguard to protect her—at least until the trial is over and the accomplice is identified and apprehended."

Not what he was expecting to hear. Todd considered his *opinion* for a moment. "Have you proposed this to her?"

The men exchanged glances that told Todd they had not.

"We were thinking of something discreet," Henry said.

Todd shook his head. "She's hyper-vigilant. She'd not only spot him but would assume he's a stalker. Maybe the accomplice himself, since she *says* she never got a look at his face. No, it will never work without her permission."

David cleared his throat. "Frankly we're…what's the right word?…anguishing about how to protect her. But from here, we just don't know how."

"Kill the messenger, if you must," Todd said, "but Kingsley's an adult—has been for years. She's mature, responsible, professional—no longer a child. I've only known her a short time, but I can assure you that she's one tough cookie, if you'll pardon the slang. I'd go as far as to say that you're endangering your relationship with her if you sneak around, trying to run her life for her."

"Well, I guess we've been told," David said.

"I apologize if I've offended you, but you asked my opinion."

"Perhaps you'd be willing to let us know if—"

"Mr. Alderson—Henry—I don't wish to be placed in the middle of a family situation. I'll intervene on the spot if she is threatened. That I can do. And I'll encourage her to keep you in the loop, even if there's nothing happening. I talk with my family on Sunday evenings. Maybe you could propose something like that. Beyond that? My answer is no."

The three looked up as Kingsley rapped on the glass and then opened the library doors. "You don't mind if I borrow him back, do you? Thanks!" To him, she said, "You've just got to see the gardens before it's too dark."

Tugging him along behind her, she grinned mischievously over her shoulder at the two best men in her life.

❧❧

By eight, most commuters had left. Others who had

traveled great distances were settling babies and toddlers in various bedrooms.

Teens had gathered on the lawn under a huge white tent with their guitars, exchanging a year's worth of stories and gossip. Her dad had lit the fire pit, and the youngsters made smores, their faces and clothes streaked with chocolate.

Nostalgia tugged at Kingsley, as she remembered Thanksgivings past. She and her cousins would visit until three, finally crashing in the fifth-floor *barracks* from sheer exhaustion. Campfires were the only thing missing, the woods being too dry. Funny—Kingsley remembered her father always said that, no matter how hard it had rained. Nobody minded.

Henry had turned on the floodlights for the adults who ambled about, deep in conversation. Kingsley watched from the patio and gestured for her mother to look. Her father and Todd, hands in pockets, were pointing toward the roof. "I wonder what they're talking about?"

Her mother groaned. "Shingles. Tell Todd not to even think about slate."

As they were leaving, Henry gave Kingsley an envelope. "Uncle David had to leave, but he asked me to give you this—it contains more details about Andrew's trust. He didn't think that today was the time or the place to get into it. He just wanted you to have fun. After you've digested it, give him a call."

Kingsley sagged, the thoughts of her visiting the Wards deflating her spirits. Fourteen months gone. Who'd ever think that the void's stinging silence could go on and on and on?

Todd appeared, lugging her coolers. "Gotta tell you, this thing is heavier than when we brought it."

Beyond the floodlights, the woods enveloped them in darkness as they trudged toward the Alderson's makeshift parking lot.

"Listen," she said. "You hear that? Acorns plopping onto fallen leaves. That first day that we spent together, remember? We ran into each other at Hawk Mountain Sanctuary and hiked the River of Rocks trail. It was warm, like today, but in late September."

An owl hooted forlornly somewhere above them.

"And you thought that I was a stalker."

"Well, it was a curious coincidence—"

"Which I invented when I overheard you asking your pal Barrie if she would go hiking with you. And she was tied up. 'Ah, ha!' I thought."

"It was a special day." *The first I'd spent alone with a man since Andy died, and I didn't think about him until I got home. How guilty I felt!*

The owl hooted again. She shivered. He laughed. "Could have been worse. He could have said, 'Nevermore.'"

"I'm glad you drove—I really am bushed."

"And I'm glad we're returning in one piece." He patted his ride. "Poor baby."

"Did you tell anyone about our 'adventure' en route?"

"No. You?"

She shook her head. "So—what was the big meeting about? Did they admonish you to obey my curfew? Grill you about your intentions? Request a criminal background check?"

He repeated the conversation about a bodyguard.

She overkilled slamming the car door. "That would ruin my life! And possibly my career." She huffed. "Like I'm a dignitary or rock star or president for god's sake? Friends, colleagues, clients—I'd be unapproachable." She jerked sideways hard enough to stutter the seatbelt. "I hope you convinced them it was a horrible idea. I've been a legal adult for a decade."

"Yeah, well—"

"My life would have been easier if I'd been a middle child."

"They wouldn't be any less protective or loving. Think how helpless they must still feel. Put yourself in their position—someday your roles will reverse—you, the parent, and they the children. That's already happening with my folks. Mom's too arthritic to drive, and Dad has macular degeneration. Had several small accidents. Took all three of us to convince them to downsize to a retirement community."

She shook her head. "That won't happen anytime soon, but I've got enough on my plate without placating them."

They fell into silence as they sped up the Blue Route in negligible traffic.

As they pulled onto the turnpike, Todd returned to the topic of her parents. "If your dad's the instigator, how about using a little blackmail?"

"Huh? About what?"

"If he's determined to intervene in your life, threaten to rat him out. He bragged that he's still agile enough to go out on the roof to make minor repairs. Clean gutters and so on. With a little cajoling, he confessed that he waits until she's away for the day. And he's very proud of the patio flagstones—says he can still lift them and plans to expand them. She doesn't approve or know about that either."

She nodded. "Renovating that house was compensation for their not having children—it was a wreck when they bought it. They've hosted Thanksgiving since before I was born. The patio and gardens have seen recitals, luncheons, and even a small wedding and reception. The only thing they couldn't get past was Christmas morning—no little people to tear into stockings. They'd host a big Christmas Eve dinner, followed by midnight church, then leave on vacation Christmas afternoon."

Todd looked over at her, and she, looking back, squeezed the hand that he offered. She chose her next words with care. "Of course they were thrilled, but after ten years of trying, they were settled, enjoying the life they had built. They had each other. That's what they say really mattered to them. It's ironic that I find myself in the same situation, having had a disastrous miscarriage."

There. She'd said it. If his intention was family, including children, he'd know to look further. They rode in silence until Kingsley remembered her godfather's documents. "Dad gave me more material to take to the Wards. Uncle David liked your suggestions. I'll understand if you've had second thoughts about coming along."

"It would be my pleasure. But, Kingsley, I've got to ask you. Did your mother think that I'd steal the silverware?"

Startled, she laughed. "Why would you ask that?"

"They were counting it after they washed it."

"Oh, that! They knew how many pieces they'd used. If the count was correct, they don't have to look through the garbage."

"Couldn't they use plastic for such a big group?"

"Nope! Using the family pattern is a tradition for the adults—Gorham Chantilly. For the kids, a chance to be grown-up and learn social graces. Then, when they're invited to the White House for dinner, they'll know which fork to use."

"Seriously?"

❧❧❧

Todd and Kingsley could see from blocks away that bright light illuminated her block. As he circled the one-way streets, the source became obvious. Floodlights illuminated the rear of her landlady's house. A medical emergency? Burglary? When she hopped out of the Explorer, however, her eye fell on her car's broken passenger window and two flat tires.

"What the hell?" she mumbled, circling the Lexus, where she discovered two more flats. The glovebox hung open, its contents strewn on the seat. "Todd!"

He closed the distance in several long strides, stooped to examine the damage, then shot to his feet, head swiveling, eyes darting in every direction. They froze momentarily, listening for running footsteps.

"Yoo-hoo!" a familiar voice called from the mansion's first-floor bedroom window. Kingsley recognized her landlady's provincial accent and relaxed. "Everything's all right, dear," the woman said. "The police have been and gone. You're safe."

Todd hoisted the coolers and nodded for Kingsley to proceed. Circling to the front door, they found Thalia Weber waiting for them, the door to her quarters slightly ajar.

"I'll drop these upstairs by your door," Todd volunteered and was back in a minute.

"What happened?" Kingsley asked.

"Please, come in and sit down." Mrs. Weber motioned them to a Victorian humpback sofa, upholstered in magnificent brocade. Half expecting horsehair on a slab, Kingsley eased gingerly onto the seat, immediately delighted by its plush comfort. Todd, sitting beside her, looked ridiculous with half his thighs extending beyond the edge of the diminutive cushions. Men must have been a foot shorter when the sofa was made.

"May I serve you some tea? Perhaps a little sherry? I must confess I'm a bit ahead of you, what with all the excitement."

"What happened?"

"Well, a little background first. We ladies have a mystery book club. We're great fans of Agatha, Sherlock, Jessica, James, and whatever author is on the bestseller list. But we're so much more than a book club. We have a little crime watch in our respective neighborhoods. Not that we'd take the law into our own hands. How foolish would that be at our age. We do surveillance. Report anything suspicious." She pointed to a pair of Nikon binoculars on her coffee table, a skinny flashlight, and an impressive camera equipped with a telephoto lens. "I heard a noise that didn't belong. I killed the hall light and crept upstairs to my bedroom window." Her eyes widened, just thinking about her adventure. "My bedroom window faces the parking lot, not like yours which face front. Oh, don't look so worried. I know where every last thing is, and I keep a clear path so I won't trip in the dark. A broken leg would spoil my fun. Anyway, with a bit of moonlight, I could make out a figure crouched by your car. So, with my flashlight in my left hand and my camera in my right, I flicked it on. The moment the culprit looked up I hit and held the button to take multiple shots." She clapped her hands in delight. "Then I called nine-one-one."

"Did you see who it was?"

"Sure did. Showed that nice policeman who patrols our neighborhood. He recognized the kid at once. Local riffraff." She handed Kingsley the patrolman's card. "He asked you to call the station in the morning. Now, how about that sherry? Perhaps your young gentleman would like something stronger?"

Todd rose. "Thank you, ma'am. That's very kind of you. But I'm driving and tomorrow's a workday."

She pretended to scribble something on her right palm with her left index finger and then shook his hand. "Your rain check." She grinned.

After exchanging departure pleasantries with their hostess, Kingsley unlocked her door. Todd snagged the coolers and dropped them on the kitchen floor. "I think I've about had it for one day. Speaking of rain checks, I haven't forgotten that extra heavenly pumpkin pie filling in your fridge."

"Come tomorrow for Thanksgiving part two. Those coolers hold enough for a feast."

"Agreed. And Kingsley, I'll bring a bottle of something suitable to review those trust fund documents. If we're going this Saturday, we better get to it."

On tiptoe, she wrapped his neck in a hug, relishing his scent and the feel of his soft cashmere sports coat against her cheek. He felt as delicious as any treat she had enjoyed at her parents. "Thank you so much for a wonderful day."

"My pleasure," he said, bending to give her a sensual kiss.

After he left, Kingsley felt enormously relieved to be back in her own sanctuary that she had built away from her past.

Chapter 6

Kingsley awoke, basking in the afterglow of her family's Thanksgiving celebration. Her family and Todd's compatibility outstripped her expectations. She had agonized over what could go wrong, but such thoughts had vanished like mist the minute they were swept into her family's embrace. What a relief and stark contrast to the previous Thanksgiving, just two months after Andy had died. In spite of her family's warmth, her attendance had cast a pall over the entire gathering.

Every imaginable detail designed to put her at ease had broken her emotionally. She'd have thought that couldn't be true. She felt trapped, claustrophobic, and wished to escape. Her compassionate mother had drawn her upstairs to her refurbished childhood bedroom, kept the family at bay, brought her a plate of her favorite food, and suggested she follow that with a nap. Lulled by the familiar rustle of the trees, hushed voices that drifted upstairs, and homey scents, she had fallen asleep and never awakened until the next morning.

One year later—what a difference! Just an ordinary day, one where her most exciting experience would be buying new tires and ordering a window for the Lexus. She would get a tow to the dealership and then fulfill her promise to babysit the Lending Department. She cherished *dull*. Employees with families should enjoy the four-day weekend, but somebody had to cover Lending, if only to answer the phones. A very casual Friday.

Thanksgiving turkey and trimmings part two with Todd for dessert? Grinning, she hopped out of bed, feeling renewed. She showered deliberately with an exquisite new gel while the coffee perked, then fluffed her unfamiliar hairstyle with a shot of the blow dryer and did her minimal makeup routine. A dressy sweater, flats, and designer denim? Scratch the denim for something corporately correct, even on Friday.

Errands accomplished, Kingsley took Keynote's elevator to Four and entered the Lending Department's domain. The scene was blissfully quiet. No phones clamoring for attention, no elevator pings announcing colleagues or clients, no staff from other departments keeping appointments. No drama. No emergencies.

She scanned the maze of gray staff cubes and immediately missed the bank of filing cabinets that used to form the clerical area's right boundary. Facilities had pulled off a miracle—for overtime pay—moving all lending's files to the new rolling system in the old conference room.

Curious, she dumped her coat and briefcase and toured the upgraded facility. With one hand she rolled the new shelving units apart until she read *Commercial Lending,* whose files were huddled in alpha order. She had feared that comingling all Lending files would invite chaos. She had voiced that opinion vociferously, even though she was a newcomer and as such usually let others lead. But she had prevailed. Lesson reinforced: trust yourself to anticipate trouble.

"You like the new system?" Kingsley jumped. Nathaniel Frazier's AA approached her. "Oh! Sorry, Kingsley. Didn't mean to startle you. A police detective came to see you a little while ago. I told him you'd be in momentarily. He's chilling in the visitor's lounge. I got him some coffee. I'll direct him to your office," she said, all in one breath.

She disappeared before Kingsley could answer.

Back in her office, Kingsley flipped on her lights, hung her coat on the stand she'd snagged at a flea market, and set her briefcase on the credenza beneath the ceiling-high wall of windows. She gazed at the panoramic view beyond the parking lot, a vista undisturbed by human intrusion. Hemlocks, pines, beeches, and nearly bare maples and oaks interlaced in a splendid design that no human gardener could replicate.

"Ms. Ward?" He introduced himself and handed her his card. A sergeant, not a detective. Someone she hadn't met. "I'm following up on the vandalism of your car yesterday evening."

Kingsley felt her heart rate settle, having momentarily feared some new information had surfaced about Miller's accomplice. Forcing her to perpetuate a lie. For her own sanity, she had tried to blot out any memory of him until she almost believed it. Pretending he never existed. Publicly insisting she never saw his face. But she had.

Miller had slung her over his shoulder, arms and legs bound with silver duct tape, and toted her toward the woods like a sack of grain where he would either bury her alive or kill her first. Even in that remote area accessed only by rutted trails, approaching engines had thwarted the plan.

He'd unlocked the trunk of his old Buick and tossed her inside like yesterday's refuse, slamming the trunk and splitting in the other guy's truck.

Her face hurt, just thinking how it had smacked against Miller's back. Arching her neck to its painful capacity, she had seen the other guy in a series of short bursts. Five-ten? Thin, middle-aged, unshaven face, grubby work clothes, a flash of light eyes, a scar, hands—something wrong with his fingers?

She would have died of thirst and exposure had not lost hunters from Ohio crashed from the underbrush and heard her screaming and kicking from inside the trunk's prison.

"I'm sorry," Kingsley said. "What were you saying? Did you find out who slashed my tires?"

He nodded. "That landlady of yours is quite a character. We're quite familiar with her and her…um…book club You wouldn't believe the useful tips those ladies report. They're having a ball."

Kingsley frowned. "Doesn't it occur to them that they could be putting themselves in danger?"

He was shaking his head, even as she was asking. "Their Wednesday luncheon is preceded by an hour at the firing range. Yep, they're licensed, and they're excellent shots. They practice, compare targets, break down their weapons, stow them in their trunks, and the loser buys lunch and the first glass of wine."

Kingsley grinned. The same lady who adamantly rejected all movie producers' offers to use exterior shots of her home. That, she said, would sully the aura of her home and compromise her Christian principles.

The sergeant sobered. "We caught your slasher, since the punk is well known to us. And your landlady caught him in the act with her camera. Now that he's no longer a juvenile, we'll be on him for any violation. He gave us a really lame story about some man offering him a hundred bucks if he'd slash the tires. Meaning yours. Said his girlfriend needed new ones to pass inspection, which would cost hundreds. But if somebody slashed them, insurance would pay for them. The kid said he waved five twenties under his nose. One hundred bucks for five minutes work, he'd be making twelve-hundred dollars an hour. And where else could he make such easy money?"

"Did the kid say what the man looked like?"

"Nothing useful. Old, which could mean anyone over thirty. Funny scar on his cheek."

"How about his hands. Anything unusual?"

The sergeant gave her a quizzical look and then shrugged. "Gloves. Black gloves, which the kid thought was odd since the evening was warm."

"I'm surprised he would notice."

"He wouldn't have, except that the gloves 'fit kind of funny.'"

಄಄಄

Nicole Smith threw her L.L.Bean jacket over her flannel pajamas to snag her newspaper from its curbside box. In addition to the latest news, she found a five-by-seven-inch padded envelope tucked between the national and local sections. From the distinctive printing in capital letters, she identified it immediately as an assignment from her new employer.

As per his instructions, she did not pull the string to reveal the contents until she locked herself in her condo. From its depths, she withdrew a cell phone, which she recognized as a burner. Cheap. Untraceable. Limited minutes. An attached sticky note instructed her in large letters, *call me from the park at ten o'clock.*

Her employer's paranoia had seemed comical at first, but now a little bit creepy as delivering gifts became more complicated. Her increased compensation, however, dispelled any misgivings as she stuffed his wad of bills into her wallet. Besides, she enjoyed the adventure. Ignoring his orders to never open the recipients' envelopes, she always disobeyed, reading and copying the contents, certain a much bigger payoff awaited decoding. At face value, it appeared that a stranger was giving great pleasure to someone worthy. She was dying to know more about the rich uncle. If she could identify him and find a way to meet him, who'd know? Well—her boss might, and she still knew nothing about him. Once she did, she would play him.

Unearthing his business card from its hiding place, she acknowledged her challenge. If she intercepted a delivery mid-destination, would she be able to pilfer its contents? No. Bad idea. The recipient might mention the amount of the gift. On the other hand, could she be involved in something illegal, like money laundering? Nonsense, she scoffed. Both employer and client appeared to have commendable motives. Psyched for adventure, she killed time until nine-forty-five. She grabbed her car keys, the burner phone, and the sticky note that included an unfamiliar number to call.

Having parked near the children's playground equipment, Nicole strolled past the mommies, grandparents, and nannies to an unoccupied baseball diamond. No doubt sports were not scheduled for Thanksgiving weekend. When she found a location with excellent reception, she dialed her employer's number. To her surprise, the outgoing message was addressed to her personally, not by her name but her condo number.

"Return home. Taped under your mailbox, you will find a tiny envelope with a key to a locker and where to find it. From the locker, remove an envelope and take it to the First Union branch that is noted on the envelope. This delivery requires a bit of acting on your part. Give the envelope to a teller and say that their customer, to whom it's addressed, is expecting it and will stop by at her convenience. Leave before she can engage you in conversation. Your compensation will be delivered as soon as our beneficiary claims her gift."

Nicole fled the park, scanning her surroundings for a glimpse of her employer, whom she had only seen once. Except for the little scar on his cheek and his expensive driving gloves, she realized she remembered little else. He was just average. And she'd been totally flustered by her humiliating ejection from the bank being witnessed by her fellow employees en route to their cars. And then she'd been followed home, not by a bank security guard as she'd first thought, but by a stranger who offered her this strange job.

She stopped before exiting the park as an idea took shape. She'd coax further interaction with the strange man. Same formula. Learn the benefactor's identity and vulnerabilities. Ingratiate herself and capitalize on any lucrative potential. Just as she had intended when luring a wealthy EVP away from his wife. It occurred to Nicole that her employer might be the rich benefactor!

She redialed. Waiting through the outgoing message, she left her own script after the beep. "Good morning, sir. Am thoroughly enjoying my work. My goal is excellent execution and your increasing confidence in me. If this new assignment meets with your satisfaction, I hope you'll trust me with even more sensitive work that requires the utmost discretion. All the best, Your Secret Santa."

Upon arriving home, Nicole detached the key and a note that specified a bus station across town. That must have been why she'd been sent to the park, although she hadn't noticed his Beemer when she headed out. She must be more observant and begin matching cars with her neighbors to spot an outsider. Another envelope was wedged in the back of the newspaper box that contained an envelope addressed to Charlotte Unger. And this time the glue had come loose. She grinned. It must have come from a box of really old stationery. A sticky note message instructed Nicole to deliver the envelope after dark Sunday evening. With gloves, Nicole gingerly extracted Un-

cle Wallace's letter and grinned. Miss Charlotte would
have an exceptional Monday.

Chapter 7

Kingsley felt each familiar bump in the long gravel driveway that bisected her in-laws' rural estate. Six years of memories unfolded like a tapestry unfurled on a vast banquet table. For all her resolve during Thanksgiving's merriment, she was losing her nerve. Todd's ease with her family, her cousins' teasing, the balmy weather, and the snugness of family now dimmed in late November's austerity and the mission at hand.

That she would be introducing their son's potential replacement after just fifteen months seemed—what? Cruel? Unkind? Unthinking? Rude? The precise superlative escaped her.

"I'd have understood if you were uncomfortable meeting the Wards and explaining Andy's trust," Kingsley said.

"It's my pleasure."

For once, his smile failed to warm her. She shivered, even though the Explorer's heated seat failed to warm her.

Wind gusts that topped twenty-five miles per hour buffeted their ride.

"I'm sorry. How many times have I asked that same question? It's just that I don't know if I can do this," she barely whispered.

"Which? Explaining my intrusion or describing the trust?"

She shrugged, gazing out the window at the wind-swept vista of southeast Pennsylvania's first dusting of snow. "You're hardly intruding. You understand the mechanics of setting it up—the advantages and the pitfalls."

"Once you start talking, you'll be just fine," Todd said. "From everything you've said, the Wards will always include you as family. Let them know that you feel the same way."

Caroline Ward, who'd stepped from the sprawling stone and cedar contemporary, approached Todd's door first. "Saw you coming from two miles away. That's the advantage of living on a perch. Thanks for bringing our girl." She extended her hand and gave his cheek a motherly peck. She circled the Explorer to hug Kingsley. "We've missed you, haven't we, Father?"

Dr. Ward had appeared, smiling but silent, and kissed Kingsley's cheek. Taking her father-in-law's hand, she brought the two men face to say. "Father Ward, I'd like you to meet Todd, formally William Todd Henning." She left out the part about his being the third. "I understand that you've met his father?"

"That I have. Welcome, young man." He shook Todd's hand. "It's freezing out here—let's go into the house."

Inside the vaulted great room, Kingsley scanned the Ward family's lineage that displayed six generations. She had wondered—but there it was—her bridal portrait still hung with the others. "Father, why don't you bring in the tray? Set it here on the coffee table."

Dr. Ward looked relieved to be given a mission and disappeared. The hitch in his gait was something new, and he looked so much older. He returned five minutes later with a pot of hot spiced tea and plates of warm cookies. "I do wish you could stay for dinner," Carolyn said as she poured. "You'll owe us a return visit if you don't."

That invitation Caroline directed specifically to Todd. She passed Kingsley a china cup and saucer but poured mugs for the men. Kingsley remembered Andy's fumbling to hold a teacup the first time she'd served him, spilling the hot contents onto his lap. Wife lesson number one: save the dainty china for her girlfriends.

Déjà vu. When Andy had first brought her home, his mother had fussed nonstop to put her at ease, almost to Andy's exclusion. She'd known intuitively that Kingsley was petrified. Now they chatted as easily as the family they had become. Gradually the conversation shifted to the reason for their visit.

Todd said, "I can only imagine what you've been through losing your son and at such a young age. My little sister died when I was twenty-two. She was just nine. My younger brother, other sister and I had helped raise her. She was our baby, too, and we hurt so deeply. But I'm sure that was nothing compared to the way our parents still feel." He gestured to the large manila envelope and nodded for Kingsley to expand on its details.

"As I explained on the phone," she said, "the fuel oil company's proposed settlement was very generous. I'm glad you agreed not to sue for further damages."

Dr. Ward sat on the couch by his wife, arms draped over his thighs, eyes on his shoes. "What murky places litigation might take us, especially now that we know that Andy's car was deliberately pushed into that truck. Even if the driver had altered his log and been on the highway entirely too long, the media would have a field day," he said.

"That's what our family's attorney, David Wentworth, admonished. Besides, the offer was generous. Between my job and my trust fund, I don't need money."

"Your godfather is right." Dr. Ward focused on Kingsley. "Is it over now? I mean, the criminal case?"

Kingsley stole a look at Todd. "Andy's killer is in jail. And he's facing charges on a number of felonies. I'd consider it over."

"If there's a trial—you *will* let us know." Andy's parents exchanged looks that told Kingsley they'd discussed this many times. Perhaps they wouldn't know if they could attend until the last minute.

"Of course," Kingsley said. "If you wish, I'll pass along any details as they unfold. Unless, of course, that would be too painful."

"Thank you, dear. We'll give that some thought."

"Dr. and Mrs. Ward—"

"Please, Todd, it's Carolyn and Ed. Do explain what you all have in mind for this money."

"Kingsley considered donating the settlement outright,

but if invested, the funds would keep growing and working."

Kingsley said, "Trustees would be chosen to write a
mission statement and direct the income each year. I propose that the Lions International Eyeglass Program be a
beneficiary since that was Andy's personal charity. The
objective would be to carry out what Andy would have
done himself. Since you're an ophthalmologist, Father
Ward, you'd be a perfect trustee. I would serve along
with someone representing the Lions. Maybe others.
We'll play that by ear. I'll leave the material with you to
read privately, then we can talk again."

The Wards scanned each page together and then set
them aside. Caroline finally said to Kingsley, "I found a
shoebox among Andy's things that I think you should
have. It appears to be letters you wrote him before you
were married. Why don't we take a look?"

Kingsley felt her insides clutch, not trusting herself to
revisit happier times and have a complete emotional
meltdown in front of his loving family and Todd.

"I have a marquetry box I'd been saving for something
special," Carolyn said. "No old shoebox for our treasures,
right? I put it and the shoebox in a Lord and Taylor bag,
thinking you'd prefer to sort the contents in private.
And," she added with a cheerful lilt, "I'm choosing new
wallpaper for the guestroom. I've been dying to get your
opinion. Come."

"I'll show Todd around," Dr. Ward said. They
shrugged back into their coats, scarves, and gloves. He
led Todd outside. They crunched down the driveway and
crossed the field where he pointed out Appalachian

ridges, gray in the distance, and other landmarks. Mostly, he walked with his hands in his pockets, not speaking. Finally, he did.

"She always said that, when she died, it would not be morning because her spirit just wouldn't leave. For that split second, before I could ask about Andrew, I was *terrified* that she'd been in that car too because it was dark and cold and wet and late. And now this, this monster who attacked her—"

"They got him. He'll be in prison for the rest of his life."

"Is there any chance that he could get free? Some clever legal maneuver? A so-called violation of his civil rights? Rights! What about hers? And Andrew's? In some places of the world, he'd have been shot."

Todd kept shaking his head. "Kingsley identified him as the killer who failed, twice, to eliminate her. That killing both her and Andrew was 'business.' If he doesn't take a plea and insists on a trial, she is adamant that she will testify. Her focus is on your son's death, not what happened to her. For everyone who loved your son and his loss to the world." Todd faced Dr. Ward. "If he ever gets free, if he ever comes near her or threatens her or harms her, I will kill him myself with my bare hands. That, I promise."

The man, Todd thought, looked so broken. He tried changing the subject to the house and the land, but the gentleman was too clearly focused. Dr. Ward scanned the mountains, then turned back to Todd.

"A death of innocence, that's what it is. Why her? Such a bright spot in a very dark universe. No one to defend her. We'd begged her to come live with us after Andrew was killed. Didn't know she was moving until the last minute. Those damn reporters, selling their papers. Prying into every corner of our personal lives. Andy was so protective, always knew where she was. Didn't want her to go out alone in the evening. He didn't care much for himself, but knew her tire tread to the millimeter, the pressure, made sure the tank and the reservoirs were full."

"Sir, she's healing, inside and out. She's making friends, likes her work and her new place. This crime that ensnared her was craziness: wrong place and wrong time. She's resilient and determined. I think she's just tired and a bit nervous about bringing me here."

Dr. Ward studied his face. "Are you close?"

"Not in the Biblical sense if that's what you're asking. We're close friends and colleagues."

"Andrew was so quiet," her father said. "She had this way of getting him talking, then stepping back. So many things I'd never have known, like his being obsessed with not wasting his gift. Hearing him say how he felt about us, his world, about God. That he'd accepted Christ as his Savior. That's such a comfort to know. We owe that to her. Now this settlement money and the trust. Most would have spent it."

"I'm glad you approve. Kingsley's determined to honor him in a meaningful way. If you'd needed the money, it would have been yours."

"She said on the phone that the trust was your idea."

"No. It was hers. She knew what she wanted to do. I merely suggested the banking mechanics."

He stopped again. "People like her were never meant to be alone and so scared."

"Does she seem scared?"

"She's changed. You should have known her before. We had to go to this charity ball, and we men couldn't dance. 'Anything's easy if you know how to do it,' she'd quoted her grandmother. We had a few drinks then moved the furniture. She taught us both. We weren't any good, but oh, how we laughed. And we stopped dreading those awful events. She taught Andy to be comfortable with himself and with others."

He fell silent again as they circled the house. "Don't make our mistake, Andrew's and mine. If you care about people, tell them before it's too late. Life is so short. Don't waste it on things that don't matter."

When the time came, Todd said goodbye, excusing himself to give them some privacy. Kingsley hugged both, and then Dr. Ward hurried inside.

"He didn't want you to see him cry," Caroline said. "I can count on one hand the times that I have. I don't know what to say, except thank you for what you're doing. And your Todd's a fine man. You always did have very good taste."

"He's not really mine."

Caroline squeezed her arm. "It's obvious that the two of you have a special bond. Dare I say it? Even more than you and our Andy until you adapted to each other. I feared that we parents promoted a family merger. If you're ready to take your life to an exciting new level, don't let what others think spoil your future. Grab it and hang on. You have our blessing, wherever your heart takes you."

❦

"You did well," he soothed her, then concentrated on finding the backcountry roads to the Pennsylvania Turnpike.

She added another damp tissue to the wad in her pocket. Finally, she said, "You never know when you're going to do something for the last time. Being back there— seeing them again—it was so much harder than I thought it would be. In my wildest imagination, I never dreamed being part of their family would be over so quickly."

"How long had you known them?"

"Since college, although our parents' charity work brought them together at various junctures. Our parents knew each other before we did, odd as that seems. Andy, so gifted, went to boarding school in New England where he thrived. Our paths didn't cross until our junior year at Penn."

"You don't have to turn them in like a used car. Maybe you could meet them someplace unfamiliar, do something new. A play or a concert, or a day trip. Avoid both the house and old patterns."

She nodded, absently kneading her palm with her thumb and gazing outside at nothing.

"They're obviously very good people who will always love you as family. That's worth more than gold."

"Andy was so like his father."

They rode in silence for a few miles.

"What are you thinking?" he finally asked.

"I was trying to remember when it all got so serious. In college, my sophomore year, a bunch of us went to a Penn State football weekend. I'd yelled myself hoarse. That evening a frat pledge perched me on the bar to help hand out the mugs. I'd croak greetings that sounded grotesque, which cracked everyone up. I wonder whatever happened to that girl."

Todd thought of the father and knew, but said nothing.

"Thing is—in those days, I was so happy. We worked hard and played hard." She searched deeper, then continued. "Friends say I'm a bit of a chameleon. That I'm like the people I'm with. I admired Andy's dedication—tried too hard to be like him. I guess that's one reason I like where I am now, however that happened. It's a chance to grow back into myself. I'm resolving to find whatever it was that once made me happy. I want to dance on the table again." She looked and caught him smiling at the dark road ahead.

Ten miles farther, she asked, "And what are *you* thinking?"

"Oh, nothing really." Then, shifting position, he kept looking ahead. "Well, that's not true. I was thinking about something Randall said, but it's rather personal."

Kingsley watched bare trees flicker striped shadows across the pavement and the hood of the car in hypnotic fashion.

Apparently having second thoughts, he continued. "After seeing us interact, he couldn't believe we weren't sleeping together. That you'd think I didn't want you, that you were undesirable. I said I thought that you needed time, or something like that. That you're being pushed, even by family who love you, to hurry up. Pull your life back together. Get on with it to make others comfortable again. I was wondering who was right."

"You were, but it's not about time. You're used to sophisticated women, which I am not. Once the novelty wore off—"

He turned, surprised, to look at her face.

"Todd, the guardrail!"

He quickly made a minor correction and cut down his speed.

"It was—the downside. We had intimacy issues. Maybe if I'd been more experienced before I met Andy, I would have known how to interest, to please him."

Todd pulled the car into a rest stop and put it in Park, engine running. She didn't look up but mechanically continued rubbing her palm.

"You don't have to go there. It's none of my business."

She continued, somewhat detached. "We were like, well, old folks at home. But someone like you—"

Todd put his hand on her arm and gave it a gentle shake. "Please. Let's stop right there. Let me say something." He looked intently into her eyes, and she saw emotions that reached to her depths. "You're an incredibly desirable woman. It's been all I could do to keep my hands off you, from dragging you off and locking you away with me. Surely you feel that."

He released her eyes and proceeded to tell her exactly what he'd told his best friend. "I don't want to be the bridge between *what was* and *what could be*. I had an incredibly bad marriage. I'm not sure I've ever known real intimacy. When it's right, pressure off, when it's fun, and we're ready, we'll figure it out."

"You have a way of making everything seem right."

He cupped her chin in his hand, and meeting her halfway over the console, kissed her. Momentarily a state trooper pulled up beside them and called from his window.

"Everything all right, sir?"

"Couldn't be better. Thanks."

Window up, Todd put it in gear and pulled back onto the turnpike.

Chapter 8

Friday at noon, the detectives who investigated both the murder in Keynote National Bank's vault, as well as the twelve-million-dollar loan scam that Kingsley Ward had uncovered, met over brauts and fries to brainstorm ideas.

"The ADA says, 'get more on Frank Ziegler.' In spite of blood evidence, he was captured on camera at the time of the murder fifty miles away. That he masterminded the loan scam would sound like enough pure speculation to raise reasonable doubt for the most challenged juror. Ms. ADA says 'break that alibi.' And 'nail him on that scam.'"

"Is it possible that he could walk on both?"

His partner batted that thought away. "We both know the man's guilty, and he's not *that* smart. We just have to prove how he managed the illusion. How about this? Suppose Ziegler reset the vault's timer?"

His partner paused mid-chew, hypnotized momentarily by that thought, remnants of sauerkraut and shredded onion sticking to his lower lip. He deftly tongued them into his mouth. He watched midday traffic stream past the busy city intersection. "Perhaps he had help."

"An accomplice? Then explain the blood evidence. It's Ziegler's, all right. He claims he snips those custom labels from his neckties because they're useless for someone his height. You're supposed to tuck the small end of the tie through the label to secure it. He claims a label got tracked into the vault."

"Right, with his blood on top of it? Explain that! It didn't just walk itself into that vault within what, a thirty-minute timeframe?"

The two munched in silence for a few moments.

"Even if the victim, Juanita, had enemies who followed her here from Columbus, how could they possibly learn enough in six months to commit the murder? With her accomplice as a minor player in the loan scam now dead, we have no suspects."

"Wait a minute. Try this. Ziegler was once a branch manager, right? That vault's an antique that they show off on tours. It came from their original building. He must know how to reset the timer."

"But Shirley Granger said once the door is closed—"

"That's not where I'm going. If I heard correctly, the timer was set sometime earlier in the day. The last person working simply closes the vault door. Slam. Click. Now suppose you were Frank and you wanted to set up an alibi. Or an accomplice that could do it while he was in Philly. That vault's in a corridor that's fairly remote. You simply reset the timer to reopen at *eight p.m.*, not *eight a.m.* Meanwhile, Frank chats up a teller, two hours away in Philly in plain view of their security camera, and returns to keep a meeting with Juanita. The time of death could be off by hours. Don't forget, they didn't find her until eight the next morning."

"He would have had to arrange to meet her." He rubbed his forehead and looked off, lost in thought. "Let's check his email and phone records, both home and at work, for any communication that day and the time that the workmen knocked off. Who arranged to have the electricity turned off and staff sent home early? And how visible is the vault's timer, anyway? Would the manager have easily noticed the change? And the vault's temperature—by how much could the time of death vary? Did Juanita have a key to the bank?"

"All tellers did."

His partner shook his head. "Why did they even *bother* with locks?"

☙❧

Later that afternoon, Keynote's head of Security, Charles "Chas" Wasleski; Shirley Granger, the senior VP under whom Branch Administration reported; and the two detectives crowded the narrow corridor outside the bank's vault. The corridor connected Shirley's back offices on the south end of the first floor with the centrally located main branch, which faced the highway.

Lew Adam, the owner of Adam's Locksmiths, was lost in thought as he ran his fingers lovingly over the antique vault's two-ton door, which stood wide open against the corridor's wall. He scrutinized the locking mechanism and whistled under his breath. He smiled.

Although he'd inspected many vaults in his career and dealt with thousands of residential and commercial locks, this beauty captured his heart.

He pondered its intricacies with the same focus that an artist would admire a Rembrandt or a Monet. The bank could have installed new state-of-the-art technology when they took ownership of the facility for its main branch, corporate headquarters, and back office facilities. However, the board of directors, employees, and townspeople had been adamant that this historically important treasure should be preserved. Thus it was transplanted.

The lead detective on the vault murder case waited patiently with the others while the expert finished his examination. "There are no safe deposit boxes?" he asked Shirley Granger."

"That function was modernized. The boxes and two private customers' rooms are behind this wall, accessible only from inside the branch. If you look into the vault's depths, you can see the old boxes. We used to bring kids in on tours after the cash drawers were pulled for the day. The boxes have little ivory buttons, onto which we used to place a black sticker if the owner was deceased. One day, when nobody was watching the kids closely, a little girl had a ball rearranging the black stickers."

"What did you do?"

"After they left, we just put them all back. We'd kept a list." Everyone smiled.

"I've seen enough," Lew said.

The security chief led the group into the dimly lit nerve center that housed the bank's surveillance equipment. He motioned them into captain's chairs that could be swiveled into a circle or turned toward a bank of video monitors.

The detective addressed the locksmith. "We understand that the timer is mechanical, needing no electricity to work. Is that right?"

Lew nodded. "Correct."

"The authorized employee sets the time for it to reopen the following day, leaving the door ajar, against the wall as we observed, until quitting time. And if it is closed prematurely, nobody—including you—could open the vault until the mechanism trips at the designated time."

"Again, you're right."

"Is it possible for someone to reset the timer for, say, eight p.m. rather than eight a.m., return to the vault at eight-oh-one p.m. after the mechanism trips, do whatever, reset the timer for eight a.m. and close the vault door? In other words, can the timer be set multiple times during the same twenty-four hours?"

"Well, yes, I suppose so. Of course, that person would have to know how."

"We've never needed to do that," Shirley said.

"Even if someone closes the vault door by mistake?"

"Then they'd be in trouble if the timer wasn't reset first," Shirley said. "From day one, new employees learn to never, ever close that door. Only the person in charge can do that. Once we had a newcomer, who was just trying to be helpful, close it prematurely, not considering that the drive-up window is open later than the branch. The tellers were unable to put away their cash drawers and supplies. A security guard had to babysit the branch until the following morning."

Everyone sighed, the point reinforced.

"Thank you for coming in," Chas said, escorting Lew to the door.

"Just give me a call if you have any other questions."

"One more thing—would you be willing to testify in court about how the vault's timer works if we need you?"

"Just that? Not about whether someone reset it?"

"The prosecutor would just need you to explain how it works in lay terms, just as you have to us."

"Of course then."

After Lew departed, the remaining four returned to their seats.

"The security cameras were off intermittently, and Ziegler's not on the tape near that time," Chas said.

"Can we check all the way back to that morning and forward to midnight?" the detective asked.

"I've cued up the entire day in question. Watch the monitors. You can see that corridor from two different angles. But remember, we had serious electrical problems. Power interruptions were so constant and debilitating that Mr. Kramer closed the bank at four and nearly every employee was gone before five."

"Juanita and the branch manager were still in the building after the bank closed," Shirley said. "Juanita was attending to last minute details, and Connie Davis, the branch manager, had made a quick run to the controller's office. When Connie re-entered the branch around five-thirty, Juanita was gone, and the vault door was close—"

The detective interrupted. "By Juanita, you're referring to the woman who called herself Juanita Rodriguez, aka Carol Drexler—"

"Let's stick to 'Juanita' for now. I still can't believe that lovely young woman was an imposter."

"As I was saying, Shirley, nobody except for the killer knew she was dead inside the vault. Here's what I need to see." He focused everyone's attention toward the monitors. "What the camera captured of that corridor for the entire day—from the time Juanita went on duty in the morning until nine p.m. or whenever the cameras cease to capture human activity. Fast-forward and stop anytime a person stops in the corridor."

"I'll show what we've got, but please understand there are gaps, some longer than others. The electricians were running new wires and replacing the old ones simultaneously to shorten the downtime. It got crazy, nerves frayed, customers angry. Not one of our best days. If only the job could have waited until Sunday. But—here goes."

From eight a.m. until noon, all images were business as usual, with tellers extracting their cash drawers and necessary materials. The traffic slowed once the staff collected what they needed, enabling Chas to move quickly unless someone lingered in the corridor. That appeared to be employees who paused to greet one another or have a brief conversation. The detective pointed whenever they spotted a male, but most appeared to be in a hurry. Shirley identified each and noted why they typically would have been in that corridor.

The digital clock on the monitor's display began skipping erratically by early afternoon as the power cut out numerous times. "Can you stop each time there's a gap so we can note the amount of lost time?" the detective asked.

"Sure." All four scribbled the math whenever the power was interrupted. The longest gap occurred after two p.m. and lasted for fifty-five minutes. Suddenly, all four jolted to attention.

"There! There she is," Shirley said, noting the clock said four-fifteen p.m. "Please back it up and proceed slowly."

After Juanita's image crawled toward the vault carrying something, she disappeared inside and emerged empty-handed. That the tiny, pretty, beautifully dressed woman looked so vulnerable startled everyone. Leaving the vault door wide open, she returned to the branch, where another monitor picked up her progress.

She was smiling, happy, and unaware that she had minutes to live.

"Freeze it there!" The detective pointed to the panoramic view of the lobby and five-story botanical garden beyond the branch's glass interior wall. A camera mounted on the branch's front wall, its function being to monitor anyone entering the branch from the lobby, recorded the scene. "Who is that?"

They squinted, finally identifying Margaret Stiles, the residential real estate lender, from the fourth floor. She had exited the elevator, turned to her left between the branch's glass wall and the elevator bank, and then disappeared toward the side parking lot.

Likewise, other stragglers were identified, smiling and eager to enjoy a few extra hours with pay.

The group watched until four forty-five, at which time

the clock jumped to six fifty-seven. The disappointment was palpable. "Please fast forward until nine p.m."

Chas did.

"…not a creature was stirring…" someone quipped.

ℯↄℯↄ

"We know how he did it," the lead detective told the ADA with unrestrained jubilation. "Forensics identified the blood on Juanita's body as matching Frank's DNA. And a label from one of his neckties, which he admits he cuts off, was found stuck to her sleeve. But supposedly she was killed within a thirty-five-minute time-frame—that is, between the time she was last seen alive in the branch by Connie Davis at four fifty-five and when Connie observed that she was gone and the vault door closed at five-thirty."

"Right," the ADA said. "And Frank Ziegler was recorded by a First Union branch camera around five p.m., two hours away in Philadelphia. We've been this route, gentlemen, which resulted in our embarrassment when we were forced to acknowledge the alibi and withdraw the murder charge."

The detective smirked. "He rose through the ranks in that bank, from part-time teller to executive vice president—through the retail side of the bank, including a stint as branch manager. That person is responsible for setting the vault's timer. He knew how to stage his alibi. All he had to do that day was to reset the timer *during* one of those power interruptions when security cameras weren't functioning, and then arrange to meet Juanita after closing time."

"Surely someone would have noticed him in that corridor."

"Evidently not. With everything in an uproar, customers needing placating, staff trying to complete transactions manually without the aid of electronics—"

"And don't forget," the other detective interrupted. "No power means no lights in that corridor. He could have slipped in long enough to reset the timer. And no one would have questioned his making the rounds during unprecedented circumstances, especially since branch administration falls under his chain of command."

"You ask how could one criminal get away with so much?" the ADA asked. "No one is alive to contradict his claim that he solved the loan scam. As EVP under which Technology falls, he has access to customer accounts. That enabled him to identify the bogus accounts. We have no evidence about who tipped him off. Then he could follow the money, change their owners' names to an alias he invented for himself, cash out, and claim both the credit and the reward."

"But he had a phony passport in his possession. Can't you do something with that?"

"He claims it was a prop. Now, if he'd been apprehended trying to re-enter our country using it—but it never came to that." She thought for a minute. "I'd love to nail him for that murder. We know Juanita was part of the loan scam. If Ziegler was the mastermind, that gives him a motive to silence her. Bring him in. Let him know we see through his so-called alibi."

"What about Connie, the branch manager?"

"Squeaky clean. And every second of her time is accounted for."

"In the meantime, we could question every employee to see if Ziegler was spotted in that corridor."

"With five hundred employees? Good luck with that!"

Chapter 9

Charlotte Unger enjoyed every morsel of her eggs, toast, OJ, and coffee, thrilled that two dozen eggs would last for two weeks. While she sipped the last of her coffee, she toasted two slices of bread, applied butter and scraped as her depression-era grandma had taught her, and then added the outermost lettuce leaf, one slice of boiled ham, and a few dill pickle chips. After cutting it diagonally, she popped her creation into a reusable plastic container, which she set on the table beside her purse.

Into another reusable container, she poured six ounces of milk. Compared to whatever she'd been reduced to scrounging, this was a feast. She'd been embarrassed to accept offers of extra sandwich wedges, pizza slices, and homemade goodies that her co-workers insisted they couldn't finish—that *"waste made waist,"* so would she please save them? She'd been too hungry to decline. But not today. She whispered a prayer for Great Uncle Wallace.

Fearing she'd become obsessive/compulsive, she'd

commanded herself to stop checking the mail once an hour. And this Monday morning she almost didn't. But there it was! Another envelope. She tore it open, right on the spot.

My dear Charlotte,

I'm sorry to burden you with my troubles on what promises to be an otherwise perfect day. My doctors are not happy with me. Something about a test result that was off by a full decimal point. I've agreed to participate in a clinical trial, which may not cure me, but could be invaluable to others similarly afflicted.

My financial advisor and my attorney both agree that the fed should not be my sole beneficiary. As a veteran, I've given enough to my country. Instead of rewriting my will at this point— something about gifts being made in contemplation of death—I've decided to start sending my bequests directly.

An individual can give up to $25,000 a year without incurring a gift tax. While I have nowhere near that amount, I would like you to have what I can spare. My representative delivered an envelope bearing your name to the First Union Bank branch listed below. I'd like you to open a safe deposit box at that branch to hold a few mementos for me.

God willing, I'll make a full recovery, and we'll meet in person.

Please enjoy the pittance I've left at First Union for whatever would make you happy.

Affectionately,
Great Uncle Wallace

Of course, Charlotte's lunch break didn't start until one, and a technical emergency forced her to eat at her desk. As it was, thirty minutes would not have been enough time to drive across town, retrieve her gift, and rent a safe deposit box. An odd thought occurred to her. She had no idea how much the latter would cost. Gifts notwithstanding, could she afford it? What did Uncle Wallace's mementos include? His military dog tags would give her a name, but what if he'd kept souvenirs like a German handgun? Jewelry? Cash? She'd know soon enough.

The second four-thirty arrived, Charlotte was out the door, risking a ticket and running stale yellow lights because she could not help herself. Once inside the branch, events crawled in slow motion. Being the end of the month, some customers might be cashing paychecks. She fretted about why everyone didn't use *direct deposit.* Finally, she got to the window.

After presenting a photo ID, a teller located a twelve-inch-by-eighteen-inch padded envelope and gave it to her.

"Is there somewhere private I can open it?" Charlotte asked, immediately feeling foolish. While another hundred dollars was a fortune for her, she'd bet that most people would rip open the envelope at one of the kiosks, in their car, or wait until they got home.

"Of course. Please follow me."

Charlotte closed the privacy door in the safe-deposit

box area, sat down, and placed her purse on the table. She stared at the envelope like a kid on Christmas morning, knowing anticipation was the best part of getting a gift. One's wildest dreams could be wrapped in holiday paper and bows.

Using the bank's letter opener, she slit it carefully. Peered in. And gasped. From its depth, she extracted a bundle of hundred dollar bills. She fanned them with her thumb and index fingers, riveted as the hundreds shuffled by like cards in a deck. She counted, heart pounding, and counted again. Ten thousand dollars!

She studied both sides of each bill. Succumbing to something primal, she buried her nose in the sweet smell of cash.

Forgetting all about the safe deposit box, she sped home to call Margaret Stiles. That dear lady would study the spreadsheet she'd created for Charlotte to budget her money. And she'd know what to do with this windfall.

♥‿♥

"Slow down! Take a deep breath and start over." Margaret soothed Charlotte whenever she could wedge in some words. "Tell me again about your Great Uncle Wallace's instructions."

"I should be thrilled, jumping for joy. Indulging in extravagant celebrating, but suddenly I'm alarmed. Why would a complete stranger give me ten thousand dollars? My family was very close, Margaret. My grandmother loved to spin tales of her childhood to us kids. She was the oldest, and as such had helped raise her younger sisters. Never once did she even hint of a male cousin. It was a petticoat world, with all the shenanigans that accompanied it. If a young suitor got out of line, her father, his brothers, and the priest would inject themselves into the drama. I'm telling you, something's not right here."

"Let's get together. How about tonight? We have choir practice, but we could come a little early at, say, seven-thirty? It sounds like you've had a shock, but we'll sort it out."

"Could you…um…take the cash to a teller and find out if it's counterfeit? Or if the serial numbers show that they're stolen? I'd be so grateful."

"Of course. That is, if you trust me not to abscond with the loot."

Charlotte hooted at that thought.

"One more thing," Margaret continued after a pregnant pause. "To the best of your recollection, would you jot down your maternal family tree as far back as you can remember? I have an idea."

Tuesday morning, as night began to loosen its grip, Margaret logged onto the Internet. Armed with Charlotte's family tree, she opened *ancestory.com* and entered the information, going directly to Charlotte's maternal great-grandmother. There, one by one, she found notices that certificates of birth had been filed in Harrisburg, Pennsylvania. From personal experience, Margaret knew that parents received such a certificate to send for official birth certificates, which were not given to the parents at the hospital. One needed to send for them and pay a small fee.

Great-grandma had five daughters, one of which was

Charlotte's grandmother. No birth or death certificate had been filed for a brother named Wallace. She followed the family backward in time, finding no Wallace. In fact, men who married into the family produced only girls. Perplexed, she rehearsed what she would tell Charlotte.

What possible motive could this man have for giving away cash to a stranger? Might he be senile and be gifting money needed for his own health and support? Might family or guardians, who lived far away, be unaware of his imprudent generosity? Might he have bad information and confused her for somebody else?

On the other hand, was there an entirely different motive, a malicious plot? And how did he get her name and address in the first place? What was the connection?

"What's my Sapphire doing so early?"

Margaret startled from concentration, causing her untouched coffee mug to slosh.

"Sorry! So sorry, Sapphire!" Margaret's husband whispered the endearment he'd chosen for his wife when they first met. He said that he'd never seen eyes that shade of vivid dark blue.

Her engagement ring sparkled with the flawless blue stone encircled with diamonds. And years later, her bifocals magnified her eyes.

He bent to kiss her, dressed to do battle in court. "Do I look okay?" the colorblind man asked.

She stood, admiring his perfect charcoal suit that draped to perfection, crisp blue shirt and striped silk tie, which she straightened just a tad. He lifted one leg, then the other, to verify that he'd chosen socks that matched.

"What's your conclusion?" he asked, motioning to

Charlotte's pile of papers.

Margaret sighed and told him how she'd struck out on ancestory.com. "Great uncle's letters and the cash look legitimate. But I need expert eyes. She's trusting me to check out the bills."

"Better let me look at her financials again. Her benefactor wouldn't want to bump her into another tax bracket if he could wait for the new year to advance her inheritance."

"She can't suggest that! It would look greedy, as if she were hinting for more."

He draped a cashmere muffler around his neck, shrugged into his topcoat, and pulled on leather gloves. He hefted a brown accordion briefcase big enough to conceal a small child, giving it a nod. "We'll run well into the evening—court, then meetings after dinner to discuss our game plan. But call if you need me."

❦

At Margaret's suggestion, Charlotte rented a safe deposit box at Keynote National Bank where she had her checking account, mortgage, and easy access to Margaret, the self-confessed vigilant mother hen. As instructed by Great Uncle Wallace, she secured his unopened envelope of personal treasures. Not being able to risk peeking inside nearly killed her, but being an honest woman, she jettisoned temptation and did as instructed.

It took her until three in the morning and a half-dozen drafts to word the most challenging letter she'd ever attempted. In it, she apologized profusely for the delay in renting the box, explaining the logistics and emphasizing that his unopened envelope was safe. She asked if he would like to co-sign. If so, she'd inquire about that procedure. Perhaps paperwork and his key could be mailed to him or his attorney.

She did not mention Margaret or that anyone was helping her, or that she hadn't used First Union's facilities. Satisfied that she'd done all she could, she'd waited impatiently for verification that the money was clean.

When it checked out, she grinned until her face hurt. Finally! She glimpsed her way out from debt's clutches.

Even after Margaret handed back the money and Charlotte deposited $1000 into her checking account and the balance into her box, uneasiness niggled. Why was that?

Margaret had tactfully relayed the facts learned on ancestory.com, admitting that she'd found no proof, one way or the other, of a relative named Wallace. She did hypothesize, however, that many babies' births that long ago happened at home or under hushed-up circumstances. Perhaps Uncle Wallace's biological father had been unknown. They'd laughed that the family's secrets might make a good novel.

Charlotte thought hard about timing. Just when had each envelope landed in her box? She just had to know the identity of her secret Santa. Her first outlandishly expensive gift to herself was a cell phone that came with a bargain account.

No matter how much sleep she would lose, she was determined to learn about Santa. Perhaps then she could trace the mysterious messenger back to her uncle and surprise him with a visit.

Just after midnight, three days later, she captured Santa's image. Elated, she forwarded the picture to Margaret's email address.

❧❧❧

Thud! Thud! Thud! Startled, Charlotte put her eye to the peephole and saw a stranger—a slender man in a black suit, white shirt, and nondescript tie. Clean-shaven with a buzz cut, he wore wraparound sunglasses, even though the overcast sky threatened a fast-moving storm. His black topcoat flapped open, revealing something black and bulky.

He raised a black-gloved hand to pound again as Charlotte cracked the door as far as the chain lock would allow.

"Yes? Can I help you?"

"FBI, ma'am." He flipped credentials toward her. "May I come in?"

Too surprised to refuse or ask for what purpose, she undid the chain and cracked the door. He stepped in, so close into her personal space that she automatically backed up. "What do you want? And please, show me those credentials again."

In the twenty seconds she was allowed to inspect them, her technology-trained eyes fixated on the number before matching the face to its owner. "What's this about?" She did not offer him a seat.

"Can we sit down?"

Only then did she motion him into her small living room, where he took the floral-print chair opposite her matching loveseat.

He leaned toward her, hands on his thighs, staring unblinkingly into her eyes. "Ms. Unger, you're in a lot of trouble. Criminal charges that will be lodged against you will land you in prison for the rest of your life. If you cooperate, however—"

"What?" she gasped, starting to hyperventilate. "What are you talking about? I've done nothing wrong."

"We know for a fact that you've been corresponding with a man whose alias is Uncle Wallace. Want to tell me about that?"

Charlotte glanced at her damp hands, onto which was stuck corduroy lint from nervously rubbing them on her thighs. "That would be my great uncle. He is—was—my late grandmother's cousin. He said he was estranged from the family and only just now located me. He believes I'm his sole living relative."

"We know for a fact that your grandmother had no such cousin, that you are his accomplice in multiple crimes, and that you are hiding evidence for him in a First Union safe deposit box."

"That's not true! And I've never met him. Our only contact has been through letters."

The man reached into his breast pocket and produced a tri-folded stack of papers that revealed photocopies of Uncle Wallace's letters to her and her thank-you notes back to him. Yellow marker highlighted words throughout every page. He smirked. "We broke your code."

"What code? There's no code. Do I need a lawyer?"

He shrugged. "If you wish. But then we won't be able to help you." The man squinted unblinking eyes at her. "The murder of a federal agent is our government's highest priority. As an accomplice, you'd be lucky to escape the death penalty. I can promise that this case will receive such international press that there will be a rush to justice."

Charlotte burst into tears. "All I ever wanted was to get out of debt, and then this wonderful old man began sending me gifts. Like a secret Santa. If I'd thought there was anything criminal, I'd have gone to the police."

The man sorted through the copies of her thank you letters, pointing to highlighted marks. He shook his head. "Nice try."

"Wait a minute. The young woman who has been delivering my uncle's letters can verify my story. In fact, she would know for whom she was delivering them."

He froze for a second and then got out a pen and a small spiral notepad. "Contact information?"

"I don't know her. She has been very discreet, as if fearing I'd force her to reveal my uncle's real name and how to reach him."

"So, how do you know it's a woman?"

"I stayed up three nights until she showed up."

"Can you identify her? What did she look like? How about her car? A license number?"

Charlotte dredged her memory, sensing that she shouldn't involve Margaret or mention the picture. He was making a circular motion with his hands to hurry it up. "Young. Late-twenties. Skinny. Dark hair cut long on one side, above the ear on the other. Her car was a navy or black Chevy with Pennsylvania plates."

"Would you recognize her if you saw her again?"

"Absolutely! She had a narrow, sharp face that was

distinctive." Charlotte shook her head. "Please. Find her. Oh! She had a bank parking decal on the right rear bumper with a key logo on it." She snapped her fingers. "Keynote National Bank. Perhaps she works there."

"That won't help. Probably some messenger service."

"I don't get it. I do not understand."

"There is a way out."

Charlotte edged expectantly to the edge of the couch.

"We want this man Wallace's co-conspirators. It may be dangerous, but if you cooperate in a sting operation, that will go a long way to help you. In fact, if you complete your assignment well, we might just make your charges go away."

"What do I have to do?"

"For your own protection, and that of any deal that we make, tell nobody about this. I doubt that you'd want your family and friends to know you're a felon anyway." He paused, as if calculating how much to reveal. Finally, he sighed and continued. "Corruption is rife in the county prison where you work. The heads must be identified and brought to justice. Your role will be to alter some records in the prison's database so that the fed can follow the trail. I can't tell you any details about the operation."

"I'd have to tell my supervisor and his boss. And does the warden know about this? Surely you don't suspect him."

"No one. You cannot discuss this with anybody inside or outside the prison. We will interact in strict confidence with the few insiders whom we can trust."

"Are any of my co-workers federal agents? Will anyone be watching what I do?"

He gave a taut smirk. "We will know every move that you make. Do not phone anybody, either, as your phone is bugged, and listening devices have been installed here and in your car. One slip up and the deal's off the table."

"How do I get in touch with you?"

"You don't. I will deliver instructions. When the mission is complete and arrests are made, you will never hear from us again."

He rose, strode toward the front door, and disappeared on foot around the corner. Only then did it strike her as odd that he never removed his thin leather gloves.

Chapter 10

The scramble in Lending was not unexpected. True to expectations, the bank would not go quietly into end-of-the-year business as usual but succumb to a frenzy of cliff-hangers. Kingsley loved the flurry of excitement, knowing the figures were exceptional—a pre-holiday gift from the entire division. Thanks to her Thanksgiving celebration with family, the launch of Andrew's trust, the Ward's blessing, and sensing where her future was heading, Kingsley couldn't help feeling euphoric. Finally. Her life was coming together.

Todd emailed: *"Parents flying to Connecticut from Colorado. Sister Linda says I can't come without you. Up for blowing this town? T"*

She responded. *"Love to!"*

The temperature plummeted forty degrees with the forecast for snow. She packed her silk long johns, wool slacks, a turtleneck, and a fisherman sweater, and set out her down jacket, ski pants, and Sorrels, gloves, scarf and knit cap. Cranberry bread baked while she showered and dressed in a black cashmere cowl-neck sweater and lined jeans. Bagel sandwiches and a thermos of coffee would suffice for breakfast on the road. Having consulted several little cousins about what was coveted by their age group, she packed new games for Todd's niece and nephew.

He arrived promptly at five in flannel and wool. Still very dark, Kingsley felt a happy aura surrounding her on their walk to the car. As they sped north on dark Saturday highways, she popped pieces of bagel into the driver, laughing whenever he licked her fingers. Country CDs warmed the darkness.

"Ten! You made great time." Todd's younger sister Linda greeted them as five-year-old Brent and three-year-old Melody threw themselves at Todd. "They've been waiting at the window since seven." She hugged Kingsley, then hurried them into the warmth of their expanded cedar saltbox home. Stained light gray with shutter-less windows trimmed in white, smoke curling from a tall stone chimney. It smelled of bayberry candles.

While the men carried luggage upstairs, Linda toured Kingsley through the downstairs and ultimately into their cozy country kitchen. From beyond a pine trestle table and patio doors, she took in a three-acre vista, its tree line of ancient maples backing to stone walls built by the settlers who'd once farmed the land.

"George and I teach high school history and English respectively," she told Kingsley as she fried bacon. "We met in college. I spend my summers being a mom while George does construction." She had Todd's eyes and dark wavy hair, but a different ancestral mouth. "You brought cranberry bread, and it's still warm? They'll fight over that. Thanks!" She scrambled eggs, then hollered to everyone, the kids jockeying for position beside Todd.

Later, the others outside, she took Kingsley upstairs. "This is Melody's room, all pink and white as she wished. At first, she was afraid of the canopy, but now she's okay. This is Brent's. We added a twin-long for Todd when he can get here, but Brent won't let us take it down in between visits. If he's very sad or misses Todd, that's his retreat."

"The children adore him."

"He's their godfather and guardian if anything happens to us. He takes that quite seriously. Across the hall is our room, and this is the guest room where you'll be staying." She pulled a yearbook off the bookshelf. "I was a sophomore when Todd was a senior," she said, flipping to his senior picture. She read, under his handsome face, *salutatorian.* "He lettered in football and track and was in student government."

"A chick magnet?"

"Surprisingly not. They phoned constantly. Pursued him relentlessly. Tried to get to him through me. He wasn't a chaser. A real straight arrow. School, sports, and his friends consumed all of his time. He never dated anyone seriously." Linda leafed through the book to her favorite candid with Randall, smiling over their science fair entry.

"I just met Randall. What a character!"

"Talk about opposites. They met in first grade. Randall had a fiery temper, and Todd might have spent his life reading books. Randall wanted to fight, but Todd would just laugh and get him involved in whatever he was doing. They became inseparable. When they got old-er, they challenged each other. Randall got Todd into sports, and Todd hounded Randall for grades.

"Randall was a gifted underachiever. Todd bet him he couldn't get the highest grade on a chemistry test, so he studied and did. When the teacher accused him of cheat-ing, Todd quizzed him in front of the teacher. Then all the teachers got on his case. At first, Randall resisted. I can still see Todd in front of our fireplace, pitching his case, both hands held out. 'Flying planes? Flipping burg-ers. Air Force Academy? Mac Academy. Seeing the world? Seeing the landfill.'"

Outside the kids began squealing, and they moved to the window to watch. Brent was attempting to hit a snowball that Todd was pitching to his small plastic bat while Melody clung to his arm. Kingsley remembered small children at Hawk Mountain Sanctuary the day they had hiked, how Todd had charmed them and told Linda about it. "We've been hearing about you ever since then. I'm glad he finally brought you to meet us."

"I had no idea I'd been worth mentioning."

"I wanted to thank you. He told me he'd told you about his ex-wife, and that you'd suggested we talk. I in-sisted he fly up. George took the kids to his mother's to give us time alone, and he dredged up the bad stuff that he'd kept buried."

Kingsley shifted uncomfortably, remembering that evening, when they hardly knew each other. Following their chance meeting at Hawk Mountain Sanctuary and spending a lovely day hiking, Todd had enlisted her help in evaluating an old stone house that had come on the market. What an amazing day! The following evening, she'd bought and delivered a book on colonial homes as a thank you gift for a lovely day.

Instead of a quiet hour talking about his project, she quickly realized she'd made a dreadful mistake. He was so drunk and spilled how his wretched ex-wife was spreading vicious, personal lies.

Kingsley quickly downplayed her involvement to Linda's compliment. "He was upset about an issue with his ex. Having said previously how close the two of you were, I suggested that he confide in you. Under normal circumstances, I never would have known the sordid details."

"I thought I was shockproof, working with teenagers, and knew Maureen had a really sick mind, but when he got graphic—that poor guy. No wonder he's burned. And to think that I leaned on him."

"He probably likes it that way."

"I'd learned about Maureen's background in bits and pieces. Parents married too young, a father who abandoned them when she was two. The mother's boyfriend who raped her when she was twelve and abused her until she was fifteen. Maureen told me how she got even, waiting for him to come into her room. She lunged at him, dousing him with lighter fluid while backing him into a corner, striking matches from a safe distance. He leaped from a second-floor window, breaking his ankles. He never came back after that. How she laughed at the memory!

"She put herself through college with scholarships and, she bragged, appreciation from older men. By the time we met her, she'd graduated, had a stepfather, and had fabricated a normal family background. I think she hates men. Each one she destroys gives her warped vindication. Builds up to tear down."

"Then how did she and Todd get together? It sounds so unlikely."

"He was a challenge. I think she saw the goodness in him and perhaps something better for herself. She was a consummate actress and played the role well. We were all fooled, except Randall, who took an instant dislike to her and wouldn't come to the wedding. We always thought Todd would be the next patriarch, being the typical oldest." Linda's face betrayed her frustration and resentment. "It was awful. She stripped him of his dignity as a man. You're the first woman he's mentioned in seven years."

"Your family must be very close."

"We are, but we've had our close calls. Randall found out how much she was cheating. I wanted to tell Todd, but Randall thought that could cause a rift in our family, so he did it himself. Once Todd left her, she kept after him. First, she was so sorry. Then it was threats. Then she'd been to therapy and had changed. Then it was a religious conversion. Pretended to have some life-threatening disease. The divorce was so ugly."

"Will he mind our talking?"

She shrugged. "I love my brother. I want more than anything for him to be happy, but there are things you just need to know. My brother has baggage. He seems strong, but there's this undercurrent he keeps under control."

"Do you think he'll ever get over it?"

"He wasn't a damaged child. He comes from a stable, caring family, but he has to stop blaming himself. Todd says that you've been married. That your experience was different—just about perfect."

"Compared to what you've just described, yes, that's true. My experience with loss was entirely different. His death was devastating, but I had the love and support of family, friends, and even strangers. There was no angry ex throwing lawyers at me. Loss by death is clean-cut, especially if the relationship was good. But I've been afraid to get involved, having lost my illusions. I hadn't considered dating, but Todd's so unthreatening, like the warmth of a fire, or the sun when the rain stops. It's fun. Who knows?"

Linda paused, turned toward the window, then turned back to Kingsley, forehead furrowed, determination replacing her placid features. "Todd spent hours, telling me about you. Your husband's murder. The killer. The loan scam. That you must testify in two different trials." Gently she grasped Kingsley's forearms. "If you ever need a safe place to hang out or hide, you'll always be welcome here."

Before she could respond, George knocked on the doorframe. "Your parents are here."

"I'm so glad you came," Linda said, hugging her.

Kingsley hung back, wiping a tear with her sleeve while the family downstairs enveloped the elder Hennings. They were older than her parents, and she was recovering from knee replacement surgery. They were cordial but formal until Todd explained their two families' banking connections. Both lit up when Kingsley slipped into the room.

Over hot mulled cider, the group loosened up, playing board games with the kids and swapping old stories. Stories became exaggerated and embellished as the men swapped cider for Scotch.

"What are you thinking?" Kingsley asked Brent, who was studying her neck.

"Mommy said that your head is sewed on."

"I think she meant that my head has stitches. Want to see? Get up on the couch, and I'll sit on the floor."

The kids scrambled onto the cushions. She tipped back her head and parted her hair with her fingers.

"I had a very bad cut, so the doctors stitched the skin back together so it would heal properly. It doesn't hurt. It just looks funny. You can touch it. It feels kind of lumpy. That will shrink in time."

"Did it hurt? Did you cry?"

"The stitches didn't hurt as much as the cut did. They put something on my head to make it feel better. I had to hold very still. I did cry because I was scared, but they were so nice that soon I wasn't scared anymore."

She pulled up a pant leg and showed them a very faint scar. "I had stitches here after I fell on the ski slope. The snow was melting and icy, and this really big groundhog got in my way. I was so busy trying to miss him that I fell and got hurt. See? The scar's almost gone."

"Did you hit the groundhog?"

"No, but he was so mad. He showed his teeth and growled at me."

Cozy. Kingsley realized she'd always remember that

evening's congeniality and cherish it. Supper was casual, plates being carried to wherever a flat surface supported a glass.

The special cups Miss Kingsley had brought in her magic tote thrilled the kids.

"Tell us a bedtime story!" the kids demanded of Uncle Todd. "Make one up about her." He gathered them onto the couch and thought for a minute. Smiling at her, he began.

"Once upon a time there was a lady who had a beautiful little cat named Pandora. The kitten had long silky black fur. But Pandora was incredibly clumsy. The very first time I visited Miss Kingsley, Pandora had fallen into the toilet, scrambled out, and landed in the clumping kitty litter. Was she ever a mess! Litter stuck all over her. Miss K and I clipped the litter from her fur with tiny little scissors. She looked so silly, and boy was she mad! Now, whenever Pandora sees me, she runs into Miss Kingsley's bedroom and hides under the bed until I go home."

"Bedtime. Come on! Both of you! Say goodnight to everyone."

When the anticipated grumbling got out of hand, Todd jumped to his feet. "Last one upstairs is a dirty sock!" He lunged for the stairs while the youngsters scrambling around his legs.

After the elder Hennings retired to their hotel and the kids were asleep, the four sank into the family room sectionals, warming their outstretched feet by the fire.

"Did you have to tell them how we *really* wrecked the transmission?" Todd asked Linda.

"They love our old stories. Besides, we were very

good teenagers. Believe me, I know. Hey, we'd better send Kingsley to bed."

"I'm awake," she lifted her head from Todd's shoulder. "Just incredibly comfortable."

"This place starts jumping terribly early, especially with my early-bird brother rattling around. You still walk at sunrise?" Linda needled him.

"I will, if anyone else will," Todd challenged.

"Sure. Just pound on my door. Really loud."

By morning, fresh snow top-dressed the countryside, enveloping the landscape in twinkling blue-white. She took his hand, and they hiked a two-mile loop. "What do you think?" he asked.

"They're great, but what happened to you?"

He scooped up a handful of snow and lobbed it at her, to which she retaliated.

"Did I pass?"

He laughed, hugging her through bundles of clothes and kissed her upturned, snow-dusted face. "They love you. *I* love you."

She grinned until the cold hurt her teeth. They walked for miles as the dawn's first light threw long blue shadows across the vast expanse. "Coming here renews me. Reminds me there's nothing more important than family. They don't slip into habits, don't take love for granted. Melody's name comes from private history they've never shared. I envy them that."

He smiled, squeezing her mittened hand. They crunched in silence awhile.

"A second chance," she said. "To grab it, you have to

let go of your favorite miserable feeling. It's possible that mine is survivor's guilt, but I'm trying."

"Mine being?"

"That you don't have what matters." She stopped, facing him. "You're the most amazing, incredible, giving person I know. If you don't believe you're entitled to happiness, she's won. Let it go. Like dandelion seeds blown on the wind. It's time."

From their bedroom window, Linda spied on the hikers. "George! Come look!" she insisted.

"Mmm. What time is it?" He peered at the clock. "Unless the house is on fire, go back to sleep."

"You've got to see this!" Eyes half closed, he joined his wife at their window. Two snowy figures had stopped in the yard, brushing flakes from each other. They were laughing and hugging, and, finally, they kissed. "All right! Now isn't that—"

George had crawled back into bed and resumed snoring.

Chapter 11

Margaret's email dashed Kingsley's post-weekend serenity: "Meeting. Urgent. Barrie's office at noon. I'll provide lunch."

Seeing Barrie's name copied, and knowing Margaret wasn't prone to theatrics, Kingsley jolted to attention. *Calm. Just chill.* She tried, but couldn't recall what could have generated an emergency that involved all three friends. Their late night ransacking of the executive area, which had led to unraveling the twelve-million-dollar loan scam, went undetected. *Or have we finally been caught? Only Todd knows what we did, and he wouldn't rat us out. Would he?*

Ever since Kingsley had recruited Assistant Controller Barrie Brown and Margaret Stiles into investigating the scam, they had become an indomitable trio. More dissimilar friends could not be found—Kingsley, the sheltered daughter of conservative Philadelphia gentry; Barrie, the former wild-child financial genius who as a teen had washed airplanes in exchange for flying lessons; and Margaret, an empty-nest parent and real-estate genius, devoted to making homeowners' dreams a reality.

Their common denominator was their love of banking, their customers, and their hatred for those who manipulated the system and robbed innocent people of their financial security. And they clicked from day one. Their clandestine investigation and Barrie's lock-picking expertise had required unquestioning trust in each other.

In Barrie's private office in the Controller's Department, the three divvied up a Subway foot-long and a liter of diet Coke. As Margaret recounted Charlotte Unger's story of her mysterious Great Uncle Wallace, Kingsley relaxed. That nobody knew Charlotte or her dilemma would be valuable if Margaret's goal was to gather independent perspective.

At length, Margaret showed the girls the secret Santa's photo, which Charlotte had provided along with copies of Charlotte's correspondence with the mysterious great uncle.

"Oh my god!" Kingsley gasped, clapping her face with both hands, her sandwich dropping onto her lap. "That's her! What's her name? The bitch with the doll and the hatpin who wanted something horrible to happen to me."

"Nicole Smith," Barrie provided with a disgusted scowl. "The *hustle*. The AA on the second floor who was fired. And now she's playing postman in the middle of the night for some old guy? That is bizarre. What's the connection between Nicole Smith and Charlotte?"

"And what does that have to do with us?" Kingsley asked.

"Charlotte says she's never seen that woman before,"

Margaret said in a controlled, steady voice. "Their lives don't intersect—school, occupation, neighborhood, church, gym, volunteer work, professional services such as doctors or dentists, friends, and so on. They have nothing in common. Charlotte works in the records department of County Prison, and never in banking."

Silence. "So?" Barrie finally asked.

"Piece it together," Margaret said. "John Miller, who killed Kingsley's husband Andy and nearly killed her, is in County Prison awaiting trial. Kingsley is the only person who can identify Miller as her attacker. Charlotte is an IT professional who works in the prison's records department. Nicole Smith, who has it in for Kingsley, is delivering gifts to Charlotte. That cannot be a coincidence. There's got to be a conspiracy. Both Charlotte and Kingsley could be in real danger."

Kingsley started to shake. "The accomplice. If only I knew who he was. All I saw was a glimpse…"

"Whoa!" Barrie shrieked. "That 'I didn't see him' shit won't protect you if that asshole is intent on payback for Miller. Worse, he might be planning his escape from County Prison. You've got to tell the cops what you know. Or make damned sure you don't let that I-can't-identify-him shit fly in public."

Margaret muttered "Language," to Barrie, pointing her thumb toward the controller's office on the other side of the wall. Barrie dropped back into her chair and shrugged, knowing HR would never come after their financial genius, whose insight made tons of money for the bank. She eyebrow shrugged consent to Margaret, nevertheless.

"My husband Pete made a discreet inquiry with a detective he knows," Margaret said. "The police can't do anything until a crime is committed. What the police can do is keep Charlotte's house under surveillance and apprehend anyone who breaches her mailbox for other than official USPS business. Mail tampering is, after all, a crime. When that person is caught, whether it's Nicole Smith or somebody else, they can interrogate her and find out what's going on and who sent her."

Barrie gave Kingsley's arm a gentle shake. "Girlfriend, you'd better ratchet up your security—at the very least, be vigilant. Pretending prison bars separate you from that bastard won't protect you if he's got a fiefdom inside and out."

⋘⋙

Charlotte took a huge chance. First, she examined every inch of her purse and her clothing. She ran a thumb and finger down her outfit, seam by seam. She wondered absently if that was how Jews, fleeing Hitler's henchmen, had hidden valuables to fund their new life, should they be lucky enough to escape. Feeling watched, she chose not to search her car but instead drove to the grocery store. From the pet food aisle, she speed-dialed Margaret on her new cell phone, praying the FBI didn't know about its existence. In less than five sentences, she texted sound bites of the dilemma she'd rehearsed in the car. She then pleaded for help.

Margaret texted back immediately.

~ We have choir practice tonight. I'll ask our minister

if we can use that small private office. We'll start rehearsing in the chancel, which will give you time to scan the sanctuary for anybody who doesn't belong. At the break, we'll talk. Do you remember that FBI man's name?

~ *Yes, and his shield number.* She typed it in.

~ *Try not to worry. To be on the safe side, may I pick you up?*

~ *Bad idea. He said my phone was bugged, but didn't ask about a cell phone. Evidently, he knows nothing about it and might wonder how we got in touch.*

That evening, after the choir was fully assembled, their minister approached the group. "Ladies and gentlemen. If I may borrow a few of you during the break and after our rehearsal, I need to update some information for our upcoming performance at the National Cathedral." That brought smiles and excited murmurs from the singers. "Margaret and Charlotte, will you meet me at the break in my office?" The two exchanged nods, then answered in the affirmative. Charlotte felt as if she might throw up and commanded her stomach to knock it off.

An hour later, the three met in a small conference room that sported no windows. The minister engaged the lock. As succinctly as possible, Margaret recounted the threat from the FBI agent, how they were holding Charlotte electronically captive, and how she must "play ball" to extricate herself.

The minister took her shaking hands in his weathered warm ones. "My daughter, of *course,* this is rubbish. I don't believe any of these charges for one second. Anything I can do, from the practical to the ecclesiastical, I will. And our facilities are at your disposal." In soft, soothing phrases, he led them in a prayer and departed their company with a blessing.

Before the rehearsal was over, Margaret felt her cell phone vibrate in her shirt pocket. A quick check of the caller ID identified Pete. She listened, nodded, and scowled, squinting her eyes to slits. She motioned Charlotte aside when the choir broke between hymns.

"Forget about any federal charges," Margaret whispered, visibly angry. "Pete phoned his detective friend who phoned his contact at the local FBI office who queried his chain of command. Bottom line: your visitor is a fraud." Charlotte gasped. "Remember I said the police would be keeping an eye on your place? Pete learned that a plainclothes policeman noticed your visitor. They got a picture."

"Did they follow him? See where he went?"

"No. Given what you were told about a bogus sting operation in the prison, the police hope to learn exactly what files that man wants to alter. Then follow the trail. It's not inconceivable that the prison's staff has been infiltrated by a criminal enterprise."

"Where does that leave me?"

"Pete wants to talk to you." Margaret handed Charlotte the phone.

"Hey, Charlotte. Here are your options," he began without a preamble. "They can either move you to a safe house while an investigation is ongoing, or—"

Charlotte waved that option off, surprising herself with the vehemence of her rage, and interrupted. "Five years of being my ex-husband's victim? Five years of scrimping and saving just to survive, only to be undone by some criminal with an agenda? No! I'm going to do what I can. Besides, I'd feel much safer inside the prison than I'll ever feel in a safe house. Count me in. Just let me know what to do."

"All right. They say to wait for his instructions and report to your job as if nothing has happened." She nodded agreement. Pete continued. "An undercover agent, posing as an old-world washerwoman, will come 'clean' your house. That is, identify the bugs. And they'll rig you up with a panic button in case you feel threatened."

"If the cleaning woman finds and removes the devices, won't that expose me? Remember I was told not to tell anyone."

"Pete's contacts say that the guy is bluffing. We'll know soon enough."

※

Steven Turner hoped that Nicole Smith would be caught off guard by his seven p.m. visit on such a dark, rainy night. Even though she had only heard his voice twice—once in person and once on a phone message—she wouldn't recognize his pattern of speech. He buzzed for admission to her second-floor condo.

As he'd hoped, she buzzed him past the security entrance and was waiting, door slightly ajar, when he approached her personal entry.

She smiled what betrayed a practiced expression, a blend of shy and slightly seductive, tipping her head to one side and letting her upstretched hand linger on the edge of the door. With a glance rehearsed many times in a mirror, she flicked her gaze from his eyes to his chin and then to his lips before turning lash-hooded eyes to his. Nothing as blatant as looking him up and down, especially down. But her intention to seduce him was clear.

She opened the door wider to admit him. "What a pleasant surprise," she murmured in her low-key contralto that fell just short of purring. "Come in. I was hoping we'd meet again." She avoided the word *personally.* "May I take your coat?"

His choice of outerwear appeared to surprise her. The weather had turned frigid for early December. It must have crossed her mind that a storm jacket or topcoat might be more suitable. When he declined her offer to hang his ankle-length raincoat, she shrugged, as if guessing he was still chilled from the wind that had blasted her windows since late afternoon. His heavily-advertised weatherproof garment insulated him from much more than the weather.

"Would you like to sit down? Can I get you something to drink? Beer, wine, soda, water, whatever?"

Hardly feeling sociable, he motioned her toward her couch. "I need you to do something for me."

"Of course! Secret Santa is at your disposal. And, as I mentioned before, may I underscore that you have my absolute discretion. Do you have a new assignment for me?"

He circled the coffee table, positioning himself between her and the end table next to the exterior wall. Happily, the drapery on the patio door that led to her balcony was already drawn, thwarting nosey neighbors with binoculars. "Actually, I have a problem, but I hope you can solve it for me."

"I'd be delighted to try. Shoot."

"My hard drive crashed, and with it, my records. I've lost all my client lists and copies of their correspondence, both coming from and going back to their benefactors. You have performed your duties precisely as instructed. That's underscored by not once failing my little tests or misinterpreting my instructions. But I am hoping against hope that, for whatever personal reason, you felt it necessary to make copies. Perhaps anticipating this kind of problem, which could have ruined my business reputation and your employment."

Her *tell* said everything he needed to know. Of course, she had! He dipped his head and shrugged as if in despair, but not far enough to compromise his peripheral vision. She couldn't help a split-second glance at a laundry hamper sitting in front of an open closet that held an apartment-size washer and dryer, and then to an open laptop on her kitchen counter.

"I'm so sorry for your trouble," she demurred. "Once I lost an entire morning's work because I failed to *save as* my document before I closed it. That lapse took me until nine that evening to undo the damage. If I'd missed a deadline, I could have been fired." She paused. Smiled sweetly. All innocence. "Can I get you something to calm your nerves? I do have a bottle of gin and some tonic water. And I think there's some scotch left by my boyfriend."

"Are you expecting him?" he asked, noting her skinny jeans and tight pink sweater that exposed an inch of taut, tanned belly on which was tattooed a flourish of roses.

She batted her hand. "No. We broke up. Now, how about that drink?"

"Please, Nicole. This isn't a social call. I need your copies. Now."

"But I didn't—"

Cold eyes cut through her menacingly. He didn't move. He didn't blink. Suddenly she looked frightened and jumped up, eying the door. He grabbed her arm and spun her around then released her.

"I'm sorry. You're not in any trouble. I'm just a bit jumpy. In fact, I'm not even going to fire you. I do understand how curiosity must have gotten the best of you." He nodded his head toward her laundry hamper. "Now get me those copies."

"I didn't mean any harm."

"Of course not. Just bring that hamper over here. Set it between us."

They must have resembled a living tableau, as neither moved for several seconds. Finally, she shrugged, turned, and repeated that she hadn't meant to disobey his orders without a good reason. She began tossing the top level of soiled clothing out of the hamper onto the carpet. She bent, doubled over, to reach farther into its depth, her voice muffled as she rummaged through the stuffed hamper.

"Bring it!"

Clutching a folder against her chest, she inched toward him. "Here."

"Good girl. Now, sit down. Let's have a peek." As casually as if he were going to view her vacation photos, he withdrew her stack of duplicator paper and straightened them with a *bonk* on the coffee table. He fanned the papers, then glanced through them deliberately. From the corner of his eye, he could see her relax.

"Very good! Now, how about that drink? Please join me with a gin and tonic. We'll toast our good fortune."

While Nicole fumbled through washing two matching glasses, dropping several ice cubes on the floor, and dealing with tonic water that fizzled onto the counter, Steven Turner looked hard through the papers. And knew what was missing.

Nicole returned with the glasses and handed him one, fussing to arrange pretty cocktail napkins on the coffee table. She sat, looking hopeful. He raised his glass in the time-honored motion, knowing that she would do likewise. "To our successful mission."

"Cheers!"

Steven Turner let the silence hang for a few minutes, knowing her anxiety would encourage her to take a few gulps. "Bring your PC over here, if you please. I'll need to see what you copied to your hard drive."

"What makes you think—"

He pointed to the stack that he'd straightened and set on the coffee table. "I'm sure you didn't go to Staples to run off some copies. Smart girl that you are, I bet you know how to scan and save, right? And a good thing, too. You can send the file directly to my PC. Spare me a lot of time scanning them myself."

As soon as it was out of his mouth, he realized his mistake.

"But—if your hard drive crashed, how can you—"

"Easy. Just email-attach them to the address I give you. My iPhone will save them to the cloud until I'm up and running again. Now—please fetch your PC over here, and we'll have a peek. If you've captured everything I need, you'll be in for a big reward."

Looking happy and enormously relieved, Nicole sprang from the couch and went directly to her dinette table. With her back turned, she didn't observe her guest introduce a few drops of colorless, odorless, tasteless liquid into her gin and tonic.

While he waited, he spotted a voodoo doll, hatpins protruding from its head, abandoned on the kitchen counter. She'd undoubtedly snagged it at some tourist trap. Nobody would ever suspect—even if they went looking for it—what potion he had acquired in Haiti.

Returning, she set the PC on the coffee table, fired it up, and navigated through her hierarchy to the appropriate folder. "Your PC isn't password protected?" he asked.

She shrugged. "Who's going to want my recipes?"

"So it's not?"

She rolled her eyes, as if he were an idiot. "I use the password *Passw0rdPC*. Isn't that clever? It's got everything—capital letter, a number, letters and—Ta, da! A clue that I can change to remember each of my devices' passwords. For instance, my Apple password would be *Passw0rdapple*."

She stared happily at her screen as she clicked open the killer's folder.

He raised his glass. "To my clever girl!"

She raised hers. Took such a big gulp that it dribbled down her chin, causing her to giggle. She shook her head as if clearing cobwebs. "I am *soooo* not used to drinking."

He waited. Five minutes passed.

Unsteadily, she attempted to set her glass on the coffee table, a smidgen splashing over the rim. "I feel so…"

With that, she slumped sideways onto the cushion away from Steven Turner. He watched momentarily. Shrugged. She was out cold, would not feel the pain. He collected both glasses, which he dumped, washed, and set in the cupboard among their mates.

Canvassing the condo, he located two smoke alarms, one by the front door and one in the bedroom. The cheap kind, battery-operated, not hard-wired. The type people rarely kept current. Pressing a dinette chair into service, he climbed to remove each cover, replacing her new-looking nine-volt batteries with long-defunct old ones.

"Stupid, stupid bitch," he murmured as he collected the printouts and her PC. Those he dropped into a heavy plastic bag which he concealed in his coat's special interior pocket. A quick scan of the condo revealed no trace of his visit.

What might he have missed? Did she keep a diary? A calendar? Blackmail material? No time to do an exhaustive search. In spite of his excellent research to the contrary, she might awaken prematurely. Better to cover his tracks and just leave. Gloved, he lit a pillar candle that decorated her coffee table and held a cigarette in the flame until one-half inch glowed sufficiently. He set it on the couch cushions a few inches from her head.

He encircled the cigarette with crumpled newspapers, which would ignite, kindle the cushions, and spread.

Foam stuffing, referred to by some as *solid gasoline*, was flammable stuff. A dangerous habit, smoking and falling asleep on such a cheap couch. In thirty minutes, the condo would be filled with dense smoke and then blaze.

Before extinguishing the lights, his eyes swept the room one final time for any trace of his visit. Before escaping unnoticed into the stormy night, he slipped black size-twelve boots over his size-nine shoes. Howling wind and driving rain would discourage even the bravest soul from venturing abroad. He hiked the short distance through the lush landscaping to the parallel row of condos where his stolen nondescript vehicle waited, its license plate splattered with mud.

Within three hours, he would arrive in the north-central Pennsylvania woods, where he would destroy and bury all trace of her stuff. He mustn't linger and enjoy his handiwork. He needed to get back and motivate Charlotte Unger to expedite springing John Miller from prison.

Chapter 12

Kingsley's phone roused her from her post-supper stupor, induced by the tedium she'd brought home from the office. This particular loan application from an agricultural client detailed his plans to build a mushroom processing plant. That, she knew, required research with an agricultural business expert. Judging from the amount of the loan, she might also need to participate the loan with another bank. Saved by the bell.

The caller ID identified Todd. When she put the phone to her ear, she heard jingling bells. "Hey! Getting into the holiday spirit?" she asked.

"In case you hadn't noticed, Christmas is two weeks away. Since we'll be heading in opposite directions to be with our families, I thought we could celebrate early. Would the lady like to dine with me this Saturday evening?"

If Kingsley didn't stop grinning helplessly, she feared her face would wrinkle permanently. He made her feel joyful and hopeful simultaneously, and that made her prickle. "I'd love to."

"I have a little Christmas present for you, just a holiday trinket, but you'll have to wait until the twenty-third if you don't mind."

"That will give me time to buy toys for you to take to the kids in Connecticut."

"One more thing. Would you consider wearing that pretty green dress that you wore to Boston? I mean, if it isn't too cold, or you'd prefer—"

"Of course." She grinned. One less silly decision to agonize over. They disconnected, leaving her hopelessly unable to scrutinize spreadsheets.

Christmas! A present for Todd. During recent months, she had selected special gifts for her parents, Barrie, Margaret, her AA, and the other family members whose names she had drawn from the traditional hat at Thanksgiving. Happily, she got Suzy and Sally, her favorite little cousins. And she had learned all about what tweens and teens would love. But what to give Todd?

Inspiration struck. She Googled his best friend, Randall Shannon, which yielded a business website that advertised his charter airline service. She lingered over his rhetoric, which extolled the prudence for clients who did not want to waste travel time flying commercial or incur the exorbitant expense of owning a corporate jet. Included in his fleet were jets that could fly cross-country without refueling. The phone number's exchange indicated a mobile. She dialed.

She hardly expected the robust, booming voice that picked up on the second ring. "Kingsley! Welcome to the dark side. Have you come to your senses and concluded that I'd be your perfect soulmate rather than my disreputable friend Todd?"

"You don't have minions to answer your phones?"

"Not when it's you on the other end of the—wait a minute—we don't have lines anymore, do we? To what do I owe the pleasure of your call?"

"I could use your advice."

"Whoa! Advice to the lovelorn is not my long suit. My exes can verify my, ah, deficiencies."

"Nothing like that. I'm hoping you could suggest a Christmas present for Todd. I'm at a loss for what he likes—or has—that wasn't already done, especially by his ex. Nothing too suggestive, but not buddy-buddy either. You've known him forever, according to his sister. Does anything come to mind?"

Silence.

Finally, she broke it. "That's okay. Thanks anyway. Calling was just an impulse."

"Just hold on now. I'm thinking. It would take a librarian to catalog his books, so I don't know what he already has." She heard what sounded like snapping fingers. "Got something. A pocket watch. Something old. He had one he loved, but he lost it on one of our trips. Never could replace it."

"He said he had 'a little something' for me, which would wait until closer to Christmas. I don't want to go overboard with a pricy gift and embarrass him."

"First off, you couldn't embarrass him if you tried. Let me give you the name of a fellow in Boston who has an antique shop in the Historic District. All those old watches, even if they run, don't necessarily cost a mint." She heard what sounded like drawers opening and snapping shut. "Got it. Write this down. Ask him if he has this particular watch or something like it. And if that doesn't work out, call me back."

"Thank you so much! I'll pursue it."

☙❧

For all her resolve, Charlotte Unger panicked, her adrenaline depleted with no dregs in reserve. December's black shadows shrouded her neighborhood, bare branches rattling her windows and scraping the side of her house. Wind howled, unleashing a storm. Even though she had splurged on seventy-five-watt light bulbs, she still kept her home nearly dark, but not for economy.

Upstairs in her two little bedrooms, she pulled blackout blinds to the sills, ensuring that no cracks exposed her movements. Then she drew the lined pinch-pleated draperies she'd lovingly sewn for this, her first real home. Charlotte had taken an adult evening education class at the local high school and transformed these rooms into luxurious nests.

A dust ruffle, pillow shams, and coordinating throw pillows let her imagine that the Victoria magazine's photographer would appear any minute to shoot a photo array. She had felt like a queen in a castle until the wolf arrived on her doorstep and threatened to snatch it all away.

Charlotte paced to the bathroom, wringing her hands, and opening the medicine cabinet. She poured a sleep aid into her palm. Not good. If anyone broke into her house, she wouldn't hear him. She dropped the little white pill back into the bottle and snapped the cap. Knowing she wouldn't sleep without help, however, she reconsidered her decision, only to scuttle the idea again. What if she overslept? Failed to complete that fake FBI guy's orders?

She checked her cell phone—again, ensuring that plugging it in would optimize its charge. She sank into her favorite goose-down pillow, picked up her mystery novel, and read a few pages without comprehending. She eyed the clock, trying not to visualize what awaited her at work. *Just show up. Act normal. Nothing will happen. Nor is it happening right now. Just be ready for his instructions.* The clock inched past midnight. She should make up her mind. Either take the damned pill or spend the night with her anxiety growing until she exploded.

Clicking off the bedside lamp, she tiptoed throughout the dark house again, sneaking peeks through slivered cracks. The neighborhood slept. Back to the bathroom. Pry open the bottle, study the blessed little white friend.

Enough!

She dry swallowed it and stuck her head under the faucet for a gulp of cool water then swiped her dripping chin on the sleeve of her white terry robe. By her bedside lamp, she reread the same pages, relieved when the words stopped making sense. Her last clear thought was an epiphany: how easily people could swap their troubles for drugs.

Charlotte woke with a start, realizing she'd actually slept dreamlessly. She peered at the clock. Six thirty. *You don't have to like it. You just have to do it, you coward*!

She pried herself out of bed, realizing she'd slept in her robe. Coffee, shower, breakfast.

She had forgotten to pack a lunch. And she hadn't brought in yesterday's mail. She knew why. Facing the reality of losing an uncle she now wouldn't know and accepting that he didn't exist had left her feeling bereft. It wasn't just the money. It was the idea of discovering family. That had given her hope. And that bastard had dashed it. Was she really that gullible? That easy a target?

Charlotte's anger and resolve rose to new levels as she stalked through her morning routine in record time.

En route to her car that was parallel parked down the street, she snagged yesterday's mail without stooping to check out the box. Mid-stride she stuffed the bundle into her canvas tote without as much as a glance because Great Uncle Wallace didn't exist.

On autopilot, she drove to the prison, parked in her spot, and arrived at her workstation, oblivious to how she got there. While performing her normal duties, she cast sideways glances at her co-workers. Most had been there forever, hardly candidates to be new FBI plants, unless, like herself, they had been coerced.

Surreptitiously, she studied their faces, which yielded nothing. Even during the lunch break, the chatter was normal, with everyone wedging in contributions the minute someone paused for a breath. Family news, TV shows, what to have for dinner—not pizza again. The lazy husband. The disrespectful teen. The bargains snagged at Black Friday sales. Critiques galore—the pricey spa, the new farmer's market, holiday plans, what to wear.

"Hey! You Okay?"

Charlotte snapped to attention, embarrassed that she had zoned out. She managed a shrug. "Just sleepy. The rain and the wind outside my window, like it will poke a hole in my wall. Times like that, I could use a landlord."

Somebody scoffed. "As if he'd do anything!"

As Charlotte was repacking her lunch containers, she remembered the mail. The holiday sales catalogs sparked her co-workers' interest as she lobbed them into the table's center. The electric, water, and sewer bills—yeah, this month she could pay them, but courtesy of whom?

Tucked among them was a number-ten white business envelope with an unfamiliar return address. G. U. W. was typed above the logo of a retirement village that was located in Harrisburg, PA. Great Uncle Wallace? The envelope was addressed to her personally, not to occupant or resident. And it bore a canceled stamp.

She glanced around the table for curious onlookers, but everyone was engrossed in the skinny lingerie model's picture, with scoffs and giggles, depending on the women's ages and sizes.

Charlotte wiped the knife she'd used to section a grapefruit and slit the envelope. Inside she found an eight-and-one-half-inch-by-eleven-inch piece of holiday stationery on which was typed a note. Beneath her address and Dear Ms. Unger, was a nonsensical paragraph, offering her a free lobster dinner if she would attend their investment presentation. Yeah, right.

Paragraph two, however, was entirely different. Void of explanation were two sets of digits, side by side, which she immediately recognized by their combinations as being inmate numbers. They were separated by the word "TO."

Beneath the numbers on the next line were the following words: "murder in the first, second-degree murder, assault with intent" and other minor charges that Charlotte recognized as pending against a prisoner. Under that line again appeared the word "TO" followed by "Drunk and Disorderly."

Finally, a third line stated "remanded" accompanied by wording about an upcoming trial. That was followed by the word "TO" and then "Time Served." A release date followed. And that day was tomorrow! She jerked to attention and commanded her face to a neutral expression. Nobody had noticed her reaction.

She was to change the records of a remanded-without-bail prisoner, awaiting trial for first-degree murder, to indicate he was in for a misdemeanor, having been sentenced to time served, and due for release tomorrow. As soon as she would return to her station, she would identify the prisoner by his inmate number.

The sting was underway, but who was involved? She wouldn't have an opportunity to notify Margaret or ask her husband Pete to contact the police. She had no choice but to enter the changes into the database. And that's what she'd do. But first, she sequestered herself in a lavatory stall to memorize the details. Should she shred and flush the instructions? No. She might go blank. Better to tuck the letters into her panties.

Charlotte approached her task chair with a nonchalance that she didn't feel, securing her canvas tote in her bottom drawer. She stretched, adjusted her position, and pretended to read papers that had hit her in-box during the lunch hour. Finally, she logged on and opened the document that listed the prisoners by inmate numbers, sorted sequentially. Fixing her face with a bored expression whenever her heart rate took off and her hands started shaking, she located the number in question.

That inmate number belonged to a prisoner named John Miller. The name was vaguely familiar. And seeing the charges, she understood why. *Oh! My! God! The guy in the news.*

Charlotte had no choice but to proceed. She changed Miller's data that was burned into her brain, expecting disaster. But lights did not flash. Sirens did not wail. Doors did not bang shut and lock. Swat teams did not encircle her desk. Deliberately, she located Miller's corresponding file and made the rest of the changes. At five p.m. she quietly gathered her things and slipped outside into the lot, half expecting armed guards to grab her and haul her to jail.

Safely in her car, Charlotte drove a half mile, diverting from her usual route into a new subdivision of unfinished tract homes. She parallel-parked beside a new concrete curb, sufficiently high to accommodate two layers of asphalt once street paving began. She feigned interest in the only finished house that bore the developer's signage.

She slipped from her car, her boots crunching on the gravel street and driveway, sidestepping icy patches where last night's rainwater was starting to freeze. Prefabricated concrete steps led to the front door. She climbed. Grabbed the knob. Prayed. It turned.

"Hello?" she called into the icy depth of what appeared to be the model home. It smelled of new drywall, freshly laid carpet, and paint that might still be wet to the touch. The furnishings looked imported, intact, from a modest furniture store's display. Doors throughout were cheap, flat veneer-on-plywood, as were the kitchen cupboards. She wandered from room to room, calling as she went, half expecting to surprise a plumber or electrician. Inside what must pass for a master bedroom, she peeked into a bathroom, which she noted had been thoroughly purged of wood and drywall dust. Retracing her steps she reaffirmed that she was alone.

Perfect! She pulled her cell phone, along with the retirement home's letter, from her storm coat's pocket and speed-dialed Margaret. While watching the street from the living room picture window, she dictated the instructions she had received, how and when she had altered the database.

"Whose name was it?" Margaret's voice whispered in her ear.

"The guy's name is John Miller. Margaret? Margaret! Are you all right? Are you still there?"

"You're very sure—"

"I am. Now, will you please ask Pete to pass it along? Otherwise, a really bad-sounding dude will be released."

"You did fine, Charlotte. You've saved the day. Now please. Go home and get some rest. I'll keep you posted."

Chapter 13

Satisfied that she had completed her assignment and negated the horrific consequences of noncompliance, Charlotte returned to her car. As she drove from the subdivision, she contemplated her situation. Would she be safe at home? Maybe. Maybe not. Go to Margaret's? No way would she endanger her friend. Maybe that safe house was the best option, after all. She'd go home and pack a small bag. Ask Pete to make the arrangements.

By the time Charlotte arrived on her street, working people were home. That meant neighbors who owned one car per licensed driver had commandeered all legal parking spaces. She circled a second and a third time, finally settling for a spot several blocks from her home. Sycamores that towered between the curb and sidewalks fronted 1920s brick homes with spacious front porches. At the sidewalk's edge, brick retaining walls separated a smidgen of grass from short hedges that abutted the porches.

Beyond the spot where she had parked, Charlotte

could make out two baseball caps and the tip of a rifle behind the porch's brick wall. They *turtled* to check her out. In spite of the chill, the good-old-boy hunters were undoubtedly cleaning their guns. It was, after all, deer season. She waved, they responded.

From her back seat she grabbed her purse and an over-sized satchel of hardbacks her friends had collected for County Prison's book drive. "Couldn't find a spot?" A familiar voice startled her as she stepped from her car. She tried not to panic but, instead, pretended she didn't recognize the man who had double-parked in the street. "Get in," he ordered, indicating his car.

One glance identified the man who had impersonated the FBI agent.

"Oh. It's you." She mustered a smile, as if she were greeting a neighbor. "You'll be pleased to know I carried out your wishes, just as instructed." She faked a little laugh. "Pretty ingenious, that letter from the retirement village. I figured out what you wanted and altered the records. Now. You better uphold your part of the bargain and not charge me with that felony."

He stepped closer to her, a gun with a long barrel pointed directly at her midsection. "I said, 'get in the car.'"

"Ah. I can't. Not with all this stuff." She pivoted, as if to show him she wouldn't fit, but heard the action slide of the pistol. "Hey! Put that thing away. You don't need it. I'll do it."

Just like the movies, she thought, as he flicked the gun, motioning her toward the open passenger-side door. Charlotte glanced helplessly for the two hunters who had grown remarkably still. Perhaps they'd finished their chore and gone into the house. She squared her shoulders, clutching her canvas tote close to her body, her right arm tightening her grip on the book bag's sturdy wooden handles.

Theatrically, she jerked her head straight up toward the towering sycamores.

"Look out!" she screamed, which is just what he did, as if a limb had just separated from the mighty old sentinel. With one fluid motion, she clobbered his midsection with pent-up rage and forty pounds of books. The gun flew from his hand as he stumbled backward, cracking his back on a neighbor's brick wall. Momentarily stunned, he recovered as Charlotte dove for the gun and then sprang to her feet.

He grabbed her arm to snatch it while Charlotte struggled to push the strong man's arm away. The deafening crack and the smell of gunpowder incongruously surprised more than scared her. Pain seared her leg, blood spattering onto the sidewalk. Still, she managed to stay on her feet, unable to process what to do next.

Two men spilled from the house, one bearing a shotgun. "Drop it!" he screamed at Charlotte's attacker.

She heard the *snick-snick* of the handgun from behind her and, simultaneously, the pump action of the shotgun. *Boom*! It took a few moments to register that her attacker, sprawled in the street, no longer had a discernable face.

Charlotte fixated on her leg, a rivulet pooling red at her feet. She didn't even feel that much pain, but was confused by onrushing people, shouting, and distant sirens approaching. She lifted her foot in a tentative step, but her leg buckled. Flat on the sidewalk, she stared at the lofty, bare sycamore branches, a lacy, black curtain against a gray sky. Lots of hands groped her, cutting her slacks and exclaiming something about a femoral artery. Her head swam, her vision blurred, darkness enveloped her. *My glasses. Where are my glasses? I cannot see.*

೮ഄ೮ഄ

Margaret tossed her keys to a waiting valet and tore into the emergency room, waving a document in the receptionist's direction. "Where'd they take her? Charlotte Unger? Gunshot wound? I'm her medical POA."

The woman leaped from behind her station, motioning for a security guard to expedite Margaret's trajectory to the trauma unit. Charlotte, she quickly learned, was receiving first aid in one of the bays and would be transported to the OR as soon as she could be stabilized.

"Ma'am?" A kind nurse gentled Margaret to a comfortable chair and sat down beside her. She pointed to the papers clutched in Margaret's trembling fist. "Your friend is in very good hands. Can I get you something? A bottle of water? Some coffee?"

"I'm all right. But—"

"Why don't you rest for a few moments? Catch your breath. I'll get you that water. And when you're up to it, perhaps you could furnish her details."

Margaret sighed, nodded consent, and waited until she could cope. Then she approached the nurses' station, taking the proffered chair to relay the details of Charlotte's life. In time she was escorted to the OR waiting room where another angel promised to keep her informed.

Time slipped away in the softly lit lounge. Its soft couches and chairs and original artwork donated by famous local artists surprised and comforted her. By daybreak, a steady stream of friends and co-workers had called or stopped by, awash with concern and offers of help.

Finally, the surgeon appeared, having taken the time to put on fresh scrubs and a positive expression.

"Margaret?" he asked, as she separated herself from the growing crowd. To the group, he said, "She's doing fine."

On the interior side of the heavy double doors that separated the waiting room from Intensive Care, he paused. "She was lucky," he said. "The bullet nicked her femoral artery. She could have bled out very quickly had her neighbors not called nine-one-one immediately, and the EMTs not been in transit a few blocks away. The artery has been repaired and the bullet removed. She was given six units of blood. Fortunately, she's AB positive, the universal recipient."

"When can I see her?"

"You can look in on her briefly, but she'll be asleep for some time. Why don't you go home, get some rest, and come back later? And suggest to the multitude out there to do likewise. Her charge nurse can give you a call when she is awake."

"Or if she, um—"

"Ma'am, of course, but we're optimistic that she'll make a complete recovery." With a quick pat to her shoulder, he was gone.

With an approving nod from her nurse, Margaret tip-toed into the glass cubicle where Charlotte lay in a sea of crisp white sheets. Charlotte's personality and her perseverance in the face of crushing adversity had always given her the aura of strength. Margaret never realized how tiny she was, dependent as she was on a room full of machines.

She ventured closer and touched Charlotte's hand, which was remarkably warm. She pulled up a chair and bent to her ear. "Everyone's here. And we love you. Just rest and get better. The bad man is dead."

She stayed for ten minutes. Then conscious of the rules, she whispered good-bye. Margaret sped through the building to outrace her tears.

⌇⌇

Two days later, Margaret located Charlotte's room on a surgical ward by following the florist. Far from the groggy victim she'd left in the ICU, Charlotte looked downright perky, surrounded by dozens of floral arrangements, balloons, and teddy bears. She belly laughed as the florist presented a bouquet of her favorite snapdragons. "It's from the prison. It says, 'To our favorite captive.' My department sent the sweetest card, which everyone signed, with a note that they would donate personal-time-off days if my benefits ran out. As if I'd had a stroke or heart attack. I only got shot."

As the florist exited, a detective replaced him. "Ms. Unger? If you're up to it, I'd like to speak with you for a minute."

"Sure. If my friend Margaret Stiles can stay. Her husband's my lawyer."

"I'm sure you won't need one," he said with a chuckle. "I thought you'd like to hear what we learned about your attacker."

Charlotte flinched and reflexively touched her bandaged leg. "Sure."

"First, there was no sting operation being conducted at the prison. The warden, his reports, and your departmental friends are not involved in a criminal enterprise. This whole charade was staged for the express purpose of breaking an inmate out of jail."

"Could it possibly have worked?"

"That's doubtful. The exiting procedure has many checks and balances to hurtle. Even starting the process would have raised an alarm, since the prisoner in question is a dangerous felon. And the warden was on it, the moment you changed the records, and he notified security."

"What happens to me now? Do you want the letters, the cash, and the envelope that my fake Great Uncle Wallace supposedly sent me? The letters are at home, but everything else is in my safe deposit box—"

Margaret interrupted. "She might want to talk to her attorney about that. Don't you need a search warrant or something?"

Charlotte waved it off. "That's okay. It wasn't mine to begin with. Margaret, would you please take him to the bank and use our key to get into my safe deposit box. Let him have whatever he needs. And do let me know what the envelope contains. I'd promised not to open it, but the circumstances no longer apply."

"I'll be back later," Margaret said then turned to the detective. "If you come to Keynote National Bank's main branch's lobby, I'll meet you there with the key."

An hour later, they reconvened and sat in a private booth, the box between them on the desk. She lifted the lid. As expected, the bundle of cash was an obvious find. "There's nine thousand dollars. Fingerprints on the bills will be Charlotte's, my husband's, the branch manager's, and mine. We all counted the money. I had the manager examine the cash. It's genuine, and the serial numbers didn't raise any red flags." She pointed to the bulky envelope, its girth having barely allowed the box lid to close. "Go ahead," she said.

The detective pulled latex gloves from his pocket, snapped them on, and lifted the envelope by its corners. With a penknife, he slit the end of the flap, taking care not to damage the glue. He looked inside and then nodded for her to do likewise. The envelope held a small revolver. He lifted it by the trigger guard with his pen and determined that it was not loaded.

"Charlotte won't be wanting that back," Margaret said. "Go ahead. Take it and the money as well." She thought a moment. "Can you return the cash to her if no rightful owner is found? She received it, in good faith, as a gift."

❦

Kingsley hung her head, unable to even look at the detective. "It's my fault! Every bit of it. I should have told you I'd caught a glimpse of that man. Maybe you could have identified him. Used a sketch artist. Tracked him down. Thwarted his endangering so many people. It was selfish of me to focus on my own safety."

The detective eyebrow-shrugged and sighed, annoyed that he wasn't getting through. "Ms. Ward. Even if you could have described your John Miller's accomplice, that would not have prevented what happened to Ms. Unger. We still have no record of him. Chemicals had obliterated his fingerprints. The shotgun blast took out his teeth and any distinguishing scars. He had no tattoos or implants. Both his car and its plates were stolen. He carried no identification. No outstanding warrants resemble that man. He was a ghost."

Kingsley kept shaking her head. "I should have done something."

"You did! And you will, by testifying against your husband's killer, for which he will be removed from society. You solved a twelve- million-dollar loan scam, and the alleged mastermind is going on trial. You risked your own life to identify both perpetrators. You cannot prevent crime from happening."

"But Charlotte—"

"She willingly went along with the imposter's demands to expose the plot. It could have been huge. She's a real hero who was tired of being a victim."

"So what happens now?"

"With Miller's accomplice eliminated and Miller secure in County Prison, you have nothing to fear. His trial won't happen for months. With any luck, he'll take a plea and be sent to a distant maximum-security prison for life. Please. Go home. Have a lovely holiday with your family and friends. And put this evil behind you."

❦

Kingsley trailed Margaret into Charlotte's tidy brick row house after setting a potted Christmas tree on her front porch. Introductions dispensed, Kingsley handed Charlotte a china plate of homemade raspberry pastries.

"Rugelachs?" Charlotte exclaimed. "My grandmother used to make them at Christmastime. I haven't had one since she passed. Thank you! But you shouldn't have—"

"If it weren't for me, you never would have been targeted. And to lose your great uncle as well."

"Grandmother used to say, 'It's an ill wind that blows nobody good.' Because of the publicity, I've heard from distant cousins I didn't know existed, and a publisher wants to buy the rights to my story for a movie."

"Pete will look over the contract to make sure your rights are protected," Margaret added. "And if you need anything at all—"

Charlotte batted her hand. "Between work and the church, my lists have lists. I never realized I had so many friends."

Chapter 14

Pass me those volumes," Todd said, directing Kingsley to the next carton. He smiled from his vantage point on the stepladder. "None of my other movers had such a cute butt."

"None could have been charmed into working on New Year's Day." She handed him the remaining reference books, then dropped into a guest chair to watch him transform the retired bank president's office into his own.

He finished the bookshelves and started arranging the top of his desk. "What I'd really like is your picture, right here on this corner."

"Come on, Todd. How would that look? Don't you grasp that because of our relationship I could be asked to resign? Or worse, pursue another area of banking? I keep waiting for that shoe to fall. I am not going over to the dark side. Branch administration is not going to happen. I'll die at my desk as a corporate lender, if you can pry me away for my funeral."

"As if our relationship is a big secret. Besides, you don't report directly to me."

"Have they decided who will replace you as Executive Vice President? And aren't they searching for a second EVP?"

"Yes. And no."

"Do you know who it is?"

"I'm afraid you'll have to learn that with everyone else. It's *insider information* that, if divulged prematurely, could affect stock prices. That would get the banker with the loose lips fired and possibly brought up on charges."

"Charges—what's the latest on our former Keynote president? I've heard rumors, but nobody knows."

"Frank's pleading *not guilty* to all charges. He's claiming credit for cracking the loan scam and recovering the funds. *And* he's refusing to resign his position. Since he's never recorded vacation days, he's also claiming months of personal time plus the insurance company's reward. Our attorneys, the Keynote National's board, and executives are scrambling for a reason to fire him. But since he hasn't been convicted of anything—"

"Could the newspaper article possibly be true?"

"About Frank uncovering the loan scam? That's sheer fabrication, but if he wins the criminal case, then he could sue. The lender who masterminded the original loan scam and forged the first round of documents—Manning Stoudt—does make a plausible scapegoat. Manning's unable to defend himself, being that he's dead, and Jeffrey Johnston, who allegedly colluded with him, has fled the jurisdiction. All efforts to find Jeffrey have been exhausted. It's even been rumored that Jeff's at the bottom of the Schuylkill River."

"That's outrageous. Can Frank succeed? And if so, what happens to your new position? Picture the headline: *Keynote National Bank Stuck With Two Presidents*."

Todd beckoned, and she circled his desk. He pulled her onto his lap.

"For your ears only," he said tracing its lobe with a delicate touch that made her giggle. "Our brilliant Technology VP may have solved our dilemma. Frank didn't know that deleted email could be resurrected from our mainframe's backup. Our tech unearthed correspondence between Jeffery Johnston and Frank Ziegler. Your predecessor, Fred McMillan, suspected Manning Stoudt was involved in something illegal which, if pursued, would have exposed the first of a dozen bogus loans that ultimately reached twelve million dollars. Frank's failure to follow procedure resulted in multiple additional felonies. Dereliction of duty at his level is a terminable offense. He'll be formally discharged first thing tomorrow. And, because of the charges pending against him, his Keynote accounts are frozen."

"Can I tell—"

"Not one word. Not even to Margaret or Barrie."

"Come on, Todd. If it weren't for them, we never would have unraveled the loan scam, much less have traced it to the bank's hierarchy."

"This is pajama talk."

"Do you ever wear them?"

"Only if there's no other way to keep warm."

She buried her face in the curve of his neck. "My silence is going to cost you—"

"I'm counting on that."

❧❧❧

Thud! Thud! Thud!

"Go away, Frank!" Dolly Ziegler screamed at her husband from inside her front door, which sounded as if it might split at any moment. "I swear! I'll call the police."

"You can't keep me out! Open this door, or I'll break it down!" Several more thuds hit the solid oak panels. "I demand my files! Now! And every other goddamn thing that belongs to me."

With the next thud and a splintering crack, Dolly grabbed for the phone.

"I'm warning you, Frank. Stay away. I'm dialing!"

A window exploded, glass spraying into the room as a rock thudded onto the floor. Terrified, Dolly ran through the house, screaming to the nine-one-one operator as she fled down the cellar steps, slamming and locking the door behind her.

She cowered behind their old chest freezer for what seemed like an interminable time. Finally, she heard angry voices upstairs.

Slowly, she abandoned the basement's safety and crept back upstairs. Through the cracked door, she saw uniformed patrolmen dragging Frank out through the kitchen.

"I'll get you for this, you stupid bitch!" he screamed at the house.

"Mrs. Ziegler, are you all right? Can I call someone?" one officer asked after cuffing Frank's hands and leading him toward a cruiser.

She shook her head. As soon as the officers finished

loading Frank into the back seat, they sped off in the direction of town. With shaking hands, Dolly managed to speed dial her best friend, Lauren James's number.

സ

Dolly's lifelong best friend paced the width of the old-fashioned kitchen. Her patience was shot. "Dolly! You need a restraining order. This is *your* house. Frank's gone over the edge." She propelled Dolly into the family room, eased her onto the couch, and hugged Dolly to her. "Please! You've got to let the police look at Frank's files. And call your attorney—what's his name?"

"Lloyd Cunningham."

"Yeah, him. And your trust officer, James Martin. Get those two together. Threaten to make what he's done very public if he ever comes near you. All those years—appropriating your trust funds, squandering your inheritance, even convincing you to sign over this house. With all the legal hot water he's in, threatening a lawsuit might protect you."

Dolly blanched. "I *can't* call the police! I won't talk to them ever! I'm scared."

"They'll protect you if we give them a very good reason."

She shook her head vehemently. "No! I can't, Lauren. You know that I can't! And you know why."

"Sweetie, don't you read the papers? You're sitting on evidence that proves Frank masterminded a loan scam worth twelve million dollars. If you turn it over to the police, that will separate you from Frank forever."

"Our children—"

"They're adults! And if they're not rallying behind their mother on this, shame on them." Lauren opened her mouth to pitch a new angle, but closed it instead as an idea took form. "Dolly, will you be okay for a minute? I'll make us some tea." With her back turned, she nonchalantly lifted Dolly's cordless handset, concealed it behind her back and strolled into the kitchen. After filling the kettle and firing the burner, she slipped outside onto the back porch. She dialed. "Let me speak to the detective in charge of the Frank Ziegler case, please."

 భాదా

"It was a slam dunk!" the detective insisted. "By the book."

"Well, apparently not," the ADA said, handing them the folded document jacketed in blue. "Mr. Ziegler's attorney is filing a motion to suppress all the evidence you took from the Ziegler residence on the grounds that the search was illegal. There was no warrant." Although the muscles twitched in her jaw, she kept her professional composure. "Gentlemen, tell me again exactly what happened."

The detectives swapped uneasy glances. The ranking one spoke. "A woman who identified herself as Frank Ziegler's wife, Dolly, phoned and said she had found evidence of a crime in her home and would we please come to see it. She said she'd heard that she could be in trouble for concealing such evidence. Something about being an accessory after the fact. When we arrived at the mansion, she opened the door, mentioned her call, and led us through the foyer."

"Exactly when was that?"

"Um—let me look at my notes. Ah, here it is. January second. We arrested Ziegler for storming their house and threatening his wife. She was in imminent danger."

"Was anyone else present?"

"Another woman was seated by the living room fireplace, but she said nothing. She looked a little surprised to see us, but she had one of those still, private faces."

"Go on."

"We reviewed with Mrs. Ziegler the details of our telephone conversation and asked if her husband should be present. She simply said no and took us into the study. 'There,' she said, pointing to the credenza. 'Go ahead.' I tried the doors, but they were locked. 'I'll get the keys,' she said, left us for a few minutes, and then returned."

"Did she personally give you the keys?"

"That's right."

"Then what happened?"

"She directed us to certain files and envelopes, and, while we examined them, she left the room. We found detailed records of the bogus loan transactions—Ziegler's phony IDs, corresponding bank accounts, and passports, and records of airline reservations, both to the islands and back here for the same afternoon."

"And you had no reason to suspect her?" She circled her hand to hurry him up. "Continue."

"It was downright spooky. Either Mrs. Ziegler had no idea what was in those files, or she's one cold fish. It was all there, including detailed records of monies paid to

Juanita Rodriguez and Jeffrey Johnston. We asked if we could take the files with us and she said 'sure.' Then she said something odd. 'And he thinks *she's* stupid.'" The detective shrugged.

"She said *she*?"

"Correct."

"Describe Mrs. Ziegler for me."

"Forty-something—smartly dressed. Petite, chestnut hair and blue eyes. Very trim, athletic—must work out on a regular basis."

"And the other woman?"

"Everything about her was plain—mousy brown hair streaked with gray that looked like it had been cut with manicure scissors. No makeup. Dark puffy eyes. Looked rather dazed. No, make that medicated."

The ADA sighed. "I can only imagine what transpired in that household, but the woman you spoke with was not Dolly Ziegler. It appears that Mrs. Ziegler was the one in the living room. Did *she* give you permission to search and take what she perceived as evidence of a crime?"

"She said nothing."

"Gentlemen, that woman who told you she was Ziegler's wife had no standing to authorize the removal of those files. We need to prove that this evidence would have been discovered inevitably or find a way to implicate Ziegler without it."

"But we caught him red-handed, having followed those account numbers into that one account, which he emptied. The check was in his possession along with his phony ID and tickets to Miami and/or the islands when we arrested him at the airport."

She rolled her eyes. "The tickets in his possession were round-trip. He claims he had already called a press conference to hand over the check as recovered funds. The editor remembers the call because it really pissed him off. Ziegler demanded he appear at the conference and didn't give him the opportunity to respond. Of course, we know this is bullshit. What," she staccatoed, "do we have without those files? Just the infamous blue list of bogus account numbers, about which he says he knows nothing. Manning Stoudt and Juanita are now deceased, without giving statements. A key person-of-interest, Jeffrey Johnston, the HR director, has vanished."

The group fell silent a moment.

"What *is* the problem?" the detective asked. "The home and furnishings belong to Mrs. Ziegler. We were told the desk had belonged to her father."

The ADA closed her eyes and rubbed her forehead in frustration. "Our Mr. Ziegler bought that credenza with his personal check and still has the bill of sale. It says 'Per customer request, one set of keys only for privacy.' Mr. Ziegler's attorney also produced the locksmith who will testify that twenty years later he made a set of keys for Mrs. Ziegler. Not from the originals, but from the locks themselves, without Mr. Ziegler's consent. The woman who claimed to be Mrs. Ziegler helped herself to those keys. At the hearing, Attorney Roth will ask that the files be ruled inadmissible, along with 'the fruits of the poisonous tree,' which, as you know, means anything you learned as a result of that search and seizure."

"I had a bad feeling this was too easy."

"Well, it *was* too good to be true. Gentlemen, we

know Ziegler masterminded a multi-million-dollar loan scam, but if the jury can't see this evidence, the case is too weak. He could walk, and jeopardy will apply." She sighed. "And I thought he was nuts to plead innocent. Please—find me a way back to those files or some other way to implicate him."

"There's Miller, that person who attacked Kingsley Ward. If he was working for Ziegler—"

The detective stopped talking when the ADA held up her hand, already guessing what she would say.

"We have no evidence of anyone working for Ziegler. Even if this Miller knows something, pleading him down would be political suicide, *if* we could convince him to testify. Even if we succeeded in running a bluff, her attacker is a dangerous felon whom the community will want locked up for life. Ziegler is a white-collar criminal. Nobody was physically hurt by this scam."

"Except for the stakeholders and the insurance company that's holding the bag for the shortfall."

"Interview the real Mrs. Ziegler. Getting her permission to have those files would solve everything, proving there was evidence of a crime in her home. At least, with the backlog of cases, the trial's not scheduled until September. And check with the Philadelphia Police. See if there's anything new on the real identity of the man who attacked Kingsley Ward."

"I wonder what else Attorney Roth will think of by then."

❧

When they arrived at the Ziegler mansion, the detectives noticed the shaggy front lawn and a small dumpster located near the front porch. They approached the open front door.

Two young people met them halfway. Although the detectives identified themselves cordially, they were not invited inside. "We tried phoning for an appointment but nobody answered. Is Mrs. Ziegler at home?"

"I'm her son and this is my sister. Sorry. She isn't available."

"When do you expect her? It's important that we speak with her." The two young people exchanged solemn glances.

"I'm afraid that's not possible," the young woman said. "Our mother has been very ill. She's not talking to anyone. We expect her to be hospitalized for some time."

"Perhaps if you'd give us the name of the hospital. I promise that we'll be brief."

Dolly's son stepped forward. "You don't understand. Our mother has had a breakdown. What my sister meant was 'can't talk.' And her doctor has left very strict orders—only certain family members are allowed to see her and that absolutely excludes strangers."

"Do you have power of attorney to act on her behalf?"

"No," they said simultaneously.

"Well, who—"

"I don't mean to be rude, but we have nothing further to add. Please leave our family alone."

The ranking detective grasped the resolve in the son's determined, hard face. He took out his card. "If your mother's status changes, we'd appreciate a call." He turned to leave.

As they were piling back into the car, he saw the son drop his card into the dumpster.

Chapter 15

A bitter wind that blasted from the north failed to chill Kingsley's euphoria as she anticipated dinner with Todd at the Olde Tavern Inn. She had splurged on a ruby red knit, which the saleswoman insisted few women could wear. It was perfect for Valentine's Day. Elegant. Classy. Accentuating her curves without being overtly sexy. One last glimpse in her bathroom mirror confirmed that her clever stylist had blended two inches of new growth where her scalp had been shorn and sutured. Had it been almost five months? So much had happened.

For its warmth, she wished she had borrowed her mother's mink coat, its generous collar doubling as a hood, but she couldn't bring herself to wear dead animals. Her ankle-length fitted down coat, while hardly elegant, would suffice.

She slipped into sling-back stilettos, remembering how she'd once towered over the boys. Today, even at five-eight, she was dwarfed by Todd. The pavement was dry. Little black spangled purse, leather dress gloves. Perfect. She glanced at the clock. Thirty minutes to kill. She laughed, which roused Pandora from snoozing on her down coverlet. Ah, yes. One last thing. She swept the lint roller over her dress and the coat.

Time crawled. Finally, a slamming car door. She hurriedly stowed her coat and purse in her office, lest she look overly anxious. The whoosh of the storm door down in the entry, familiar footsteps ascending, and his signature tap-tap-ta-tap-tap on her private door. She opened it so quickly that he hadn't had time to lower his knuckles. She almost said *wow*. He was wearing a cashmere topcoat, charcoal suit, and white shirt, his red tie matching her dress. He held an old-fashioned felt hat by its brim. Bitter wind had flushed his face.

"I love that dress!" he said, helping her on with her coat. "It matches your spirit."

After the short drive to the Olde Tavern Inn, Todd snagged a prime parking spot. He opened her door with a flourish, exaggerating the role of a colonial gentleman. Built of native limestone, the historic inn dated to the late 1700s to accommodate weary businessmen en route from Philadelphia to Pittsburgh. Its designation as an historic landmark saved it from being bulldozed to construct a new superhighway.

Antique coach lights on tall black standards lit the cobblestone walkway that meandered to the inn's oak door. Guiding her by the elbow, Todd shortened his steps to ensure that her heels wouldn't slip into the cracks. Soft lights spilled through original wavy glass windows. She could hear muted laughter.

Inside, while Todd confirmed their reservation, Kingsley took it all in. On the massive wood mantle, Douglas fir garlands, decorated with gold and white lovebirds, sparkled with thousands of tiny clear lights. The scent of apple wood burning in the massive stone fireplace, the aroma of pine, bayberry, and spices mingled with the Inn's signature prime rib.

A table waited for them by the hearth. When a waiter lit their candle, its light reflected on tiny red hearts sprinkled on the white linen cloth.

She realized that the Inn's old-world charm recapitulated Todd's dream of finding just such a place. While they scrutinized the wine list, Kingsley's mind drifted to an earlier adventure, touring Hopewell Furnace. She remembered how Todd had photographed architectural details inside and outside the manor house for future reference. She smiled at him, closing the folder. "A white wine. You choose."

The waiter returned. "A Dewar's on the rocks. And the lady will have a chardonnay." He pointed. Nodded. "This one."

"What were you thinking?" he asked.

"About the day we toured Hopewell, and your dream of restoring an old farmhouse. I didn't realize how serious you were. What a day. And where it led! On the way home, we checked out one of the properties that turned out to be on the bogus loan list."

"And you found that your loan customer's facility, supposedly under construction, was nothing but a vacant field. And that night you and your buddies broke into the Executive area looking for evidence." He shook his head. "It might not have turned out as well as it did."

"Assuming I testify convincingly."

Todd held up his hand in a stop-traffic gesture. "Enough. Poof. Tonight the bank does not exist. We have years to sort out our jobs." He stopped and, giving her a sheepish look, motioned to the menu. "How about something other than turkey or ham?" The waiter returned with their drinks, took their orders, and withdrew.

Time slipped away in a comforting haze. One personal story eased into another as they shared the threads that brought them together to this time and this place. Finally, she realized that the surrounding tables had turned over twice.

"Dinner was outstanding," she murmured, as they finished their coffee and amaretto. "There's something intoxicating about historic settings that makes me feel connected to the ages and traditions that last."

Todd straightened a bit, his demeanor shifting to a more serious posture. She thought reluctantly that he was signaling it was time to go. She picked up her purse, preparing to leave, but he wasn't moving.

"This year will bring big changes for me," he said, beginning a new thread. "Doug finished his last presidential duties and passed the baton to me. By this time next week, he'll be in California. I'm ready and eager to take up the challenge. But—I have far more important things on my mind." He set his glass aside. His smile warmed her more than the crackling fire. She waited, intrigued by the firelight reflected in his eyes.

"I want to pick up the search for a real home, which I've neglected since October when the one on the highway was sold. Think you could help me find it?"

"Of course. It'll be fun. I know how important it is to you. I'm sure the right one is out there, waiting." She smiled indulgently, running a finger down the back of his hand that rested beside hers on the table.

"How long would you say that we've known each other?" he asked.

She smiled at his hand that was now holding hers and answered truthfully. "That depends upon how you calculate time. I can't remember when I didn't know you."

"The old house, no matter how perfect, would be just stone and mortar without a family to make it a home. It's Valentine's Day, and you've run away with my heart. Surely you must realize how much I love you. I want to stretch our time into forever. I can't imagine a future without you." He paused, holding her eyes. "Kingsley, will you marry me?"

His words hung, suspended like magic, and Kingsley realized she'd been holding her breath. When she tried to speak, her brain couldn't process the myriad of emotions she felt at that moment. All she could manage was "Yes! Oh, yes!"

They grinned stupidly at each other, then he bent across the table to punctuate the moment with a kiss.

He chuckled, almost to himself, then confessed with a sigh. "I'm so relieved. I didn't have a Plan B." Then his tone became more serious. "I want to give you something special to mark the occasion. Something that's unique to us." From his pocket, he pulled a small heart-shaped leather box whose oval lid was inlaid with a tiny circle of gold-leaf flowers. He set it before her. "My great-great grandmother brought this from England and kept her earrings in it. Go ahead. Open it. Oh, it sticks just a tad. Wiggle it a little."

She opened the box in which a pair of blue-white diamond earrings released fire against the box's rose silk lining. She gasped. "They're gorgeous!" She looked up at him in wonder.

"There's something special about each one. Take one out and turn it over, then let me check the back." She did so and saw where he pointed to a tiny *h* engraved in the gold. "I had the jeweler mark them so that you'd always know which one was which.

"My full name is William Todd Henning III. My grandfather went by W. Todd, and my father by Bill. That stone was in Grandfather's stickpin. He always said it would be for my bride. Dad kept it for me after Grandfather passed away. When Dad met you in Connecticut, he gave it to me and said, 'Don't let her get away.' And I don't intend to. Ever."

Happy tears welled up in her eyes, and she dabbed them with her linen napkin. "It's a family heirloom. Are you sure?"

"I've never been more sure of anything in my life. Now, look at the other one. Engraved are the letters is *t to k.* That stands for "Todd to Kingsley.' The jeweler matched Grandfather's stone with this new one, which I bought for you. That's for your left ear."

"Like wedding rings on the left hand?"

"That's right. You can have whatever kind of wedding band you like. I thought we could choose them together."

"I can't believe you did this for me. I don't know what to say."

He took her hand again and held her eyes. "Just say that you'll have me, you'll love, me and be faithful to me. And never leave me."

"That is *so* easy."

He bent over and kissed her again, while a white-haired couple looked on, smiling, then smiled at each other. "Let's make it a very short engagement. Like next week or next month or whenever you wish."

"Can we keep it simple, just family and best friends? Plan something unique that's meaningful to us?"

"My thoughts exactly. If you like, we can start calling family tomorrow. Your parents must know something's up. I had to find out what kind of gold you could wear, and I'm a pretty bad liar."

espeso

They drove back to her place, climbing the steps to her door, arm in arm, for once not talking at all. As the heavy door chinked closed behind them, they kissed in the dark vestibule. Finally, she said, "Let me fix you a drink, then maybe you'll help me try on the earrings."

"I'd better pass on that drink. I'm already skirting the limits, and I have to drive."

She took his topcoat, then kicked off her shoes. "Not if you stay." She thrilled at the look that passed over his face. Kingsley unearthed her grandmother's cut glass snifters, poured two Bailey's, and curled next to him on the couch. In between sips, he showed her the secret to opening the box, then handed each earring to her.

"How long have you been planning this?"

"Truthfully? Since our dinner at that Hawk Mountain diner in September after we hiked the River of Rocks trail. I consider that our first date, when I accidentally-on-purpose ran into you, although I felt like a stalker. No. It was when I first saw you at the gym. You'd dropped your gloves. I just had no idea how to get from there to here until so many bizarre events threw us together, compressing time. And then, there you were, at the newcomers' luncheon for new bank officers. I thought I was dreaming."

"I need a mirror," she said, taking his hand and leading him back to her bedroom vanity. She sat while he straddled the other end to watch. He handed her each earring, and awkwardly at first, she managed the screw backs without dropping them onto the carpet. "They're gorgeous," she said, turning to show him."

"*You're* gorgeous. Don't be afraid to wear and enjoy them."

"What if I lost one, or somebody stole them?"

"The jeweler promised that screw backs are secure. And they're insured." He brushed a curl back from her ear. "Besides, what they represent cannot be stolen or lost. That's yours forever."

"Are you that sure about me? About us?"

"I've never been more sure of anything in my life." He kissed her with that same passion that flashed her back to that evening at his condo when she'd dropped in unannounced, ostensibly to give him a book that she'd found on historic renovations. He'd been terribly drunk, guard down, and shared a glimpse of his dreadful failed marriage. And he had kissed her passionately.

"I've wanted you so badly," she said, as she turned the hurricane lamp down to a glow, lowered the shades, and returned. Taking his hands, she smoothed, then kissed, the tips of his fingers. He was holding her eyes, time in suspension. Words, she realized, had simply run out and a backlog of feelings begging their due overwhelmed her.

"I'd have waited forever for you," he whispered, then gently kissed her upper, then lower lip and then both.

"I love you so much," she responded to his raw expressions of love and of lust, the craziness overtaking her, losing herself in it, in him. Nothing existed outside her senses, the frenzied stripping, and exquisite intimacy, nothing denied.

Afterward, dozing and then waking, the rest of the world drifted back in sensations: the rumpled sheets' texture, the warmth of his body, his now gentle breathing next to her ear. Lost in a dream, he was resting a strong, gentle hand on her arm. She found herself grinning, unable to stop, and she sighed to the depth of her being. Was she the same person who had spent that first night right here in this bed, terrified of every strange noise?

She slipped into the bathroom, lit scented candles, and then dropped fluffy towels onto the floor. Leaving the door to the bedroom ajar, she stepped into the shower and let its luxurious warmth envelop her.

Shortly, his shadow darkened the glass, and he stepped in. Cupping her face, he bent down to kiss her. "You are amazing," he dragged out the syllables, his voice one with the water and smooth with the echoes. He took the scented soap that she offered, lathered his hands, then slowly caressed her slick body with his hands and his eyes. Then he handed it to her. "Don't be afraid to look at me, to touch me," he said, guiding her soapy hands.

They lingered awhile, then soothed and revived, toweled each other. "I rushed you before," he said and carried her back to the her bed. Deliberately, playfully, he built the momentum until, exhausted, they slept.

৩৩৩

A sliver of light cracked through the shades, bringing with the dawn and fresh awareness. She touched her ears, remembering, and rolled into his warmth. Finally, she opened her eyes. "You're beautiful when you're asleep," he said, gathering her in his arms. "Let's have a very short engagement. I don't want to let you out of my sight."

They snuggled awhile amid jumbled sheets and uprooted blankets.

Finally, he said, "Why don't I rescue what's left of my clothes and go make us some coffee? Take as long as you want getting dressed, then let's go to my place and I'll cook you breakfast. Perhaps you'd like to call family? How does that sound?"

"Mmm. Lovely." Through slit eyes she admired his nakedness crossing the room and wondered how she could ever keep a straight face at the bank. "What's your hurry?" she said, barely audible, but the question was not lost as he retraced his steps.

৩৩৩

"Sarah, what's wrong?" Henry Alderson leaped from

his recliner, dropping the Sunday *New York Times* on the floor. Picking his way around it's scattered sections, he hurried toward his wife. She was crying, tears streaking the makeup she had applied for church. Only as he got closer did he see she was laughing and crying at the same time.

"What?" he repeated.

With a poke of her manicured finger, Sarah hit the phone's speaker button. "News! Kingsley has news!"

Henry smiled, knowing full well it wasn't about a silly promotion or some exotic adventure that she had planned. Todd. It was about Todd, and he knew it.

The parents digested the gush of euphoria, which was tempered with emphatic details of what would not happen. With Kingsley's deep hatred of newspaper reporters and their history of prying into her life, there would be no engagement announcement, showers or parties, or an elaborate ceremony.

Sarah listened, understanding, tempering her opinions until they mentioned a simple ceremony with the Justice of the Peace. "Absolutely not!" Sarah couldn't contain herself any longer. "That would be like taking a meeting."

"Or, as an alternative, a small ceremony in the garden the first Saturday in May."

Sarah beamed at her husband. "Of course! Just leave everything to me."

"Mom?"

"Oh. I am sorry. Just tell me what you'd like me to do, and I'll help. Henry, stop rolling your eyes!"

Kingsley had not intended to broach the subject within

twenty-four hours of their engagement. "Mom, we may still need that JP. Widows can remarry, no problem, but Todd is divorced. Wouldn't we need the Bishop's permission to be married by an Episcopal priest?"

"Is he a Christian?"

"A Baptized Lutheran. And his brother's a minister."

Todd spoke up. "Under the circumstances, and with no children involved, I planned to seek an annulment. I put those wheels in motion some time ago."

"Any idea where you'll live?"

"We're going house hunting," she said, her bouncy voice audible over the miles.

"Contemporary? Colonial?"

"Old. Really, really, really old. Wish us luck."

Following more loving rounds of congratulations, Sarah and Henry hung up simultaneously. "That's a smirk if ever I saw one," Henry said. "You're not surprised?"

"After Thanksgiving? There was an easiness, a friendship, but the electricity!" Sarah opened the end table drawer and extracted a folder. "Now, Henry—if we're going to have a wedding on the patio, we'll need to garden much earlier this year. I'll see if they still have bulbs that bloom the first week of May. And I'd better nail down our caterer. And who's that photographer the Gilberts used? Their daughter's pictures were phenomenal."

"Didn't I hear *small*? Immediate family and a few close friends?"

"Now, Henry—small can be lovely. Imagine! The idea of going to a Justice of the Peace. No bankers' meeting for our daughter."

"I should know to simply say 'yes'm' when you start with 'now, Henry.'"

"*You* don't act surprised."

"You're the one with the folder. It's the way Todd acted at lunch."

"Lunch?"

"Well…ah…we ended up at the same meeting, then went for a bite. He admired my ring—mentioned that Kingsley seems to have so much trouble with her hand. An allergy of some kind. I said her engagement ring was an antique alloy, no idea what. Then he asked about fourteen or eighteen karat."

"He wouldn't have dared ask me such a question."

"Just let me know what you want me to do." He kissed her cheek then ambled away.

Easing into his library chair, he looked at the double-frame photo of Kingsley, age five, playing banker in his office, the other at her first Philadelphia firm. *My child, my daughter, light of my life*, he thought. "Sir," Todd had said, "if she'll have me, I want to marry your daughter. If I don't have your blessing, I'll work hard to earn it. Family is my first priority too." He had continued. "I had intended to honor my wedding vows, come hell or high water, never anticipating how high the water or how depraved the hell. The marriage was over in a matter of months, but I tried—lord knows I tried. I believe in commitment and want you to understand why I couldn't go on."

"Really, you don't have to explain. Your past is none of my business."

Todd had held up his hand, then handed Henry the operative's report, including the photos. "Sir," Todd had said. "I will honor and cherish your daughter."

Henry thought he was shockproof, but wasn't prepared. Not for Maureen. "First, since we're going to be family, call me Henry." Now he set Kingsley's photos back on his desk, thinking he'd need one of them together.

<h1 style="text-align:center">Chapter 16</h1>

Todd's quest for finding the perfect old house consumed their weekends. They had seen stone, brick, and frame; old mills, barns, and stores; and even a church. Houses on highways, encircled by condos; in place or to move; too big, too small, or too botched to salvage. Building with vintage and salvaged materials began creeping into their conversation, but not without disappointment.

The fourth Sunday in March, Kingsley's phone rang at six. "This may be it—and it goes on the market tomorrow." Kingsley groped for her robe as Todd gushed the details, his customary cool nonexistent.

"It's limestone, early eighteen hundreds, on twenty acres, six miles from the bank, bordered on three sides by Mennonite farms. The fourth side has been rezoned for a subdivision, but issues between the buyer and the seller may tie that up for years."

"I know you were hoping to find something big."

"About four-thousand square feet, if you include a finished third floor. It has four large rooms downstairs, four bedrooms upstairs, but only one bathroom. I'll call the architect. He'll get the inspector. Can't get the contractor until Monday. He's Mennonite, and they never work Sundays."

"What's it like? Should I call my folks?"

"Absolutely. We'll need all the eyes we can get. We may have to make a snap decision or lose it."

"Why are they selling?"

"The owner suffered devastating losses in the market but not before spending a bundle on structural necessities. He has to raise cash. It still needs lots of work, but what has been done sounds meticulous."

Kingsley sprang to the bathroom, showered in haste, and threw on lined jeans over silk long johns, a turtleneck and cable knit wool sweater. She stuffed woolen socked feet into tall hiking boots, having learned from painful experience that neglected country farmhouses could be borderline inaccessible to foot traffic. By the time Todd pulled around front, she was approaching the sidewalk, a bag of yesterday's donuts and travel mugs of coffee stowed in an insulated bag.

As soon as Kingsley spotted her dad's Suburban, Todd pulled onto the berm to follow the realtor's car west on the four-lane. Exiting onto a secondary, their small caravan followed the meandering rural road deeper into the country. Where the realtor's right turn signal indicated, they crunched down a long gravel lane that bisected virgin woods.

A hundred yards farther, the woods gave way to a clearing on which towered their possibility. Magnificent oaks, which obscured the house from the two-lane, separated the dense woods from an overgrown front lawn. Greg, the young realtor who leaped from his Jeep, hurried to meet them, clipboard in hand.

Making a sweeping motion with his free hand, he began to pitch it. "The house was built in 1803," he said, pointing to the date stone carved above the front door. "The walls are twenty-nine inches thick, and the windows are original. See that mortar line?" He pointed to a vertical seam that bisected the house. "Everything to the right of the door was added in the eighteen-thirties, which doubled its size. The original house includes the foyer and staircase. To the left, it included two rooms downstairs and two bedrooms upstairs. The bathroom, above the foyer, was added much later. Only four families have owned it, including newlyweds who stayed sixty years. While the widow spent her last five in a nursing home, it stood empty. Her heirs sold it to the present owner four years ago."

Greg unlocked the massive walnut door and led them inside. Dim and quite cold, its surfaces were smothered with dust. The smell of old wood and well-used fireplaces mingled with drafts that occasionally whistled. "Foyer's about twelve wide by twenty," the architect said. "Great staircase back there."

Greg circled them through the downstairs. "To our left would have been the front parlor and behind it, the family's sitting room." He led them across the back, through an archway, and past a back door. "Here, beneath the staircase, is the cellar door and a possible spot for a *Harry Potter* powder room off the center hall. Through this door, into the right rear, is the kitchen."

"Todd! A walk-in fireplace!" Kingsley tried unsuccessfully to keep her voice calm. "And the kitchen is huge!" It was bare except for two wooden cupboards toe-nailed to the ceiling and a porcelain sink flanked by twin draining boards supported by old metal cabinets. Greg steered them into the front corner room. "And this is the dining room."

"This would make a great library," Todd said to the architect. "Install glass doors that would open to the foyer."

They completed the circle, and climbing the staircase, paused on a landing at a window that overlooked the backyard and the farmland beyond. Turning right again they trooped up six more steps into the broad upper hall.

"Before indoor plumbing, there would have been a center front window. Each bedroom has its own fireplace with new closets partitioned between the front and back rooms."

Greg motioned them into the bathroom, renovations for which stopped before a huge claw-foot tub could be removed. A 1950s white toilet and washbowl remained.

Todd, with his architect and inspector in tow, rounded up Greg. "Give us a rundown on what's already been done, then we'll talk about what else we've found."

Greg referred to his clipboard. "The house has great bones. New copper pipes, which were no easy trick, and an original slate roof, which has been repaired, should last a lifetime. The well and septic check out. The structure and timbers are sound. As you can see, the stone's been repointed. That's a big plus and probably what bankrupted the present owner."

The inspector was frowning. "The electric's obsolete and squirrels have been chewing the wires. The furnace is shot. Doubt you'd want radiators anyway, but there's a solution—two heat pumps, one for downstairs, one up. Run the duct work for downstairs up through the cellar, the ducts for upstairs down through the third floor."

"Third floor?"

"That door in the upstairs hall, Kingsley," Todd said. "The attic is floored." Turning back to the men, "What else?"

"Paint's got to be lead. I'd let a professional deal with that. You'll want to install a second bath and a powder room. And total redecorating. The floors, unfortunately, have been varnished, which is half on, half off. The fireplaces need restoration or sealing if you don't intend to use them. If you want to use the bank barn as a garage, it needs a new roof and secure doors. That's all the big stuff."

"Kingsley, a minute?" They left the others and sat on the stairs. "What do you think?"

"It's simply fantastic. I love it."

"Are you quite sure? I promise, a project like this will take over our lives."

She beamed. "Nothing else has even come close, and you know it. And the setting is perfect! Let's do it."

"Hey, Greg, tell the seller that you have a buyer."

"You mean it? Really? My first big sale—"

"Why don't you nail it down first?"

Greg disappeared then returned shortly, looking dejected.

"What happened?" Todd asked.

"The seller already has an offer. I'm sorry. We simply weren't fast enough."

Kingsley stole a look at Todd, whose face was perfectly calm. "What *exactly* did he say?"

"'There's an offer on the table, and I think the seller is taking it. He needs to sell quickly.'"

"Did he say he'd *accepted* the offer?" Greg looked blank. "Call him back and ask," Todd ordered.

Greg dialed and, in just a minute, covered the mouthpiece and said, "No, not yet."

"What's the offer?"

"The bid is five-percent below asking price, and he wants an allowance for the wiring. And it's contingent upon his mortgage approval."

"Tell him you've got a cash customer who's willing to pay asking price and take the property as-is. I'll give him a ten-percent nonrefundable down payment today and the balance in a week if we can sign the agreement *today*. Tomorrow the deal's off the table. Tell him to call you right back."

Greg's eyes widened. "Are you sure?"

"She's picked the spot for our Christmas tree."

Kingsley grew nervous and, to kill time, wandered upstairs while Todd examined what would be involved with stripping the floorboards. Through a back bedroom window, she gazed at the perfect checkerboard farmland bordered by tree rows.

How many people in 200 years had gazed out that window? The walls were covered with layers of wallpaper, water-stained before the new roof arrested further damage.

She found a loose corner and, rolling back the paper, saw a blue and then a pink layer.

Children, how many, had stood here, watching the birds or the snow? She bit her lip hard, then licked where it tasted salty. What to do with this room since there wouldn't be any children? Is such a big house insane for two people?

Never in her dreams, from earliest childhood, had she imagined her life without children. She wiped her eyes with the hem of her sleeve. At least the problem was both of them.

"What a great little room—actually, it's still rather big. Kind of easy to lose perspective without any furniture," Todd chattered. "Kingsley? What's wrong?"

She fabricated a quick lie that was partially true. "I was just thinking of that poor dear old lady, alone in a nursing home, her husband dead. Sixty years? I'll bet it went by in a heartbeat."

He hugged her, then smoothing back her bangs, kissed her forehead. "We'll make time our servant and this, our haven: a retreat from the rat race. Rats—I suppose we get rodents as part of *as is*. Exterminator—we'll add that to the list, unless you like pets or have a great recipe." She swatted his arm.

Greg hollered, and they hurried to the staircase, colliding with him. "Can we go to my office to sign the agreement? You've got yourselves a house!"

Kingsley threw her arms around Todd, nearly toppling them both down the stairs. Releasing him, she eyed the vast empty interior. "Do you see what I see? It's our future."

"Yep. And a whole lot of work."

⁂

The third Wednesday in April, Kingsley took a deep breath and entered the vast ballroom to witness Todd's first shareholders meeting. On stage, a long-skirted table bore Warren and Todd's nameplates along with one for the corporate secretary.

Long tables for sixteen, dressed in white linen, were already filling with 500 shareholders whose line snaked from the lobby to the sign-in table. Todd and Warren greeted them, many by first name, as they inched toward the waiting officers' table to collect their nametags and annual reports.

Barrie wormed her way through the crush and grabbed her arm. "Over here," she directed Kingsley toward a major shareholder who needed some courting. Suddenly a hush rippled through the room. "My god," Barrie hissed. "It's Frank!"

Kingsley followed Barrie's stare to the group moving toward a reserved table at the front of the room. "What's he doing here?"

"He owns a ton of our stock. And look who he's with—our largest shareholder! Know what I heard? He's filed a lawsuit for the reward money and Keynote for damages."

"Does Todd know that?"

Barrie grinned. "Roll over and ask him." She glanced at her watch as the lights blinked several times. "Showtime."

The room grew quiet after seats stopped scraping and the executive officers took to the stage. As Chairman, Warren took charge, dispatching the minutes of the previous year's meeting, the election of new board members, and giving a brief update on the holding company. He then turned the meeting over to Todd. Since Keynote National Bank was the bulk of the financial corporation, most of the accountability was Todd's.

Two large screens in the room's front corners magnified Todd's face in such detail that Kingsley was transfixed. Built-in ceiling speakers amplified his voice, and, for the first time, Kingsley could detect a trace of New England. His importance stunned her, his message compelling, his words succinct and on target. Black-tie language, grammatically precise, subjects and far-flung verbs all agreeing.

Finally, Todd fielded questions, two from the audience and two from reporters. He was gathering his notes when a man shouted, "I have a question."

One of the directors called, "I can't hear him. Run the cordless mike over to him."

Kingsley caught Barrie's eye. Barrie mouthed *Frank*.

The question rang through the ballroom. "Todd, is it true that the board has a lucrative offer to sell Keynote? That your sole purpose for joining Keynote was to get it ready to sell?"

Alarmed, Kingsley slipped from her chair and duck-walked to Barrie. "That's it! That's the voice! It's Frank's!"

Barrie's eyes widened. "Seriously? The loan scam?" she mouthed. "No way."

Kingsley bobbed her head up and down frantically. "I'd know that voice anywhere!"

Barrie bent to her ear. "But it can't be—you would have nailed it by now."

"That's not true!" she whispered. "I've never had a conversation with him, nor been in a meeting at which he has spoken." Kingsley refocused on Todd. Composed and relaxed, one hand in his pocket, he could have been chatting with an old friend.

"There is no offer on the table, Frank, and none in the pipeline. I was brought to Keynote to continue the tradition of increasing profits and earnings for our shareholders, as my predecessors did for decades. Last year, we exceeded projections and our first quarter figures are good. At the risk of making a *forward-looking statement*, which I'm not intending, we're well on our way to another fine year.

"The board, Warren and I, as Doug before me, feel the best value for our shareholders, employees, and community is to remain independent. In short, we're not planning to sell. You can count on our being a sound investment, a good business partner, and a community leader."

"Todd, I—"

Warren stood, and with ballet precision, replaced Todd at the podium. "If there's no further business, the meeting is adjourned." He clicked off the podium mike.

Servers swept into the ballroom and began dealing free chicken dinners while conversations rose to a din. A reporter cornered Todd as he dismounted the steps. "Todd, a question. You didn't mention the loan scam. The public has a right to an update. Is it true that the perpetrators are all dead? And that the shareholders are out a ton of money?"

"First of all, the bank has insurance to cover the short-fall, for which they will be compensated as funds are recovered."

"Doesn't that make Frank Ziegler a hero? Is it true that he's suing the bank to regain his position, the reward, and compensatory damages? Don't those demands represent conflicting interests?" He shoved the mike in Todd's direction.

Todd smiled benignly at the reporter. "That's five questions, Ed. I have no new information to share. As for any alleged legal or criminal actions, you'll have to ask Frank about the former and the police about the latter. The loan scam is still under investigation, and the bank never comments on open police investigations. Now, you'll have to excuse me."

"Thank you." The reporter scanned the multitude, lit on someone of particular interest, and darted toward Frank.

Kingsley followed his trajectory but lost track of both in the crowd. Perhaps the reporter had left to file his story. Rather than eat, Todd worked his way from table to table, shaking hands and chatting. Kingsley hung back to watch him.

"Kingsley! There you are. Where are you sitting?" She pointed. He moved close to her ear. "How'd I do?"

"You were wonderful. You make it look easy. But—can a reporter who's sent to cover the meeting work the crowd after it's over?"

"The event is two-part. Reporters are welcome to cover the business portion, but when the business meeting concludes, they must leave. The dinner is for shareholders by invitation only."

"What if that reporter owns Keynote stock? What then?"

"If you look around, you'll notice our employee-shareholders are scattered around the room, keeping tabs on our guests by designated area. They'd move in swiftly to convince an intruder that it's time to leave. Come. I want you to meet the directors with whom you'll be sitting next year." Hand on her waist, he took her from table to table, introducing them to his fiancée. She basked in their good wishes, all problems with Frank set aside.

cseco

Back in her apartment, Todd couldn't stop pacing. "Frank's was the voice? Are you sure? That's too bizarre."

Kingsley nodded emphatically. "Absolutely."

"But it's been months—"

"Think back, Todd. I never heard him speak at a meeting. My first day on the job, when he walked through Lending, I approached him to introduce myself. I thought he had come to meet me, since I was the new head of Commercial Lending. He just batted his hand to dismiss me and kept on walking toward Nathaniel Frazier's corner office. Two weeks later—you remember my baptism by fire—I reported on Lending at the Department Head meeting. Nathaniel had been called away unexpectedly." She smiled. "You chaired that meeting and were so gracious to me. I was so nervous! Frank dropped in briefly but never spoke. Then in October, I was late to my first officers' meeting. Frank had already finished speaking. On my way out, I recognized his voice from behind a screen. No way I could intrude on an executive meeting. And by Christmas, he was gone."

"He's been on TV."

"I never caught it. And he avoids me. Todd—I have to tell the police. I know what I heard. His voice is so distinctive that I nearly jumped to my feet."

"I'll go with you."

"You can't. That would scream conflict of interest, to say nothing of politics, which could hurt your career."

"Let me worry about that. You know he's pleading innocent. If the case goes to trial, you'd have to testify."

"I'll do it."

He studied her face then finally nodded. "If you're sure."

She patted the sofa beside her. "Let's move on to more serious business—chilled wine, fruit, French bread, and cheese—a light snack to get you down off the lights. You were wonderful tonight."

Chapter 17

The following morning the ADA welcomed Kingsley into her office, eager for details begun on the phone. Her demeanor belied her churning insides. Could they finally be getting a break?

"Is the red light on?" the ADA asked about the small recording device. Kingsley said that it was, knowing it would preserve their conversation and establish her consent. The ADA stated the date, the time and place, and the names of those present, including the spelling.

"Start at the beginning. You said you suspected a loan scam in progress and that the suspicious paperwork was somewhere in Manning Stoudt's office?"

"Correction. The junior loan officer who called himself Manning Stoudt."

"Of course. Continue."

"When the documents weren't in our central file, and knowing he was the originating officer, I looked around his office and found the paperwork in a box under his desk."

"Was that unusual?"

"Absolutely. On a subsequent evening after everyone had gone home, I took a folder from the box to our copy room to duplicate the contents. Afraid I might be caught, I planned to take the copies home to read at my leisure."

"Is that illegal or unethical?"

"Neither. All loan documents belong to the bank, and as head of Commercial Lending, Manning reported to me."

"So why didn't you simply insist that he turn over the files?"

"Initially, I'd made a big deal about what should have been a minor clerical error. It appeared Nathaniel Frazier, the head of Lending, and Jeffrey Johnston, the vice president in charge of Human Resources, had reprimanded him. At best, a black mark could have been put on his permanent record. No, I wanted to research that paperwork before making any accusations, in spite of my suspicions."

"And the loan in question turned out to be bogus?"

"Yes. And part of a much larger scheme that ran into millions."

"Which, because of the scope, indicated multiple people."

Kingsley thought for a minute to phrase her response carefully. "I do recall one twelve-million-dollar loan scam at another bank that was perpetrated by one person alone. I thought that might be the case until I heard Manning Stoudt discussing the scam with a second person. The other man was angry. And loud."

"Tell me again exactly what makes you think the voice belongs to Frank Ziegler. A jury will find it hard to believe that after six months you could identify him from—what? Inside a cabinet? How did that happen?"

"I was about to copy the contents of the file when I heard the elevator door open and two voices emerge in heated conversation." When the ADA looked puzzled, Kingsley explained. "Our department is laid out like a big rectangle. Elevators by the front left wall, copy room on the left wall, my office on the back wall, and Manning's on the right, directly in line with the copy room. The staff *cube farm* is in the center, with a walkway separating them from the other lenders' offices along the back outside wall."

"And your boss's office…"

"Back right corner. It was dark. As I said, everyone had gone home."

"Continue—you were in the copy room…"

"Correct. I hid behind the door, my only option being to wait them out, unnoticed. After they'd leave, I'd copy the files. The argument continued in Manning's office. I thought I was home free. Manning's voice was a rumble. The unidentified voice was insisting 'there's no tie to me—that you alone are going to prison unless you do as you're told.' Manning's light was snapped off, and they approached the elevator. But instead of getting on, they bypassed it, rounded the corner, and entered the copy room.

"I heard them coming. There was no place to hide, except in that empty cabinet. I was terrified I'd sneeze or my muscles would spaz. But they continued to snarl at each other over the sound of the copier, duplicating papers, using several reams of paper. So many that they had to reload the machine."

"Why didn't you just pretend to be working late?"

"With all the lights off? I know it sounds crazy, but I honestly thought I might be in danger or, at the very least, embarrass myself. It was too late for a do-over. That's why I hid."

"Tell me about the voice."

"It's distinctive. He has a slight Pennsylvania Dutch accent. For example, rather than 'get out now' it comes out 'git awt naw.' He has a faint lisp and speaks as if his tongue's too big for his mouth. And he pronounced *sw* like *th*. *Sweet* would be *thweet*. He's a baritone, but just barely. The resonance of his voice had a raspy-saw quality and was thin, shallow, and airy in tone. The tambour was covered, not bell-like. And the way he handles his diphthongs—"

"What?"

"Vowel combinations, like the o-y in toy. He drags them out."

"You're a singer?"

"Just in the shower. I did study voice but didn't pursue it. I have a very good ear—for volume, range, distance, and speech patterns. Movies are way too loud."

"Are you *very* sure this was the voice."

"Absolutely."

"Would you be willing to do a voice line-up if we can get a judge to issue a court order?"

"Of course."

"The defense attorney will try to discredit you."

Kingsley rose, gripped the edge of the desk. "Just let

him try. I know what I heard, and I'm *not* backing down." She set her business card on the desk. "Whenever you're ready, just give me a call, and I'll clear my calendar."

The ADA escorted Kingsley to the elevator and thanked her again. The second Kingsley was gone, the ADA snapped her door shut, punching the air with her fist. Kingsley Ward would make an excellent witness. The ADA summoned her staff to fine-tune their strategy and get a warrant for the lineup.

ↄ๏ↄ

Todd unlocked Kingsley's empty apartment, sidestepping the invisible bloodstain that was seared into his mind from the dreadful night of her attack. Finally, May had arrived. In five days, he'd be in St. Davids, watching her descend the staircase to marry him. Six more days and they would be cruising the ocean, finally alone.

In her kitchen, he quickly located the stool she'd forgotten then made one last loop checking closets. His brain knew she was home with her family, but he was unsettled by how gone she was.

He remembered the first time he sat on her couch, the meals that she fed him, the hours they'd spent simply talking. The way that she fussed over him. Why had it taken so long to find her?

He paused at her bedroom. Valentine's Day. The first time she'd drawn the shades. How fast they'd turned into a couple! He checked out the bathroom and tightened Pandora's slow-dripping faucet. Their first dinner date, when a frightened Pandora took a flying leap into the toilet and then scrambled into the clumping kitty litter. Snipping litter from yowling Pandora, who had yet to forgive him. He resisted the urge to phone. Collecting the stool, he locked up and turned in her keys.

"Mr. H. Thought I might miss you." Todd's squat cleaning woman had been singing a hymn at the top of her lungs when he entered his condo. "If only all of my clients were like you. Most men are such slobs. Well, it's ready for inspection."

"Thanks for all that you've done and especially for your honesty. Here, this is for today, and the envelope's my thanks."

"Mr. H? Don't forget the box in your study. And call me when the new missus needs me." She opened the envelope. "Thank *you*. I really appreciate this."

"And I, you." She bustled out. Todd's eyes swept the vast empty space—the hours they'd spent on the carpet, the architect's plans strewn everywhere. Intimate times, discovering real love. He looked at his watch and shouldering the box, closed the door on his past.

Todd drove to their rental, a lucky find on a gracious old street overhung with a tunnel of sycamore trees. On the Victorian wrap-around porch a massive swing creaked on its chains. Inside everything was just as they'd left it, organized chaos of their combined worlds. Henning Home and Warehouse, she'd joked, all their spare furniture stowed in spare bedrooms. She'd been right. They got it all in. He walked through the living room, back to the dining room, stacked five feet high with double rows of cartons, labeled in marker, for their home in the country.

He opened kitchen cupboards, remembering how they'd debated whose stuff went where. She'd nabbed the duplicates she'd need while they worked on the stone house.

The pantry closet that ran the length of the room had looked enormous before she'd filled it with mysterious staples like ten kinds of curry. No more eating alone. He looked at his watch. This time, five days.

Upstairs a huge empty place between the two front windows was stacked with new bedding. What was keeping the truck? He killed time, inspecting closets, his suits and shirts abutting hers. Yesterday it had all seemed so practical, but now so personal.

He cracked her top dresser drawer, closed it and opened another. Silky things, folded up small, smooth to the touch. He searched with his eyes, then carefully lifted the black petticoat, edged in deep lace. She still had it. He held it up by the elastic, then carefully refolded and put it away.

He sat down on the floor and pulled out his cell phone to dial the local priest's number. "Just wanted to thank you again for helping me get the bishop's permission to remarry. I wasn't comfortable with a priest she'd known all of her life. My situation was just too ugly."

"Son," the priest said, "the divorce was appropriate. You did the right thing. Just try to forgive yourself. And maybe in time, you'll find your way back. Your experience, you know, was not about God, but about people who'd gone astray."

"I'll try to attend with her—give it a chance."

"Give *Him* and yourself a chance."

Todd said thanks one more time, then disconnected. Another wrinkle in his rumpled past. Would he tell her about it? Probably not. To his ears, he sounded weak and naïve, and he'd beaten the Maureen subject to death. He knew what Kingsley would say—just let it go, like dandelion seeds blown to the wind. But go back to church?

Maureen's new religion he'd never heard of. The way that they gushed, touched, looked at him and each other. That horrible night he'd walked in on the orgy. He'd bolted, having no recollection of how he got home. She hadn't returned for two days, and when she did, she was shameless, rerunning the old tape of how he was prudish, uptight, too buttoned down, a dinosaur.

His envy of Andrew crept to the surface. Andy had been perfect for Kingsley. For most women, in fact, since Andy didn't have Todd's kind of baggage. What if his best was a distant second? What if he failed her? He speed-dialed the security company. "Are you positive the system is foolproof? Good. Turn it on now, even though we'll be gone for two weeks. I expect action, even if the disturbance is caused by a mouse."

"Your landlord owes you a favor since you upgraded his rental property. Will you be needing a bodyguard again?"

"I want one I can call on a moment's notice. I suspect there are more people involved with the man who attacked her. Desperate people with access to muscle."

"You can count on us, sir."

He disconnected, then jumped when it rang immediately. "Did I thank you enough for making last rounds?" Kingsley asked.

"How did you know I was thinking about you?" He could hear women laughing, the sound growing dimmer as she must have been walking away.

She sighed. "This sounds silly, but I hated to see our apartments all empty. So much of our history took place in those rooms. I felt like I was leaving part of us behind."

"I understand."

"Did the mattresses come yet? Did you find all the bedding? Don't forget, box springs first, then the dust ruffle in between the mattress and box springs, then the vinyl cover, the comfort pad, then the sheets—"

"Don't worry. I'll get it right. Oh, the truck's here. Kingsley? Have fun today, but call me tonight. I miss you."

She lowered her voice to a breathy whisper that aroused him instantly. "Do you have any idea how I'm going to show you how much I love you?"

"Be explicit."

✂✄

Late afternoon sun splashed the Alderson's sunroom with rainbows as Jeannette Henning opened another photo album that she and Sarah had spread on the coffee table. "'What have you got in this suitcase, bricks?' That's what Bill said. Todd favors his father, don't you think?"

Sarah smiled at her new friend. "This time has been precious. Can't thank you enough for coming early. We could have been ogres, and you'd have been stuck here for days."

"Not a chance!" Jeannette opened the last album, her face clouding over. "Here's our little angel. Todd saved us from self-destructing after she died. I'd been afraid my pregnancy would embarrass adolescent kids, but they were thrilled. When she was born, they practically fought over her. I can still picture that boy making up stories and rocking her until she was so old her feet dragged on the floor."

She paused, taking a sip of iced tea. "We couldn't spoil her. She always wanted to be one of the grownups. That trip to Lake Erie was her first big-girl vacation without us. Her friend's family were expert sailors. A sudden squall, the boat capsized. They never found any of them." Jeannette struggled for composure. "I'm sorry. You'd think after all these years..."

"Believe me, I understand."

"It was Todd who envisioned our memorial project. Our township had committed land for a children's park, but had no money to build it." She leafed through the album to pictures of them with their friends and neighbors on tractors, hauling lumber and wielding paintbrushes. "He insisted we needed to do the labor ourselves, and he was right. We started to heal. When Todd hurts, he finds someone to help." Jeannette changed the subject abruptly.

"I blame myself for Maureen. Didn't think to warn Todd about women like her. We were clawing our way out of our grief when this pretty, bouncy creature swept into our lives. I remember how she made Grandpa laugh, pinching his cheek and teasing the guys. She sparkled. Looking back, even then I don't think Todd knew quite what to make of her. She was aggressive, catering, and fussing nonstop." She bowed her head, quietly adding, "We all promoted it. After all he had done, we just wanted him to be happy." She looked away for a moment.

"The wedding preparations were a blessed distraction. Her mother was nice, but that stepfather…" Jeannette batted at the memory with her hand. "I didn't let myself think *dysfunctional family*, but in retrospect, I'd need a new term."

Sarah nodded. "We mothers do blame ourselves, even for what's beyond our control."

"When do our children become our parents? Our daughter Linda knew long before Bill and I did. Todd and Maureen came home infrequently—demands of their work, or so he said—but within that first year I was shocked by the change in them. He was so distant, she, well, so mean. By the second year, he was coming alone. Then my Bill learned something that made him so furious he put his fist through the drywall. Some incident involving one of his friends and that girl."

"Speaking of mothers…" Sarah paused to retrieve a letter from the end table drawer. "This is for you. It's from Caroline Ward, Kingsley's mother-in-law. When the Wards heard of the engagement, they were happy for her, but said they would decline an invitation to come. That this was your day. Here. Oh, there's Kingsley. Excuse me?"

Jeannette scanned the note, then read it a second and third time of their blessing and highest regard for Todd and the hopes that they would meet. She rummaged for a tissue.

Kingsley sailed into the room, strewing shopping bags in her wake, then settled beside Todd's mother to give her a kiss. "List says I'm ready," she said, producing pages with columns of check marks. "Have my folks run you ragged?" She looked sheepishly over her shoulder at the mess that she'd made and got up to collect the debris. "Mom, may I borrow her for a few minutes?"

She turned her attention back to their guest. "I have something for you." Jeannette followed Kingsley up to her room.

"I wanted to give you something special to remember this week. Go ahead. Open this one first." She directed Jeannette to the wing-backed chair in a sunny corner. "I know you have plenty of family photos. I call this album 'A Day in Todd's Life,' although it couldn't possibly happen the same day."

Jeannette opened to the first picture. "That's him, cooking breakfast. You can make out the clock. Five-thirty a.m. Next is Marketing's desk shot, then he's off to a meeting. He was hurrying to his car, briefcase in hand at the exact moment I snapped him looking at his watch. The next two are in the bank's atrium. He's up at the second-floor rail holding forth with two colleagues, then down by the fountain with kids who were touring.

"Now he's conducting the Department Head meeting, then at lunch over Chinese with staff. In the hard-hat photo, he's touring a manufacturing plant—they sneaked me the photo—then there's Marketing's official photo with the Board of Directors. Dinner—he's the guest speaker at a community function, then back at his office where he's shed his coat. See the dark windows? Finally, back at his condo, having traded his contacts for glasses, papers strewn everywhere."

"What's he doing here?"

"Practicing a speech. He makes it look easy, but he rehearses, down to the gestures. Check the tall clock—one a.m. The rest of the photos are priceless—the shock on his face when he was presented as the bank's next president. A profile headshot of him in deep thought. The shareholder's meeting, delivering his speech, fielding a press question and laughing at somebody's joke. And finally, his new formal portrait."

"It's beautiful! Do you think I could order a big one?" Kingsley smiled and handed her a second package. "Is this what I think it is?" Kingsley nodded. "You are as dear as everyone says."

"The last one is Todd's humility shot."

"What's that all over him?"

"Motor oil. He insisted, 'I can too still change it.'"

Kingsley turned serious eyes to Jeannette. "My whole life I've been surrounded by family who love me. I know how little I have to do to show up his ex. I just want you to know that I love Todd and will cherish and take very good care of him. He is a prince. I'll thank God every day for the rest of my life that we found each other. Thank you for taking a chance on me. I'll be honored to be part of your family."

Their hug was interrupted by horns on the driveway below. "That could only be Randall Shannon," Jeannette said, rolling damp eyes.

"He can help with your overnight bags. We thought you'd enjoy having Todd to yourself at the hotel this evening. He'll bring you tomorrow at ten, then Mom and I will take you to lunch with my aunts while the men golf. We'll regroup for dinner at the club, then settle in early. The place will start jumping early on Saturday."

Randall bound upstairs. "Yo, Mom!" He swept Jeannette off her chair, squeezed her, then moved on to Kingsley. "Please tell me that gorgeous little blonde bundle of energy is Barrie. And I thought you'd have all the fun!" He offered both arms. "Ladies, let's see if the best man can fake being a gentleman."

Chapter 18

Moonlight bathed the Alderson's garden as Kingsley and Todd shared their last single moments. "Even in the dark I can smell the flowers and see their glow. Our day will be perfect," she murmured.

"*You're* perfect and precious. You've taught me the real meaning of intimacy and how good life can be." He smoothed her cheek with one fingertip and slipped a deep sigh through his smile.

"We'll be standing right on this spot…" she said.

"And after our vows, I'll kiss you like this." He passionately ran his hands down her ticklish spots.

She giggled, breaking away. "Do that and Randall will hoot something obscene."

They hugged, neither wishing to call it a day. Finally, he broke away. "I'll be here by nine. If I never show up, you'll know I've been hit by—um—abducted by aliens. No, wait. I'll just bring them along." She shivered. "Are you chilly?"

"Excited. Happy. This is really happening, isn't it?"

"It is." They kissed again. "I've never loved anyone as much as I love you."

ͻ҂ͻ

Saturday's sunrise illuminated daffodils, flowering crabapples, and azaleas that rose from the patio's freshly mulched gardens. Both mothers, hidden behind the sunroom's drawn sheers, drank coffee while watching the caterers transform the patio. Exquisite details seamed into place. After tying white padded cushions onto each chair, they placed them in curved rows facing the garden then disappeared into the kitchen to finish the nuptial buffet.

Sarah took Jeannette into the foyer to inspect the round antique table that was draped in vintage Battenberg lace. Their cake was trimmed with fresh roses. Jeannette beamed. "Even the cake is a garden." Glancing into the dining room, Sarah winced as a gloveless novice handled her grandmother's sterling, but she let it pass. The doorbell clamored and Henry, already dressed in his new navy suit, responded.

"Delivery for Kingsley Ward?" She swept barefoot downstairs, tying her robe, and stopped long enough to kiss her dad's cheek before taking the long silver box.

"It's from Todd." She untied the bow. "Yellow roses! He remembered that's my favorite. He has to be the sweetest man on the planet. I'll never be able to do enough for him."

"Dear—the time?"

Kingsley grinned at her mom and retreated. Alone in her room, she reread his card:

> *My dearest K*
> *A few more hours—*
> *Then forever—*
> *All my love,*
> *T*

She remembered her first wedding, inextricably tangled with finals and graduation. Her mother had gloried in meeting the challenges that threw Kingsley's ulcers into high gear.

Two cousins' dresses didn't fit; the club manager quit abruptly; the floral order got lost; and there were hurt feelings, although their culled guest list had exceeded 300.

After the extravagant rehearsal dinner dragged on until midnight, she had gulped Maalox and hardly slept.

Today seventy guests would share their sanctuary, enjoy gourmet nibbles, cake and champagne, then wander the gardens while they slipped away.

Kingsley laid her ecru Victorian lace dress on her coverlet and smiled. In her hair, she tucked one yellow rose and secured a sixpence into her left shoe for luck. She felt she'd already had hers and somebody else's.

Sarah knocked. "Look. Below in the yard." Standing in profile, Todd had arrived and was sharing a joke with the fathers, a new brown suit jacket draped over one arm, a dark brown silk tie perfectly knotted at the neck of his crisp ecru shirt.

Kingsley caught her breath and thrilled involuntarily.

"You'd better think about getting ready," Sarah urged, returning her hug, then fluffing Kingsley's hair from her earrings. "We begin in an hour." Sarah turned, her pale blue silk dress rustling.

"Mom?"

Sarah turned back.

"You're the best."

For the twentieth time, Kingsley checked her suitcase, her purse, and her carry-on luggage. Passport. Photo ID. A sundress, short-sleeved sweater and cork sandals she'd wear to the airport also lay on the bed. She retrieved her cosmetics bag from her suitcase and dropped it onto her vanity to redo her makeup after the ceremony. *Please God, don't let me bawl,* she prayed, then chided herself for being so frivolous. Eleven days at sea. She could only imagine.

At five minutes to ten, Henry knocked. "You look beautiful, honey. May I escort you downstairs? There's a man there who claims that he loves you. Let's not keep him waiting."

"Thanks for everything, Dad. Not just for today but for being there for me all my life. I love you." She picked up her flowers.

As they descended the long, curving staircase, Todd extended his hand to meet hers. "Good morning, Sunshine. Oh, you are gorgeous."

As they stepped from the sunroom, she froze momentarily, but when goldfinches broke into glorious song, Todd whispered, "Can they be trusted?" She laughed, and relaxing, returned the smiles of those she held dear, the joy of the morning soaking her being.

Her childhood priest beamed, his rich voice and message imparting the dignity and joy of the morning. To her: "Kingsley, will you have this man to be your husband..."

She smiled through damp eyes. "I will."

To that corresponding question, Todd's clear, unfaltering voice echoed through their green cathedral. "I will." He took her right hand in his. "I, Todd, take you, Kingsley, to be my wife..." She read the love in his eyes as she repeated her promise. She noticed he'd taken a deep breath and held it.

The priest continued, "Bless, O Lord, these rings..."

Todd placed hers on her finger. "Kingsley, I give you this ring. And with all that I am and all that I have, I honor you."

෧෩෪

Randall shot up Route 95.

"Hey, buddy. We don't have time for a ticket," Todd said.

"Let me worry about that. Kiss your bride or something."

"Got your passport, hon?" Todd asked.

"Right here, but—Todd! I left my cosmetics bag on my vanity."

"You don't need anything to make you pretty."

"But I need my pills."

"If we go back, we'll miss our flight *and* the ship. If there's something you need, the ship has a store."

"And a pharmacy?"

He nodded yes.

Randall squeezed into curbside check-in, hopped out

and flagged an attendant. "He says run for it. They've called your flight. They'll send out the bags."

The man at the gate who had been paging their names signaled the attendant, who took their boarding passes. "The beauty of flying with me," Todd explained as they sank into first class seats, "is that I don't fit anywhere else." He bent over and kissed her. "Finally. Alone."

"How did I ever talk you into marrying me in the first place?" she asked.

"You brought me a special book on old houses. And you signed my book K with no period, meaning no ending."

❧❧❧

"This time last week we were saying our vows," she reflected as they watched their tender ease from the ship. "Before we know it, a month, a year, a decade will fly by." She smiled up at her husband, tanned and relaxed. He put his arm around her waist and squeezed.

"Happy?" he asked.

She nodded, grinning. "We'll have many special times. And every May, after you dispatch the shareholders' meeting, let's get away."

The small boat chugged toward the uninhabited island's pristine inlets that promised excellent snorkeling.

Todd took the agenda out of his bag. "They'll ferry us back to their private island for a picnic, then we can swim, hike, or just lie on the beach. And there's something special to see."

"What?" She caught his impish smile.

"It's a secret, but I'll give you a hint. It's on your fantasy list."

"How did you know that I had one?"

"Gotcha. Now let me get your picture—"

"I'll do that for you," a fellow passenger volunteered. "If you stand by the rail, I can capture the island in the background." Haitians manning a small boat with patchwork sails broke from their fishing to wave. Absently, she rubbed Todd's arm, and he quickly responded by covering her hand with his.

"This is the best—being able to touch you in public," she said, rubbing the back of the hand that held hers.

"You're so affectionate. I love that. Men need it and just don't know how to ask for it. I noticed that about you early on—you reaching, then checking yourself. Now we don't have to." The enthusiastic chirping of their snorkeling instructor broke their reflection.

"Got the underwater camera?" he asked, and she rummaged in her bag to produce it.

"Now remember our deal. None of these surface at work."

"I'm not planning on sharing my wife with anyone."

After the picnic, they broke from their shipmates and followed the curve of iridescent sand that wound farther and farther from the sound of steel drums. "That barbecue! Didn't know I could eat that much. And the piña coladas! And just look at this island. The ocean. The beach. I could stay here forever," she said dreamily, taking his hand.

They walked thirty minutes, and, finally, she asked, "Where are we going?"

"Should be around the next bend." Shortly they stopped, having found a semicircular cutout, pure turquoise water, sparkling with sunlight that gently lapped on white sand. "Does this remind you of anything?"

She giggled. "It's what I described that night you brought the Chianti to my apartment to help heal my wounds. I was thinking of running away."

"I believe you said something about skinny dipping. We're all alone."

She scanned the shoreline skeptically. "There's got to be people."

"The only inhabitants are cruise line employees. They work and live on the opposite side of the island. And at the moment they're entertaining our fellow passengers. We *are* all alone. I asked."

"Just what did you say?"

"I told the social director the truth—that my bride wanted to swim au naturel."

"You didn't!"

"Well, no. I just asked where we could swim privately. Let her fill in the blanks. Her only reminder was that there was no lifeguard and that they couldn't be responsible for us. I assured her that I was a strong swimmer." He dropped their totes and arranged their towels close to the water. "The last tender doesn't leave for hours."

"You don't think I'll do it, do you?" she teased. He chuckled, shaking his head, then stretched out. "Pass me the sunscreen," she said as she slipped off her suit, then efficiently oiled herself while pretending to scan the vegetation nonchalantly. "Now look who's shy!" She waded into the water, the shallows taking their time to reach her knees and finally her hips. Turning, she called. "It's glorious! Come join me."

Shedding his suit, he followed her as she stroked out farther, teasingly keeping her distance. Testing, she eased to the depth to her shoulders, then paddled to where the color deepened. When she tried standing, she dropped off a ledge. Spluttering and laughing, she held up a hitchhiking thumb. He pulled her into his arms, and she locked her tightly onto his neck. "Does this fit your fantasy?" he teased.

"It's a start."

"Tell me."

"There's the part about you."

"Back then I was in it?"

"It was your fault. You wouldn't stay out of my dreams."

"And just what was I doing?"

She kissed him, working her way to his ear, nipped it while encircling his waist with her legs. "Can it be done in the water?" she breathed in his ear.

"Oh, Baby, come closer…"

∾∾∾

They lay face to face, sharing one towel, exhausted. Shadows lengthened, and even the birds eased their chatter. "Today's been fantastic," she whispered. "I wish we could freeze it."

"We have forever." He stroked her arm with one fingertip. "You're quite a woman." Reluctantly he pulled himself up on one elbow and, shading his eyes, studied the sun that had slipped perceptibly. "If we don't start back soon, we'll miss the last tender."

"Let's skip formal dinner," she said. "Just be private. Have room service or hit the buffet a lot later." They gathered their things, then hand-in-hand, walked very slowly without talking. She finally said, "I thought I had some idea, but this!"

⌘

She woke up abruptly. Looking through their balcony doors, realized the moon was too high. "How long did I sleep?" she asked in alarm.

Todd, feet propped on the bed, was already dressed in a silk camp shirt and shorts. He put down his paperback. "Wore you out, did I?" She dropped back on the bed. He came to her and kissed her lightly. "You can fantasize about me anytime."

"You must be starving."

"Rounded up snacks and a beer. If you're hungry, we can hit the buffet. It's very casual. Steel band. Dancing."

"I took a shower." She pulled the damp towel from under her hair and groaned. "That's the last thing I remember." He laughed again.

"You can go back to sleep if you want to."

She sat up, finger-combing her tousled curls. "No way. I can sleep for all eternity. Let's go find that band and celebrate. I don't want this day to ever end." She hopped out of bed and rummaged the closet for a sundress, chattering a nonstop review of their perfect day. Permissive eyes followed her details. She stopped. "What?"

"Loving you is the easiest thing I've ever done."

Chapter 19

Somewhere en route from their jobs and rental property to the old stone house, the working-world stress began fading along with the last days of May. As Kingsley and Todd threw open the doors and windows, woodland scents and nocturnal sounds replaced the hot, stagnant air. By flashlight, they ferried their tools and supplies into the cavernous space they'd call home.

Todd unlashed mattresses from the Explorer's roof rack, and together they muscled them through the back door. "Could we ever use those cabin boys now," he joked as they wrestled a pair of unwieldy box springs onto their future guest room's floor. "I'll unpack the Explorer if you make up the bed," he said and disappeared downstairs.

In sharp contrast to the overall disrepair, she smoothed a thousand-count contour bottom sheet onto the king-sized mattress. She stuffed the edge of its matching flat sheet between the mattress and the box springs and scrunched king-sized pillows against the back wall. Without electricity to power a fan, the coverlet was best left in its package. After she finished, she unpacked candles and globes and placed them on the deep windowsills.

Slowly Kingsley circled throughout the upstairs, then paused on the staircase. Moonlight splashed a silvery path through the foyer below, washing their future library to its left and living room to the right of the foyer. She inhaled the scent of the smoke-steeped old fireplaces, ancient wood, and plaster and digested the magic of first-time awareness compared to what she had only imagined. This was far better.

"I'll pick up the sander first thing in the morning," Todd called, dropping tool boxes in the hall. "I should be able to do the downstairs this weekend, then put on the finish by the middle of June. When the wiring is completed, we can move in some furniture—tarp it as necessary—while we paint. Weekend camping *will* get more civilized, I promise."

"The wiring's not done?"

"They'd hoped to fish-hook the new wires through, using the old wires as guides, but unfortunately, the old wires were junctured in sections. There's an alternative to poking holes in the horse-hair plaster and risking it cracking." He picked up a discarded piece of hollow metal tubing and beamed his flashlight down its back side.

"The electrician can run this *raceway* along the baseboard. The wires go inside it, then down a hole in the corner into the basement, where the wires are attached to the new breaker box. Once painted, the raceway looks like quarter-round molding. It'll hold lots of wires, and it's accessible. I told them to go for it wherever necessary."

"But they promised we'd have juice by tomorrow."

He shrugged helplessly. "Another small challenge—our reserve generator is still on back order."

She groaned.

"Hey, cold water will feel great if it's going to be 90 and you are so pretty in candlelight."

She faked a scowl. "Yeah, it'll hide my blue lips and goosebumps."

"Come here." He pretended to munch on her neck till she laughed. "That's my good sport." She wriggled away, still laughing and wiping her throat. She went to the kitchen to deal with enough food to suffice throughout Memorial Day weekend.

Todd stepped out front. Beyond the overgrown yard, the woods brooded darkly, and something wild uttered mournfully. He breathed slowly, weighing his options. Should he tell her about Miller's threat? Just how reliable was a jailhouse snitch anyway? He couldn't ignore it, even if Miller couldn't make bail.

Miller had an accomplice when he'd tried to kill her. And now it sounded as if he had another, whose escape plot had landed the accomplice in the morgue. Perhaps he had help in the prison itself. Todd decided to call the security company first thing tomorrow and brainstorm alternatives for safeguarding the property until they had sufficient power to boot up and operate the new high-tech system.

He unearthed his cell phone and found reception excellent, having spotted a tower near their exit. He thought of the wiring delay. They could have stayed at the rental until the security system was active, but no way in hell would he spoil her first weekend in their new home.

He gritted his teeth and renewed his vow. No one would ever, *ever* get at her again. He peered one last time into the darkness, memorizing its wild, normal sounds, and then went inside. He bolted the door and checked every window latch throughout the downstairs.

Satisfied, he put his agitation on hold. "Where are you hiding?" he called to his bride and followed the sound of her laughter.

⌘

"You look like an alien," Kingsley shouted over the sander and small rental generator he'd managed to snag at a rural hardware store. Protected in jeans, work boots, long-sleeved shirt, earplugs, and respirator with dual HEPA filters, he was attacking the library floor. "You're sure I can't help?" He waved her off while keeping both eyes on his monster.

Outside, the crystal air was void of humidity and smelled of fresh earth. Goldfinches and cardinals, robins and blue jays filled the air with joyous racket. Today she was free to plan her gardens and liberate what she hoped were old roses and perennials that had somehow survived many decades. Armed with stakes, string, shovels, and an edger, she tested the ground with a spading fork. In the center backyard, she quickly found the delineation where hard-pack clay ended and loam began, proof that yester-year's gardener had amended the native soil.

Kingsley uprooted waist-high grasses and weeds, exposing old treasures. Years of neglect had failed to strangle vintage roses. She pruned back the canes to emerging sprouts, imagining them in full bloom. She labored all morning, breaking to swap her jeans and work shirt for shorts and a halter and to gulp cold well water from the outdoor spigot.

"One floorboard can't be salvaged, but I know where to get vintage replacements from guys who repurpose materials from structures being torn down," Todd called. Heat, dust, and flies hadn't dampened his enthusiasm. He gulped the water she brought him. Returning to the garden, she marked new boundaries, then edged and spaded its meandering shape.

A fountain and pond, she thought, *and a birdbath, a butterfly bush, crepe myrtle, some step stones, and a sundial. And oodles of flowers that riot from March till November.*

At noon she assembled a picnic under the maples. Hot, sweaty and dusty, Todd came outside, stripped naked, and hosed himself off. Then, unscrewing the nozzle, he drank deeply, water coursing down muscles and tan. She watched him, intrigued—the consummate banker replaced by a sexy day laborer.

Returning to work, Kingsley searched the foundation for other lost treasures. On the west side, she found remnants of iris and daffodils, Shasta daisies and peonies, and even more roses. She edged six feet from the house, then painstakingly stripped sod and uprooted weeds. Lost in thought, she remembered Grammy's sprinkler and how the wet grass had squished under her bare feet. She hosed herself, loving its shocking contrast to the heat. All afternoon, spurred by results, she broke the hot work with trips to the spigot. She'd plant mums and bulbs in the fall. Some perennials this summer. By the time the sun began its retreat, she had completed her three-day goal.

Todd stripped at the spigot, hosing and soaping himself. She came up behind him and grabbed the soap, taking over. "Do I detect an invitation?" he asked.

"Later," she promised before retreating to brave a cold bath. Feeling human again, she inspected their future library where Todd had attacked the old pine floors. Haze hung throughout the lofty front rooms. In the kitchen, she opened the first cooler they'd wisely lined with dry ice. Rising vapor coated her face as she liberated chicken, pasta and potato salads, and mixed fruit. Adding rolls, she piled paper plates. She ferried their feast to the blanket, returning for drinks.

"Now that's a sight," Todd said, brushing damp curls from her ears. "You look as delicious as dinner." He gave her neck tiny licks. "Yep, tasty, all right."

"Did you see our gardens?"

"Certainly did. Did you see what you managed to duck? There was so little finish that this puppy chewed right through it. At this rate, I'll definitely finish this weekend. We've got to decide—unfinished wood, wax, or polyurethane?"

Ancient maples cast longer shadows across the backyard, a fresh breeze stirring the edges of evening. He took a deep breath. "Man, it was stifling in there! Bet it was ninety degrees. If I'd known you were so strong, I'd have traded you jobs. Hey! You're really burned. Doesn't it hurt?"

"It's prickly, that's all."

He put down his plate and looked closer. "Didn't you use sunscreen?"

"Before and after lunch."

"That's *it*? In this heat, you'd sweat it off in thirty minutes. Let me look at you." He squatted and lifted her sundress's strap away from her neck. "Wow." He touched her arm gently, which left white fingerprints. "Looks like you're wearing a scarlet sweater. I'll run to the drugstore for something. Why don't you soak in cool water? Take down the heat." He was gone before she could object.

Inside, she found a tall glass, filled it with ice, then carried white rum and a liter of tonic upstairs. With candles lit, she let the cool breeze soothe her wet, sunburned body.

A sip, then one more and another. She refilled the glass, then feeling no pain, let her mind drift.

By the time Todd returned she had poured a third glass. He watched from the doorway as she cupped gentle waves over her skin. Seeing him, she sat up, extending her hands, blue-white against red. "I got something that sprays," he said, staring at her. She rose from the water.

"I'll have to drip dry," she said, attempting to pat here and there, then letting the towel slip to the floor.

Attempting a joke to dismiss his arousal, he put out his palm. "I'll need a rain check." She kissed his palm then reached for the other. Without letting go, she backed him out of the bathroom and on down the hall. "I can't touch you. I'll hurt you."

"Not where it's white." Slowly she maneuvered him toward the mattress on the floor. When he tripped, she followed him down, kissing his forehead, his eyes, his lips, and throat, then worked her way downward. Directing his hands, she whispered "White—white."

Intensity mounting, she abandoned herself to his gathering momentum, slowing and picking it up, timing her rhythm to his ragged breathing. Then, as he started holding his breath, she let herself go for synchronized pleasure. Exhausted, she dropped on his chest.

"Phenomenal," she breathed, then flopped on her back and within minutes was gone. Awake in the night, he turned her gently and sprayed her again. Grinning, he wondered how she'd feel in the morning or if she would even remember, given how much she had drunk. She was full of surprises, this conservative lady who had learned quickly how to let go.

He remembered her saying that her first husband Andy, now dead for two years, needed to initiate. Once when she'd had a little too much wine, she had confided that sex was few and far in between. Had Andy found her that undesirable, as she had feared? Or was he a low-T kind of guy? Or was he that determined to father no kids? Damn, what a fool!

The next morning Todd looked up from his paper and coffee as she breezed into the kitchen, already dressed in casual silk and strappy sandals. "If I hurry, I can make eight o'clock church, then maybe we can find a cooked breakfast somewhere. I'm starving already, and you'll need sustenance to keep up with my pace."

"How's the sunburn?"

"Fading—doubt it will blister. You found good stuff, Doc."

"*You* are good stuff! Just how stiff were those drinks

anyway?" She glanced at the half-empty fifth on the counter and shrugged innocently.

"I was just minding my business, relaxing, when this gorgeous hunk of a man seduced me." She smiled smugly.

"Come here, you," he motioned her onto his lap. "Think you're pretty cute, don't you, having your way with me?" He kissed her again. "I love it when you initiate."

"You taught me." She snuggled into his shoulder then sat up abruptly. "Todd, we need to talk."

He looked up, surprised by the change in her voice.

"A detective called me about an incident at the prison."

"You know then? I didn't want to upset you. Thought we could put off talking about it, but, Kingsley, I do accept that you're not a child."

"Did you also get a second call about an informant?"

"A second call? When was that?"

"Yesterday. On my cell. Unless he called twice, you wouldn't have received the message as well. Seems the informant was killed."

Todd jerked. "What? When? How?"

"The detective said they'd found him dead in his cell. A stab wound of some kind. What a shame! Seems he was just a kid who was awaiting trial for a minor incident that would likely be reduced to time served. Trouble was the public defender's office was too overwhelmed to deal with it quickly. Just twenty-one. They'd have let him go in exchange for his information. But the wheels ground too slowly. The detective said he pushed to get him out, becoming friendly with prisoners who had information, because his widowed mother was ill."

He shook his head. "Well, that does it! My strategy is to have professionals dig deeper into Miller's history. Does he work alone or with others? Who are his known associates? What raps has he beaten? How best to protect you?"

"Okay."

"No argument?"

"No, that makes sense, but that's going to cost a fortune."

"Look at it as an investment. Now that it's settled, why don't I throw on some decent clothes and take you to church?"

"But you have issues with organized religion."

"If you can keep your faith after all you've been through, maybe I can find my way back."

Chapter 20

Kingsley dropped her briefcase in the rental house foyer, sank onto the couch, and dropped her head on the back cushion. Eyes closed, she pried off her shoes with opposite toes.

"Didn't hear you come in." Todd emerged from the kitchen, already in jeans and a tee, his sockless feet in docksiders. "You must be starving. It's after seven."

She shook her head without opening her eyes. "Sorry I'm late. Party at work. If you'll put the potatoes in at four hundred, then light the grill in twenty minutes. There's London broil marinating, bottom shelf of the fridge, and a cornbread casserole that just needs nuking. Salad, bottom shelf."

"And I thought cooking was hard." He left smiling and returned in a minute. "Potatoes are in. What kind of party?"

"Shower."

"Wedding?"

"Baby. Lori in Real Estate." A long pause followed without Kingsley moving.

"Was it nice?"

"They know it's a girl. Lots of pretty pink things. She's so excited. Husband came with their new minivan to help her pack up."

He sat down beside her and thought for a minute. "Honey, maybe sometime, not right this minute, but later, we should talk about adoption."

She slit open her eyes. "We *just* got married. It's all I can do to keep up with you."

"But the process—it could take years. I did a little research and learned it could take a decade."

She put up her hand, eyes closed again. "Right. Get in line, hope and pray for ten years only to have a sixteen-year-old birth mother change her mind. Reclaim our little girl from her second birthday party. No thanks. I will never, *ever* go there. Besides, we'll be fine, just the two of us. It's not like we didn't know that neither of us could have children." The room fell silent again. Finally, she rallied. "If you don't mind, I need a shower. Could you manage the kitchen? Yell if something's not clear, okay? I *promise* I'll be better company in about twenty gallons." She pried herself up from the couch and gave him a perfunctory hug, then trudged to the stairs.

"Sure." He watched her ascend then went to the kitchen where he pulled out the meat and lifted the plastic. One of his favorites. The vegetable was something entirely new, but the salad—another favorite.

He set them both on the counter then sat at the table to study the calendar. She'd circled June ninth, his birthday, in hearts. She'd planned something special, but wouldn't give hints. Thirty-seven. Another ten years and he would be closing on fifty. And if they didn't get on waiting lists soon—

If only he were younger, he wouldn't feel compelled to start pushing, yet she sounded emphatic.

He took a deep breath, massaging his temples. Finally, he realized he hadn't heard water. Maybe she'd fallen asleep—better check before lighting the grill. Barefoot, he slipped up the stairs, avoiding the creaks, but halfway up, stopped as he saw her. She'd shed her clothes down to her underwear and was dragging her robe by the collar. Even in profile, he could see she'd been crying. He waited, motionless, until she was past, then quietly retreated downstairs.

ფოჩ

"Of course you did the right thing to call," Sarah Alderson said to her daughter. "The reason you couldn't reach your gastroenterologist in Philadelphia was because he retired. Dr. Herman has your records. Isn't he the one—"

"He didn't believe that bacteria could cause ulcers. That's why I finally went elsewhere. I still think he didn't back down because Andy was rude after Dr. Zachen, the next guy I saw, proved he was wrong. Rude? Andy was furious. He had no patience with incompetent doctors who don't keep up to date."

"Our doctor says if you're throwing up blood, you should go straight to the emergency room."

"It's nothing like that, but I keep thinking of Grammy and about my being attacked last November. If it's the ulcer making a comeback, at least I know how to treat it. Who knows how long bacteria can lurk? And I'm run down from that virus."

"Honey, I know that you're scared, but you're a lot younger than Grammy was."

"Mom, did she have stomach cancer?"

"Well, yes, but that was so long ago, and she ignored symptoms entirely too long. There's no comparison between her health and yours. I promise. Um, dear? Your dad and I can't help wonder if you're experiencing post-traumatic stress. That horrible attack when you were nearly bludgeoned to death. The kidnapping. Now, don't be mad, but Todd told us about the threats. That's got to be taking a toll."

"I couldn't have anticipated that white-color crime like a loan scam could get me attacked and nearly killed."

"And then learning the truth about Andy's death—that a kind, gentle ophthalmologist was killed by a hired killer over a grant. That's enough to traumatize anyone."

"Maybe I should see a shrink."

"Honey, it can't hurt. Lots of people who aren't mental cases benefit from counseling."

"What would Grammy have said?"

"She'd say, 'It's like the buttons on your shirt. You own them. They're touching your skin. But somebody else can see them better.'"

"Thanks for the pep talk, Mom. I hate to see you so worried. As soon as I feel better, things will get back to normal. The guys who specialize in removing lead-based paint have finished the wood trim. I can start painting the windowsills. There are twenty-six altogether, and if I paint four per evening and more on the weekends, I'll finish by the Fourth."

"Listen to yourself!"

"It's great therapy, Mom. I'm never happier than when we're out in the country. Already it feels like home."

"I'd love to come help you paint if Todd's tied up at his conference over the weekend. We could talk about stenciling a border in the kitchen—that is, if you'd like the idea and Todd doesn't object."

Kingsley laughed. "He'll leave the decorative touches to us. And yes, I'd love you to design something for us. He hopes to be home late tonight."

"Sorry, Henry," Sarah called to her husband. "Todd will be home, so you're stuck taking me to the opera."

Hearing her father's pretend agony, Kingsley grinned.

৩৩৩

The engines roared, projecting Randall's Gulf Steam away from Chicago. "That's gotta be better than sex," he rejoiced then, catching Todd's look, qualified. "Maybe as good as. Speaking of which, I'll have you home to your bride before ten."

"I should have left early this morning. The wrap-up was redundant. Thanks for waiting. With my flight canceled it could have been Sunday before I got home."

"Purely selfish, my man. I needed the keys to your rental, and I have high hopes for an excellent weekend with Kingsley's pal, Barrie. How was the conference?"

"Great presentations, but the timing was terrible." Todd studied the darkening sky and fell silent.

"She okay?"

"She sounded infinitely better by Thursday. Had blood drawn on Tuesday. The new doctor faxed her a diet to follow. No caffeine, alcohol, chocolate, spices, dairy, raw stuff, and so on. There's some awful test that involves snaking a tube to the stomach, but she won't have to take it, whether it's ulcers or not. The specialist says that antibiotics are the first course of action regardless. She's very relieved."

"And her appointment today?"

"I should have been there. I'm not convinced it's a bacterial infection. For someone so tolerant of other people, she's entirely too hard on herself. She'd have thrown off that virus a whole lot sooner if she'd only stayed home. The bank would have survived. And Miller's upcoming trial has maxed her stress level."

"No plea was worked out?"

"Surprised the hell out of me." Todd stared at the darkness. "I've never seen anyone as sick as she's been, and she would not let me help her."

"Maybe when she's down, defeated, ill, scared, wounded, she needs to hide that from you. Look, Todd, talk to her. Haul out those feelings we hate to admit. I didn't do that with Janie and look where it got me. I should have insisted."

"Could she have convinced you to stop flying? Or could you have overridden her paranoia for your safety?"

"Had we communicated, Janie and I would have ended it sooner. An eight-year engagement—where was my mind?"

"Stay as long as you want at the rental," Todd said. "You're seeing Barrie?"

"Seems she learned to fly as a teen. Washed planes in exchange for lessons. What an opening! I'm taking her up tomorrow."

"Randall, a word of advice. Move too fast and she'll hand you your head. Kingsley says she belted the last guy who got out of line. Imagine that little scrap decking a six-footer and breaking his jaw."

Randall laughed. "Understood, but who knows? If you could get lucky, there's hope for me too." The men exchanged looks that encompassed decades of friendship.

✡✡

Kingsley awoke to broad daylight and peered at the clock. Nine-thirty. He was still peacefully sleeping. She watched him until he finally stirred, as if feeling her gaze.

"Good morning, Sunshine." He drew her in closely and kissed the top of her head. "You wore me out last night. Oh, it's so good to be home."

"With the fourth on a Wednesday, we have five days to do whatever we want."

"Just tell me you feel as good as you look."

"I'm so very much better. And I have lots to tell you."

He drew himself up on one elbow. "I see they finished tiling the bathroom."

"Then you also saw there's no sink. I suppose we'd better go shopping." She flopped onto her stomach and closed her eyes. "On second thought, wake me up when you get back." He slapped her rear playfully through the rumpled sheets, then crawled over to kiss the back of her neck.

"Someone dropped a greenhouse in the front hall."

"Perennials for the new shade garden out front and annuals for the western foundation. I'm going to plant them today."

"If we ever get up."

"Or we could stay…"

"Kingsley, if we really want to be in by September, we'd better hop to it."

A hot breeze wafting through screens brought the essence of advancing summer. From the front porch, Kingsley identified the scent of clover and honeysuckle. She breathed deeply, feeling at one with the ages and grateful to be a trustee of this precious spot.

First the chores on her list, a rewarding soak, then a picnic out back, after which they would lie in the hammock and swap tales of their week. The Monet swing from Tidewater Workshop had arrived in time for his birthday. They'd hang it between the two giant oak trees near the shade garden she had staked out. She studied the spot beyond the front door. Impatiens in the front, hostas and ferns interspersed among dwarf azaleas in the middle. Rhododendrons in the back.

Todd called from the foyer. "Come see what I brought you." Freeing a carton from its metal bands, he eased out a vessel, watching her face.

"The tulips! Who told you? Oh, it's just gorgeous." She ran her fingers around the hand-painted vessel that bloomed with vibrant red tulips. "But it cost the earth! Imagine spending that much for a washbowl. You spoil me rotten. How can I ever thank you enough? You are so thoughtful."

"I'll think of something." He collected a kiss, then mounted the stairs, whistling. "Now let's see what kind of a plumber I am. All I have to do is set it over the hole in the cabinet and hook up the hardware."

Kingsley lugged cardboard flats of perennials from the foyer to the western foundation: asters, her birth flower, and roses for Todd, including a Peace and a Pristine. As a comic reminder, three dozen tall snapdragons. Out front by the oaks she set flats of shade lovers—astilbes and foxgloves and mixed-color impatiens would produce a riot of color in front of the perennials. She dragged gallon pots of Gerard Fuchsia and Delaware Valley White azaleas and set them in lazy curves behind the annuals' spots. The Cunningham white rhododendrons from Barrie and Margaret she set at the edge of the woods. Bulbs—they had to wait until fall.

After setting each pot where she thought it should go, she returned to the living room to admire another project that screamed for attention. New shutters, stacked with existing ones, awaited primer and paint. An Amish craftsman had perfectly replicated the original ones that couldn't be salvaged. She made a note that she'd need to jury-rig several more sawhorses. Monday she'd paint.

With the house emerging, the move within reach and everything she wanted under that roof, she dreamed of the years, like ongoing circles, full of fun and discovery. Life breathed in that once empty house. She'd miss it— their first golden summer, its adventure and challenges, but somehow every step forward brought something better. That they had known each other only ten months was inconceivable.

Her musings were interrupted by an approaching roar and rising dust cloud that mushroomed over their lane. From the front door, Kingsley identified a stranger's Mustang convertible. How odd. Family and friends always circled around back, but this car stopped by the path that connected their lane to the front door.

Instinctively, Kingsley stepped back inside, though she couldn't pinpoint what had alarmed her. A petite woman with long, dark hair and a dour expression erupted from the car, slamming the door. She yanked off Jackie-O sunglasses and jammed them on top of her head. Dressed in skinny white jeans, a bare-midriff floral-print top, and stiletto sandals, she picked her way through the mowed weeds as if avoiding meadow muffins. Stepping onto the porch, she headed through the open front door without pausing to knock.

"Todd!" Angry. Demanding. Her eyes swept the interior, dismissing Kingsley as if she were invisible.

"He's upstairs. Can I help you?" The woman ignored her, eyeing the staircase, and began moving toward it. Kingsley maneuvered to block her path. She didn't want to be rude, but the woman's attitude made Kingsley bristle.

"He's busy right now. Can I tell him who's here?"

The woman dismissed Kingsley with an icy stare. Her tanning-bed skin appeared greenish-brown. She looked thirty-five, maybe forty, although her sun-damaged skin made her look older. Pale blue eyes were hardened with black liner, her lipstick too blue for her golden skin tones.

There was something exaggerated, defiant about her, but she had been, could still be, very pretty.

As Todd's whistling floated downstairs, the woman began to brush past her. "Excuse me?" Kingsley reached for the woman's arm, but she yanked it away. "You can't just barge in here. Who are you and what do you want?"

The woman cut her with frigid eyes. "I don't have to explain myself to Todd's bimbos."

Kingsley heard footsteps approaching the stairs. "Hey, hon, do we have any…" He halted on the landing, freezing the motion of toweling his hands.

The woman flashed a deprecating scowl. "Get down here! Now!"

Anger flashed on Todd's face. "Maureen—what the hell."

Kingsley jolted. *My god. It's her! What's she doing here? What should I do?* Stepping into her line of vision, she spoke to the intruder.

"I'm *not* his bimbo. I am his wife. And this is our home. Please leave. Now!" A statement, not a suggestion.

The woman ignored her and started to walk around her, but Todd, who had recovered, descended the stairs and stopped beside Kingsley.

"What do you want?"

Angrily she thrust a photograph at Todd, which he trapped against his stomach. He righted it for a look. He eyebrow-shrugged his recognition then shoved it back at her. "I've seen it. Your adulterous porn collection never interested me."

She thrust a second eight-by-ten glossy at him. "Try this."

"So—someone captured your orgy. What do you want me to do with it? File it with the rest of the divorce proceedings? The scene was bad enough in person when I caught you and your friends *in the flesh*."

"And this?"

Todd jolted. "What the hell? That's photo-shopped, and badly at that." He glared at the transformation, his image super-imposed into the grotesque scene. "Explain!"

"Call off your buddy, Randall Shannon. Tell him that unless he stops showing the photos his PI sneaked on your behalf, I'll post this one of you on the Internet. How fast do you think they'll fire your sorry ass? I mean a bank president is supposed to be beyond reproach, am I right?"

Todd stared at her in disbelief. "I don't get it."

"That asshole buddy of yours may not give a shit about himself, but you're his weak spot. Tell him to stop 'warning' his friends about me. Or I'll ruin you."

"Maureen—it's been eight years. Why now? What the hell—"

"That sleazy PI, who Randall hired for your divorce attorney, archived the photos. Now he's supplying them to other clients who want background checks. And guess who's spearheading that little enterprise to ruin my life? Randall! Seems my ex-boyfriend, emphasis on ex, is being considered for a federal judgeship. Your buddy decided to do him a favor. Supplied him with information that could ruin his chances. My lover was sooooo sorry, but he can't be tainted by negative publicity."

"Maureen—as fast and loose as you were, there's got

to be hundreds of pictures floating around. You want someone to blame? Look in the mirror."

She smirked, hand on one skinny hip, throwing out her augmented chest. "But, as you said yourself, that was years ago. Nobody remembers—unless dear Randall stirs the pot. Call him and his sleazy PI off my case. Or else this lovely picture of you goes viral."

Dead silence hung in the air. Finally, Kingsley spoke up. "Get out of our home. And don't bother my family again."

"Your home! He hooked you on *this*? That's so ridiculous. Probably fall down around your ears. And family?" She turned on him. "Better tell sweetie here about your little problem before she starts knitting booties."

Kingsley stepped into her personal space and Maureen backed up a little. "We don't have a problem."

"Oh, really," Maureen drawled, eyes hard and hateful, mouth snaking vengeance. "He didn't tell you he only shoots blanks? Or was he going to ask good ol' Randall to do it for him? A sleaze like Randall would know where to get some Rohypnol. Maybe you'd never know." She grinned triumphantly. "Until the little, redheaded bastard arrives."

"Maureen, she knows. Always did. Now get out. Leave us alone," Todd responded, his voice low and measured, eyes steely and frigid.

Maureen shot Kingsley a look that said she hadn't anticipated that.

Breaking eye contact and darting black looks, Maureen turned and flounced out the door. She halted halfway down the path, stabbing the air with a blue-lacquered nail. "Call him off! Or read all about your demise on the Internet."

She flung herself into the Mustang, slamming the door, and floored the convertible up the lane. An orange cloud of dust drifted toward the house, settling on the front yard.

Todd stood transfixed, leaving Kingsley to grapple with what she could possibly say. He looked, unseeing, into the yard. That magnificent man, whom she'd seen hold captive a room of five hundred. Undone by a hundred-pound witch.

Chapter 21

Todd, I am so sorry. I handled that badly. I shouldn't have let her in. Should have kept quiet. Slipped out. Let you deal. She made me furious."

Motionless, he focused on the settling dust. "Sorry you saw it. Guess you can't help wondering how I got mixed up with someone like that."

She rubbed his crossed forearms. "I suppose she wasn't always like that. If I'd lost you and knew you were out there, having a life that didn't include me, I might behave badly." She pried his clenched arms apart enough to reach around his waist and hug him until he relaxed. "Now, how about installing my tulips? I've never slept with a plumber before."

"I—need to make a few calls. Be by myself. If you don't mind."

"No, sure. That's okay. I'll go plant those perennials before they start wilting."

He nodded then turned and walked back toward the stairs.

She called after him. "I'll set out sandwiches for

lunch. Just help yourself whenever you're ready."

He waved acknowledgment without turning then disappeared. His footfalls traversed the upper hall above where she stood, methodical and deliberate. She heard something pounding, but it wasn't a hammer.

Clutching her trowel like a weapon, Kingsley strode outside, attacking the rich soil and planting perennials quickly as if to outrace her anger. Their beautiful weekend. Theirs! What had that woman hoped to accomplish? Did she only want what she couldn't have? If Kingsley had harbored one tiny doubt about Todd's having leftover feelings for her, that was gone.

As twilight settled, Kingsley busied herself, sectioning grapefruit for breakfast at the old draining board.

"Kingsley?" Todd approached her so quietly that she jumped, dropping the serrated knife into the sink. Fresh from a bath, his deepening tan made his white tee shirt appear to glow. "I spoke with Randall. Seems that judge-elect did his own background checks. Randall had nothing to do with it."

"But—can't she still—"

Todd drew his iPhone from his pocket, keyed several screens, and then scrolled. Hit play. "As soon as she started, I hit record. Since it was in my pocket, the sound's a bit muffled, but her blackmail attempt was recorded. That I forwarded to Randall. He says graphic threats can lead to criminal charges. That she won't want to go there."

"Then it's over?"

"That part." His eyes looked pale gray and unusually solemn, his voice deep and serious. She dreaded whatever came next. He took a deep breath and expelled it slowly. "We need to talk."

"Why don't we try out the swing?" She attempted normalcy and nonchalance that she didn't feel. "The evening's quite lovely."

She slipped on her flip-flops and led him outside. The air was velvety, the first stars of evening brilliant in a sky that swept from navy to black.

They positioned themselves, side by side, on the new swing. She scooted back while he walked the swing backward. Gliding forward, like little kids on the playground who pretended they were flying, they arched skyward.

As the swing passed through pockets of changing air temperature and began to slow, he finally spoke. "The opposite of love isn't hate. It's indifference. And that's how I feel about her. I'm beyond being hurt by whatever she says. I'm just sorry if she spoiled your weekend." He turned to face her. In spite of his calm, she thought he looked broken. "Honey, Maureen's untimely appearance underscored something we need to talk about. I assumed at some point we'd make some decisions. At first, I thought it was my imagination, but it became more and more obvious that you've finally faced a painful reality. I did a very selfish thing marrying you."

"You're not saying you're sorry!"

"Good heavens, no. If there are two things I'm sure of, it's that we belong together and there's nothing that I wouldn't do for you."

"Todd, you don't have to go there."

"Please. Just let me finish." He paused, looked away,

then back at her, holding her hand, absently twisting her ring. "I want you to think about something very seriously. Just because I can't father children doesn't mean you can't have one. When you think the time's right, we could consult with a fertility specialist about using a donor. I love kids and would quickly forget our baby's origin, just as adoptive parents do. But no one could show up to reclaim our child. We'd have to decide what to tell our families, but I'll do whatever you want. You don't have to say anything now. Just think about it, okay?"

"You'd really do that for me?"

"Nobody has ever loved me the way that you do. You've gladly put me ahead of everything else."

"Todd, I—"

"She—Maureen—knows all too well how to push my buttons. My divorce had just been finalized when my family had a reunion. My mother bragged to everyone about my accomplishments, she was that proud. My great Aunt Pauline blindsided me in front of everyone. 'I don't understand you young people today. No interest in family or children or commitment. Why is money and work more important? In my day, family came first.'

"What could I say? I loved and respected her. I escaped and went home, had a few drinks and finally called Randall. He bet me that before I turned forty, I'd find the right woman and I'd have a family. I told him it was too late. That I was too damaged. The women too scary, too needy, too opportunistic. Too like Maureen. That my aunt hadn't said it in so many words, but I knew what she meant. When it came to what mattered, I was a failure.

"And then you came along, and my whole life

changed. The right woman. There isn't anything I wouldn't do for you or give you if I could. So, give it some thought—for both of us." He paused, the only sound being the swoosh of the swing as he nudged it into motion again.

She studied his face. "Do you trust me? I mean *really* trust me?"

"You know that I do."

"Do you think I could ever cheat on you?"

"Absolutely not."

"There's something I'd like to know about that test with the zeroes. Did you open the envelope the report came in, or was it already open? Try to remember."

"I'll never forget that ugly scene. Remember, she was suing me for fraud since she couldn't tap into my trust fund. I was so angry that I told the lab not to call me. Just mail me something I could use in court. She still had a key. I came in and there she was, waving the report, yelling victoriously. I scanned it quickly and saw the results. She snatched it back, balled it up, and threw it at the fireplace. I stormed out, and when I returned, she was gone, and the fire was out."

"You know I had a dreadful miscarriage around the time Andy was killed," Kingsley said. "Multiple specialists I consulted about ongoing problems deemed it unlikely that I could ever conceive again. Something about scar tissue which, if removed surgically, would render me sterile. I told you about it when I barely knew you so that you could look elsewhere if you wanted children. I want you to check on those zeroes for your own peace of mind." The swing glided back and forth for several more swipes, the only sound being crickets and peepers.

Suddenly Todd put his foot down, stopping the swing so quickly they almost fell off. "What *are* we talking about?"

She turned his face gently. "Your bet with Randall. I hope it wasn't for a bundle because you're going to lose. I'm pregnant."

Kingsley would always remember Todd's speechless moment. His eyes sweeping over her, then quickly returning to her face, overcome with emotion. "Are you sure?" She nodded yes. "How long have you known?"

"Since yesterday. I was torn between saying 'Honey, guess what' and waiting until I was sure I wouldn't miscarry. This morning I almost blurted it out, but that wouldn't have been right. It was none of Maureen's business."

He wrapped her up in a hug that lifted her off the swing, making a complete circle before setting her down. "Are you all right? Do you feel okay?" She nodded yes. "You tried to tell me, and I just kept talking."

"I'm overwhelmed by the lengths you'd have gone to for me. What you said meant so much. You know something else? You're going to have to rethink your self-image. Let's see—the man who just needs to take off his swimsuit."

"Seriously?"

"Had to be. I felt the twinge that very morning, meaning prime time. If I'd only known why I've been feeling so lousy, I might have enjoyed it."

"Only you would say something like that. Promise me something."

"Anything."

"That we'll talk, no matter what's wrong or how serious. Whatever it is, we can handle it. You don't have to protect me." He paused. "Are you *really* sure?"

She laughed. "Oh, definitely. February. A Valentine present."

"We should celebrate."

"Let's go in the house and turn on some music. I want to dance."

☙☙

"Doctor, Kingsley Henning is calling from work. She's very upset. She says that she's bleeding."

"Put her through."

"Kingsley, what seems to be the problem?"

"I went to the ladies' room," she sobbed, "and I think I'm miscarrying. This just *can't* be happening again. What should I do?"

"Are you in pain? Having contractions or cramps?"

"Well, yes and no."

"Tell me about the bleeding. Are you soaking pads?"

"It's more like serious spotting."

"First, I want you to calm down. It doesn't sound serious, but we're taking no chances. Is there a couch in your lounge? And is anyone with you?"

"Yes. My friend Barrie is with me."

"Good. Lie down. Is Todd at the bank?"

"Someone's getting him out of a meeting."

"I'm at the hospital. Have him bring you directly, and someone will meet you at the ER entrance with a wheelchair. Now Kingsley, don't worry. There's any number of reasonable explanations that don't necessarily spell trouble. Think calming thoughts, and I'll see you shortly."

For once Kingsley couldn't focus on what others were thinking as the EMT's gurney rolled her to a waiting ambulance. By the time the triage nurse took down the details, she was beginning to feel foolish. Once in a bay, however, the nurse taking her blood pressure was scowling and saying something about two-hundred-something over—what? She felt her heart thud, a flush of panic heating her face. *Not again. Oh, dear God, no. Not again.* She began making rash promises, bargaining, begging, while willing herself to calm down.

"Let's get that again," a second hovering nurse was saying, utterly calm. She smiled at Kingsley. "Get white-coat hypertension much?"

Now Kingsley felt foolish.

"Try to relax. The doctor will be in shortly. In the meantime, we'll keep hubby busy with forms."

Relax. Right. When their dream could be wiped out. No! That was not going to happen. She willed the voices screaming in her head to shut up. White noise enveloped her in its monotony as she concentrated on pleasant thoughts. When was the last time she'd let herself stretch out and just chill?

She thought of the beautiful gardens, the roses blooming in her imagination. She wandered through the shade garden where hostas were blooming. She imagined the scents, the sounds, and the soft breeze on her face. Burying her face in the soft pillow, she fell asleep.

⌀⌀

"It's superficial," her doctor reassured Todd. "And it's nothing you did. Both she and the baby are fine. However, I am concerned about her blood pressure."

"She's always joked about how low it is."

Frowning, the doctor riffled through her medical records. "You're right—ninety over sixty, one-hundred over seventy-four, eighty over forty-eight. The latter is how low it was on her first visit to my office. I remember she'd had a virus. Today it's quite high. Is there anything going on in her life that I should know about?"

"She's excited about the baby and following your instructions religiously. She's letting me do things for a change. But the trial and the threats. The nightmares she once had as a child and again after her first husband died. They're recurring. She cries in her sleep or wakes up in a panic."

The doctor straightened in his chair and leaned closer. "What threats?"

Todd pushed out of his visitor's chair and slowly paced between it and the bookshelf. "The beast who attacked her threatened to kill her if she testifies against him. We're afraid that he might have people on the outside. There have been hang-up calls."

"I could write a letter explaining that the trauma of testifying will endanger both her and her baby."

Todd shook his head. "She's convinced that her only safety is having him behind bars." He continued to pace. "Our security company is on alert in case he escapes or is being transported, but look what he's done without leaving prison. I can't protect her from that. Do you have any idea how that makes me feel? If I could just get my hands on that bastard, I'd settle it once and for all."

The doctor buzzed for the nurse. "If Kingsley's dressed, send her back, please."

Kingsley slipped in and, sitting beside Todd, took his hand. "Did I overreact?"

"Not at all. If there's a challenge, we want to intervene immediately," her doctor said.

"I told him about the nightmares," Todd admitted.

"Why is it so important that you testify?" the doctor asked.

"There's no doubt in my mind that he'll want revenge, and if I don't testify, he might get off. What happens to my baby when he's released? Will he be safe in our home? Or anywhere else? We can't take that risk."

"If you change your mind about my writing the DA on your behalf, just say the word. In the meantime, let's take each day as it comes."

"Can I go back to work?"

"I want you off your feet for a week. Walk a bit for your circulation, eat healthy food, and take your prenatal vitamins. Call me if you have any pain or if the bleeding resumes. Also, I want your blood pressure watched."

"I'm supposed to attend a banquet with Todd on Thursday evening. Can I?"

"Let's play it safe. Stay home and rest. There will be years to attend those rubber-chicken dinners."

Chapter 22

The assistant knocked and entered the warden's office apologetically. "I'm sorry, but this cannot wait. Leon Paschal's attorney called and said Paschal is livid. That you've been holding his son Dillon incognito for over a month."

The warden jerked to attention. "That's crazy! I'd know if we had that mobster's kid in our custody." He flipped through screens to the list of current inmates. "Nope. No Dillon Paschal. He's wrong."

"Sir, I took the liberty of checking with the police. There's no outstanding warrant for Dillon, but they do have a missing person's report dated last month. We have a young John Miller who landed here about the same time who fits the description. The attorney's faxing Dillon's photo."

"The same John Miller who's being held for murder?"

"No, this one's just a kid. What shall I tell the attorney?"

"Stall. No, tell him I'm out until three. That should give us time to investigate."

A secretary rapped on the door with the fax and then left. The two studied the grainy printout of a young man's slender face with a five o'clock shadow, a near-shaven head and low, dark brows.

"Check our mug shots," the warden told the assistant.

"Be right back, sir."

Within twenty minutes, he returned. The warden could tell the depth of the shit by the look on his face.

"Call down. Have this young man who calls himself John Miller brought to me at once, but don't tell anyone why."

Thirty minutes later the kid was led into the warden's office and put in a chair. "Son, there seems to be some confusion about your identity." The young man stared at the floor. "Are you Dillon Paschal? And if so, what are you doing here? Your father and some very important people are quite upset. According to our computer, you aren't here."

"You didn't tell them you found me, did you?" the boy cried in alarm. "They'll kill me."

"Son, whatever you did, I'm sure they'll forgive you. They must be terribly worried. Besides, that's just a figure of speech." The warden eyed the young man whose agitation was mounting. "Why don't you start at the beginning? How did you get here in the first place? And why? People don't just break into prison."

"Please, just don't call them. You've got to promise."

"Talk to me, son."

The kid dropped his head and began. "I was doing badly in school. I'm just not that bright. Father wanted me to become a lawyer and hounded me about grades.

Finally, he put me in a prestigious prep school. Paid them a ton of money to take me and tutor me." The boy dropped his voice to a whisper. "I thought that kid was my friend—was, you know, like me. He wasn't. He told his father, who called the headmaster, who called my father. Headmaster told my father they'd forget the whole incident if he'd quietly withdraw me."

"What did you do?"

"It's not what I did. It's what I am. I'm gay."

"Did your father know that?" The boy shook his head. "What about your mother?"

"He threw her out when I was little. I have no idea where she is."

"So what happened next?"

"Father was livid. Way beyond reason. Said I was worthless to him as a son. That if he couldn't talk some sense into me, he'd beat it in."

"And?"

The boy hesitated and, with a little prodding, stood up, turned, and shrugged his jumpsuit off his shoulders. Healed scars crosshatched his back. "He did that to you?"

"He's got these goons. One day, about a year ago, I overheard them talking about where some body was buried. The kidnapping was in all the papers. I didn't let on that I knew until I was desperate. I told my father if they ever touched me again, I'd tell the cops. Huge mistake. He came after me, but he was too slow. I got away."

"Why didn't you go to the police?"

"They'd never have believed me. I'd run away too many times, but he always found me. Besides, Father has important friends in high places. I have this buddy who put me in touch with some dude who makes fake IDs. I met him in a bar, and we were just completing our transaction when some guy pulls a gun on the bartender. There's a big scuffle, shots fired, and we all ran outside, right into the cops. I was arrested."

"Did you get an attorney?"

He shook his head. "I refused to give them my real name. So they called me John Doe. They put me in a holding cell with a bunch of other guys who told me the cops would run my picture in the paper or on TV if I didn't give them a name. When I was interrogated, I was so nervous, I went blank. But they had my fake ID among my personal effects. The name was John Miller. Plain and simple. So I confirmed it. And they believed me. I ended up here."

"Were you ever arraigned? Did you see an attorney?"

"I thought I'd be discovered any minute, but several days passed. Then I was put in with these really mean dudes. One of them wanted me to be his girlfriend, so I told him I had AIDS so he'd leave me alone. That backfired. Now they want to kill me. I've got to get out of here."

"Are you infected?"

"No. I just thought if I said—"

The warden dragged his attention away from the boy's face and scrolled his PC for John Miller.

"You're in here, all right, but it says you're 42. Must be a typo." The warden switched to other screens and compared information. "Wait. I see the problem. The two of you got merged into one file. How old are you really?"

"Just turned eighteen. I thought if I hid until my birthday, they couldn't call Father without my permission. I just don't know how to get out."

"Dillon…"

"John. It's John Miller now."

"Okay, John. Here's how I see it. A first-year public defender can resolve this in minutes."

The boy jumped to his feet. "Please, sir, if you have any compassion, you'll just let me out of here. I'm dead if you don't."

The warden went to him and, taking him by his bony shoulders, settled him gently back in his chair. "Where would you go?"

"Far away. Just give me my clothes and some bus fare. Drop me at the station. I have friends out of town who can help me. Just don't make me say where I'm going."

"If you tell the police what you know about the body, I'm sure they'll protect you. Get you into the witness protection program."

The boy shook his head violently. "I wouldn't live to testify! And if you quote me to anyone, I'll deny it. Please, can't you understand? I must disappear."

"This is unprecedented."

"I *promise* you'll never hear from me again!" Miller paused, then looked through tears at the warden, who was shaking his head *no*. "Sir, you know the case they're comparing to Jimmy Hoffa?" The warden's head jerked to attention. "If you'll let me go, I'll tell you where the body is buried. And after I'm safe, I promise I'll call and tell you who I heard did it. You could help the police by working backward for evidence once you know where to look."

The warden's mind whirled, political opportunities blooming like fireworks. His cooperation in thwarting Charlotte Unger's coerced crime to help free a murderer had added big points to his personnel record. But solving the crime of the decade? "Wait here," he addressed the frazzled young man. "If you tell no one else, I think I can help you."

He approached his assistant's desk and spoke quietly to him. "I'm sending young John Miller back to detention, but cut the order for the segregated area for his protection. Just until I plan how to deal with his family." He snapped a glance at his watch, darted into his office, and shut the door.

❦

The police caravan converged on the neighborhood of rundown row houses that undulated for blocks in the working class part of the city. Detectives in a Crown Vic, uniformed officers in squad cars, and workers in coveralls and steel-toed construction boots disgorged from a police utility van. They approached the house with the number provided by the warden from a confidential informant. The detectives approached two young men who were enjoying a beer after a long working day, their feet propped on the porch's concrete half wall. Reacting to the invasion, the pair jumped to their feet.

"Whoa, dudes," one of them shouted as they descended the front steps two at a time. "What the hell?"

The detective in charge approached the men cautiously although neither appeared to have weapons. Slight and skinny but well muscled and tanned, neither topped five-foot-five. From the looks of their clean tees, jeans, and wet hair, they must have just showered and changed from their jobs.

Both stood on the sidewalk, arms crossed over puffed chests, piercing the cops with identical black eyes and don't-mess-with-me attitudes. Looks that said cops are not welcome. "What do you want?" the older one demanded. He appeared to be in his mid-twenties and spoke in accented English.

"We have a warrant to search for evidence of a crime on this property. Is either of you the owner?"

"We rent."

"Do you know where we can find the owner?"

The spokesman shrugged. "We mail the checks to some company in Baltimore. Property Management something-or-other."

"Who's your contact if something goes wrong? Like a water pipe bursts or the head stops up?"

They laughed, quite amused at the cop's stupidity. "Lowe's knows. They got the duct tape. We get electric, water—anything else is on us."

"How long have you lived here?"

The two exchanged glances. "Six, eight months?"

"Where are you from?"

"New York. We found work in the mushroom houses. They let us work double shifts, six days a week. Sundays, we go to church."

"Anyone else living here? Family?"

"Soon," the younger one said. "When we got here, we stayed at the shelter. Walked ten miles each way for two weeks. Then we found jobs at the mushroom houses. They gave us a trailer to stay in. When we got enough money, we came here. We got savings accounts, bus passes, a church, and friends. Family joins us. Very soon." Pride in their piece of the American dream showed on their faces.

"Where are you from originally?"

"Puerto Rico. Born and raised. That's America, too, you know. It's all your fault, what happened to Puerto Rico. Before the War, Puerto Rico supplied the Spanish Empire with coffee and sugar. After, you bought coffee from South America. Sugar from Hawaii. Wrecked the economy. Today, it's the poor who come to find work. Rich? Very rich. They stay put."

"What you want?" The younger man asked. "Where you have to go?"

"This warrant specifies an area out back. These guys—" He motioned to the team in overalls. "—they need to do some digging. While you've lived here, did anyone lay a new patio out back?"

"No. It was here when we got here. You're not going to wreck it, are you? Oh, man, that's why we rent this unit. Our families, when they get here, we hang out, have parties, eat, and dance."

"Sorry, guys."

The workers converged on the backyard while the young renters hung at the periphery. With hammers, picks, and crowbars they attacked the concrete slab, beginning at the corner. Chunks, they piled on the scrub of hard-packed clay, grew.

As the workers approached the center, one called to

the others. "Look at the color. It's newer in the center."

"Easy does it then," the detective said, stating the obvious.

A six-foot by four-foot rectangle delineated an area of interest. Judiciously, they pried at it. The thin, uppermost layer shattered, revealing boards that must have been chosen to cover a hole and level the masonry. All hands bent to the task, freeing the thinner concrete layer and exposing the boards.

With a pry bar, the edges of the planks were cracked and loosened from whatever lay beneath. A black rubber bundle, too thick for a garbage bag, came into view. One worker slashed the edge with a sheetrock knife.

A stench roiled from what lay inside. In unison, everyone jumped back, hands grasping their faces. The decaying remains of the missing mobster lay scrunched in a fetal position. Rawhide strips secured the body in a shroud made of the material used to line water lagoons on farms and golf courses.

"You don't suppose they buried him alive."

"Not with that hole in the back of his head."

"Call the warden. Give him the good news."

The detective scanned the sky's gathering gloom and pulled out his cell phone to get the ME, the coroner, and CSIs on board before the storm wreaked havoc with trace evidence. Others anchored a tarp with a necklace of concrete chunks to protect the scene.

"What about us?" the renters asked.

"Go in the house and make yourselves comfortable. We may have some more questions. When we're finished, we'll keep you company while you pack a few things and find temporary housing until the crime scene is released."

ↄ∞ↄ

"Prepare release papers for our young John Miller," the warden instructed. "If anyone asks when you retrieve him from segregation, tell them the warden needs to see him. Find him some civvies, a cap, and bus money. And here." He emptied some bills from petty cash into a number-ten envelope and sealed it. "Give him this. Arrange for a discreet drop at the bus terminal. And make very sure he's there before three."

The assistant stared, dumbfounded. "Couldn't we get into a shitload of trouble?"

The warden grinned. "Focus on the press conference when we take credit for solving the crime of the decade, thanks to an anonymous source that I developed."

"Don't know which would be worse—dealing with the boss, the press, or those goons if this thing goes south. What do we do about Leon Paschal?"

"We'll tell his attorney the truth—that our records show we do not, nor have we ever, had anyone named Dillon Paschal incarcerated here." The warden returned to his inner office and closed the door, killing what seemed like an interminable amount of time until young Dillon was brought before him and ordered to sit. "Son, I'm granting your release."

Joyfully, the boy leaped to his feet.

"*If*—you tell me who did it. Right now!"

"Oh." He sagged and slumped back into his chair, studying his sneakers for a moment.

"Going once. Going twice…"

"Okay. I'll tell you."

"But make no mistake. If you're lying to me, I will track you down and see that you're prosecuted to the full extent of the law."

After the boy did as he was asked, the warden summoned his assistant to expedite young Miller's release.

Chapter 23

Kingsley lay on the couch at the rental house, feet propped on its back, laptop and papers strewn on the coffee table. Todd came in from the kitchen, unrolling and buttoning his sleeves. "Mozart?" He smiled as she absently rubbed her belly.

"An oboe concerto. They say he can hear it." She extricated herself from the papers. "Come here, Dad. We need a hug. And I should warn you that I've been reading some very creative literature about keeping Daddy happy. Something to think about while you're listening to those boring speeches at dinner."

"You are one evil woman."

She giggled. "Why don't I pack a few clothes and after the meeting we'll head for the country?"

He grinned, then kissed her and reluctantly approached the mirror to deal with his tie. "You've got my numbers?" He nodded at her cell phone while knotting his tie. "Arm the system and don't forget, it won't work when the windows and doors are open. Use the air conditioning instead. And don't leave the key in the deadbolt. Your track record on that isn't cool."

"You worry too much. I'll be fine. And I'll be busy. I have a conference call scheduled for one o'clock, and they're patching me into the loan committee at three." He picked up his briefcase and swept the rental with critical eyes.

"Hey! I know that look. I'll be fine. Todd?" she called after him. "One more thing? There's a storm coming in."

"Don't worry, hon. I have great incentive to come back in one piece. Don't forget to lock up. I'll call at the dinner break."

✃⋑✃⋑

John Miller skulked through decaying back alleys whose sparse gravel had lost the battle with weeds. As he passed sagging detached garages, he read bumper stickers, then locked on an old F150 that made him smile: *Protected by Smith and Wesson* and *We don't call 911*. Cap pulled half-mast, he chose the most promising property and scanned its backyard for signs of activity. When there was none, he proceeded. Spotting neither human nor beast through the flimsy screen, he eased the back door open and slipped into the kitchen.

He paused, eyes adjusting to the approaching storm's gloom, then crept across the split linoleum, past a humpback refrigerator, and chipped painted cupboards. The scent of baked ham with pineapple nearly derailed him. Later, he thought, he would appropriate the perfect antidote for prison food. A purse on a maple dining room table drew him into a small front room. He rummaged then pocketed her cash.

Beyond, in the living room, built-in bookshelves displayed family photos—WWII portraits followed by decades that marched toward old age. A closet under the stairway caught his attention. Before crossing to it, he checked the shallow front porch, obscured with lace curtains. No one was home out there either.

Inside the closet, he pushed aside caps, gloves, and papers stacked on a shelf on which was concealed a forty-ounce Maxwell House coffee can, filled with assorted shotgun shells. He grabbed a handful and grinned at the deadly potpourri ranging from number-six squirrel loads to vicious twelve-gauge double-aught buckshot. A quick sweep of the closet's interior revealed a twelve-gauge Mossberg-500 shotgun neatly bracketed over the door. He snatched it down, stroking it lovingly. Next, he dumped the coffee can's contents, retrieving only the buckshot. As he slid those shells up the Mossberg's loading tub, he planned his revenge.

He leaned the shotgun against the doorframe then stuffed his pockets with more ammunition.

"Who are you? Get out of here!" He wheeled to face one furious, charging, white-haired woman, wielding an umbrella, wrath of God boiling in angry eyes.

He sprang and in one motion backhanded the woman who crashed into the banister and crumpled to the floor. As thunder growled in the distance, Miller grabbed the Mossberg and disappeared into the gathering gloom.

The heat wave was losing ground to the fast-moving cold front. Kingsley moved to the porch swing to capture the thrill of approaching wild weather. She was braced, along with the entire Northeast, for the havoc a direct hit would cause. The sky grew darker, pulsing heat lightning off in the distance, the accompanying thunderclap still beyond hearing. Premature darkness tricked on the streetlights, and even the birds had grown quiet. By seven, swirling winds hurtled lawn chairs and trashcan lids into the street, where large raindrops splattered.

Reluctantly, Kingsley went inside and watched wet globs bounce off the walkway and smack at the panes. She thought of her garden out in the country, parched and in need of a soaking, and hoped that the sump pump could handle the deluge. She wished she was there— would be as soon as Todd could escape.

She microwaved chicken and poured orange juice that he'd squeezed and left with strict orders that she should drink it. Time dragged. She killed it by watching the weather channel that confirmed they were in for it big time. Lightning and thunder exploded simultaneously, the storm setting down overhead. Rubbing her belly, she soothingly told Baby, "It's just noise. Mommy will protect you. Go back to sleep."

As another flash-crash vibrated the house, the lights died, leaving an eerie pocket of silence amid the storm's fury. Her cell phone clamored. "This is your security company. Your power has been interrupted."

The lights came back on, and the air conditioner's compressor struggled to life. "It's the storm. Everything's fine on our block. Thanks anyway for the call." She went to the control panel, re-entered numbers, then snapped off the TV and pulled the plug. Fifteen minutes later it happened again, and again the security company called. "I'm fine. It's the storm. No need to keep calling."

"I'm sorry, Ms. Henning. We must. It's our job." The next time, the current stayed off, but the phone did not ring. Without air conditioning, the room became stuffy, so she cracked the windows facing the porch, hoping the wind would not tear up the house.

Kingsley went to the kitchen to hunt candles and matches, afraid that she'd taken them all to the country. A sole flashlight remained under the sink. After retrieving it, she wandered into the dining room, stacked high with cartons. Poking through boxes, she found the proofs from their wedding.

Sitting cross-legged against a tall carton, she relived the morning. The formal pose by the fireplace, staged to look like her grandparents' portrait, was perfect and made her feel connected to them. Her favorite, however, was one of the candids, out in the garden, facing each other, heads haloed by sunlight. That perfect shot she would enlarge and hang in their bedroom.

eɔɛɔ

At the banquet where Todd braved rubber chicken, his pager vibrated. Not recognizing the number, he waited until the break then went to the lobby.

"Mr. Henning, I'm sorry," the detective said. "I don't know how it happened. John Miller was released from County Prison by mistake. Seems there were two inmates with the same name. Thought I should warn you. I called your home, but nobody answers. We've got people out looking for Miller."

"You mean to tell me they just let him go? How the hell could that happen?"

"Well, actually, they dropped him at the bus station."

Alarmed, Todd paced the lobby, his bellows reverberating throughout the vast atrium. "When?"

"Around two."

"Two!" Todd snapped a look at his watch. "It's going on eight."

"Mr. Henning, we're doing everything humanly possible to trace his whereabouts. Please try to be patient."

"Patient! He attacked her last year. Bludgeoned her, cracked her ribs, and left her for dead. After she identified him as her assailant and found evidence that he'd killed her husband, he kidnapped her and nearly killed her. She escaped, but he's making long-distance death threats. And you just dropped that dangerous felon at the bus station? You've got to send the troops to our rental property immediately! She's all alone. He knows where we're staying. I'm heading there now."

"We'll send a patrol car as soon as we can, but this storm's wreaking havoc. Multiple bad accidents blocking major roadways."

"You've got to protect her."

"Sir, I don't mean to make light of it, but with everything he's facing and cash in his pockets, Miller won't stick around. He's probably halfway to Virginia by now."

"Are you checking passenger descriptions? Destinations?"

"Of course, but he could have hitchhiked or stolen a car."

Lightning struck a nearby transformer, its accompanying clap shaking the building. Lights went dead, followed by the hollow sound of nothing electrical running. Todd raced for the doors. An eerie darkness enveloped the area, pinpointed by headlights futilely aimed by frantic drivers inching without the order of traffic lights.

He jabbed the rental's speed-dial number. *Phone out of service.* He tried her cell phone. *The party you are trying to reach is not available. Please leave a message.* Damn! Shoving the phone into his pocket, he raced through the parking lot, tore open the door, and jumped into his truck.

ပာ

Kingsley didn't know what caused her to prickle, but simultaneously Pandora hissed and tore up the stairs, fur and tail bristling. Poor baby, scared by the noise. She ought to go soothe her, but she knew the kitten would head for the hole under the box springs and stay there for hours.

A creepy sensation tingled her core. What was it? Something was different, like a noise out of place. A branch on the roof? Blowing debris? The wind playing tricks on her nerves? She slid the proofs back into their envelope and rubbed her belly, breathing slowly and thinking calm thoughts to stem the adrenaline rush through the baby.

She jumped as the tall clock chimed its Westminsters,

the three-quarter hour, going on eight. White lightning exploded, illuminating the living room. The window! She'd cracked it, but now, wide open, something appeared to be dangling. Squinting, she realized the screen had been torn. How could the storm have done that much damage? Her little voice warned: *Do not investigate*!

She backed into an aisle between the stacked cartons. *Get a grip*, she demanded, even though she sensed she wasn't alone. It couldn't be Todd. He'd park in the alley and come in the back door, calling her name. Instinctively, she shrank farther into the boxes' protective maze. She felt for a weapon, anything available, trying to remember just how the room looked.

Out in the living room, something crashed, followed by stuff that slid from a surface in seeming slow motion. Where was her phone? Idiot, out there! She cursed herself, then felt in her pocket for keys. Should she try to escape? She'd locked both the deadbolts, front door and back, and it was simply too far and too many motions to slide the kitchen door's chain, unlock the knob, then the deadbolt. Her escape route via the front and upstairs to the fire escape were between her and the unknown.

∽∾∽

Todd yanked at his tie as he sped through the industrial complex's parking lot, but gridlocked, stalled motorists blocked the exit. Without traffic lights, they inched forward, trying to outfox drivers, whose turns should have been next. With a rush of adrenaline, he shot over the curb and sped down the median, uprooting huge chunks of grass in his wake as he aimed for the highway. Three miles from home, horrifically far. Squeezing the truck between two sluggish cars, he caught the first functioning green light and sped south, sending water walls in either direction.

Slowing for traffic, he punched nine-one-one. When the operator asked entirely too many questions, he lost his temper then apologized quickly and begged for somebody, *anybody*, to please check the rental. Two miles to go—10,560 feet between him and her. He hit speeddial for home. Nothing. No way the phone should be out of order, not with the lines six feet underground. Her cell phone, but *the party you are trying to reach…*

♧♧♧

Suddenly it hit her—the smell of wet fabric mingled with sweat and…could it be?…Ham! Like Grammy's, with pineapple. Someone inched closer. Now she could hear, over the rain, the squish of wet soles on the hardwood floor. Her ears prickled as they detected deep, ragged breathing. Cold tingles spread from her scalp to her shoulders.

"I know you're back there!"

She jumped, smothering her gasp with her hand.

"I seen you, know you're alone. Come out! Just want to talk. We got matters to settle."

She didn't dare breathe.

Frantically, she tried to remember which floorboards squeaked and whether her bare feet made any sound. Visualize! Where had she seen that bulky old tool? The one Todd used to work on the laundry tubs down in the cellar? Feeling her way, she touched cardboard boxes' surfaces. Think! Where was it? In the third aisle, down near the back? She crept, touching, until her hand found hard, cold metal. Ever so gently, she retrieved the six-pound pipe wrench, grasping its head to keep it from jingling.

The baby fluttered. Left-handed, she rubbed her belly until she realized that, too, made a scratchy noise. *Calm. Stay calm*, she demanded. *You've got to escape.*

"Games is it? Won't work. I can smell where you are."

Lightning flashed, and, in that brief moment, she saw that same ugly face in the same mirror, like back in her apartment. Just before he'd clubbed her with Grammy's vase. But unlike that November, he brandished a shotgun. At least his head had been turned. This couldn't possibly be happening again, but it was. *Dear God in Heaven, protect us*, she prayed. She'd been lucky before but the odds were against its happening *twice*.

Her baby couldn't possibly survive, even if they found her at once. What would happen to Todd? His baby destroyed? He'd never survive it. So many things left unsaid and undone. Anger overrode fear. *You bastard*, she vowed. *I'll stop you or die trying.*

She crept down the aisle, rounded the corner, and flattened herself against the wall that separated the dining from the living room. She inched toward the doorway. He'd have to pass through it.

She'd get just one chance. If she lifted the wrench over her head, she'd be wide open. *No, swing it, aim for his skull. Go for a homer beyond center field.*

ფოფო

A mile and closing, what's up ahead? Todd spotted the pileup, lights flashing, cars halted, truck jackknifed and chain reaction, then gapers and gawkers. His eyes swept the roadside, obstructed with barricades. There was no berm. No way to pass. He swerved into a 7/Eleven, jumped from the truck and took off on foot. Three-quarter mile, a half, four-tenths, then three. He raced down the asphalt, heart pounding, rain pouring down over his eyes, dodging the potholes that threatened to throw him. The distance closed in slow motion. *What if he's in there? Hurting her? Killing her?* His beautiful lady, love of his life, strapped to a gurney, bloody and battered, impersonal hands zipping the bag.

Faster and faster—in all of his races, no goal as crucial. Down on the right, the street came into view. Maples and sycamores, peaceful sentinels belying the danger. Two-tenths, one-tenth, the house looming ahead. My god, why was theirs dark when the others had light?

ფოფო

Miller's stink moved in the saturated air, sometimes halting, then inching closer, his breathing irregular. Could he spot her in that same mirror, hung on a nail so conveniently left by a previous tenant? The irony stunned her.

Focus, she demanded. *Club him as hard as you can, then race for the door. Throw the chain with my left hand, deadbolt with my right, then the knob left...or is it the other way around? Run like hell. No, hide in the alley.*

You know it. He doesn't. She flexed stiffening fingers, silently breathing. *Slowly, deliberately, baby don't move.* She saw a dark sleeve, followed by his profile. *Just one step more, don't risk a backswing. He'd see the windup and lunge. One fluid motion, decisively accurate.* With all her might she wielded the weapon, shrieking, holding nothing back. Impact! Bone-crushing connection.

⌘

Three houses, two and up on the porch, he grabbed at the doorknob, which was still locked. A horrible scream broke from inside, followed by the crashing of metal on wood. Todd plunged through the window.

"Kingsley!" he bawled as he lunged toward the creature who was scrambling and cursing and lunging at her. Lightning flashed as the wounded bull, clutching his arm, groped for the shotgun.

"You'll pay! You'll pay!" the beast howled.

Todd dived for his knees and tackled the varmint, who crashed to the floor, taking down two rows of cartons. In an instant, Todd grabbed his throat with his left hand and flattened him with a crushing blow to the bridge of his nose. "You bastard!" Todd smashed at his face. Hit him! Again! Again! Bash his brains to a pulp. Grind his head into the floor—

"Todd! Stop!"

Miller's eyes had rolled back, blood gushing from his nose and his ears. Chancing a glance over his shoulder, Todd saw her behind him, braced for the fight with a cast-iron skillet grasped in both hands, his wrench at her feet. He looked back at Miller, suspended, then back at her. Senses returning, he let Miller crumple to the floor. Quickly, he grabbed her and hugged her to him, burying her face in his chest.

Voices erupted as emergency vehicles disgorged en masse and spilled into the house.

"In here!" Todd yelled.

Police quickly took charge of the scene and the assailant passed out on the floor.

Todd pried the skillet from Kingsley's hand, while keeping his eyes trained on Miller.

She lifted her head and started to turn. "Is he?"

He stopped her. "Don't look." He backed her away, skirting the boxes, then took her upstairs. "Are you both all right?"

"The baby is moving. I feel okay. Just hide me." She buried her face in his shoulder until she stopped shaking. "So many things flashed through my mind. Why now, when everything's perfect? I thought of Andy, just before the impact at the top of the ramp, and wondered what death would feel like. Promise me that if anything ever happens to our children or me, you'll never give up. That you'll go on for us. Promise me that."

"I don't know if I could."

"Oh, please. If I thought that I'd ruined your life by coming into it, my soul would be tortured. You're such a fine person, loving and giving, with so much to offer. We've both survived terrible times, however different, and that has taught me we've got to trust that things will work out. Now promise me, please."

He gathered composure and sighed. "I promise."

She wiped his wet cheek with her fingers and kissed him.

Michael, an EMT and her next-door neighbor from the apartment, thundered upstairs. "Heard your address on the scanner. Quite a zoo downstairs. You two okay?"

"Check her blood pressure, will you? And could you get someone to help retrieve my truck and pull it into the alley? I want to get her out of here before the reporters show up."

When they slipped back downstairs, a detective stopped them and motioned them into the kitchen, where someone had lit an emergency light. He swung the door shut and studied them with expressionless eyes. He penciled a notation on a small notepad. "I have a few questions."

"That's got to wait," Todd said. "She's in no shape. I'll tell you whatever you want to know in the morning."

The detective ignored Kingsley, who had put her forehead down on the table. "Just tell me what happened here."

"Am I under arrest?" Todd asked.

The detective looked startled.

"Because if I'm not, we're out of here." Todd turned to Kingsley. "There's Mike with the truck. Now, Detective, you got questions? Ask the idiot who let Miller go. Ask your buddies who didn't respond. Ask yourself if you want to be responsible for stroking her out."

The detective closed his notepad.

"Come on, honey," Todd whispered once out of earshot. "We've got better locks in the country."

Chapter 24

Outside, the alley-turned-river gushed an orange quagmire, but that didn't deter curious neighbors. Todd hustled Kingsley toward the truck's privacy.

"Our bags—"

Todd shook his head. "No time."

"I've got to know where to find you," the detective called after them.

Todd dropped his arm from her shoulder and shook his fist. "Leave us alone. If you try to stop me, there will be hell to pay. We're leaving. It's preposterous to think anyone could live and work in this god-forsaken place."

Amid wind-whipped torrents and flashing strobes, Todd pushed Kingsley into the truck and splashed through the muck to the driver's side. Slamming the truck into gear, he sped down the alley.

ʚꙅɞ

Rain settled into a steady downpour, the lightning retreating, as Todd's truck sloshed down their lane. He pulled around back then fumbled with keys while the rain plastered their hair and their clothes. Inside the kitchen's welcoming darkness, Kingsley hugged his damp body, feeling his heart thuds and shivers. "You're freezing. Let's get out of this wet stuff and into the tub."

They dropped their shoes and most of their clothes on the kitchen floor. Shivering, they went upstairs.

Kingsley turned on the water and let it start filling while they finished stripping. He got in and she slipped in behind him while the tub filled. She reached for the soap and lathered his back then soothed it away with small handfuls of water, then soaped herself.

Rinsed, she pulled the chain and let the gray water centrifuge down, along with their terror. She refilled the tub to the top. "Just lean back against me." She worked her thumbs from his scalp down his spine to the porcelain, the clean, hot water providing resistance. Finally, she hugged his back to her chest.

At last, he spoke. "I swore last November I'd kill him. Dreamed of it, obsessed, lust for vengeance. I used to be a peaceable man. I've never hit anyone. I don't even hunt. There's a monster inside me, dark and ugly, capable of inhuman destruction. Doesn't that make me as bad as him? I wanted to beat him senseless, till nothing was left of my rage or of him. I've done it, God, help me." He dropped his head. "You'll carry that image of me forever."

She hugged him tightly, displacing the water that lapped against them. "He was just seconds from grabbing me, killing me. I hit him as hard as I could, but it wasn't enough. In that split second, I knew I was dead. It was your fury that saved me."

She laid her cheek against his wet back, rocking, while ripples of water gradually cooled. "Let's go to bed," she said. "It doesn't matter whether we sleep." She reached for a towel, then got one for him and dried his chest, back, legs and feet, then wrapped herself up.

"God, help me," he said. "The promises I made, the oaths that I swore—"

"It's over and done. Whatever follows, we'll deal with tomorrow."

Back in their bedroom, she cracked the top sash to hear the rain's finale. "Hold me. Just hold me," she said, sliding in between welcoming sheets and the quilt. "They say if we lie heart to heart we can synchronize beats."

Entwined, she kept a vigil until his heart finally slowed and exhaustion took over. The rain's lullaby, now soft on the roof, lulled her to sleep.

Kingsley awoke to broad daylight and peered at the clock. Seven-thirty. Todd came into the bedroom already shaved and wearing a clean dress shirt and slacks, carrying a fast food bag. "You must be starving. Didn't know what would taste good, so I brought everything— scrambled eggs, English muffins, pancakes, orange juice."

"That looks wonderful. But didn't you get anything for yourself?"

"If you can't eat it all—"

She laughed. "Bring it on up, and we'll picnic."

He unfolded the newspaper, reality displacing the moment of levity.

"Did we make the morning edition?" she asked.

"With Keynote's file photos of us. They had until midnight to file their stories, and it was all over by nine. Come on, eat your breakfast before it gets cold."

"What time did you get up? I never heard you."

"Four-thirty. I wanted to call our families before the news broke. A reporter from the *Philadelphia Inquirer* had already talked to your dad." He picked up the newspaper, the headline blaring under the banner. "Honey, he's dead. I killed him."

She crawled over to see for herself. "He would have killed both of us, you *know* that. You had no choice."

"The police want to talk to us. Separately."

She searched his face in disbelief. "Then we better review our stories."

"I must have told a dozen people since a year ago November that I'd kill him if I got a chance. I think I even said that to the police. I have no recollection of what I told the nine-one-one operator. I was that frantic. They might say I went too far."

"But he was a wild animal."

"The media attention will be intense and that, unfortunately, will spill onto you. A person in my position must be above reproach, especially in our conservative business. The board could feel that my life's too flamboyant, that I attract the wrong kind of publicity, or that my distraction from duty could harm the bank. They wouldn't fire me, but I might be asked to resign."

"That would be outrageously unfair. This is my fault. If I'd left Manning's files alone, none of this would have happened."

"No, you did your job and were helpless to change events already in motion."

She tossed the paper aside. "Whatever happens, we'll face it together. And if you resign, we'll simply go somewhere else."

He hugged her and held her briefly. "Your dad called David Wentworth, who agrees we should have representation. He'll go with us to the police."

"But he's not a criminal attorney."

"And we are not criminals."

"Clothes! I have nothing to wear for a business meeting."

"I stopped at the rental. They let me grab our bags and the clean laundry basket after they searched them."

"Todd, I'll tell the police in graphic detail just how it was. And if they don't believe me, I'll talk to the media. They've used me to sell papers. I can use them."

He shook his head. "That would just fuel the fire, which is the curse of being a public person. But we're getting ahead of ourselves. Let's see what David says first."

Pandora jumped onto the bed. "Baby!" She scooped up her cat. "I forgot all about you!" She buried her face in her fur and cried with relief.

⌒⌒⌒

The detective greeted them with surprising deference. "Mr. Henning. Ms. Ward. Thank you for coming."

"It's Mrs. Henning," Kingsley corrected him icily.

"Yes, of course. I'm sorry. I would have come to your

home, but Mr. Henning made it clear that it was off limits. Why don't we sit down?"

Todd introduced David and his partner, a pert young woman in an impeccable navy pantsuit.

"I know you've had quite an ordeal. Are you sure you're up to this?"

"Perfectly. And I remember every second if you'd like to get started."

"We do need your statements, but first I want to fill you in on what happened. The newspaper report was sketchy, especially about the other victim."

"What other victim?" Todd asked.

"When Miller escaped, he broke into an old couple's home. Feisty old lady tried to stop him from stealing their hunting rifle, and he attacked her. She's in the hospital with broken bones, but will recover."

Kingsley backed off the attitude. "That's awful!"

"By now, we have the medical examiner's prelim. Miller was high on drugs that gave him inhuman strength. You were lucky he didn't kill both of you."

"Did the drugs kill him?"

"No, nor did a fractured left arm and shoulder and a broken jaw. Here's what did: a bridge-of-nose blow that forced bone into his brain. The arm and jaw wouldn't have stopped him, and, without that third hit, he would have kept coming. Untrained, you probably couldn't duplicate that blow if you tried, or so says our martial-arts expert."

"You mean Todd's not in trouble?"

"It's justifiable homicide. I regret help couldn't reach you in time. Your husband left a trail of distress calls.

The storm, the mix-up with Miller's name. That's never happened before and won't again, I can promise you that. At least, now, you don't need to testify against him."

After giving their statements individually, they left the building.

"Come on, admit it," Todd said. "You're disappointed. You were ready to fight, and they wouldn't. I'm glad you're on my side."

When they reached the steps, several strobes fired, reporters converging with mikes and recorders, all asking questions at once. Kingsley took Todd's arm and tried to look pleasant as they escaped without comment.

As they drove away, Todd said, "Warren wants to see me at four. I can take you home first."

"No, I'll go to the office. I'll wait for you there."

Walking through the bank's lobby, Connie, the branch manager, hurried to catch them. "Todd, I just heard. I'm so sorry. We'll miss you."

Todd's cheek twitched involuntarily before he could mask his reaction. "Thanks, Connie," he said, steering Kingsley toward the elevator, then knuckling the button for the executive floor. As soon as the doors closed, he looked up at the ceiling and let out his breath. "So. It begins. Or it ends."

Kingsley pulled the stop button, halting the elevator in between floors. He looked up, meeting her eyes. For a brief moment, neither said anything. "Todd, do what you have to. Beg for your job, or tell them to shove it. I do understand that men are known for the work that they do. I am so lucky. All I have to do is raise one healthy child, and the world will salute me. Throw in a successful career, and I'm a role model. I can do that anywhere as long as you're with me."

She rubbed his arm gently. "If they don't appreciate all that you've done, your potential, your commitment to doing what's right, then they don't deserve you. Just don't lose your resolve, your confidence in yourself and your abilities." She reached for the button, and as the elevator began its crawl, a grin crept across his face.

He followed her into her office and closed her door. "I don't think I ever realized until this moment how much this job means to me," he said. "This quiet, provincial place, populated with old-fashioned people, substantial values, all of the beauty that surrounds us. But in the end, you and our children are my priority. Everything else is unimportant."

Marle knocked, then opened the door. "Mr. Kramer's on my line looking for Todd. What shall I tell him?"

He looked at his watch. Four o'clock. "Tell him I'm on my way." Todd stood, buttoned his jacket, and squared his shoulders. Then he left for the stairwell.

Todd stared into his office, absorbing its comfort, then nodded to his secretary who looked very solemn. She started to approach him then retreated instead.

Quiet rippled through the executive area, heads turning, eyes quickly averting, as Todd neared the back corner office.

He rapped twice and opened the door, which brought Warren to his feet. Seated in visitors' chairs were the board chairman and the corporate attorney who specialized in human resources.

"Todd, you've had an ordeal. Are you all right? And

your wife, how's she doing?" Todd answered fine to all. "Sit. Please."

The chairman was looking anywhere but at him, and the attorney, one leg crossed with its foot on his knee, fingered its tassel.

"This is—so difficult." Warren began. "When we hired you, I thought you'd be here long after I left. We had no idea it would end so quickly. I am so sorry. I don't know what to say that will change anything. If there were only some way—"

"Warren, I understand. I've pushed hard for decorum and professionalism. If I can't project the image that's needed, then someone else should."

Warren nodded. "On the issue of married couples, you've been our first and have set an example that others will appreciate. But now, we must address practical matters."

"You'll need my letter of resignation, I know. And I do have a contract with four years to run. I expect that will be honored."

"Now wait just a minute," the attorney jumped into it. "Under the circumstances, I don't think that's appropriate."

"I don't want to quibble," Todd said. "I'll have my attorney contact you. I'm sure we can work something out."

Warren put up his hand for silence. "We'll honor your contract if I have to pay it myself."

"Warren, you certainly don't need to."

The old man glared at the attorney. "Leave us alone for a few minutes, both of you."

"I don't recommend that."

Warren stood and stared down the attorney until he retreated, trailed by the chairman. Warren closed the door then dropped into his chair, his face weary and drawn.

"Todd, I feel responsible for everything that's happened because we brought you here under false pretenses. Doug had threatened to leave two years earlier because of problems with Frank. Problems I'd fueled by refusing to acknowledge them. I'd indulged myself in intellectual pursuits, distancing myself from day-to-day challenges. When Doug's wife became ill, he lost the ability to fight on two fronts. We compromised. Doug agreed to stay for a while to give us time to recruit someone of your caliber and create an additional position to shift power away from Frank. We hoped Frank would simply retire. There weren't sufficient grounds to fire him, and a leadership shakeup, coupled with a lack of succession, could have brought down the bank."

The old man dropped his chin, took a deep breath, and exhaled.

Todd sighed. "Warren, I'm no virgin. I did my homework. Read the situation and the personalities. I still feel there's nothing I couldn't have dealt with, given the opportunity. I've made a good start."

"A great start. Just look at the figures," Warren ruefully picked up a printout as if to illustrate hundreds of points, but thumped it back onto his desk instead. "We're way ahead of this year's projections."

"I'm just sorry my personal life became such a circus."

"Have you seen the morning edition?" Warren

dropped Section A in front of Todd, which showed an elderly man kissing his wife's cheek at her hospital bed. "Article says how grateful they are to you. She's quoted as saying she would have been afraid to go home, had you not stopped that lunatic. And they had nowhere else to go."

"I hadn't seen it."

"That's the one unprofessional thing I've ever known you to do, Todd. Giving your decision to resign your position to the media instead of to me."

Todd jerked to attention. "What are you talking about?"

Warren flipped the paper, revealing the article below the fold, which showed Todd bundling Kingsley into the truck behind the rental. The headline read *Henning Resigns*.

Todd leaped from his chair to scrutinize the article. "What the hell? Warren, surely you know me better than that. Wait. Back up. You mean you *aren't* asking me to resign?

"You mean you're *not*?" Warren broke into uncontrollable laughter.

Todd skimmed the article while Warren took deep breaths. Finally, he said, "Get those two back in here. Let's restart this meeting." Twenty minutes later, Warren dismissed the attorney.

Todd addressed the two who remained. "If I'm to stay, I need to know I have your confidence. I need to focus on two things—what I was brought here to do and my family. You must understand, however, that while Kingsley and I won't pursue the media unless it benefits the bank and the community, we cannot be held accountable for their fascination."

They agreed and shook hands, after which the chairman left.

"We should ask the paper to print a retraction," Warren said.

"And get two lines in the Saturday edition that nobody reads? There's a better way, and, fortunately, the stock market was closed before this article hit. If we address it now, it will be a non-issue by the time the market opens on Monday. Get Marketing on the phone. Let's use our newswire's thousand-point destination list to send our own story. The local paper can read the facts with the rest of the world. Tell Marketing to email it here first for approval then to employees with a red-button flag."

Warren rose to the occasion. "I'll dictate a great quote."

When it was finished, buttons were pushed, and Todd got up to leave. "Todd—next time."

"There won't be a next time."

Kingsley was sitting at her desk taking off voice and emails when he walked in and closed the door. He filled her in.

Kingsley looked at his still face that showed no emotion. "Hon, are you okay?" He looked into the distance beyond her window.

"Everyone thinks I'm a hero—that the situation justified my actions, but that doesn't change the fact that I intended to kill him. That's wrong."

"There's a voicemail from our priest who saw the paper and wants us to call him. Shall I?" Todd nodded, she dialed. "He says to come over, or he'll come to us, now or whenever," she said when she hung up. "He's at the church."

Eyes brimming, he acquiesced.

Chapter 25

Jeffrey Johnston was going broke fast. The former head of Keynote National Bank's Human Resources Department sat on the sand, his minions reduced to scurrying crustaceans.

Oblivious to the dampness soaking his shorts, Jeff considered his plight. He could strangle the person who'd somehow diverted $180,000 from his *retirement account*. All these months later he raged over accounts, now frozen, that had slipped from his grasp. Frank—goddamn Frank! In spite of the contribution paid for Jeff's service, to say nothing of silence, Frank's horrendous timing had forced Jeff's departure with no time to choose the best solution. Frank owed him huge.

Jeff could kill Jimmy Buffet for luring him here with delusions of tropical paradise, exotic women and a sea of Margaritas. Where minimal work bought a simple existence while bumming around.

The truth was, the islands were too damned expensive, except for drug lords, celebrities, and trust-fund brats. He had stupidly based his impressions on banking perk trips, insulated from reality by corporate credit. His redheaded skin hated the heat, the sand sliced his city-boy feet, and his ears distrusted strange accents as much as they did his.

He missed simple things like the Super Bowl, snow, the smell of wet springtime, and leaves that died in the fall along with those damned biting bugs.

Jeff yearned for Montana or Washington State. To get some little job, find guys who played poker, and women who'd stay through breakfast. He missed his kids, but they'd hate him by now. Maybe someday they'd forgive him or at least understand him.

But her? Not Ms. Perfect, the twenty-year mistake who had made him feel small. She'd known from the start he was average at best—unambitious and slothful, no good with money, someone who'd squeaked through a no-name college.

She'd been happy to fit him in as the groom, never grasping that her mission was not to reform him. He'd have been happier with a cocktail waitress, except that Suzanne was so damned good with money. Could he go back? Beg her forgiveness? He'd rather starve.

Why hadn't he simply divorced her, taken his share and gone somewhere else? But no, he had to get greedy.

Somehow it always came back to the money. He'd have to risk hitting Frank up one more time. Convince him that his continued freedom rested, in part, on Jeffrey. He needed a plan and without a clue as to where he stood legally, some new ID and a place to get lost. The island boys who ran the small businesses—they'd give him direction.

"Hey, ma man, what'll it be?" the congenial bartender's gold teeth flashed beneath ebony skin as dark as his hair that blended into the thatched roof's deep shade.

When Jeff's eyes had adjusted from the sand's harsh glare, he dropped onto a stool and feigned nonchalance. "Red Stripe." Jeff took a sip then bought some time tracing lazy squiggles on the bottle's condensation. "Say, I could use some information for a friend who's in a bit of a jam. You know, ex-wife and attorneys pursuing him back in the states. Wants to go home incognito till he can work his shit out, you know?" He paused, taking a sip of his beer. "Thought maybe you could put me, him, onto a specialist who makes IDs. For a price, of course."

The bartender's eyes showed white as he rolled them, his mouth forming an O for a whistle that didn't make a sound. He locked Jeff's eyes in a brotherly manner. "I can give you a name…" he whispered.

"Someone confidential?"

The bartender grinned, looking both ways, then leaned toward him. "Ain't no other kind, ma man."

"How much?"

"Oh, just fifty American for me. A little finder's fee."

"And for him?" The bartender grinned and lowered his voice one more notch.

"Gonna run you two, maybe three."

"I guess my friend could swing two hundred bucks. It would be worth it."

The bartender's raucous laugh startled Jeff half off his stool. "Thousand, ma man. Thousand."

Jeffrey shot him a look, both mad and embarrassed, realizing once again how badly he'd misjudged these supposedly stupid, uneducated people. "I'll pass it along."

"anytime. Hey! You finishing that?" As Jeffrey slouched from the hut, the bartender shrugged, wiped the bottle's rim on his shirttail, and treated himself to a gulp.

Jeffrey returned to his metaphorical rock, pulled out his wallet, and checked the expiration date on his PA driver's license. December, five months away. Did states cross-reference requests for new licenses against outstanding warrants? If he went out west and got himself acclimated, he'd have time to surf for instructions on how to acquire ID. Hell, if someone could learn to make bombs on the Internet, surely Jeff could learn something far simpler.

Even if he did invest thousands down here, could he trust these characters to do more than just pocket his money? He'd learned in HR to read people's eyes, and he knew that *they* knew he was out of his league.

The plan of action snapped into focus so suddenly that Jeff leaped toward its execution. At his local bank's box, he grabbed what remained of his cash, his papers, and that all-important evidence envelope.

Next, he bought a one-way ticket on the puddle jumper to Miami. Back in that hellhole they called a room, he spent five minutes stuffing his few possessions into a duffle bag, then grabbed a cab to the airstrip.

Arriving, Jeffrey scanned Miami's yellow pages for used car dealers located on the bus route. Smiley Joe's caricature, with an ear-to-ear grin and beguiling promises, jumped from the page. Jeff hopped onto a bus and studied a map as the bus inched from red light to red light, blazing heat nullifying the air conditioner's attempts to cool sweaty bodies crammed into its confines.

"You've come to the right place!" Smiley Joe pumped Jeff's hand. "We'll fix you right up."

Jeff returned the grin of the man whose horsey teeth so closely resembled the ad.

"This would be perfect. These Hondas were built to go three, four hundred thousand." Smiley Joe embellished this with a confidential hiss. "It's those damn labor unions that ruined American automakers. But Hondas, now they're made to last, especially these older ones."

Jeffrey eyeballed the senior citizen that claimed 74,000 miles and hoped it wasn't off by more than one rollback. "It's been in an accident," he noted, pointing out various homemade repairs. "I couldn't go two thousand dollars for that kind of risk."

"How far are you traveling?"

"Haven't decided." Jeff knew he was on far safer ground bargaining with American riffraff. "I'll give you a thousand."

Smiley Joe's grin broadened, as if that were possible, as he clapped Jeff on the back. "Cost *me* more than that. I suppose, just for you, I could go fifteen hundred dollars?"

"Make it twelve and you've got a deal."

Smiley Joe agreed with a silky handshake and a quick run inside to wrap up the paperwork.

Jeffrey exited from the lot but got less than four blocks before the Honda spluttered its last, giving just enough warning to drift into a McDonald's parking lot. Powered by nothing short of pure rage, Jeff erupted into Smiley Joe's office, sweating and dragging his duffel bag. "You son of a bitch! Think you can screw me because I'm a stranger? I'm not that naïve. Now I'll tell you *my* deal. I'm exposing you for the fraud that you are. To the cops, the *Herald*, whoever the hell licenses you, the Better Business Bureau, consumer advocacy groups. You shouldn't have messed with someone who has corporate savvy." Jeffrey went on and on, venting months of frustration on Smiley Joe, who was somehow incapable of a really straight face.

The consummate salesman pulled on a contrite expression. "Sir, I'm terribly sorry. I had no idea. The guy who checked out that little Honda will be fired immediately. My reputation's important to me and my family. For the very same price, I'll give you a better one. Here." He led an exhausted Jeffrey to a loaded three-year-old Honda Accord with pristine silver paint.

"Sir, I'm an honest businessman and don't want any trouble. Here's what I propose. Take the keys and drive it around—give it a really good spin. I'll give you the address of my favorite restaurant thirty miles down the highway. Give my name to the owner and tell him you've come for a Smiley Deal. He'll know to bill me. Then after you've eaten, relaxed, and made friends with your car, come back, and we'll fix up the paperwork, okay?"

Jeffrey silently congratulated himself for finally, *finally* prevailing. He masked his euphoria by thinking *bla bla bla*. Feigning concession, he accepted the deal, shook Smiley's hand, then loaded his stuff into the trunk. His ride purred down the highway. For twelve hundred bucks, this obvious beauty would last him for years. At last, his luck was changing. As he opened the moonroof, he idly wondered if this kind of car had really good pickup—of the female variety.

Idiot! Smiley Joe cursed the man silently, a genuine grin overtaking his face. He looked at his watch and waited twenty minutes before he picked up the phone. "Smiley Joe here. I'd like to report a vehicle stolen right off my lot. A silver Honda Accord with Florida plates. Saw it going north toward the highway. Yeah, I can describe him. Better be careful. When he opened his duffel bag, I think I saw a gun. He threw the bag into the trunk. Thanks, officer."

Meanwhile, as Jeffrey caught three consecutive green lights, he realized his beauty's V6 engine and Michelin tires made forty-five miles per hour feel like twenty. Out on the highway, following Smiley's directions, he stuck to the speed limit. Fifteen miles later, he chuckled at the idiot in the hot yellow Corvette who'd blown by him, attracting the cops.

When the officer got on *his* bumper and motioned *him* over, Jeff panicked, realizing he hadn't checked the glove box for Smiley's registration. He prayed that wouldn't cause any problems. The cop sat in his car for what seemed like forever then approached Jeff, hand close to his weapon, and directed Jeff to get out of the car and to spread 'em. Bewildered and unable to explain, Jeffrey was cuffed and stuffed into the cruiser and whisked away.

✿✿✿

Jeffrey repeated, in tiniest detail, exactly how he came into possession of Smiley Joe's car. He'd been printed and shot and then cooled his heels in a holding cell, stripped of possessions to say nothing of his dignity, then finally questioned by the detective who appeared to be an astute judge of people.

He seemed to believe Jeff's story—even alluded to complaints about Smiley.

At Jeff's pleading, they checked the McDonald's lot and, sure enough, found the dead Honda for which Jeff had the papers. Jeff finally confessed to an edited version of the tongue-lashing he'd given Smiley Joe. That his redheaded temper had, once again, gotten him into trouble.

Back across town, Smiley Joe was playfully toying with just how long he'd make that idiot twist in the wind before discovering his unfortunate mistake. Or maybe he'd just play it out. The cops would never believe the restaurant story—it didn't exist. And he'd thought today would be dull. Tomorrow—he'd be generous tomorrow and withdraw the complaint.

The detective was contemplating Jeffrey's fate when another officer rapped on his door. "Mr. Milk Toast?" He motioned to Jeffrey's file. "He's wanted in Pennsylvania in connection with a twelve-million-dollar loan scam."

The detective's eyebrows shot up. "Really! Let's take another look at that envelope he was so concerned we not lose. If the documents contain evidence of a crime, we might have probable cause to hold him. If we've caught a live one, I want no mistakes."

"He had the papers in his duffel bag, which we searched in connection with the weapons tip." While they were reviewing the details, Smiley Joe called, which ironically cleared the way for Jeff's extradition to Pennsylvania.

☙❧

Jeffrey sat contritely across from his wife in the county prison visitors' room. He was surprised by her objective attitude that more closely resembled a former colleague with whom he'd done minor business and was now adding a postscript. She had lost weight, done something with her hair, and was wearing makeup. She looked downright attractive.

He was expecting a tirade, but, instead, she ticked through an organized agenda.

"Sorry about bail, Jeff. The judge says you're a flight risk. Your attorney says he'll try again since you left the jurisdiction before you were wanted for questioning in the loan scam. That you left to divorce me. That there's proof of previously establishing a presence down there, and that you weren't getting the news. It helps that you re-entered the states on your own."

"It was good of you to find someone of his caliber. The public defender's office is understaffed and underfunded. I wouldn't have stood a chance."

Suzanne shook her head. "We're still married, and, as such, our combined assets disqualify you for the PD's services. Margaret at the bank and the folks at my credit union worked out a financing package for me. When we split up our assets, you can subtract whatever this costs from the sale of the house. If the attorney can get the charges dropped or make a deal, that could be settled soon and relatively cheaply. If you stand trial and are convicted, and we appeal—"

"I don't want you to have to sell the house! You practically paid for it yourself."

She ignored that and hurried on to the main reason for her visit. "The children want to see you. Our versions must dovetail. And you need to know what they've been told."

"I don't know how to face them. What do I say?"

"When you first left, I told them you had an impromptu invitation to go deep-sea fishing off the coast of Florida. That you'd be gone two weeks. I used that to buy time, having no idea where you'd gone. They thought that was neat. I relayed all the special messages you supposedly sent to my office. Of course, I knew. I just needed time to sort it all out. Then the loan scam hit the fan. When you didn't return and your name was in the paper, I told the kids you were innocent. That you had critical information and couldn't return until arrangements could be made for your safety and testimony. That if they discussed it with anyone, they could be endangering you."

"Didn't that scare them?"

"They're practically adults. I reasoned that was better than telling them nobody knew where you were or that you could be dead."

"But now…"

"Jeffrey, did you have anything to do with the deaths of those people?"

"Suzanne, I swear, I was wrong not to turn Manning Stoudt in when I learned he was an imposter and suspected what he was up to. But the last contact I had with John

Miller was the report he gave me on Stoudt's identity. And I turned that over to Frank. Juanita? After her initial interview, I had no contact with her. I cannot believe she was murdered—in the vault, of all places."

"Can you prove that? Plead it down in exchange for your testimony? Maybe get probation or even charges dropped?"

"The DA has the documents I kept for insurance—hell, for blackmail. For the moment, nobody knows that I'm back. Impress that on the kids, Okay? They must keep quiet. The DA wants Frank so badly that they just might give me total immunity. If my case goes to trial, he wants you three lined up in the courtroom looking supportive."

"We'll do it. But let's get back to the kids and what you should say. Jeff Jr. has been accepted to Penn State's architectural program at the main campus and is thrilled. He just visited Frank Lloyd Wright's Falling Water. Ask him about that. Just don't mention his girlfriend. She broke up with him after…well, I think it was her parents' influence. Jenny won first place in the science fair. She sampled water downstream from a manufacturing plant and found a pollutant that wasn't supposed to be there. She can tell you how she analyzed the data and, if you listen, you might understand it. She's decided to major in microbiology and has crammed next year's schedule with science and math. She's not seeing Brad anymore and don't mention any of her friends except Caitlin, got it?"

"Yeah. About us—"

"They somehow feel the divorce is their fault. I want you to talk to them about that."

"How could such smart kids think that?"

Suzanne shrugged. "Being so bright, they're very imaginative—have been around friends' parents who don't get along. They seem to feel they're the cause of our friction, that they were too noisy with all of their friends, bickering, scratching the car, breaking curfew—"

"All kids do that. They're fantastic. Have never worried us about anything important."

"Jeffrey—" She impaled him with icy eyes. "*You* tell them that, and since you've got time, think of expansive examples of everything they've done to make you proud. *They* haven't done anything wrong. Make sure they know that."

Jeffrey nodded. "You've done a yeoman's job with them and all of this. You always were an excellent manager."

"Yeah, right. I just never realized how badly you held that against me." She looked at her watch. "Gotta go. Eat something, Jeff. You're terribly thin."

"Suzanne?" He called after her as she motioned to the guard. "Thanks. Thanks a lot."

"Don't misunderstand, Jeff. I'm not doing this for you. It's for the kids. They have to live with the fallout."

Chapter 26

Frank, *please* sit down and stop pacing. You're making me seasick." R. Samuel Roth drew deeply into his reservoir of patience and waited for his client to park it. "Let's dispense with the easy part first—the vault murder. Your second polygraph was, again, inconclusive. I propose, if the DA persists, we release certain parts to the media. Let the court of public opinion chew on that for a while."

Frank squirmed in his chair. "I still don't see why you won't let me take a police polygraph. I know it's not my answer but my reaction to the question that makes the needle jump. I've practiced by imagining a brick wall."

"In the first place, Frank, you can't control how panicked you get. But, even if you pass with flying colors, the police could lie about the results."

"They couldn't do that!"

"They could, and they have, so we won't go there."

Frank jumped to his feet and resumed pacing.

"At least we have time since the police are still trying to build a case." Sam switched gears. "Jeffrey Johnston.

Now he's a huge problem. You'll notice I didn't use the word 'challenge.' My private detective learned that the police are holding him incognito. I filed for discovery and here—take a look. He kept every email and note that you ever sent him."

Frank riffled through it and scowled.

"I want you to go through every damned word and come up with a reasonable explanation or double meaning for all of it. Otherwise, the jury can't help but conclude that you're guilty. Do it quickly, before the public learns he's been found."

Frank waved his hand at the documents. "It's just my word against his, and he'll cop a plea to save his own skin. Tell *that* to the jury—he's the real criminal."

"I will underscore that, but his records are terribly damaging. Frank, I still recommend that you take the plea. With Jeffrey back in the mix, it's a gift."

"And spend a few years of my life in some god-damned country club prison? Be unable to sue for my job? Face civil litigation?"

Sam glared at him darkly. "It wouldn't stop there. Jeffrey Johnston will testify that you ordered him to hire John Miller. We've unearthed his ads as a soldier of fortune, a.k.a. hired killer. The DA will charge you as a co-conspirator in the bludgeoning of Kingsley Ward Henning. The jury will see those graphic photos of her attack, allegedly under your orders.

"You had motive to kill her, not only for linking you to the loan scam, but for overhearing your complicity with Manning Stoudt. The embezzlement is more than twelve million dollars! We're talking about maximum security hell for the rest of your life."

"No! I won't take a plea!"

Sam sighed. "All right. Sit down. Let's concentrate on developing some wiggle room. About the voice Ms. Henning claims she heard—are you continuing to work with the speech therapist? It's the vowels and that stutter. That should have been corrected years ago. Your speech *must* sound different from what she describes to the jury."

Frank jumped up, leaned over Sam's desk, and shouted at him. "You've *got* to discredit that woman. Make her look like the opportunist she is, using that face and big tits to seduce the man who stole my promotion."

"Sit!" Sam bellowed back. "Do you know who she is? Her family? Her attorney, David Wentworth? Attack her, and Wentworth will eat you for breakfast."

"She used Daddy's connections to get her job," Frank said.

Sam handed Frank a report. "Read this." When Frank merely tossed it aside, Sam raised his voice several notches. "*Read it*! You paid for this research, and you damned well better know what you're up against. Her credentials are sterling, her character impeccable, and the media will play on her late husband's murder. And— Miller, whom Jeffrey says he hired at your behest—killed Andrew Ward. Quite the damaging package. But besides being credible, she'll appear sympathetic. Something else, Frank. She's articulate. I wish we had a witness like her. But, more to the point, she's very sweet. And her pregnancy shows."

"Oh, terrific. Bet they planned that too. Look, Sam,

you're working for me. I say find some way to discredit both her and Jeffrey Johnston, even if you have to make something up. Maybe it's not Henning's baby."

Sam banged his fist on the desk. "I will not go there! And if you insist, then you'll have to find a new lawyer." He quieted a bit. "Frank, my best advice is to salvage whatever you can of your life."

ങ്ങ

The swing's lazy motion passed through the scent of wild grasses and corn drying down in the adjacent fields, as August inexorably succumbed to September.

"I think we're ready," Todd said. "Ice tub's out back under the trees. Brought up the beer and the soda. Put the tarps under the tables in the front hall like you asked. I love what you did with the tables."

"It's the flowers. Just think—we had gardens before we had electricity." She leaned her head on his shoulder. "Same Saturday next year, we can put his playpen under this tree and swing while he naps. How could it be any more peaceful?"

"I'm glad you caved in and let people bring food."

"*They* planned the housewarming picnic. Guess we have been pretty reclusive. If we don't entertain, we won't have any friends."

"Just so we keep business out of the house. Do that kind of entertaining at a restaurant or a club. Our home is for family and friends. Speaking of which, what's the tally?"

"At least sixty. Now, about Christmas parties—we could do back-to-back Friday and Saturday. Have friends one night then family the next."

"That's pretty ambitious. You'll be seven months."

She smiled happily. "It'll be wonderful. Let's decorate early. We'll need a bartender, but I'll do the food. It's all I can think about lately."

"How are we handling food today?"

"We'll run lines in the front door, down the hall and out the back door. I hope everyone remembers lawn chairs. Our first party. Isn't this fun?"

"You make everything fun."

"Remember the house on the highway? I envisioned myself in that picture, away from my dragons. I was startled and shook off the feeling because I knew that just couldn't happen. Yet here we are."

They were quiet awhile, then she asked, "Did you ever check on that lab report with the zeroes? Or did you just trust me?"

"Yep to both."

"Bet the number was billions."

"There was another number, *way, way* before the zeroes." He grinned pathetically.

"Think you're quite the stud, don't you?"

"Your words, not mine…"

eↄeↄ

Lauren James edged her Chevy into the lane marked with colorful balloons tied to the mailbox. A plaque by the front door read:

HOUSE OF HENNING
WELCOME FRIENDS

They rose from a swing and crossed the front yard to greet her. Lauren panicked, but it was too late to turn back.

She was immediately struck by the incredible contrasts between the Zieglers and the Hennings. The Hennings' heads had been together, relaxed and smiling, sharing something private. She'd seen their photos but was surprised by how much more attractive they were in person, even in play clothes. She felt a pang for Dolly Ziegler that ranged between jealousy and grief. Why couldn't Dolly have met someone like Todd?

Kingsley extended her hand. "We *do* know you! Todd, you remember Lauren James. She's the phlebotomist who was instrumental in organizing the blood drive."

Lauren was taken aback, not remembering their having met.

"I certainly hope you plan to repeat it," Todd said. "Call me when you're planning next year's. We want to host it again."

"Why, thanks. I dread making corporate calls, and I'm expected to do so."

"If you need to approach other companies, I'd be happy to make introductions on your behalf. It's the least I can do when you're ensuring an adequate blood supply for our community."

Lauren recalled Charlotte Unger being shot and needing six units of AB-plus blood but decided not to mention it. Thank God, there had been an ample supply.

"Todd, Lauren called about the Ziegler Mansion, which will be renovated as a library. She's interested in our architect, and that's why she's here."

"We hardly know where to begin," Lauren said, finally relaxing.

"He's a really nice guy and devoted to historic preservation," Todd nodded. "Tell him I suggested you call. He won't charge for a walk-through to give you some ballpark estimates. Make sure to tell him the library's a nonprofit. He might even donate his time."

"Let's go inside, and I'll get you his card," Kingsley said.

Todd shook his head. "If you ladies will excuse me, I must go deal with the drinks. I'll be around back if you need me."

Lauren gazed at the large center hall, strung with a line of abutted card tables that were covered with sheets. She caught a whiff of fresh paint. The floors to the room to the left were tarped. Huddles of furniture, also covered, were clustered in what must be the living room, the dining room in similar condition behind it.

"Let's go into the library," Kingsley said, motioning her to the right. "It's done, except for the bookshelves. Can I get you anything? We have lots of cold drinks, or I could make coffee."

"That's very kind, but no thanks. I can't stay long." Lauren gazed around. "This is—beautiful!"

Kingsley directed Lauren toward a small sofa. "We've finished our bedroom, the upstairs bath, and this room. The kitchen cabinets will be installed in two weeks. It's been quite a challenge. We joke that insanity must run in both families." Kingsley rummaged in the coffee table drawer. "Here's the architect's card. He thought of everything. Imagine if I'd stripped and sanded lead-based paint not knowing I was pregnant. Those posts in the corners may interest you. They mimic New England architecture, but hide water pipes for the guest bath upstairs."

"The Ziegler Mansion is special for me," Lauren said. "Dolly Ziegler has been my best friend since we were little." She tipped her head slightly and changed subjects awkwardly. "I understand you're testifying at Frank's trial. I've followed the developments. The papers have been full of it since last November."

"I'm sure the Zieglers appreciate having a friend to stand by them. It's a real family tragedy."

"You don't understand. I said *Dolly* is my friend. She's a victim in every sense of the word. She's divorcing him for unbearable cruelty." Lauren fought building anger. "Frank's guilty as sin. Mrs. Henning—you *are* going to testify against him, aren't you? I heard a rumor that you were too ill."

Kingsley scowled and shook her head. "I had a scare with the baby, but I'm fine now. And yes, I've been subpoenaed to testify."

"Frank claims Jeffrey Johnston's the mastermind. I feel so sorry for his wife and kids. Some say Jeffrey's living it up in a banana republic, but others say he's at the bottom of the Schuylkill River." She leaned closer and lowered her voice. "Dolly showed me Frank's files. I've seen detailed records of the loan scam. He kept them locked in their home. But Dolly and I found them. Because of some technicality, they've been excluded as evidence. And this town believes he's such a saint! If only they'd let me testify, but the files were ruled inadmissible. If he gets off…"

"If you can't testify and the files were in the Ziegler's home, and they're divorcing, why can't Mrs. Ziegler testify?"

Lauren's shoulders drooped. "Dolly had a breakdown, and her doctor won't let anyone near her. She was that traumatized by Frank. Someone else has to win this for her. I'm sorry. I don't mean to sound like I'm trying to tamper with your testimony, but the case could go either way, and that would be a travesty."

"Perhaps Mrs. Ziegler could contact the DA. If there was evidence of a crime in her house, she should remove any suspicion from herself. If she's not well, perhaps she could write what she knows in a letter."

"Really? Is that possible? I—she—hadn't thought of that. But she's in no condition to deliver a letter or answer questions about it. She's terrified."

"She could use a private mail delivery service—like an armored courier for important documents. In fact, I have a card here somewhere if you think she might be interested." Kingsley riffled through the drawer, located the business card, and gave it to her.

"Thank you!" Lauren jumped awkwardly to her feet, nearly tripping on a desk's Queen Ann leg. "I have to go." She hurried through the front hall, but stopped and turned at the door. "I love my friend. It's just that, well, it's so frustrating. I want justice, if only for Dolly." She held up the pair of cards. "Thanks for this. And please thank your husband about the next blood drive."

"What was that all about?" Todd asked, returning from the backyard.

"Mrs. Ziegler's best friend. My sense is that she wants me to exaggerate. I would love to know what she saw. Todd, if he gets off, then wins the civil suit, can he get his job back?"

"Not with the proof of dereliction of duty, but anything's possible."

A tooting horn and joyful voices announced Randall's arrival with Barrie beside him, ready to party. Randall slowed, then hopped from his Jeep to help Barrie wrestle a cooler. "Hey!" Barrie bubbled into the kitchen. "He is so cool! He let me fly upside down!"

Kingsley scowled after hugging her. "You've been holding out. You owe me details."

"For starters, he wears silk—the really short ones—and we are ultra compatible."

"You better get out here," Margaret warned Kingsley. "Todd and Randall are swapping stories about you two." She propelled Kingsley toward the shade of the maples where their friends were convulsed with laughter. Immediately Kingsley spotted the three-tiered fountain with cherubs in playful poses.

"Ahem! Attention! A little housewarming gift for the family who had roses before plumbing."

Todd pried himself from his lawn chair and thanked everyone.

"It's wonderful! Thank you," Kingsley said. "I even know a pretty good plumber who can hook it up."

The group quickly reverted to gabbing. Kingsley stepped back, scanning the scene, lost in thought.

"Todd, it's all here. The stone house, the yard and trees, our friends, the garden and even the fountain. It's the dream I had in the hospital."

"I guess you're more likely to get what you want if you know what it is."

From under the maples, the voices got louder. "Hey, Kingsley," Randall called. "I hear you like picking strawberries."

"Todd, you didn't tell them that story…"

"It's cute!"

"It's private."

"Okay then, you tell it."

"It's not that remarkable. Barrie and I went berry picking one morning in June. A cold front with rain swept through early. We'd worn shorts and tee shirts, but didn't bring raincoats or jackets and got chilled to the bone. We gave up by eight. Todd had worked on the water heater but hadn't thrown the breaker. So, no hot water. I decided to crawl into bed to warm up. That's about it."

"That's not how it went," Todd set down his beer. "I'd been up until three trying to figure out why the water heater *wouldn't*. For once in my life, I went back to sleep. I opened my eyes and coming toward me is the gorgeous creature I married, wearing only a towel—on her head. 'Oh, man!' I thought to myself. She crawls in beside me and I am a-wake! She hugged me. I never knew skin could be quite that cold. I bet they heard me scream miles away."

"Tell them *what* you screamed, Todd."

"Why, nothing in particular."

"'You scared it!' That's what you screamed." Everyone laughed, then she whispered to him, "Tell stories on me, will you."

"Then I won't tell what you did next."

Chapter 27

Lauren James drove slowly back from the country into her subdivision of eighth-acre lots. For the first time, her rancher looked tiny. She sank into a chair. Scanning the room with fresh eyes, she realized her living room could be dropped into the Hennings' foyer. Funny. She'd always thought hers was spacious, stretching across the front of the house, but now she felt claustrophobic.

Such beautiful people, making her feel important and equal. Lauren felt guilty, her sole purpose for going to learn the extent of Kingsley's testimony and to encourage embellishment, but there had been scant opportunity to pitch it. If only, *if only*, there was some other way to get those files in front of the jury.

She dropped the architect's card into a drawer. Her need for his services had been purely creative, but maybe she'd call him anyway. Lauren went to the kitchen, took a beer from the fridge, then replaced it to fix something stronger. Why, oh why, had she ever thought Dolly could break with the past? What a horrible friend she, Lauren, had turned out to be, goading her onward, as if Dolly could ever stand up to Frank. Now, at least, Dolly was free.

Lauren pulled Dolly's letter from its hiding place and wondered again why they called it the South of France, and not southern France. Reality clutched at her throat. How Lauren missed her! When Dolly had finally come home from the hospital, she had holed up, despite the urging of her church family, and friends. Everyone assumed she was shamed by the scandal, but Lauren knew better.

Dolly's attorney completed arrangements to transfer the mansion to the Library Association, and her children divided the antiques and keepsakes at Dolly's direction. Meanwhile, Lauren brought groceries and ran errands, but mostly just sat with her. By the time everyone missed the recluse, several months had passed. Only her children and Lauren knew where she'd gone, and they kept her secret. Again, Lauren read:

Dear Dearest Lauren,

I'm declaring this modest country house settled and am beginning to feel at home. The pace is so leisurely that I'm finally relaxing. What few neighbors I have are pleasant. They let me practice my French on them, but find it amusing. I've taken up painting. My teacher thinks I have talent, but you know all too well how few illusions I harbor of myself.

Dr. Gordon's retired American associate lives nearby and, with him, I'm trying to purge my de-

mons. Our goal is quite simple—make peace with the past and myself. After much soul-searching, I have embraced Catholicism. My priest has given me absolution, but forgiving myself is not quite that simple.

I can't tell you how much I'm looking forward to your visit this fall and what a blessing it was to see my children. There will never be enough words to thank you for all you have done. Pray for me, please, as I will for you. I love and miss you, my dearest friend.

Dolly

Lauren wiped her eyes. That horrible day. She flashed back to Dolly's terrified voice, shaking and barely intelligible. Lauren had torn over to her house to find Dolly cowering in the corner of the garage, blood on her jacket, still clutching the phone. Frank's car door was open. "What happened? What did he do to you?"

Dolly sobbed in ragged gulps and shook her head. Lauren had eased her into the house and cradled her, rocking until she quieted. "I didn't mean to. I didn't. I didn't. She just came at me."

"Who, Dolly? Who?"

"That girl. Frank's." Dolly looked up, brown irises encircled in white. "She's dead."

"Where? How?"

"At the bank." Dolly sucked air in between sobs and blurted it out. "Everyone was gone except her, alone in the vault. I confronted her. 'You want blood? I'll give you his.' I took the letter opener, stabbed a hole in the bag I'd swiped during the blood drive. She just laughed at me. Said I was stupid, just like Frank does. I was holding the letter opener. She lunged, and I—I—"

"You what?" Lauren shook Dolly's shoulders, gently but firmly. "What did you do?"

Dolly focused terrified eyes on her friend. "I must have killed her. The letter opener—it stabbed her."

"Dolly—the blood on your clothes—"

"She clawed me, and the bag squirted. Then she fell down."

"We've got to get you out of here." Lauren swept Frank's car with her eyes and, seeing no blood, she ran back to her friend. "Where's your car?"

"Frank took it to Philly."

Lauren stripped Dolly's stained coat, balled it inside out, and shoved it into a garbage bag. After loading Dolly into Lauren's own car, she sped home, garaging her car, and lowering the door before getting out.

Dolly had glazed over, was babbling unintelligibly as Lauren stripped her, dropping her clothes and her canvas sneaks onto spread newspapers, then half carried her naked body to the tub. She bathed her, shampooing her hair and taking a nailbrush to every finger, her palms, and her wrists, all the while humming the songs that she'd sung to her children. She toweled her and then bundled her into bed.

Out in the garage, Lauren studied Dolly's clothes and then dumped all of them, including the coat and the garbage bag, into the washer set on *hot* with Tide and a half-quart of Clorox. In between cycles, she sat with Dolly, who was now lying in a fetal position, staring. Lauren phoned Dr. Gordon. "Bring her," he'd said. He'd arrange immediate admittance to a private hospital.

The clothes and the sneaks, Lauren washed a second, then a third time, with more Tide and more Clorox. Finally, she dried them. With shears, she cut each piece into scraps. She divided the snippets into four paper bags and locked them in her trunk. The newspapers she burned on the barbecue grill. After leaving Dolly in Dr. Gordon's care, Lauren circled south Philly, leaving each paper bag in a different fast food dumpster. Finally, she made her way home over lazy back roads.

Two mysteries continued to haunt her. Where was Frank's blood bag and where was the other cloverleaf earring? They had belonged to Dolly's mother, and Dolly always wore them for luck. Lauren had found one, smashed by Frank's car door, on Dolly's garage floor, and had dropped it into her pocket. Its mate was nowhere. Dolly remembered thrusting Juanita's note at her in the vault and believed the label might have stuck to it, but she mentioned no other details.

Now, so many months later, Lauren wiped her eyes on her sleeve and put Dolly's letter under the paper in her dresser drawer. She'd answer it tomorrow, but mail it from Philly.

She ached for her friend and could drown in a sea of *if onlys* and *should have beens*, but that wouldn't do any good. At least she was out of harm's way.

This was Frank's fault. Every bit of it, but nobody would ever believe Dolly. Frank had to pay.

Sinking back into her chair, an idea struck Lauren as she remembered something Mrs. Henning had said.

❧❧❧

Buck and Smitty began tooting and yelling the minute they turned onto Smitty's street of cookie-cutter twenty-four-by thirty-six-foot vinyl ranchers. Buck braked then carefully backed his old pickup down Smitty's driveway and onto the carport. Smitty's wife Julie and Buck's wife got the message big time.

"You got it? You really got it?" Julie hugged one, then the other. "That fridge is gorgeous! How high did you have to go? Oh, I'm almost afraid to ask."

Smitty faked a grimace, but couldn't contain himself. "Twenty-five bucks."

Julie threw herself into his arms and kissed him, oblivious to the neighbors across the street sitting in lawn chairs on their driveway.

"Nobody bid against me. Can you imagine? Buck, get the dolly and help me muscle it into the kitchen. Had a chance to look it over and I don't think there's a scratch on it. Has to be cleaned out, though, and the left hydrator sticks, but that I can fix."

"Buck, thanks for the help with your truck," Julie enthused. "We sank our last dollar into the down payment, assuming the fridge came with the house. The new ones, whew! Can you imagine a beauty like this, twenty-four cubic feet, practically new, just for beer and soda in some rich dude's garage? Go figure."

"What was it like—the auction? Did you get inside the Ziegler mansion? I hear it's a museum," Buck's wife asked.

"Everything for sale was out in the yard. I peeked into

the living room, but it was empty. There was this big freezer that we could have used, but that brought over two hundred. Hey, let's get this thing in. Then we gotta split and relieve Mom before the baby wakes up."

After Buck and his wife blew back down the street, Smitty and Julie returned to the kitchen to gush over their treasure.

"One little drawback, Julie. Inside's pretty gross. It's empty, but boy does it smell. If you get the Clorox, a bucket, and my rubber gloves from the basement, I'll figure out what we need to fix the hydrator. We can run by the hardware store on our way to the grocery. By then, the fridge should be cold."

"Oh, ice cream, milk, juice! Fresh meat! This is so cool."

By the time Julie returned from the basement, Smitty had the hydrator out on the floor and, on his hands and knees, had reached to his shoulder into its depths. "Ha! Here's the problem. We're lucking out. It isn't broken. Just some sort of bag wedged in the back. Hey, what the hell."

Julie got down on all fours to look. "Why, it's one of those bags they use at a blood bank. See? There's the logo. Wait—there's part of a name. 'Fr' something. What on earth is this doing here?"

"That's disgusting. Watch out! There's a hole. Hand me a trash bag, then we better scrub." After they disinfected themselves and the fridge, they sailed off to the store, plotting the acquisition of a washing machine.

৩৩৩

Shirley Granger's assistant swept into her boss's office for the third time in ten minutes. "If you don't get out of here, you'll miss your plane. How would that look?" She eyeballed the cartons. "Facilities will move those to Five while you're gone. We'll finish your desk. You look great, Shirley. Take some deep breaths. You'll be fine."

"I'll be one of the few attendees at the conference who's not a bank president, but Todd insists that I'm ready. Said the HR SVP 'expert' should attend, and he has to stay here for the trial. And if I'm to make EVP in my lifetime, I need to grow into the role."

"How did finals go?"

"Pair of As. That means the bank reimburses one-hundred percent. I thought Todd was wrong about my getting college credit for on-the-job experience and from a big-name college at that. But one more semester and I'll have junior standing. And I'm not even the oldest. I realize now how conceited I was. My knowledge was like Swiss cheese. No wonder some of my ideas bombed, yet others were excellent. And the prof kept asking me to share anecdotes with the class."

"Leave the desk, Shirley. We'll finish packing."

"Imagine, getting Todd's old office. Hope you won't mind the executive fishbowl." Her secretary picked up Shirley's briefcase and cleared her throat. "Thanks, Kiddo. Oh—do me a favor. Page me a few times in San Diego so I won't feel out of place."

"Out!"

Shirley scurried away. The assistant and her AA opened Shirley's desk drawers to wipe them out with damp paper towels.

"What do we do with the flotsam and jetsam?" the AA asked.

"Salvage the paper clips, post-its, and notepads, but throw out the bitties. Here—make it easy." She hit the release, and the belly drawer popped out. "Just bonk it into the trash can."

"Who gets this office?"

"The incoming VP. We'll want to restock with new supplies before we move to the Executive area."

The AA released another drawer. "What about this? Looks like a four-leaf clover."

"Probably came off a cheap logo pen. Trash it."

Chapter 28

A warm, gentle rain dueted with Mozart as the Hennings celebrated Labor Day reading new books. With their backs propped at opposite ends of Todd's leather couch, which they'd slid from under the living room tarp, their feet crossed somewhere in the middle. Finally, when classical segued into country, she set her book on her chest. She slid lower and closed her eyes. Don Williams was singing, "Hold me so close that I feel your heartbeat…"

Kingsley smiled at the beautiful images. When she opened her eyes, he had stopped reading to watch her. "What thoughts go with that expression?" he asked.

"When I'm really old and recall our best times, this will be one of them," she said dreamily, snuggling lower under the chenille throw that covered her bare legs.

"One of mine will be trailing you through the grocery for the first time thinking, 'I get her *and* dinner?'"

"How's your book?"

"So good that I'll have to ration it or I'll have it devoured by evening," Todd said.

"Would I like it?"

"Probably not. It's guy stuff." She abandoned her cushions and crawled to the opposite end of the couch. He snuggled her under the throw, then balanced the book on his stomach. "The bad guys are loading their weapons and drugs into the hearse while the good guys are taking up their positions across town. They don't know their mole's been found out, nor does the mole."

She read a few paragraphs where he was pointing. "You're right," she said, shaking her head. He set the book on the back of the couch and shed his new reading glasses. "I like them," she said. "You look so distinguished."

"It's creeping middle age…"

"Good. Then I can afford a few stretch marks."

"As long as I get a tour."

They cuddled and listened awhile.

"The smell of the rain, bread in the machine—how many days will we get like this?" she asked.

"We've earned it and need it. You did a great job painting the molding. As soon as the carpentry's completed, we can set up this room. And we'll finish the dining room in October.

"Things will get hectic this week—Frank's trial starts tomorrow, your ultrasound's on Tuesday, the dinner dance is Saturday, and your testimony will land somewhere in between."

She gave him a kiss, then crawled back to her book. She read one more chapter, then flipped to the end and read something there.

"That's cheating."

"This couple keep messing it up. I had to know. Now, at least, I can enjoy it." She readied some tissues and returned to her chapter. "This is going to get sad before it gets happy." She peered up at him. "Go back to your drug dealers and stop laughing at me." He continued to smile, and she set down the book. "The heroine's so possessive. Do I keep you from doing guy things? You spend all your free time with me."

"I've had years to do guy things, and besides, I spend most of my waking hours with men. I should warn you, however—you've never lived through a football season with this old quarterback. But if you want me out from under your feet…" She braced hers against his.

"Our feet are just fine." She returned to her chapter, absently rubbing the arch of his foot with her toe. Finally, she looked up and met his gaze. "What were you thinking just now?" He looked off through the window and didn't respond. "That's okay. You're allowed private thoughts."

"Randall said something on our flight from Chicago— that you might feel you have to be perfect. The truth is, I think that's backward. Sometimes I'm startled that you're here at all. I have this dark thought. If Andrew could walk in right now—if you could revert to your former life—whom would you choose? I know, that's stupid—"

"If I'd met you both on a level field, I'd say that you and I have a lot more in common. And you love kids."

He smiled, playfully trapping her foot between his, and then returned to his book.

"I better go check on dinner," she said, getting up. "I'll leave the cellar door open to torture you with the aroma of beef burgundy."

She pulled his old dress shirt down over her panties and padded toward the hall.

"What color do you call that?" he asked, pointing downward.

"Peacock."

"Is there a top?"

"Too tight—nobody told me that these would grow faster than that," she said, patting her tummy. "Enjoy it while it lasts," she called from the kitchen.

He inserted a marker and dropped his book to the floor. Shortly, she reappeared at the kitchen door, holding up one bare foot.

"Am I cliché or what?" She fussed with the bread maker then decided to check the oven, temporarily installed in the basement.

"Put something on your feet if you're going downstairs. There's nails." From the end of the hall she waved beach sandals then clopped downward.

When she returned, Todd had moved to the window, lost in thought as the thickening clouds and rain-drenched oaks spread premature dusk. Raindrops, falling great distances, foamed puddles beside their swing. She slipped up behind him, hugging his back to her cheek.

"Rain getting you down, or is it my sappy music?"

He continued to look out the window. "Sometimes I feel like I'm living another man's dream—that fate dropped me into his place."

"I thought that was it. You asked me something important. I want to give you a much better answer."

"You really don't have to…"

She turned him and looped her thumbs through his

belt carriers, hands on his hips. "Andy's loss to the world was unfathomable. He was destined to do something huge. When I met him, he was so quiet, so introverted that it was a pleasure drawing him out, helping him share his ideas with others. He loved that, and we became very close. But as he got deeper into his work, he withdrew, and I lived on the periphery.

"That was fine. I was happy, I thought. I loved him, and I always will. I loved the idea of marriage and being in love. But I would return from class or from work and tell the ten-minute story of my day while he waited politely until he could escape. I could sit in the same room with him and be lonely. I worked at the relationship, terribly hard, but never could figure out what was wrong. I verged on depression. I finally decided I was the problem and filled up my time with work, study, friends, family, and activities.

"At the time of his death, I knew he was unhappy with some of his choices, and I couldn't help him. I believe we can love someone deeply, value their fine qualities, care passionately about what happens to them, without being good marriage partners. We'd have gone on forever, and I'd never have cheated or dreamed of divorce. It's painful giving it words, but Andy and I should have been cherished friends. My first marriage was a mistake. We were failing."

He looked up at the ceiling, then back at her.

She continued. "When I least expected it, there you were, bringing all that interaction, the fun, the day-to-day sharing of mutual interests, the joy of being alive. And yes, the intimacy. I felt both excited and scared, yet terribly sad because you were so far beyond me. Yet somehow we zigzagged into place. The love that I give you I feel coming back, and that overwhelms me.

"My first thought when I awake is, oh boy, I get one more day. I've never loved anyone the way I love you. Our marriage isn't something to work at. It's play—a child's skip-and-go-naked joyful experience. I knew we'd be good, but I never dreamed just how good. I survived Andy's death, but I could never survive losing you."

"Oh, honey," he breathed more than said as he drew her against him. "That's one answer I never expected."

"Pretty deep for a rainy Monday," she said. She took his hand and led him back to the couch, then wriggled into his arms. "I had my first erotic dream about you after the first time I sat on this couch."

"Was I any good?"

"Outrageously. Did you ever dream about me?"

"We were back at the gym, walking toward each other, but I was unable to close the distance. Then, after that first department head meeting, I dreamed of you wearing nothing but a black lace petticoat. But my dreams never prepared me for the real thing."

She slipped her hand under his tee shirt and rubbed her finger back and forth slowly above the top of his jeans. "Did I ever mention that you're every inch a man?"

He grinned. "Once or twice."

"And that I know which inches are ticklish, even though you try hard to hide it?"

"That does something other than tickle," he said, moving her hand down over his jeans.

She gave his belt a small tug.

"This thing is tough…"

"How about those little front closures?"

"That just takes practice. But if you'd rather read…"

"I'd rather practice. Come here, you."

ⱥⱥⱥ

The obstetrician guided the ultrasound wand over Kingsley's abdomen as all three watched the grainy images sweep on the video monitor. Enthusiastically, the doctor translated their baby's intricate details. "That's the head, the forehead, nose, chin, and there's the backbone."

The parents stared, and, finally, they saw.

"It looks like a skeleton, right down to the eye sockets. This is so weird, Todd. I can see and feel him at the same time." She grabbed his hand and squeezed it. The doctor continued describing the heart, exclaiming about its perfect chambers, then moved the wand.

"What's that? Looks like crossed baseball bats."

"Your baby's legs—up here's the knees and down to the feet. We'll measure his femur to determine his size, but I can tell you now that he's developing normally, looks perfect, and has all his parts. Would you like to know the sex of your child?"

"I'm sure it's a boy. And you're saying 'he,'" she said.

"Well, let's see if you're right." Gently he tapped Kingsley's belly, and the baby obligingly parted his knees. "Know what that is, Dad?"

Todd stared. "It *is* a boy!"

"I'll print out the pictures for you to take home."

"What happens next?"

"Whatever you're doing is working quite well. Go home and don't worry, be happy, enjoy. Paint his room blue. Think tee ball and soccer. I'll see you next month. Sooner if need be. And you, Todd, you call me too if you're worried or if the little mother is misbehaving."

Chapter 29

Kingsley tossed the form-fitting knit onto a pile of maternity clothes, feeling ridiculous that she'd even considered playing the pregnancy card. Ms. Assistant DA would just have to manage without her baby bump. Her other new clothes were too voluminous for her fourth month. From the closet, she selected her favorite gray suit, worn shortly before the Labor Day break, but the buttons strained on both jacket and blouse and the waistband bit into her flesh.

Todd hollered upstairs. "Breakfast in five!"

Kingsley snipped the tags from a soft knit dress and slipped into the last candidate. She smoothed the sleeves into position while approaching the full-length mirror. Heather-taupe knit draped to perfection, instantly justifying the outrageous price tag.

This is it, she thought, feeling the edges of panic beginning to rise like a wave. She took several deep breaths attempting to quell it. *In an instant,* she told herself, *it will be this time tomorrow, then next week, then next month.* The trial would be history with her testimony completed. She went to the front window and gazed at the tranquil picture below. By the lamppost, rioting mums competed vibrantly with pumpkins and gourds that she had lovingly grouped for their first party.

Last year, alone, she had gathered such treasures, screwed up her courage, and invited near-strangers to her apartment.

Her mind flashed pictures of their first fall, hiking Hawk Mountain, visiting Hopewell, her fears of the dying light being replaced with new associations. Calmed, she went looking for shoes.

"Your eggs and toast won't survive nuking. Just close your eyes and grab something."

Hurriedly, Kingsley unearthed her comfy old alligator heels and went downstairs.

"Did you see the message?" Todd asked. "They want you by nine for a final briefing. They think you'll be called to the stand around ten." Kingsley sat down and studied her plate, but made no attempt to taste it.

"They must have finished opening arguments."

"I guess. So you'd better eat. Proceedings could be protracted, and I doubt they'll let you snack on the stand." He smiled at his joke as he went to the counter to refill his mug. She didn't move.

"Kingsley, are you all right?"

"I never dreamed it would go quite this far. Everyone assured me that Frank would cave in, especially since Jeff reappeared so dramatically. I know Frank can't hurt me, but he is so scary and will be watching me, impaling me with those lizard eyes. His angry presence is so pervasive."

"I doubt he's been making those hang-up calls. They're probably wrong numbers, telemarketing malfunctions, distracted friends..."

She sighed. "They had me try out the witness chair. It is so high! The chamber has a really weird smell and an echo. I practiced answering questions using the mike, but every syllable sounded exaggerated. I forgot to look at the jury box, lapsed into ten-dollar words, and embellished my answers into confusion."

"You'll do just fine once ordinary people occupy that box. You've survived more hostility at work."

"I've been warned that it could get nasty—questions about my emotional stability, Andy's death, and Miller's attack. Then there's our relationship, bank politics—" She paused. "The media is expected to show up en masse. I'm so afraid that I'll panic, go blank, cry, or throw up. Ruin everything."

"Sweetheart, do you want to back out? If you think this could endanger you in any way—"

"I can't, Todd. And not just because I've been subpoenaed. Frank can't get away with all the grief that he's caused. That man is evil."

"I'll cancel my meeting. Take you to the courthouse myself."

"No, let's stick with the plan. Uncle David's coming for coffee at eight and insists on driving me."

"Then I'll go to the bank and have someone run me to the courthouse."

"Do I look all right?"

"Perfect, and your haircut is pretty, all layered like that."

"You're going to love Uncle David's bill—dinner for him and his wife. I'll ask my folks to join us for 'celebration gourmet.' I did insist on making a generous contribution in his firm's name to the American Red Cross's Disaster Relief Fund."

"Great idea," Todd said. "Now, do you think you can eat? And the cook needs a hug."

"You are so patient. How can you stand me?"

"That's easy. I can't cook dinner."

⧼⧽⧼⧽

Frank paced the corridor, furious with himself for his bad timing. He'd allowed for traffic, road construction, parking, and one more trip to a pay phone. Much to his dismay, he was two hours early. Damn it, Sam should have brought him so he wouldn't be here alone like some pathetic low-life criminal. But Sam's mangy mutt had needed a vet, or so went the excuse. Frank walked city blocks, explored the old courthouse, and checked out the view from the lofty law library before planting himself near the chamber door.

A small knot of people at the far end of the corridor caught his attention. Todd Henning strode past. A woman rose to link arms with him. Two attorneys in exquisite suits had to be the lawyers from Philly, and he recognized a woman from the DA's office. Frank watched the small gathering then focused on her. She looked like someone's sweet wife, or somebody's daughter, in a simple knit dress of obvious quality that modestly accentuated her curves. From time to time she touched her belly. A manicured hand tucked a wisp of stray curls behind her ear. Fear rose like acid as Frank acknowledged that the jury would love her.

As a fourth man approached, Frank watched Kingsley, who had returned to her seat. She rose and extended her hand to the newcomer. Frank recalled a similar time when she had extended her hand in greeting on her first day. He cussed himself for his crucial error in judgment—his complete lack of interest in junior officers. She was the woman he'd thought a receptionist instead of someone he should be cultivating. Too late. Much too late.

The little group rose and headed his way en route to the chamber's great oaken door. Transfixed, he watched her—head up, eyes somewhere beyond, perfect poise, quick resolute step, obviously ignoring him. The great R. Samuel Roth had been a wise choice. Only he could crush her and Jeffrey Johnston as well. It only took one of twelve jurors.

Frank looked at his watch—fifteen minutes to go. Where the hell was Sam?

"Frank Ziegler?"

Startled, Frank jumped to his feet.

"Special delivery."

A man in uniform handed Frank a number-ten white envelope then quickly departed.

Frank stared at it then looked back for the man, but he had vanished. He extracted a single sheet of white stationery on which was typed an undated letter.

Frank, it began without *dear*. Dolly! What the hell! Where was she? He checked the envelope, but it was blank. *You'll never hear from me again and don't try to find me—*

Jolted, Frank darted down the corridor, searching for the messenger. He hammered the elevator button, but the floor number seemed to be stuck on one.

He bolted for the stairwell, taking the steps two at a time. Jostling and shoving his way through the lobby, he searched in vain, realizing he'd failed to note the uniform's logo.

He ducked outside and raced around the courthouse's perimeter, but the man had vanished.

Frank looked at his watch—five minutes to go. He had to get back. Opting for privacy, he took the stairs, rereading the letter.

> *Frank—*
>
> *You'll never hear from me again and don't try to find me. I have one final present for you—the second set of keys to 'our' desk and credenza, along with the store owner's dated receipt and note to me, expressing his apology for not sending my duplicate keys at the time the desk and credenza were bought by my father.*
>
> *I always believed you when you said I was stupid, stupid, stupid. Therefore, I knew I couldn't figure out what to do with my keys and those files you left in 'my' office. So I'm having my attorney send the salesman's note, along with my permission to forward the files to the district attorney. Maybe he's not so stupid. RIH U SOB.*
>
> *Dolly*

R. Samuel Roth appeared at Frank's side. "Showtime. Let's go."

Frank grabbed his arm. "Wait! We've got to talk."

☙☙

Kingsley stared in disbelief at the ADA then back at Todd. "They don't need me to testify?"

"That's right, Mrs. Henning. It's over."

"What happened?" she asked.

"All of a sudden he's in a big hurry to accept a plea bargain before the DA changes his mind and takes it off the table. No idea why, but the plea bargain includes all charges related to the loan scam."

"He'll have to confess before the judge as part of the plea, won't he?"

"That's right," the ADA said. "But you must understand he's steadfast in his denial of any wrongdoing in connection with your attack, Mrs. Henning. And Jeffrey Johnston was unable to offer any proof to the contrary. We believe that John Miller acted on his own volition, for whatever reason."

"But why?" Todd asked. "Why attack Kingsley?"

"The police traced his activities to a base of operation in western Pennsylvania. It appears he tried to blackmail Manning Stoudt for fifty percent of his take in the loan scam. Manning misread the danger grotesquely and not only refused but threatened to expose him. We believe Miller killed him then ransacked Kingsley's apartment for any material that could link him to Manning or that he could use against the loan scam's mastermind. Unfortunately, you saw Miller and lived to identify him."

"What about the vault murder?" Kingsley asked.

"The investigation is ongoing, but, to date, we haven't been able to link Frank to any co-conspirators. And his alibi is on a Philadelphia bank's tape."

"Frank will go away for a long time," Kingsley's godfather said. "We could put an army of private investigators to work on linking him to your attack."

Kingsley raised a hand to stop the discussion. "Enough. I don't want to spend one more minute of our lives on Frank Ziegler."

David chuckled. "Then it's back to Philadelphia where other fish await my frying. Speaking of which, we'll look forward to dinner." The group quickly disbursed.

"What now?" Todd asked, once they were outside hailing a cab.

"Food. I'm famished. Then back to the bank—I can't wait to dig into that either."

ⅇᎯⅇᎯ

Lauren James was lying in wait for her husband, whose sports coat hung from his finger. "Out here," she called from the patio, latching the stockade gate behind him. "I'm declaring this husband appreciation weekend," she murmured, kissing then nipping his ear. His battered briefcase hit the concrete.

"Whatever's gotten into you, I like it."

"Check the newspaper's evening edition. Frank has pled guilty. I can't help but think of the contrasts between Frank and you. You're such a good person, good husband, and good father. You've worked tirelessly for us. I practically have to push you out the door to go fishing or bowling. All these years, all those check marks, the house, college for the kids."

"I enjoy it, Lauren. It's not the destination but the journey that matters, and the trip has been great. You're the smart one. Before I met you, I didn't know what a phlebotomist was, much less how to spell it. I'm just a salesman, but you've always made me feel so important."

"That's 'cause you are. Salesman of the year, how many years running? Have you forgotten the trips that you won for us? Remember Hawaii?"

They embraced and kissed again.

"Go dump your stuff and change. I made a pitcher of Margaritas and some little hors-d'oeuvres for the grill. Later, a steak."

He disappeared then reappeared in what she realized was record time. She lowered her jump suit's zipper a smidgen and pulled on an innocent look.

She plucked two salt-rimmed glasses from the freezer, filled, and then carried them out to the patio. "I think you need a new car."

"Aw, honey, I don't think so."

"In March, I planted a big lipstick kiss on the envelope mailing our son's last tuition check. It's your turn. I know you've left drool marks all over a certain Corvette."

"That would be frivolous. Besides, I don't need a new car."

"We're not talking about need." She dropped her sandal and massaged his shin with her toes. "We have the whole weekend. Let's start with a few drinks and a nice dinner. You can have whatever you want for dessert."

He started to salivate. "Can I come back for seconds?"

She giggled. "I'll fire the grill. How about turning on some music for us?"

He disappeared, and she lit the gas. The perfect end to the perfect day. She thought about Dolly and savored revenge as she slipped the out-of-town messenger's receipt from her pocket and watched the flames consume every trace. Would she ever tell Dolly the yarn she'd concocted? Perhaps, if Dolly figured it out or got wind of Lauren's devious solution, but Lauren wasn't worried. Sometimes it was easier to beg forgiveness than to get permission. And what was so wrong about meting out justice? *RIH, Frank. Rot in hell.*

Lauren focused on her sweetheart who, after twenty-five years, still made her tingle. "I love you, my prince. Tomorrow we're going to buy that Corvette, but tonight, you're all mine."

Chapter 30

Todd angled an armchair in their center hall and arranged his arms like the statue of Lincoln. How had she described the stairway at Hopewell Village last fall? '*A lady in a beautiful gown is descending to meet the love of her life.*' He had asked at the time where the couple was going, and she had answered, '*To influence fair-minded people to care for those whom society neglects. They have that gift, and they use it wisely.*'

Now here they were, doing just that. He listened for her step overhead.

Tonight the community leaders who held the purse strings—captains of industry, quiet old money and some noisy new, and trust fund administrators—would gather. Without their ongoing support, tonight would be just another gala event, and the Family and Youth Center wouldn't be built.

Todd glanced at the tall clock. Kingsley had admired his tux and fussed with his tie, then shooed him downstairs while she finished dressing, wanting to make a grand entrance. When he heard her, he moved toward the stairs to watch, her right hand skimming the rail, her left lifting her skirt. He forgot the joke he had practiced when he saw his elegant lady, her hair up in curls like that evening in Boston. Long, sleek lines of black crepe flared to make room for the baby. As she smiled that smile she kept only for him, he extended his hand.

"Oh, you look lovely!"

"You don't think the neckline's too low?" she asked.

"It's perfect. You're perfect. Here, let me do that." He smoothed fine curls from the nape of her neck to clasp Grammy's cameo band.

"We mustn't be late," she said. "Your speech—do you have your notes?"

He patted his pocket.

"It sounded great in the kitchen," she said. "And those who hear you will want to help."

"I did my research, have the right stats—how many children and families who need us, the limited re-sources—but something's not right."

"Everyone attending knows and respects you. You're capable and worthy of what you're requesting. Just don't be afraid to show them your heart." She held up her lip-stick tube. "Quick kiss?" He did, then she moved to the mirror and in four quick strokes was ready to go.

"Take my arm," he said. "You don't want to trip in those little shoes."

ⲉⳁⲉⳁ

As they entered the club, Todd's mind swept back to the luncheon with Warren, over there, in that little room, five men and a lady, light picking up highlights in her shiny, dark hair. Narrow shoulders, straight back. His first glimpse of her profile. *It's her!*

A week of evenings he'd hung out at the gym. His early bird, he learned much later, had been and gone fourteen hours ago. The price that his stomach had paid for that lunch, just sitting beside her.

Todd was aware, the minute they entered, that heads started turning, his regal lady returning their smiles. Kingsley paused at the first couple. "Todd, you remember the Wilsons—we met at the symphony. Edna, how's your mother doing? Oh, I'm so glad." A couple yards farther, "How's your son like his new job? You must be so proud."

Her rhythm established, they paused for each couple, taking forty-five minutes to reach their table. If pride was a sin, his place was reserved by the fire. Throughout dinner, she focused on others, laughed at his jokes, and followed his lead.

At last, the time came. Approaching the mike, he took out his notes and took stock of his guests, finishing their coffee, seemingly glad to be there. He glanced at Kingsley, whose eyes said *Go ahead. You'll be fine.* He welcomed them, asked for the lights, and watched with them the artful video that laid out the mission. Short and sweet. The lights came back up. He made a small joke, and when they grew quiet, he spoke of the numbers—stats about kids, their families, resources, the cost of facilities, and the price of neglect. Left-brain stuff. He knew he was missing the mark.

He paused for a second then looked at her. She'd laid

her left hand on the table and touched the hearts entwined in her ring. It caught in his chest. Light of his life, everything that mattered, right there at that table. He pushed the note cards aside.

"I'm sure you'll agree. There's nothing more important than family. This is the anniversary of the day my wife and I met. I thought we should do something special, so I asked her what she would like. 'Two things,' she responded. 'Take me dancing,' so I brought her here." He paused, taking a sip of water until the chuckles subsided. "She gave me this envelope and asked me to give it to Stuart, our campaign treasurer. It's her personal donation, in memory of her grandmother, to benefit kids. Here, Stuart." He handed it down to the table below. "Her second request was that I match it." He reached into his pocket and handed that down too.

Returning to the mike, he looked back at her. She had glanced down then back up at him with that sweetness, unchanged by the evil that nearly killed her.

He swallowed. "Some of you know that Kingsley and I are expecting our first child this winter. We're told it's a boy, perfect and healthy, and we're so excited. I'm a fortunate man. We'll welcome him; love him; protect him; keep him warm, dry, and fed; provide for his needs and some of his wants. We'll do our best to teach by example what's right and what's wrong, good morals and values, and, as all of us know, that to whom much is given, much is expected. And he'll know as he passes through life, that, no matter what happens, he had two parents who wanted and loved him."

He paused, looked at her, and felt the spark jump the

distance between them. Clearing his throat, he bought a few seconds of grace.

"But." His voice changed with staccato precision. He waited for pin-dropping silence. "But. There's a child out there, right here in our town, who hasn't been hugged today, nor will she be tomorrow. A fourth-grade boy being approached by drug dealers for lack of an after-school drop-in center. A single dad in the park, tending his toddlers, who just lost his job for lack of a sitter. A twelve-year-old bully beating up smaller kids because no one's teaching him sportsmanship and fair play. A bright little girl who doesn't get math who's destined to slip through the cracks.

"There's much we can do right here at home. This Family and Community Center's not about yanking kids from their homes or telling poor families they're doing it wrong. It's about shoring up families with daycare and counseling, wholesome activities, tutoring and sports, a safe place to build healthy lives on small successes—to understand what it means to pay back. And hugs. Did I mention that?" He looked over at Kingsley, and to her said, "We all need that in our lives.

"Will you please take our message back to your companies, your churches, and neighbors? Please let them know that each dollar is precious. That every donation, no matter how small, is greatly appreciated and will be spent wisely. We'll need volunteers now, to make calls and get out the message, to roll up sleeves, wield paintbrushes, and, by this time next year, to tutor and coach. And yes, did I mention? Give hugs.

"We have a great band. They'll play till we drop. I

hope you enjoy the rest of your evening. And now, if you'll join us, I've promised my lady I'd dance."

Kingsley slipped from her chair, met him halfway, taking his hand as the audience applauded. "You were wonderful," she whispered, as they led the others onto the floor. "Thank you for all that you said. You make me so proud."

"It came from the heart, every word."

✸✸✸

The Following February, an arctic swirl of fresh snow followed Todd into the back hall. He pulled off his ski goggles and dropped his caked Sorrels onto the rag rug and hung his cap, jumpsuit, muffler, and gloves on the pegs.

"Man, it is frigid!" He glanced at the remote thermometer that read zero outside and seventy-two in the kitchen. "Factor in the wind chill and flesh could freeze just like that. How are you holding up?"

Kingsley sat as well as she could at the old wooden table, fingers laced on her tummy as if she were balancing an enormous beach ball. "I think he's waiting until it gets warmer." She struggled to get up and then reached way over herself to give him a kiss and warm his cold cheeks with her hands. "You've got to be starving. There's beef-barley soup, sandwiches, and I baked an apple pie. What's it like out there?"

"I can't believe twelve inches can drift like it does. There are bare patches out in the fields and dunes approaching five feet by the driveway. I've got to keep up with it—thought at the time it was overkill, but I am so glad we paved the lane and that I talked you into that truck."

"Now wait just a minute. Who talked whom into what?" She needled him until he conceded.

"I just wish I'd erected snow fences, but we're right on the line where snow doesn't happen. It usually tracks up the Appalachians to the west and north or stays east by the coast on its way to New England. Did you call Penn DOT?"

"I gave them our location and asked them to *please* not plow us in again. Michael called. Another foot's in the forecast. He thinks we should go to their house since they live five minutes from the hospital. He said all the EMTs are on call, but he'll reach us if his neighborhood gets snowed in. He even mentioned that he had experience delivering babies. I thanked him but told him the Valentine Blizzard will be over and melted before we must go."

Suddenly Kingsley's face contorted and she bolted for the powder room, slamming the door.

Alarmed, Todd trailed after her, calling through the door, "Are you all right?"

"My water just broke. Hey, now we'll have action." She emerged after what seemed to Todd like forever, smiling all over herself.

"Should we go now?"

She shook her head, laughing at him. "I haven't had a single contraction. It could be twelve, twenty-four hours before anything happens. You go eat lunch. I probably shouldn't, and besides, I'm not hungry."

She lumbered upstairs, grinning mischievously over the rail.

"What are you going to do?"

"Take a leisurely shower, wash my hair, get partially dressed, and maybe lie down for a while. Don't look so worried. First babies simply do not fall out. Do something for me? Call the doctor's answering service and tell them my water has broken, but make sure they understand that twelve-thirty is noon—today—and not midnight last night, okay? And, Todd, do eat some lunch."

When she called thirty minutes later, he tore up the stairs three at a time.

"This is so cool. Look!" Seeing his face, she apologized for scaring him then parted her robe and pointed to spots on her belly. "That's got to be feet." The baby obligingly kicked where Todd touched. She wiggled her toes. "And I can still see my feet."

"You're rather enjoying this, aren't you?"

"It's a miracle, and I'm getting to live it. Do you realize this will be our last day alone? Tomorrow we'll be a family."

"Kingsley, please. If you're going to take a shower, go do it."

"Right. Go finish your lunch." She kissed him quickly then shut the bathroom door.

Within three minutes, he was back upstairs, bringing the rest of his sandwich and pie. He paced from window to window while he chewed. A leaden-gray sky had settled in closer, and the wind had picked up perceptibly. He took up a vigil by the front window and frowned at snow wisps circling into the lane.

In twenty minutes, she re-emerged in a terry robe and slippers, toweling her hair.

"I want to take one last look at his room," she said passing between the two closet doors. "Didn't the walls turn out beautifully? The ark is so perfect with all those dear little animals marching toward it. Mom came back last week to finish the faces. See? They have lashes." She checked the crib for the umpteenth time, the dressing table, and thanked him again for the bentwood rocker with deep down cushions.

"Did you really think we couldn't have children?" Todd asked.

"I wasn't ready to accept it, but was terribly afraid to investigate."

"But you married me anyway. Why, when having a family was so important to you?"

"Grammy used to say that children are only lent to us, to do our very best and then let them go. Give them roots, and then give them wings. But you. You, I could keep. Will we ever tell him our story?"

"I want my son to know how badly we wanted *him*. Had we known, we might have waited awhile, and our first child would be somebody else. Besides, we need to keep a few secrets."

She returned to the window and drank in the wind-swept white beauty beyond their snow-covered garden.

"Honey, you still haven't dried your hair. Please— you're making me nervous."

She did then begged his help with her socks. She then pulled on the only pair of slacks that still fit and his hopelessly over-stretched woolen sweater. She stopped, braced herself with one hand on the wall. "There. A contraction. When they're five minutes apart, we'll go."

The telephone rang, and Todd took the message.

"Doctor's office says, 'because of the weather, make that every ten. Sooner if it starts snowing harder.' The doctor is packing an overnight bag and will stay at the hospital till the roads are passable."

Kingsley lowered her head, made a face, and froze where she had been stepping. "That's two. If that's all there is, it will be easy. And when I get there, an epidural. Piece of cake. One thing, though—I reserve the right to scream, and you'd better not pass out on me, okay?" She grimaced again and held her breath until it passed.

"Aren't you supposed to be breathing or something?"

She gave him a dark look and told him to cool it then returned to the vanity to put on some makeup.

"Should we be timing those? They seem close together."

"They're only Braxton Hicks practice contractions. They'll settle down. Maybe the hot shower had something to do with it. They may even stop for a while. Since you're obviously not going back downstairs, why don't you time them?"

"The second and third were three minutes apart."

She shook her head, dismissing it, but felt a fresh wave, stronger this time and steadied herself.

"Honey, I get another three minutes. We're going—now!"

"I'll get my bag."

"It's by the back door."

"I'll need my coat, cap, and some gloves."

"Hung them on the kitchen chair."

She took the handrail and his arm, stopping mid-flight. "Earrings! I can't have this baby without my earrings." She turned but stopped to grab the rail for another contraction. Todd took the steps two at a time, retrieved the earrings and separated the pieces for her.

"There," she said, tilting her head for his blessing. "How do I look?"

"Like a widow, if you don't give me a break."

"Then let's do it."

By the time they reached the hospital, Kingsley was having trouble determining where one pain ended and another began, walls of pain enveloping her like twenty-foot waves. The obstetrical ward oozed upbeat tranquility, as confident professionals glided seamlessly through their well-practiced drill. Kingsley and Todd were quickly separated over her protests and their reassurances.

"Dad, come with me. I'll get you ready, then take you back," a motherly nurse said. "We won't forget you."

Before he got settled, someone in scrubs reappeared, tossing directions at the desk. "Page her doctor. She's fully dilated."

The woman reappeared, and taking Todd's arm, hurried him down the hall where he caught up with the procession. Kingsley craned her neck, looking quite frightened until she caught sight of him. She stretched out her arm to close the distance.

"You don't believe in shaving it close," her doctor kidded her in between pushes. "Now give me one more good one. All right!"

What Kingsley remembered all ran together except for

three things—her first glimpse of her baby, the feel of his warm little body, and the look on Todd's face as he held his new son for the very first time.

"Seven pounds, two ounces, twenty-two inches. He is so cute." Kingsley bubbled to her parents. "Has a mop of black hair and new-kitten gray eyes. Looks just like his father. I feel great. Scared Todd half to death, waiting so long. He'll never let me hear the end of it. We'll probably rent an RV for the parking lot next time."

"Next time?" Todd mouthed to her.

She winked and continued to chatter, then finally gave up the phone.

"She's already in trouble for running around when they wanted her to rest. Wait till you see this baby. He's half legs, and his fingers fit between two of my knuckles—grip of an orangutan. No, he looks like her." Sleet pelted against Kingsley's window. "Even if the governor hadn't closed the roads, it's treacherous. Nothing will move for two days. As soon as I can clear the lane, go straight there."

They finished their call, then rang the next number.

"Hey, Grandma, got William Todd the Fourth here," Todd said, bragging the particulars to his parents. "He's got Henning toes—could have picked him out of ten thousand. I'll call my sibs, if you'll call the others, but I'll call Aunt Pauline myself. We need to continue our chat about the importance of family."

Kingsley held Billy and, together, they unwrapped their child to look closer. He'd been fed, changed, and rewrapped, then crashed in her arms. "His skin feels like rose petals," she said as he opened his eyes. "Look at him looking at us. You're right. He *can* focus. Isn't he amazing?" They talked nonsense to him and imagined the future, grateful to have the time to themselves.

"The toes—what's that about?"

"I'll show you," he said, taking one tiny foot that curled to his touch. "Between his fourth and fifth toes, there's a web. That makes him the eighth generation that we know of. We'll record it with identifying marks and make sure nobody removes them. Even if his footprints are lost, we could identify him. I'll tell him the story when he's old enough to understand."

"Todd, do you realize it's Valentine's Day? Last year, over dinner, you proposed. And the next day, we were iced in and had to miss the symphony. You fixed hot dogs in your fireplace and told me that next year it was my turn to plan something special. Now it's your turn again.

He grinned. "I'll never top this."

Todd looked at his watch. "It's after ten. You must be exhausted. Please try to sleep."

"I can't get down off my high." She held out her arms, and he squeezed in beside her. "I don't want to miss a second of this."

"Thank you," he said. "For him, for loving me, for making us whole. I love you."

He smoothed back her curls and kissed her eyelids and the tears that coursed down her cheeks. After she settled, he returned to his chair, kicked off his loafers, and propped his feet on the bed rail.

Outside, the moonlight broke through the clouds, sparkling on pristine blue-white moguls that covered all trace of man-made inventions. The sight, the feel of the moment, spread a peace that she'd seldom known. Her mind slipped back to another storm and the night she was sure her life was over and that she'd never be happy again. How wrong she had been! Emotional tears coursed down her cheeks, and she hoped that Todd wouldn't notice.

Todd tiptoed over to check on Billy and finding bright eyes connecting with his, lifted him into the crook of his arm. "If you're a night owl like your old man, you're going to get me for company." He carried the baby back to his chair and propped his sock feet on the side of her bed. "What shall we talk about? Football? You're not much bigger than ones that I've carried."

Billy wriggled into Todd's arm and then broke his gaze with a jaw-splitting yawn.

"Todd, tell him a story. You know, like the ones you tell Brett and Melody.

"Let me think." He smiled at his baby whose eyes held his own, but crossed when Todd raised him to kiss his soft forehead. "I've got it." He snuggled lower with Billy. "Once upon a time, there was a man. Everyone said this man had everything. But the man was so lonely. He wanted a family but couldn't find one. Then one day he met a special lady. She was so beautiful, but more than that, she was kind and reached out to him. And the man said to himself, 'That's her! I have found her!'"

Todd stopped as his baby yawned, his eyes drifting then closing in sleep. He smoothed his downy head and kissed his baby goodnight. Then he added two more words to his story, "The Beginning."

Epilogue

Kingsley stood apart from the briefing that prefaced Keynote National Bank's media event. Today the bank would unveil its long-awaited daycare facility. Todd was briefing the staff who shortly would be meeting with reporters and photographers. He reviewed talking points, referring to the press release and fact sheet, advance copies of which had been transmitted by Marketing with the reporters' invitations. EVP Shirley Granger; Paula, the marketing director; and Alicia Wright, the newly hired head of Keynote's daycare, seemed anxious yet excited about their fifteen minutes of fame.

Kingsley strained to pick up his words, although she would not be participating. Her attention pricked when he mentioned the word *vault*.

"…under no circumstances," he was saying, "mention that our little charges will be as safe as the money in our vault. If anyone poses a question about the vault murder, I will interrupt and reiterate that we cannot comment on an ongoing police investigation. A savvy reporter might try to stop you in the hall or in the parking lot. Do not get sucked in."

"Are there any new developments?" someone asked.

"I cannot comment."

That brought chuckles.

Todd glanced at his watch. "Questions? All right, then. It's show-and-tell time."

At ten o'clock sharp Sandy, the bank's community/ media relations officer, led the reporters into the daycare. Kingsley hung back at the door, feeling somewhat bereft. This was the very first time she'd gone anywhere without her newborn. Just the thought of Billy made her breasts tingle, and she pressed her forearm against them to discourage her milk from letting down. He would be fine for a couple of hours, she reminded herself, at home with his Grammy Sarah, who would spoil him rotten.

The guests filled the space, gazing at the cream-colored walls on which were painted a secret garden with woodland creatures, flowers, ferns, and foaming ponds. The photographer set up his equipment behind the low dividers, which picked up the motif and separated areas for arts and crafts, stories, and games. Play centers lined the far exterior wall where light streamed through the parking-lot windows. A hint of fresh paint, floor wax, and new furnishings permeated the air.

With introductions dispatched, Todd expanded on Ms. Wright's sterling credentials that included a master's degree in early childhood education and years of teaching experience. Her wide-set brown eyes were wrinkle-fringed from decades of smiling at children, but her crisp, well-chosen words underscored her authority.

"We'll separate then subdivide our little ones by age," she said. "To the left will be all manner of baby equipment—rockers, bouncers, and walkers on this colorful flat-napped rug. Along the far-left interior, the nursery is softly lit for napping babies and nursing mothers. Every day, babies get fresh linens, and while they are sleeping one of our staff checks on them every few minutes. Each day, parents get a report card telling when they slept, ate, were changed, what songs and games we played and so on. Upon arrival, parents bring us their forms. We need to know what our little ones did while they weren't with us."

"What is the staff-to-child ratio?"

"We will have four adults for our children from six a.m. to seven p.m.

"Can you elaborate on this statement about security?"

"Everyone bringing their child must show their ID, both coming and going, until we know them by sight. When collecting the children, no one may take one step over that yellow line without signing the child out *in our presence*." She pointed to the three-inch stripe painted on the only door to the corridor. Even though she spoke in a little-girl voice suitable for addressing small children, there was no doubt in Kingsley's mind that the woman meant business.

"Our exterior door is locked at all times. The security cameras are monitored by real people, and nobody can pass unobserved into our daycare."

"But what about fire? There's only one door. That corridor looks rather narrow, and hundreds of people occupy this building."

She smiled indulgently. "In the first place, most employees exit elsewhere. We would be the first ones out. Our double-hung windows, across the room, are wired. If the electricity's out, we can override the system, opening them and stepping over the sills."

The facility was even nicer than Kingsley imagined—bright, new, and squeaky clean. And safe. Safer, in fact, than any other place in the bank.

"Hey, Todd. Did you start the daycare for your own family?"

Kingsley stole a look at her husband and recognized the posture he assumed when taking a difficult question about the bank's financials. Left hand in his pocket, one foot slightly ahead of the other, knees flexed to tell his body to chill, a friendly smile on his face. He responded. "I saw the need for this daycare immediately upon my arrival. At that time, I was single and childless. Sandy, tell us about your research."

"As community relations officer, I surveyed our employees who have small children and followed up with personal interviews. I coordinated with HR and reviewed exit interviews. Quality daycare surfaced as being of paramount importance for employee retention. We also must credit our friend, customer, and shareholder, Paul Yokum, president and owner of Wire Products, Inc. He took our fact-finding group on a tour and let us copy his best daycare ideas."

Kingsley jolted to attention. *Paul Yokum. Of course. The customer with the bank's posting error that was the tip of the loan scam's iceberg. Had I not gone to meet him, or if Manning Stoudt had waited for me to return and simply fixed his error, how different our lives might have turned out.* Kingsley forced herself back to the moment.

"As a result of our research we also have instituted *paid time off*," Shirley added, "which replaces two separate, non-interchangeable entities, vacation versus sick days. One fellow in Trust hasn't missed a day's work in twenty-five years, while in other companies—not ours of course—employees have been known to call in sick to finish holiday preparations."

"Todd, what's it going to cost?"

"The daycare? We are committed to retaining our quality employees. Turnover is an expensive business. For the parents, we've worked out a scale, based on salary, to make our daycare affordable, from free to an hourly-based fee based on community expectations."

"Is your son enrolled?"

"I can think of no better way to underscore the value and safety of our new daycare than with my family's support."

Fearing Todd might draw her into a testimonial, Kingsley ducked into the corridor and didn't stop moving until she reached the lobby and the parking lot beyond. In spite of the rhetoric, the excellent facility, and the state-of-the-art security, her anxiety level approached panic. A sense of foreboding, of impending danger, blindsided her. No amount of mental chatter could calm her fears.

As she put miles between herself and the bank, she commanded her right brain to have a talk with her left. *Of course, Billy would be safe in the daycare. Why wouldn't he?*

OTHER BOOKS BY
NANCY A. HUGHES

The Dying Hour

A Matter of Trust

About the Author

Nancy A. Hughes, a native of Key West who grew up in Pittsburgh, lives with her husband in south central Pennsylvania. Following graduation from Penn State, where she majored in journalism, she spent most of her career in business writing, specializing in media, community, and public relations for small to midsized businesses.

In recent years, Hughes turned her attention to murdering people—on paper, that is. *A Matter of Trust* is the first of a three-part mystery series. It follows *The Dying Hour*, which was released October 15, 2016. Hughes's focus is character-driven crime-solving mysteries.

When she isn't writing, Hughes is devoted to shade gardening and to volunteering at the veteran's hospital. Visit her on her website at www.hughescribe.com.